Cheryl Holt

Heart's Demand

Copyright © 2015 by Cheryl Holt

All rights reserved under International and Pan-American Copyright Conventions

By payment of required fees, you have been granted the *non*-exclusive, *non*-transferable right to access and read the text of this book. No part of this text may be reproduced, transmitted, downloaded, decompiled, reverse engineered, or stored in or introduced into any information storage and retrieval system, in any form or by any means, whether electronic or mechanical, now known or hereinafter invented without the express written permission of copyright owner.

Please Note

The reverse engineering, uploading, and/or distributing of this book via the internet or via any other means without the permission of the copyright owner is illegal and punishable by law. Please purchase only authorized electronic editions, and do not participate in or encourage electronic piracy of copyrighted materials. Your support of the author's rights is appreciated.

No part of this book may be reproduced or transmitted in any form or by any electronic or mechanical means, including photocopying, recording or by any information storage and retrieval system, without the written permission of the publisher, except where permitted by law.

Thank you.

Cover Design Angela Waters
Interior format by The Killion Group
http://thekilliongroupinc.com

PRAISE FOR *NEW YORK TIMES BESTSELLING AUTHOR* CHERYL HOLT

"Best storyteller of the year…"
Romantic Times Magazine

"A master writer…"
Fallen Angel Reviews

"The Queen of Erotic Romance…"
Book Cover Reviews

"Cheryl Holt is magnificent…"
Reader to Reader Reviews

"From cover to cover, I was spellbound. Truly outstanding…"
Romance Junkies

"A classic love story with hot, fiery passion dripping from every page. There's nothing better than curling up with a great book and this one totally qualifies."
Fresh Fiction

"This is a masterpiece of storytelling. A sensual delight scattered with rose petals that are divinely arousing. Oh my, yes indeedy!"
Reader to Reader Reviews

Praise for Cheryl Holt's "Lord Trent" trilogy

"A true guilty pleasure!"
Novels Alive TV

"LOVE'S PROMISE can't take the number one spot as my favorite by Ms. Holt—that belongs to her book NICHOLAS—but it's currently running a close second."
Manic Readers

"The book was brilliant…can't wait for Book #2."
Harlie's Book Reviews

"I guarantee you won't want to put this one down. Holt's fast-paced dialogue, paired with the emotional turmoil, will keep you turning the pages all the way to the end."
Susana's Parlour

"…A great love story populated with many flawed characters. Highly recommend it."
Bookworm 2 Bookworm Reviews

BOOKS BY CHERYL HOLT

HEART'S DEMAND
HEART'S DESIRE
HEART'S DELIGHT
WONDERFUL
WANTON
WICKED
LOVE'S PERIL
LOVE'S PRICE
LOVE'S PROMISE
SEDUCING THE GROOM
SWEET SURRENDER
THE WEDDING
MUD CREEK
MARRY ME
LOVE ME
KISS ME
SEDUCE ME
KNIGHT OF SEDUCTION
NICHOLAS
DREAMS OF DESIRE
TASTE OF TEMPTATION
PROMISE OF PLEASURE
SLEEPING WITH THE DEVIL
DOUBLE FANTASY
FORBIDDEN FANTASY
SECRET FANTASY
TOO WICKED TO WED
TOO TEMPTING TO TOUCH
TOO HOT TO HANDLE
FURTHER THAN PASSION
DEEPER THAN DESIRE
MORE THAN SEDUCTION
COMPLETE ABANDON
ABSOLUTE PLEASURE
TOTAL SURRENDER
LOVE LESSONS
MOUNTAIN DREAMS
MY TRUE LOVE
MY ONLY LOVE
MEG'S SECRET ADMIRER
THE WAY OF THE HEART

PROLOGUE

"Stop! I command you!"

Bryce shouted the order, but he was only five, so no one paid him any heed.

Etherton shook his head, pierced by a wave of grief. As he had a thousand times the past few months, he wished he had power or influence or even a magic wand that could wipe away every dreadful event that had occurred.

But he was just a man, an ordinary bachelor with no ability to change Fate or right a single wrong that had been done to the people he loved. The custody of Bryce and his three siblings had been forced on Etherton by circumstance. While he would gladly assume the job of watching over Julian's children, he hardly felt proficient to the task.

They were at the docks. Bryce's mother, Anne, had just been dragged onto the prison ship that would transport her to the penal colonies in Australia. Bryce and his siblings—Annie and the twins Michael and Matthew—would be enrolled in boarding schools where they'd grow up as orphans.

They'd be fed, clothed, housed, and educated. It was a better ending than most in their dire situation could hope to attain.

Yet their father had been a viscount, would eventually have been an earl. His children should have been raised in mansions and groomed for greatness. They should have been friends with the children of princes and kings. Now they would simply be charity cases with no history or ancestry that mattered.

How could the universe be so cruel?

Etherton would accompany Bryce to his destination, and his servants, Mr. and Mrs. Wilson, along with their daughter, Miss Wilson, would convey the others. With the twins being three years old and Annie only two, they were much too young for boarding school, but there had been no other option.

Etherton hadn't the means or aptitude to care for them, so he'd bribed reluctant headmasters to accept them as students. Mr. and Mrs. Wilson had loaded the twins into the carriage that would whisk them away. Etherton had his hand on Bryce's shoulder, but Bryce jerked away and ran after his brothers.

"Stop!" Bryce shouted again. "You can't take them! You can't! I forbid it!"

The Wilsons were already inside with the boys, and Etherton could see Mr. Wilson wrestling with them as they fought to look out at Bryce. They were sturdy, rambunctious scalawags, and if they wriggled free and climbed out the window, Etherton wouldn't be surprised.

Mr. Wilson glanced out at Etherton, his gaze exasperated, and Etherton motioned to the driver. "Hurry, would you? We're finished here. There's no need to tarry."

The driver clicked the reins, and the horses started off. Bryce bellowed to his brothers. "Michael! Matthew!"

But the carriage was quickly down the block and around the corner, and if the twins yelled back to Bryce, Etherton didn't hear them.

Bryce's fury distressed Annie—called Sissy by her brothers. She was being carried to another carriage by Mr. Wilson's daughter. She began to wail with dismay, and Etherton couldn't blame her. He wanted to wail too.

Their grandfather had ripped their world apart merely because their father had wed for love—and without permission—to a very unsuitable actress and singer. Had there ever been a more vicious fiend?

He'd been determined to prove his authority over Julian, but his vengeance had crushed his own grandchildren. Did he realize the harm he'd inflicted?

Etherton was sure not.

Julian had died in a hunting accident that Etherton didn't believe to have been an accident at all. Then their mother had been accused of stealing from the exalted Blair family, of pilfering jewels and money. She'd been prosecuted simply to prevent her children from inheriting a single farthing of their grandfather's fortune.

Well, Etherton certainly hoped the ogre found happiness in the next life, for he definitely didn't deserve it in this one. If there was any justice, the aged tyrant would rot in Hell.

"By-By! By-By!" Annie said to Bryce. She couldn't yet pronounce his name.

Bryce whipped around and rushed over to her. He yanked her from Miss Wilson's arms and clutched her to his chest.

Miss Wilson glared at Etherton, flashing the same exasperated look her father had just exhibited. She couldn't decide if she should grab Annie and continue on or if she should halt and extend the torturous moment.

The prior six months had been a long slog of horrific days, but this day was the most ghastly by far. None of them was immune, not even Miss Wilson who had a significant but unpalatable role to play in the unfolding debacle. She would deliver Annie to Miss Peabody's School for Girls, a dank, crumbling edifice that reminded Etherton of a prison.

Bryce was kneeling in front of Sissy. She was pretty as a porcelain doll, with curly blond hair and big blue eyes. Poignant tears dripped down her rosy cheeks, their blatant affection agonizing to observe.

"Don't be afraid, Sissy," Bryce murmured as Etherton walked up. He asked Etherton, "Can't she stay with us, Mr. Etherton? Can't she? Please?"

"No, Bryce. You're going to a boy's school. She can't go with you."

"Please, Mr. Etherton! She's too little to be off on her own."

"She'll be fine, Bryce."

"She won't be fine," he fiercely replied, and he leapt up and whirled on Etherton. "Mother ordered me to watch over her and the twins, yet you're sending them away."

Etherton shrugged. "I'm sorry."

What else could he say? Their plight was incomprehensible.

Bryce's grandfather had been insistent that Julian not wed Anne, but he'd married her anyway, and the old coot had gotten even. After Julian died, he'd declared there had been no marriage, that the children were illegitimate bastards. As an aristocrat, no one had argued with him, and Anne's witnesses had been her fellow actors who were considered disreputable and dishonest.

Now Julian was dead, Anne transported, and their children...

What would become of them?

He peered down at Annie, and his smile was forced. "You want to attend school, don't you, Sissy? Won't that be fun?"

Her gaze was distressed and condemning. Bryce shoved Etherton away and knelt in front of her again.

"I'll visit you all the time," he advised her. "Won't I, Mr. Etherton?"

"Yes," Etherton lied.

"How often, do you think? Every day?"

"No, no, probably every Saturday."

The school where she'd be housed was a four-day journey from London. If Etherton was able to take Bryce once a year, it would be a miracle.

Bryce didn't recognize the promise for the falsehood it was, and he turned to Sissy. "Every Saturday," he repeated. "When I arrive, you can tell me about your teachers and your new friends. You can show me your new room and your new bed."

Sissy scowled. "By-By."

"Yes, I'm By-By, your big brother. You'll never forget, will you?"

Sissy shook her head, and Bryce clasped her hands. They stared and stared, nose to nose, chin to chin.

Finally Bryce peeked up at Etherton. "I'll never see her again, will I?"

"Of course you will."

"No, I can feel it. She'll go away—as Mother went away. As Father went away. What if she grows up, and I don't remember what she looks like? How will I find her?"

Etherton sighed. "You're being ridiculous, Bryce. We'll visit regularly."

"I don't believe you, Mr. Etherton. I don't believe any adults anymore. You're all liars."

"I'm doing the best I can," Etherton complained.

"Your *best* is not good enough," Bryce scolded. "You told Mother you'd protect us. You swore it to her! I heard you."

"And I meant every word."

Bryce pointed to the ship where the sailors had cast off. A tug was towing the vessel out into the main channel of the Thames. "She hasn't even left yet, and you've already proved your vows are worthless. I can't rely on you."

He spun back to Sissy, and for an eternity they continued to stare, as if committing each other's features to memory. Then he dug in his pocket and pulled out a small ivory statuette that had belonged to his mother. It was an ancient goddess, a protector of musicians and artists. His mother had set it on her harpsichord.

Etherton hadn't realized Bryce had secreted it away. Every other possession had been sold to pay for their maintenance and education. The statuette was a precious treasure, and Etherton almost warned him not to give it to her. How could she appreciate its value? How would she ever keep from losing it?

But he doubted he could dissuade Bryce from parting with the dear artifact. And at this late date, how could it matter?

"Let's go, Bryce," he said.

"In a minute, Mr. Etherton," Bryce snapped in response. He held out the statuette to Sissy. "This was Mother's."

"Mama."

"You must always hide it in your pocket. You must never let it be taken from you. It's very important, Sissy. Do you understand?"

"Mama," she said again.

"I have no idea when I'll see you again. Maybe never. You must promise to be a very good girl."

Sissy nodded. "Good."

"You must make Mother and Father proud."

"Dada."

"I will come and find you someday," Bryce insisted. "Despite what anyone tells you, I will search for you and I *will* find you. I swear it."

As if she grasped the weight of his comment, she reached out and caressed his face. "By-By."

"Yes, Sissy, I'm Bryce Blair, and you're Annie Blair. Don't ever forget your name, and you must never lose the statuette. When we're grown-ups, I'll know who you are because you have Mother's statue." He turned it over and showed her the initials *AB* that were printed on the bottom. "These two letters? They stand for Mother's name. Anne Blair."

"Mama," Sissy murmured.

Bryce put the statuette into her plump little hand and wrapped her fingers around it. Then he drew her into a tight hug. Both of them were crying, and Miss Wilson was weeping too.

"Mr. Etherton," she said, "may we go? I can't abide much more of this."

"Yes, please be off."

Etherton grabbed Bryce, and Miss Wilson grabbed Sissy. They pulled, having to yank the siblings apart to separate them. Miss Wilson lifted Sissy and hurried to their carriage. A footman helped her in as Sissy screamed and begged in her toddler's language to stay with Bryce.

But the door was slammed shut, and the driver whipped the horses into a trot. They lurched forward and the vehicle rumbled away.

"Don't forget me, Sissy," Bryce called. "Don't forget."

Blessedly, Miss Wilson didn't let Sissy look out the window, so Etherton didn't have to have that final image in his mind. He tried to steer Bryce away, but the boy refused to budge, watching the fleeing carriage as if he was rooted to the ground.

Etherton glanced down the busy wharf. He didn't expect Julian's relatives would arrive to cause trouble. He didn't think Bryce's grandfather or uncle wondered about the fate of Anne's children. The two despicable men had simply been determined to have her sent away so no claim could ever be made against the estate.

Yet with such fortunes at stake, Etherton couldn't be sure what a malicious person might attempt.

"You'll see her soon, Bryce." Etherton's lies were getting easier to voice. "I promise."

"I told you I don't believe you."

"We must be off. We have many miles to travel today."

"We'll depart after Mother's ship has faded from view."

"It's not safe for us to remain here."

"I don't care. What could happen to me that hasn't already happened?"

It was an adult's sort of query, and Etherton had no answer, but Bryce's firm resolve was clear. He was five, but he was so imperious, so like his father whom Etherton had adored.

"I suppose we can wait a bit," Etherton mumbled.

"Yes, I suppose we can."

They stood together, gaping as the ship was moved farther and farther away. There were a few other stragglers on the dock, strangers who also had family members sailing to the other side of the Earth. They all appeared stunned.

"Might they permit Mother to come up onto the deck and wave goodbye?" Bryce sounded devastated and forlorn.

"No, I'm certain they won't."

Bryce nodded heavily, as if the cruelness of the world had just been revealed. A grueling half hour passed, and ultimately the vessel was swallowed up by other river traffic. Once it vanished, Bryce turned away.

"We may leave now," he stoically said.

"Fine. Let's do."

Feeling awkward and aggrieved, Etherton started toward the carriage. He tried to take Bryce's hand, but Bryce wouldn't let him. Bryce was quietly crying, and Etherton was struggling to keep his own tears at bay.

He'd loved Julian so dearly and missed him so much. Anne had been Julian's great amour and cherished friend, but despite their joyous marriage, Etherton had been closer to Julian than anyone. He'd known Julian all his life, and Julian had been the center of Etherton's universe. The hole left by his death was too big to ever be filled.

Still though, he was compelled to say, "It will be all right, Bryce. You'll see. At the moment, matters seem chaotic, but everything will eventually work out for the best."

"You're wrong, Mr. Etherton. My home is gone. My sister and brothers are gone. My parents are gone. Nothing will ever be all right again."

CHAPTER ONE

"Who may I tell him is calling?"

"Katarina...ah...Webster."

Katarina—known as Kat to her friends and family—kept her expression carefully blank. She hadn't meant to stumble over the surname of Webster, and her hesitation made her sound like an idiot.

Webster was her mother's American maiden name. Since Kat was traveling in disguise and not eager to be recognized, it seemed the best choice.

In reality, she was Her Royal Highness, Katarina Victoria Sasha Morovsky, Princess of Parthenia. In ordinary circumstances, she would have proclaimed herself and used her title to obtain whatever boon or aid she sought. But her treacherous cousin, Kristof, egged on by his advisors, had revoked her status and designation. At that moment, she was no one of consequence at all.

She was staggering about, trying to figure out how to proceed in a normal fashion when the entire foundation of her life had been destroyed.

"Why do you request an appointment with Monsieur Valois?" the butler asked. "What is the purpose of your visit?"

"I'm newly arrived in Cairo," she replied. "I was apprised that he is the person to approach when assistance is required."

The butler studied her, obviously finding too many flaws to count. "Have you a recommendation?"

"A recommendation for what?"

"The Monsieur is an important man. He does not deal with anyone who will waste his time."

"I need a reference to vouch for my...what? My character? My veracity? My position in the world?"

He gave a very French sort of shrug. "Any of those will suffice."

Kat glared, her green eyes shooting daggers. If she'd been a male, she'd have pounded him into the ground. If she'd been lumping along in her usual condition, she'd have snapped her fingers and had him dragged off to the dungeons.

Well, not to the dungeons. She'd never behaved that way, but it was satisfying to imagine herself having some authority. At the very least, she might have demanded he apologize.

She took a deep breath to calm herself. She was now living as all common people lived. She was being treated as all ordinary women were treated, and she had to remember and accept that fact.

She flashed her most winning smile, the one that had once charmed royal suitors from all the minor courts of Europe. "Please inform Monsieur Valois that I am simply new to Egypt, and I am desperate to receive his shrewd advice."

"On what topic?"

"I will be traveling to the pyramids to locate my uncle who is digging there. I'm hoping to hire a guide and bodyguards, but in such a foreign place, I don't feel competent to handle the interviews myself."

"Very wise, mistress."

"I was told at my hotel that the Monsieur could suggest suitable employees."

The butler studied her again, then nodded. "Wait here. I will see if he is available."

The ornate doors of the grand villa were shut in her face, and her temper flared. She wasn't invited into the shady foyer. She wasn't offered a chair in the garden or a sip of lemon water to cool her parched throat. A dog wouldn't have been so shabbily abused, and she'd just raised a fist to knock and give the rude oaf a piece of her mind when he yanked the door open.

"The Monsieur is busy today," he claimed. "There can be no appointment."

"But...but...you haven't been gone five seconds," she huffed. "How could you have spoken with him?"

"You come tomorrow."

"What time?"

The door was already closing, and she was so furious she nearly wedged herself into the threshold so she could force him to display some manners. Yes, she was in Egypt, and yes, habits and routines were very different in the hot, dreary land, but she was positive no servant in any country—even in Egypt—was allowed to be so insolent.

She whipped away and stomped off, refusing to embarrass herself by begging for an audience. Apparently Monsieur Valois had resided in Cairo for ages and was the most savvy European in the city. If he couldn't be bothered to confer with a damsel in distress, surely there was another man in the teeming metropolis who would be happy to assume the role.

She yearned to shout her true name, but she kept silent. Not because her cousin, Kristof, had ordered her to stop using her title. Not because she'd become a political pawn in his mad scheme, but because she didn't want it known that she was in Egypt.

Kristof was insane, and she'd had enough of his devious machinations. He'd declared her deceased parents' lengthy marriage null and void. Then he'd ruled Kat and her two younger siblings—Nicholas and Isabelle—to be illegitimate bastards. But his most grievous sin had been committed against Nicholas.

Nicholas was her father's son and rightful heir to the throne, but he was only twelve. When Kat's father had died a year earlier, there had been a few months of uncertainty as a regency was discussed for Nicholas. Who should help him to rule? Who should supervise him until he reached his majority?

Kat's mother had perished birthing Isabelle, so for the prior decade, Kat had reared her siblings. She'd avoided her own marriage to stay in Parthenia and care for them. At age twenty-five, she seemed more like their mother than their older sister.

She'd expected to be picked as Regent, but councilors had vigorously derided the notion. As the debate had swirled, Kristof had seized power and crowned himself king. He'd installed his supporters in positions of authority and disinherited Kat and her siblings.

Kat was simply a female, from a very small, very peaceful country. She didn't have an army. The kingdom itself didn't have an army. She didn't have legions of soldiers to impose a just ending for Nicholas. There had been no hue and cry from the citizenry to demand Kristof step down. In fact, he'd been roundly hailed for taking action, so she'd been forced to accept what had occurred. It had infuriated her, but she'd accepted it.

They might have remained in Parthenia, but a friend of her father's had pulled her aside and whispered that Nicholas might be at risk from Kristof. Initially she'd refused to believe it, but gradually she'd decided she couldn't discount the words of warning.

So long as Nicholas was alive and underfoot at the palace, he was a daily reminder to everyone that he was the lawful king, that Kristof was a deceitful usurper. It wasn't the Middle Ages so the chance of a royal murder was very likely preposterous to consider, but Kristof was a fiend, and she would put nothing past him.

It would be simple for a twelve-year-old boy to be poisoned or suffer an accident. Who could ever prove that treachery had been involved? Especially with Kristof's loyalists handling any investigation.

Kat would do anything to protect her siblings, and once she'd admitted that perfidy could transpire, there had been no reason to stay in Parthenia. She still had her own fortune from her mother's dowry, so she'd had the funds to sneak away with Nicholas and Isabelle.

Her mother had been a fetching, elegant American heiress. On her grand tour of Europe when she was eighteen, Kat's father had met her and made her his bride.

Kat's father had been handsome and dynamic, and she imagined her mother had been swept off her feet by his regal proposal. But Kat had been fifteen when her mother had passed away in childbed, so they'd never had an adult conversation about her parents' marriage.

It was entirely possible that her mother had been unhappy as a queen in a foreign land. She'd been pragmatic and level-headed, possessed of very American ideas about equality and egalitarianism. She'd scoffed over the concept of one person being better than another merely because of the blood in his veins, and she'd frequently waxed nostalgic about the life in America she'd abandoned.

Her only brother, Cedric Webster, was an archeologist who'd been digging in Egypt for decades. With Kat's world in shambles, she'd decided to seek him out. He was the sole Webster relative who'd ever visited Parthenia, and he and her mother had been close. He'd help Kat, wouldn't he?

She needed advice from someone she could trust. She needed to rest and regroup under her uncle's watchful eye. She needed consoling from someone who would tell her she wasn't crazed to worry about Nicholas's safety. Most of all, she needed his opinion as to where she should go with Nicholas. London? Paris? Rome? Boston?

Was it necessary to put an ocean between him and Kristof? If that's what it would take for Nicholas to be out of danger, then that is what she would do.

Monsieur Valois's spectacular villa was nestled on the banks of the Nile, the long driveway leading to a busy city street. She'd rented a chair, and four natives had carried her to her destination. They had remained outside the gates and would convey her back to the hotel where Nicholas, Isabelle, and Kat's friend, Pippa Clementi, were waiting for her to return.

She'd brought a parasol to shield herself from the sun, but she'd left it in her rented chair so the sun's rays beat down unmercifully. She hadn't walked twenty steps when the temperature began to be oppressive, and it occurred to her that she had to alter her wardrobe into one that was more suitable for the tropical climate.

She was wearing layers of petticoats, woolen stockings, a jacket, a tight corset, and the air was so heavy and so still that she felt as if she was suffocating.

The villa's grounds were quiet, verdant, comprised of lush gardens of green foliage and fruit trees she couldn't identify. She slipped under an arbor, pausing to fan her heated face, when she heard hearty masculine laughter, swords clanging, vocal jesting, and affable insults being hurled.

She crept farther into the foliage, pushing a palm frond away so she was staring out at a smooth patch of lawn. There were two men fencing, several others lounging in the shade and observing the combatants.

They spoke English with a British accent, and they were a bit older than she was, probably thirty or so. They were much the same size, six feet in height, with broad shoulders, muscled arms, and long, lean legs. One was dark-haired and one was blond, but they were both handsome as the devil.

They were in trousers and boots, their shirts off, their chests bared, and it was inordinately thrilling to see all that male flesh. Their torsos had been bronzed by the sun, providing stark evidence that they spent an extensive amount of time strutting about unclad.

She tried to imagine what it would be like to be so promiscuous with one's person. In Parthenia, where the terrain was mountainous, cold, and snowy, people were always buttoned up from chin to toe, usually bundled in sweaters and coats.

She was attired in garments she'd brought from home, and she wished she could be so free and easy with her clothes. She wished she could strip to her petticoat and find some comfort.

The blond man in particular held her attention. He was arresting as a Greek god, his dynamic qualities almost tangible. They wafted toward her, and she was rooted to her spot and couldn't move.

His golden locks hadn't been trimmed, and they were loose and curling over his shoulders. He had an aristocratic countenance, his face clean-shaven and pleasing to view, with sharp cheekbones, a strong jaw, a wide, generous mouth that was creased with laugh lines as if he was humored by life and smiled often.

But it was his eyes that most intrigued her. They were a deep blue color like the waters in the Mediterranean Sea she'd crossed in her flight out of Italy. She'd never seen such eyes, and she wished she had the temerity to bluster over and gaze into them from a few feet away.

No doubt it would be an exhilarating experience.

Their swords crashed together, steel banging on steel, as the blond man worked the dark-haired man backward over the grass. He kept up the onslaught, hitting and hitting the other combatant until finally, with a hard flick of his wrist, his opponent's weapon flew away. The onlookers cheered and clapped.

One of them shouted, "Hoorah for Mr. Blair!"

"You dirty dog," the dark-haired man scolded, but in a cordial way. "Can't you let me win at least once?"

"No," the blond man, Mr. Blair, said. "The point of these lessons is to improve our skill with a blade. How can it benefit either of us if I mollycoddle you?"

"When you constantly beat me like this, you're bruising my ego."

"That's not possible. Your ego is entirely too large to ever be dented."

A servant hustled over to Mr. Blair and held out a bucket of water. The virile fellow grabbed it and dumped the contents over his head so he was wet and slippery, and the sight did something funny to her innards.

Her pulse raced. Her fingers tingled.

In her sheltered, coddled existence as a princess, she'd had limited contact with men. She couldn't recall ever seeing a man's bare chest before, and witnessing it was exciting but disturbing.

His shirt was lying in the grass, and he picked it up, using it as a towel to dry his face and shoulders. As he tugged it on, a spectator stood and ambled over. He was older, probably fifty-five or sixty, but he was slender and spry with graying hair pulled into a tidy ponytail. He sported a thin mustache, and he was very elegant, his hands expressive as if he might be an artist or musician.

"Under my tutelage," he told Mr. Blair, his French accent clear, "you are both much improved."

"Yes, Valois," Mr. Blair replied, "your instruction has been impressive."

Kat bit down a cluck of offense. So this was the notorious Monsieur Valois. He couldn't be bothered to meet with her because he'd been playing games.

He retrieved a sword and demonstrated several lunges. He was graceful as a ballet dancer, very quick and assured.

"Monsieur Hubbard," he said to the dark-haired man, "you must balance your feet to level your thrust."

Mr. Hubbard responded, "Or Bryce could simply stop being such a vain brute and permit me to win every so often."

Mr. Blair flashed a glower so crammed with imperious authority that Kat was stunned by it. Who was he? What was he? Why would such a magnificent male specimen be dawdling in Valois's garden, engaged in a paltry fencing lesson? He was already stupendous. Why would he feel himself in need of training?

"Egypt has changed me, Chase," Mr. Blair said to Mr. Hubbard. "And your grating personality is wearing thin. I've lost my inclination to be nice to you."

"I could help you find it," Chase Hubbard complained.

"No, thank you," Mr. Blair retorted. "I rather enjoy beating you."

"Now we're getting to the truth of the matter," Mr. Hubbard groused. "You're becoming a veritable one-man war machine."

"Well, so long as I remain in this accursed country, I'm not about to have another miscreant take advantage of me. I've suffered enough catastrophe for ten lifetimes. If a brigand ever again dares to glance in my direction, he'll be sorry."

Valois beamed with approval. "You are definitely your father's son. I see him in every move you make."

"*Merci*, Valois." Mr. Blair nodded. "That is the highest compliment you could ever have paid me."

Mr. Blair turned then, and for just a second, he was staring right at her. She froze and held her breath, praying he wouldn't notice her lurking in the foliage. She planned to visit Valois again and would hate to have to explain why she'd been prowling in his bushes and spying on him and his guests.

For a few seconds, Mr. Blair observed her, as if checking to be certain she was really there and not an apparition. Then he grinned and motioned with his index finger, indicating she should step out onto the grassy lawn.

He was such an imposing figure that it was difficult to ignore his summons, but she could be quite imposing herself. She was a princess after all.

She spun and dashed away, racing out to the bricked drive and hastening to the street. Behind her, Mr. Blair said, "Did you see that?"

"See what?" Mr. Hubbard asked.

"There was a woman watching us."

"A woman?" Valois said. "Why would a woman be hiding in my garden?"

Kat heard naught more than that. Terrified they might come after her, she increased her pace. Yet as she reached the gates, she stumbled to a halt and frowned.

When she'd arrived, the boulevard had been busy with traffic, with donkeys and camels and carts and pedestrians. Now it was quiet, no vehicles or animals in sight. Her rented chair was down the block, leaned on a garden wall, the porters having fled.

She peered about, wondering what had happened. Tentatively she walked toward the abandoned chair, when suddenly she was grabbed from behind. A burly, pungent man lifted her and swiftly carried her to a waiting carriage, and it took a moment for reality to settle in.

She was being kidnapped!

Throughout her life as a princess, she'd been counseled that such an insulting misfortune could befall her, but she'd never heeded the warnings. She'd grown up in safe, tiny Parthenia where this sort of thing would never have been contemplated.

The prior year had been a hideous grind of disasters. After all the indignities inflicted on her and her siblings, this ignominy was the last straw. She was more livid than she'd ever been.

Her attacker shouted in Arabic, but she didn't understand the language so she couldn't guess what he'd said. But his remark caused several other brigands to appear.

She kicked at his shins and screamed at the top of her lungs. He tried to cover her mouth with his filthy hand, but she bit him, her teeth latching on firmly enough to draw blood.

He bellowed with outrage and loosened his grip sufficiently that she wiggled away and plunged to her knees. Before she could scamper off, she heard quick, angry strides approaching. More words were shouted in Arabic and fighting commenced around her.

She was too frightened to look up so she threw her arms over her head and hunkered down, anxious for the horrid episode to conclude. Finally there was a loud thump on the cobbles, and she peeked over. Her assailant was unconscious in the gutter, and his accomplices had vanished like smoke.

Mr. Blair, the man from Valois's fencing lesson, had a sword at the criminal's throat. He was magnificent, tough and deadly, like a Crusader knight from days of old.

My hero! She'd never been happier to see another person.

She pushed herself to a sitting position and assessed her condition. Her palms were dirty and scraped, her skirt torn. Her bonnet had been knocked off, her brunette hair tumbling down her back in a messy chestnut wave.

Too disoriented to stand on her own, she continued to sit, to stare at Mr. Blair. She was embarrassed to be so weak. Six months earlier, she'd been relieved of her title of princess, and already she'd forgotten how to muster royal fortitude.

"Is he dead?" she asked Mr. Blair.

"No. Should I kill him for you? I can if you'd like, but I'd rather not proceed while you're watching."

Kat felt giddy at the notion that her dear champion would kill for her, but she replied with, "I don't suppose we ought to murder him out here on the street."

Mr. Blair chuckled. "No, probably not. I'm not clear on the local laws, but I'm quite sure the authorities would frown on foreigners committing a homicide."

He took the scoundrel's weapons for his own, then riffled through vest, trousers, and turban. He found a string of prayer beads but naught else, and he tossed them aside.

"Do you know who he is?" he inquired as he straightened.

"I have no idea. I've never seen him before."

"Was he following you?"

"I don't think so. I was simply walking along and he grabbed me."

"Most likely, he was hoping to rob you. Was he after your purse?"

"Perhaps, but you arrived too fast so he didn't have time for much mischief."

She tamped down a shudder, wondering if the bandit *had* been following her. Had Kristof sent him? Was she being spied on? If so, Nicholas and Isabelle weren't safe! At that very moment, other bandits might be on their way to kidnap *them*! She had to get back to the hotel. She had to...to...

As rapidly as the frantic thoughts careened in her mind, she shoved them away. She'd been very furtive in her departure from Parthenia. No one except her friend, Pippa, had been apprised of her plans. Not even Nicholas and Isabelle.

Pippa had helped her make the arrangements to travel, and she would never have betrayed Kat. They'd been raised together, were close as sisters. Pippa hated Kristof even more than Kat, and she'd have cut out her tongue rather than tell him a single detail.

So...Kat had to calm down. She wasn't being followed. No one was spying. Her lazy, unreliable porters had sneaked off and left her on her own. A random miscreant had seen her and pounced. That's all it was.

Mr. Hubbard from the fencing lesson rushed up to Mr. Blair. A gaggle of servants trailed after him, including the rude oaf who'd guarded Valois's door and had refused to let her inside. She glanced away, not inclined to have him suppose she cared enough to recognize him.

"What happened?" Mr. Hubbard asked.

Mr. Blair answered, "This idiot assaulted her."

"What shall we do with him?"

"Take him to Valois. He'll know how to handle the situation."

Mr. Hubbard snapped his fingers, and the servants seized the bandit by the ankles and dragged him away, his head banging on the cobbles. Shortly the whole group vanished through the gates into Valois's estate grounds.

She was alone with Mr. Blair, still staring, still sitting on her bottom and too disordered to rise.

"Are you injured?" he asked as he came over to her.

"Just my pride."

"Can you stand?"

"I'm sure I can."

But she didn't move. He extended his hand, and she reached for it and clasped hold. She shouldn't have allowed him to touch her—at least not according to her prior rank. It was forbidden for anyone to touch her exalted royal anatomy, but she *wasn't* royal anymore, and she had to get over the snobbery that had been instilled in her at birth.

Besides, though it was silly, she wanted him to be in charge so she didn't have to be. She was near to weeping, as if the attack had been her own fault, which was ridiculous. She'd done nothing wrong and needn't feel guilty or afraid.

He was very strong, and it was easy for him to pull her up. In a thrice, she was on her feet, but she was off balance and she smacked into him, the entire front of her body suddenly pressed to his.

For an instant, they were frozen in place, and she gazed up into his blue, blue eyes. The strangest sensation swept through her. It seemed as if they'd always been friends, and her heart leapt, as if they were lovers who'd been separated then reunited.

He appeared to perceive the connection too. He studied her and frowned. "Have we met before?"

"No," she said.

"Are you certain? I could swear I know you from somewhere."

She smiled. "You don't."

He dipped his head and stepped away. "Pardon me."

"Yes, absolutely."

She tried not to regret the small distance he'd imposed between their torsos, but there was a peculiar and thrilling wave of energy surging from him to her, as if their proximity had enlivened the surrounding air. The second he retreated, the atmosphere calmed.

He was still holding her hand though, and he bowed over it.

"Bryce Blair, formerly of London, England, at your service, madam."

"I'm very pleased to make your acquaintance, Mr. Blair. I am Miss Katarina Webster."

She provided her fake surname with no difficulty, but she didn't provide her town of residence as he had.

"Where are you from, Miss Webster? You have the most unusual accent. I can't place it."

French was the official language of Parthenia, but with its central location, she was also fluent in Italian and Spanish. And of course her mother had been from Boston, so Kat had grown up speaking English in the queen's apartments. But she wasn't about to mention Parthenia.

"I'm an American," she claimed.

"An American! My goodness. How exotic."

"Is it?"

"Yes, very exotic. What were you doing in Valois's garden?"

"I have to discuss a private matter with him, but his butler turned me away."

"How rude."

"I certainly thought so."

"You were spying on me," he said.

"I wouldn't call it *spying*. I heard your swordplay as I was leaving, and I peeked through the palm fronds to discover what was occurring."

"No, you were spying, you scamp. I've recently become quite the swordsman, and I'm amazing to watch. You can admit it."

"Not in a thousand years, you vain beast."

He laughed, the merry sound of it washing over her like cool rain. As she'd suspected when she'd first seen him, he appeared to be contented and happy. Very likely, he laughed often and joyfully, and she wished some of his jollity would rub off on her. She felt abused and aggrieved and nothing was amusing or fun anymore.

The street was busy again as if the inhabitants had been hiding until the spectacle ended. With the excitement concluded, pedestrians were rushing past. She and Mr. Blair dawdled in the middle of it, their hands still inappropriately clasped together. He seemed in no hurry to release her, and Kat wasn't about to pull away either.

He exuded strength and power and ability, and just then it was exactly the kind of support she needed.

"Will you come into Valois's villa?" he asked.

"I'm a mess, Mr. Blair. When I meet him, I'd like to present myself in a better condition."

"I understand. Where are you staying?"

"For now, at the Hotel Cairo."

"The European visitor's sanctuary in the desert."

"So I'm told."

"It's some distance away. How did you get here?"

"Porters brought me in a rented chair." She pointed to the abandoned vehicle. "They conveniently vanished when I was assaulted."

"Yes, that was convenient of them, wasn't it?"

"They work at the hotel."

"I'll have a word with the management about it. I doubt they'll be working there tomorrow."

"You needn't bother. I can speak up for myself."

"Of course you can, Miss Webster, but you are a female and this is Egypt. May I escort you to your hotel? I'm determined that you arrive safely, and it's obvious I shouldn't trust the task to anyone but myself."

She probably should have demurred, should have worried about his motives or intentions. As he'd mentioned, this *was* Egypt, and it was a renowned haven for slavers, criminals, confidence artists, pirates, and other low types. What if he was a kidnapper too? What if he had wicked designs on her person?

The inane notion flitted by, and she ignored it. He was courteous, faithful, and trustworthy. She stared into his mesmerizing blue eyes and was absolutely certain of it.

"I would appreciate it very much if you would see me to my hotel."

"It would be my pleasure."

He turned to a servant who was walking by and barked out a few orders in Arabic. Several men hastened to pick up her chair. They carried it over, and Mr. Blair helped her in. He rattled off another string of commands, and her new set of porters raced away at a trot.

They departed very rapidly and, suddenly panicked, she glanced around, afraid they'd left him behind. But he was jogging along at their swift pace.

"Stay with me," she said. "Don't let them go off without you."

He flashed a grin that was devastatingly beautiful. "No, I won't let them. I'll be right by your side the entire way. You couldn't be shed of me if you tried."

CHAPTER TWO

"What brought you to Cairo, Mr. Blair?"

"It's a long story."

"Will you tell it to me someday?"

"I can tell it to you now."

He was walking beside the rented chair that was carrying Miss Webster to her hotel.

He was incredibly intrigued by her. During her visit to Valois, she'd been unaccompanied by a maid or footman so she was either very brave or very foolish.

Valois had lived in Cairo for decades, having come exploring as a youth, but while he'd been away from France, the revolution had heated up, and most of his relatives were murdered. There had been no home to which he could return, so he'd remained in Egypt, preferring the rough and tumble city to the cold, dangerous palaces of Paris.

He was apprised of every event that happened in Cairo, instantly learned when Europeans arrived, knew when they were in trouble, knew when they needed help or advice. He traded in information and was often involved in unsavory and clandestine activities.

Bryce's father, Julian, had come on his own adventure thirty years earlier. For a short while, he and Valois had been partners, and when Bryce had experienced his own series of disasters, he rushed to Valois for assistance.

Why had she sought out Valois? People never called on him for innocent reasons.

"I'm adventuring," he told her.

"How wildly extraordinary."

"I signed on with a group of acquaintances in London. My friend Chase Hubbard—I was fencing with him at the villa—convinced me I should."

"And now that you're here, are you glad you listened to him?"

Bryce shrugged. "Yes and no. My father traveled in Egypt as a young man. I wanted to follow in his footsteps."

"Good for you, Mr. Blair."

"But since I arrived, I've suffered naught but catastrophe. Valois has kindly let me stay with him until I can arrange to depart."

"What catastrophes have you encountered? I'm only just arrived myself. Describe some of the hazards so I can try to avoid them."

"Well, let's see. Our boat crashed on some rapids and broke apart. Three fellows drowned."

She gasped. "Seriously? You're not jesting?"

"No. A few others contracted a fever and perished."

"Mr. Blair! You're scaring me."

"Yes, it's been quite scary. We were robbed of everything but the clothes on our backs. We were nearly slain by some villainous Bedouins. We were abandoned for dead in the desert and almost perished from thirst and starvation."

"That can't be true. No single trip could involve so many calamities."

"It's all true, I'm afraid. We started out with a dozen investors, and we staggered into Cairo with six men. Four of them had the money to head for England, and they left as fast as passage could be purchased."

"What about you?"

"Chase and I spent our money getting here, then our meager reserve funds were stolen from us. We haven't the means to leave so we're still figuring out what to do."

She peeked out at him, her dark hair gleaming in the bright light. It was an unusual shade, appearing to be a very normal brunette until the sun shone on it in a certain way. Then he noted that it was shot through with strands of auburn and gold. He'd never seen hair like it.

In her tussle with her assailant, her bonnet had fallen off and her combs scattered so the curly locks had tumbled down her back. Was she aware of it? She seemed a bit disoriented so she must not have noticed. He was being treated to a lovely sight.

Though he was pretending he wasn't affected by her, she was extremely beautiful. At about five-foot-five or so, she was just the right height for a woman, and while very slender, she had curves in all the right spots. With her bright green eyes and dimpled cheeks, she was a joy to behold.

She was distressed though. He could sense it in her, almost as if he'd always known her, as if they were so intimate that he could perceive her fretting. Could he soothe her woe? Should he try?

From her speech and mannerisms, he suspected she was raised in high circumstances, and it had been a very long while since he'd encountered a real lady. In the months he'd been in Egypt, he'd met only whores and doxies so it was a very nice change.

She frowned at him. "I think I'm angry that you shared so many sordid details about your failed journey. If I was a timid, wilting sort of female, I'd likely have swooned."

"I wouldn't take you for the swooning type."

"I'm delighted to hear it."

"I spoke frankly with a purpose."

"What was it?"

"It's dangerous here. It's a strange land filled with unseen perils we never considered. I'm concerned that you visited Valois without an escort."

"I thought I was safe enough. The concierge at the hotel insisted I was."

"He's an idiot then, to send you off alone."

"I had my porters."

"Who vanished at the first sign of trouble."

"Yes, they did, the blasted miscreants. They'll definitely get an earful should I ever have the misfortune to see them again."

"I've learned—in the worst possible ways—that nothing is as it seems in this country. Disaster can strike in an instant."

"I realize that now."

"Please tell me you won't venture off on your own again. If you won't give me your vow, I'll worry constantly."

She smiled a smile that was charming and full of mischief. "My dear champion, will you truly worry?"

"Every second—unless you promise to be more careful."

"I promise. I called on Valois because I must hire a guide and bodyguards."

"Clearly you need the bodyguards. But why the guide?"

"My uncle is in Egypt, digging at an archeological site, but I'm not certain of his exact location."

"It shouldn't be too difficult to discover. He's an American too?"

"Yes."

"Valois knows everyone who's important. He'll be able to point you in the proper direction."

"That's what I was told. So you see, in my contacting him, I was trying to be cautious, but I was assailed before my retinue of guards could be put in place."

He breathed a sigh of relief. She wasn't reckless or negligent. She'd been seeking the appropriate assistance. There were modern, independent women who assumed they could behave however they liked, but they were riotously irresponsible and regularly got themselves into jams that men had to get them out of. Thankfully she wasn't one of those thoughtless types.

The moment he returned to the villa, he'd speak to Valois. He'd be sure Valois provided whatever aid she required.

Much too soon, they reached her hotel, the porters carrying her under the shade of the impressive portico. They set down the chair, and he waved them away. Yet they hovered, hoping he'd toss them a few coins, but he hadn't a farthing to his name, and he was galled by his own foolishness.

In London, he'd never been overly rich, but he'd always earned sufficient income to support his bad habits. He'd taken occasional jobs as a singer and actor, but he also gambled. He was a shrewd card player, but he'd never been addicted to gaming as some fellows were. So he never bet more than he could afford to lose.

Never for a single second had he ever been completely bankrupt, and it was a humiliating state of affairs to find himself penniless.

When Chase had suggested the trip to Egypt, it had sounded like a grand lark. Bryce had been at loose ends in London, feeling as if he was wasting his life, and he'd welcomed the chance to flee.

He'd grown up believing he was an orphan with no family or past worth mentioning. But totally by accident, he'd found the sister for whom he'd been searching for twenty years. As young children, she'd been Annie Blair, and he'd called her Sissy.

Now she was wealthy and settled, married to a viscount, and her name was Evangeline Drake, Lady Run. She'd helped him to fill in the blanks in his memory, to recollect who and what they'd been before tragedy had struck when he was five.

His father, Julian Blair, had been a viscount and would have one day been Earl of Radcliffe. Bryce should have been first in line to inherit that title. Instead he was standing on a dusty, hot street in Cairo and wondering how he'd ever leave.

If his sister could see him, broke, exhausted, irked beyond measure, what would she think?

It had been risky to traipse off with Chase Hubbard. His friend was a rascal and troublemaker, with no morals and a penchant for excess. Chase had a rough background too. His father was a French count, his mother the man's favorite mistress. When he'd died, Chase's French relatives had abandoned him quickly enough.

They'd paid for his schooling—that's where he and Bryce had met as boys—but they'd never provided a farthing beyond that. Chase scrounged and gambled and swindled to earn his living, choosing to walk a more despicable road than Bryce in order to survive financially.

Bryce liked him very much, but didn't trust him and never had. It was insane to latch onto any scheme Chase hatched, but he had—and look where it had landed him!

He'd disgraced himself by writing to Sissy to beg for funds to come home. With sea travel and mail so unreliable, he didn't know if she'd ever receive the letter. If she did, she'd send money, but with the way his luck was running, it might be years before it arrived.

Valois had graciously allowed him to stay at the villa, but Bryce couldn't impose forever. At least Valois was teaching Bryce some of the battle skills he should have acquired prior to departing London. If he'd had any idea how dangerous the journey would be, he'd have prepared himself a little better.

He hadn't understood that he'd have to fight murderous bandits or rescue himself from pilfering brigands. Well, he was learning his lessons swiftly and thoroughly. The next time a miscreant glanced at him, he'd be sorry.

His father had been a tough, valiant adventurer and explorer, and Bryce could feel the man's blood flowing in his veins. Day by day, he was more powerful, more assertive, more ready to protect and defend himself and others, but power and assertiveness didn't pay the bills.

What to do? What to do?

It was the question he constantly asked himself now.

While still in London, he'd insisted to Sissy that he would never sing for his supper again. But perhaps he ought to find a European cabaret and revert to his old forms of employment. If he was singing and playing the pianoforte in a reputable business, no one would stab him in the back and steal his purse.

He reached into the chair and helped Miss Webster to climb out. The porters were still lurking, and she leaned in and murmured to Bryce.

"I'm not sure of the customs here, and I don't know how you persuaded those men to carry me. Would they be offended if I compensated them?"

"No. I would have done it myself, but I'm ashamed to admit I haven't a penny in my pocket."

She waved away his comment. "It's not your debt. It's mine."

She opened her bag and pulled out a wad of money, and he nearly groaned aloud. She couldn't have every greedy passerby realize she was flush with cash. With how she was acting, he would have thought she'd never been out on her own before.

He stepped in, shielding her hands.

"Don't let everyone see your money," he whispered.

"Oh."

Her eyes widened with surprise—as if the prospect had never occurred to her, and maybe it hadn't. Maybe it was her first trip abroad, but then if she'd come all the way from America, she'd been traveling for ages. By now she ought to be more savvy.

He picked out an appropriate amount and gave it to a passing servant who hustled over and distributed it. Other servants emerged from the lobby.

They recognized Miss Webster as a guest, and they began fawning over her, grabbing her parasol, her fan, motioning for her to follow them inside. They were all smiles, all obsequious submissiveness that was faked. The Egyptians who worked in the grand hotels were courteous and civil to your face, but you wouldn't like to bump into one of them at night in a dark alley.

Miss Webster started after them, as Bryce lingered behind and shared a few harsh words with a servant who was in charge of the rest. He explained the assault, the porters who'd vanished. The man oozed dismay and apology.

He hurried after Miss Webster, and Bryce stood under the portico, watching her with a curious sort of nostalgia. He wanted to accompany her inside, wanted to escort her to her room to guarantee she was safely sequestered, but he didn't really know her. No doubt a father or brother or fiancé was waiting for her to return.

Still though, he was a little irked that she didn't bother to glance back. Yet just as he suffered the irritating notion, she halted and whipped around.

"Mr. Blair, aren't you going to say goodbye?"

"I was thinking the same about you."

"It's been marvelous to chat. Won't you stay and join me for a cup of tea?"

He'd relish nothing more than to enter the fabulous establishment, to sit in a shady spot while the servants fanned him with palm fronds. He'd fill his eyes with odd, pretty Miss Webster.

But when he'd intervened in her attack, he'd been dressed in his traveling clothes, his shirt untucked, his trousers torn. He was sweaty and cross, and he was armed with a sword and a knife, both dangling from his belt. He had a small pistol in his boot too.

In light of his rash of misfortunes, he never went anywhere without it. He looked no better than a chimney sweep and felt no better than some of the brigands he'd encountered on the road.

He took her hand, bowed over it, and kissed her fingers.

"I can't come in," he murmured.

"Are you certain? I hate to have you leave. It seems wrong."

Yes, it did. "May I visit another time? May I call on you when I'm in an improved condition?"

"Why yes, you may call on me. I'd like that very much."

She smiled the most beguiling smile, and he caught himself falling into it, mesmerized by it. He wanted her to keep smiling at him and to never stop.

Was he smitten? How could he be? They'd only just met. But then there was no accounting for romance, and he'd always loved women. It had been a very long while since he'd had a chance to flirt with someone who might flirt back.

He'd definitely return at the earliest opportunity.

He stepped away. "Now I'll say goodbye."

"No, not goodbye. Let's say, until tomorrow."

"Yes, until tomorrow."

She hovered, both of them eager to add something else, something more, but ultimately she spun and left. She climbed the three stairs into the lobby, the servants trailing after her. At the last second, she looked over and waved.

He nodded then hastened away so if she glanced again, she wouldn't see him moping and dawdling like a fool.

He missed her already.

⁂ ⁂ ⁂ ⁂

"You were assaulted?" Pippa shrieked.

"Hush," Kat cautioned. "Nicholas and Isabelle might hear you."

"But assaulted!" Pippa hissed more quietly.

"Yes."

"By whom?"

"A scoundrel on the street."

"What was his reason?"

"Apparently it was a robbery."

"Oh, my Lord, Katarina. Attacked on the street like a…nobody! Didn't I tell you we should have stayed in Parthenia where we belonged?"

"Yes, Pippa, you did. A thousand times or more. And didn't I tell you I was worried about Nicholas and we didn't dare remain?"

"And didn't I tell you that you were silly to fret over it? Kristof is insane, but he's not smart enough to concern himself with Nicholas. He's twelve. It would never have occurred to Kristof that he was a threat."

"What if you were wrong?" Kat asked.

"I wasn't," Pippa staunchly declared. "I suppose your being molested by a villain hasn't changed your mind."

"No."

"We'll press on to the desert to find your uncle."

"Yes."

"To do what? Live in a tent and take baths in the sand? No doubt we'll be eaten by crocodiles or stung to death by scorpions."

Kat couldn't completely conceal her exasperation.

Pippa had been Kat's best friend for twenty years. They'd grown up together, had shared the same tutors and governesses and dance masters. Pippa was an orphan and Kat's father had been her guardian. She'd been treated like a member of the royal family.

When Kat had decided to leave Parthenia, Pippa was the only

one in whom she'd confided, the only one she'd trusted.

In the beginning, Pippa had agreed with Kat's scheme, but as they'd journeyed farther and farther from home, Pippa had started to question everything. Recently her complaints were more spurious and annoying. Kat had offered to send her back, but she refused to go, claiming she would stick with Kat through thick and thin.

But with their finally arriving in Egypt, Pippa's qualms frequently bordered on hysteria. She was positive they'd be murdered in their beds or sold as harem slaves in the local market. Kat's encounter with the robber confirmed Pippa's worst fears, and Kat wished she hadn't mentioned the incident.

"Pippa, it will be fine. Uncle Cedric will be glad to see us, and he'll help us however he can. Please calm yourself. Your constant chastisement exhausts me."

"What if you'd been killed? Answer that, would you? What would have become of me and your brother and sister?"

"You have your instructions as to how you should proceed. You would deliver Nicholas and Isabelle to Uncle Cedric, then access the funds I set aside for you, and you'd return to Parthenia."

"With you dead and buried! And me on my own and having to carry on without you? How is that a valid plan?"

"I'm not intending to pass away for many decades so stop fretting."

They were at the hotel, in their sitting room that had a small balcony overlooking the Nile. It wasn't the grandest suite available, which was what Pippa had insisted they request. But Kat was trying to be inconspicuous and not stir any gossip. It was odd enough for two women to be traveling on their own, and she couldn't draw extra attention.

Luckily Cairo was a busy, hectic city with foreigners from all over Europe, so it wasn't difficult to blend in. When she'd checked into the establishment, she'd told the proprietor she was a grieving widow, and it was presumed Nicholas and Isabelle were her children. So she probably shouldn't have been loitering in the lobby and mooning over Mr. Blair.

"Did you speak with Monsieur Valois?" Pippa asked.

"No. His butler wouldn't let me."

Pippa bristled with offense. "Ooh, I can't wait until I'm allowed to reveal your true status to all and sundry. I'll inform that wretch of who you really are."

"I'm sure he'll be impressed," Kat sarcastically retorted.

Kat might have been a princess with royal blood in her veins, but often when she talked about her homeland, people appeared confused over what it was and where it was located. She'd given up explaining.

"What now?" Pippa inquired. "You were hoping Valois would recommend an escort. I'm not stepping one foot into that desert unless we're surrounded by an entourage of hale, burly guards."

"I'll call on him again tomorrow. I was thinking I'd write first and request an appointment, which I should have done anyway. From the rumors I'd heard about him, I assumed I could bluster in unannounced. I know better, and I usually have better manners."

"He should be grateful to have you visit," Pippa loyally stated. "He should be thrilled."

"I'm just a lonely widow, remember? I'm the least thrilling visitor in the world."

There was a knock on the door, and neither of them moved. They'd grown up pampered and spoiled, so they'd never had to open a door in Parthenia. It was a minor but silly change in their life situation, and each time Kat realized how out of touch she was with daily living, she was shocked at how isolated she'd been from reality.

She started to rise, then Pippa noticed, and she rose instead and hurried over. A servant held out a silver tray with a letter on it. Pippa tried to take it, but he insisted it was for Kat and no other. She motioned for him to enter, then shooed him out before she examined the handwriting on the front.

She couldn't imagine who would contact her. No one knew who or where she was, and for an instant her pulse raced with alarm. Was it from Kristof? Was he about to order her home? But quickly, she saw that it was addressed to Katarina Webster and she relaxed. Kristof wasn't aware that she was using her mother's maiden name.

"Who is it from?" Pippa asked. "Who discovered that we are here?"

"It's from Monsieur Valois."

"The rude lout himself! How marvelous that he deigned to correspond."

"Be nice, Pippa."

"What does he say?"

"He's sorry he missed me earlier today, and he's very sorry about the incident outside his gate."

"As he should be."

"He's invited me to supper tomorrow night."

"Perhaps he's not so bad after all." Pippa hesitated, then asked, "May I accompany you? Am I included?"

"I'm certain it would be all right, but let me think on it."

Kat didn't like to leave Nicholas and Isabelle alone. She only trusted herself or Pippa to watch them. It unnerved her to have hotel servants or a hired nanny care for them, even if it was for a short interval.

"It's just supper, Kat. What could happen if I go?"

"That's what I thought this morning, and I was attacked in the street."

"You claimed it was random."

"It was."

"We'd be away for a few hours. How could it hurt?" Kat didn't respond, and Pippa begged, "Please, Kat? It's been ages since I've had any fun."

Pippa liked to dance and make merry. Of all the sins Kat had committed against her by convincing her to tag along, Kat most hated that Pippa couldn't enjoy her favorite entertainments.

"Let me think on it," she said again.

Pippa bit down whatever else she might have added. They both knew Kat would relent. She'd never been able to put her foot down about anything. It was the reason she'd had to flee Parthenia. She was a mediator and problem-solver. She didn't like to fight or argue, and she had trouble saying *no* and meaning it.

She glanced at the bottom of the letter and smiled. Pippa saw it and smirked.

"Why are you suddenly grinning like the cat that spotted the canary?"

"Valois has a guest staying with him, a Mr. Bryce Blair."

"How very British-sounding."

"He was the one who rescued me from the bandit."

"Was he tall, dark, and handsome? You have to tell me he was, and if he wasn't, lie about it."

"He was tall and handsome, but not dark. He had glorious blond hair and big blue eyes. He looked like a Greek god."

"A Greek god? If you noticed, he must have been splendid."

"He was." Kat pointed to the letter. "He penned a postscript. He says he hopes I'll come to supper."

"*He* hopes you will?"

"Yes."

"We've been in Egypt for a whole day and romance is already blossoming."

Kat scoffed. "Don't be absurd. When have I ever been smitten?"

"Never?"

"Precisely. He's not available to me. He'd have to be of royal blood."

"Not anymore," Pippa caustically griped. "Have you forgotten? Thanks to your despicable cousin, you're no longer a royal person."

"You don't have to remind me."

"You can flirt with whomever you like, and the great thing about being away from Parthenia is that there's no one to order you not to."

Kat sighed.

If only it were that easy. She'd love to be an ordinary woman who could be swept off her feet by a dashing fellow. But she'd spent too much of her life being counseled as to her rank and station, and even with that station revoked, she still heard those old voices warning her to be careful in her actions and attentions.

Besides, she might not always be disavowed. Kristof had quickly raised himself up, but he might just as quickly be cast down. Kat might have her title returned someday. Kristof had ruled that—because Kat's mother had been a foreigner and a commoner—her marriage to Kat's father was invalid. It had been the basis for declaring Kat and her siblings to be illegitimate.

Yet another king—Nicholas for instance—might decree otherwise. Another king might wish to have the prior heirs back in the palace. Even if that never transpired, even if she was never able to restore Nicholas to his rightful position, she would be busy rearing him and Isabelle. There would never be an opportunity for a frivolous endeavor such as amour.

Still though, at the thought of seeing Mr. Blair again, she couldn't tamp down a flutter of excitement. He was the most dynamic man she'd ever met. In the short period she'd been with him, she'd felt safe, protected, and very, very happy. He'd seemed to enjoy her company too. They shared a potent, magnetic attraction, and she couldn't help but wonder what it portended.

She looked over at Pippa. "I've made up my mind. We'll both go."

"Thank you, Kat! Oh, thank you. I'm suffocating in this room."

"Let's send for a maid. I want to buy new dresses that are more in line with the climate and temperature. And we'll find someone to style our hair. Valois and his male friends will be very glad we've arrived."

"I should hope so. You're one of the most beautiful women in Europe, and I'm not far behind."

Kat laughed. "We're humble too."

"And intoxicating. And rich. And mysterious."

"Yes, yes," Kat mockingly agreed. "I'm sure Valois's guests will be enthralled."

"I'm sure they will."

Kat had never considered herself to be particularly vain. Nor had she ever been especially taken with any suitor. Her interactions with the opposite sex had always been vigilantly proscribed.

She'd managed to be kissed a few times, but they had been hasty, furtive gropings carried out in dark hallways when she was sixteen and seventeen. If she'd been caught, her daring swains would have been whipped and maybe even imprisoned, and Kat had rapidly realized she couldn't recklessly put a boy in such jeopardy. She'd halted any flirtations. So...she'd never had the chance to suffer such a giddy rush of pleasure.

Bryce Blair...Bryce Blair... It was a fine name, befitting a very fine man.

CHAPTER THREE

Kat stood on Valois's balcony. It looked out over the dark, meandering waters of the Nile. The moon was rising in the east. It was full and round, the desert air making it glow an odd orange color.

Valois was an impeccable host. The food had been delicious, the wine superb, the service excellent, but the company had been the most intriguing. Twenty guests had been present, an interesting mix of foreigners from many places on the globe. They were all travelers seeking something in Egypt they couldn't find anywhere else.

The oppressive afternoon heat had cooled, and with the full moon shining down, she was possessed of an odd and urgent energy, as if she might commit any wild deed. She yearned to yank off her shoes and stockings, to run on the sandy shore. She'd let down her hair and strip to her petticoat, then jump into the swirling current.

It was a pretty picture to ponder, of herself alive with joy and verve. Of course she'd never behave so outrageously, but the tropical flowers and temperature were prodding her as if she was constantly being poked with a pin.

Footsteps sounded behind her, a man walking across the tiled verandah to the spot where she leaned against the balustrade. She glanced over her shoulder, relieved to see Mr. Blair approaching. So far he'd given very little indication that they were acquainted.

After he'd rescued her from her attacker, she'd assumed they'd established a bond. She'd been so excited to attend supper, to be with him again, but during the interminable repast he'd barely noticed her.

As she and Pippa had socialized before the meal, he'd been present but had hardly spoken to her. Then he'd been seated at the opposite end of the table so there had been no chance to chat. He'd spent the whole supper flirting with the women surrounding him, and Kat had been surprised to realize she was jealous and envious, which was ridiculous.

When the ladies had excused themselves and left the men to their port, she'd snuck outside so she could regain her equilibrium and control her careening emotions.

What was wrong with her? Anymore, no matter the issue, she flitted from one extreme to the next, never able to discover any middle ground in her attitude, wishes, or conduct.

She had no hold over Mr. Blair, and apparently they possessed no heightened fondness. She must have misinterpreted their prior encounter, and it was certainly typical. Life as a royal princess insured that relationships were stilted and awkward.

Yet here he was, and her heart fluttered with exhilaration.

He kept coming until he was directly in front of her, close enough that his trousers brushed her skirt. She wasn't accustomed to anyone standing so near, but she wasn't about to protest. The sparks she'd noted the prior day had already ignited, the air practically sizzling with anticipation.

He was dressed formally in black trousers, a black coat, a snowy white cravat. It was an expensive suit tailored from exquisite fabric, and she wondered if he'd brought it with him for adventuring down the Nile. It was a frivolous piece of clothing to cart along on such a trip, but she was glad he had. He was stunning.

She stared into his amazing blue eyes. The moonlight made them sparkle like diamonds.

"Hello, Mr. Blair."

"Hello, Miss Webster. Katarina. May I call you Katarina? Will you swoon if I do?"

"As we've previously discussed, I'm not the swooning sort. Yes, you may call me Katarina. Actually my friends call me Kat."

It was a heady moment for her. Only Pippa and her immediate family used her Christian name. Others simply weren't allowed, and she was giddy with astonishment over taking such a bold leap.

"Kat," he murmured and studied her. "I like it."

"What may I call you?"

"Bryce."

"Bryce Blair—a very masculine name."

"Is it? I've never thought so."

He stepped even closer so his leg was pressed to her own, and he eased her into the balustrade, her bottom wedged against the marble stone.

She was astounded by his brazen advance. She wanted to put a palm on his chest and push him back and inch or two, but her anatomy was almost singing with elation at having him touch her.

"You didn't talk to me when I arrived." She sounded as if she was pouting. "I decided you were ignoring me. Or perhaps we weren't really friends."

"I didn't think I should hog your attention. If I'd spent a single second by your side, I wouldn't have let anyone near you."

"You're flirting with me."

"I definitely am."

"I don't believe I've been flirted with before."

"With you being so beautiful? That can't be true. Are the men in America idiots?"

"No, but my father was a ferocious ogre. Any possible beau was too terrified to glance in my direction."

"I'm not afraid to look."

He laid a hand on her waist, which was shocking. She felt overcome—by the heat, by the full moon, by his gazing at her so intently—and she slid away.

"You might be a bit too much for me," she said aloud when she'd meant to keep the comment to herself.

"Too much *what?*" he asked.

"Too much man."

"No, I'm betting I'll turn out to be just the right amount."

She laughed, and it dawned on her that it had been ages since she'd laughed about anything.

"Did you survive the assault all in one piece?" he inquired.

"I'm stiff from when I fell to the cobbles, but other than that I'm fine."

"I'm relieved to hear it."

"What happened to the reprobate who accosted me?"

He flashed his devil's grin. "We probably oughtn't to discuss it, but he won't ever bother you again."

"Thank goodness."

Her nerves were getting the better of her, and she sidled away, but every time she moved, he moved too.

"Are you scared of me?" he asked.

"No."

"Then why keep skittering away?"

"I told you you're a bit much for me. I wasn't joking."

"Have you a father or brother traveling with you, Kat?"

"No, just my friend, Pippa. You met her earlier in the dining room."

"Two females? How daring you are."

"I'm a widow. My children are with me too. Nicholas and Isabelle."

"How old are they?"

"Ten and twelve."

"They're waiting for you at the hotel?"

"Yes."

"You don't have to be back soon, do you?"

"No."

She rattled off her lies with ease. Long before she'd fled Parthenia, she'd concocted an entire fake history she could recite if she was peppered with questions about her life or family. The only thing she hadn't changed was their first names. She'd suspected it would be difficult to remember who they were and they'd stumble into fibs.

"Valois sent me to fetch you," Bryce said.

"How kind of him to make time for me."

"But I'm not delivering you just yet. Let's walk down to the water. I want you all to myself for a few minutes."

She peered over her shoulder. "Is it safe down there?"

"Is it...*safe*? I'll be with you. There can be no peril when I am by your side."

"You're awfully sure of that."

"Since I arrived in Egypt, I've been learning new tricks. I can now be deadly when riled, and I exude a definite sense of menace. No criminal would risk approaching me."

She was positive he was correct and that she'd accompany him. Still though, she asked, "What if you're wrong?"

"Then we're both in trouble." He held out his hand, and when she hesitated, he said almost like a dare, "Come on, Kat. Live dangerously."

"I never have."

"Maybe you should start."

She snorted. "You're teaching me an important detail about myself."

"What is it?"

"I can't imagine telling you *no*."

"And you shouldn't tell me that. It's just a walk on the beach in the moonlight."

"You have the most wicked gleam in your eye. I'm certain you're contemplating much more than a pleasant stroll."

"You'll never know unless you come with me."

He was so delectable, so impossibly vain and magnificent, that she shuddered to consider what sorts of mischief he might ultimately convince her to attempt. If she'd had any prudence remaining, she'd have refused to go, but apparently her prudence had flown away.

As if they were adolescent sweethearts, he linked their fingers and gave a slight tug. It was all the persuasion she needed.

They left the verandah, following the path to the river. Burning torches marked the route so it was easy to see the way. The sounds of the party faded. All she could hear was the breeze rustling the leaves in the trees, a few night animals calling to one another, and her pulse pounding in her ears.

The trail ended at an ornate dock complete with benches in secluded alcoves where a person could tarry and stare out at the view. Lamps twinkled from boats at anchor, but also from houses on the other bank. She was in the middle of a large city, but felt as if she was isolated on a sprawling country estate.

They sat side by side on a bench. Water lapped down below, a cool gust of wind riffling her hair. Their arms and legs were nestled together, and he was still holding her hand. It was the most intimate, thrilling moment of her life.

For a long while, they enjoyed a companionable silence. She was dying to open her mouth and blather on about topics she couldn't address. She wanted to mention her father's death and Kristof's perfidy, wanted to mention how alone she was and how afraid that she was making all the wrong decisions.

She wanted to disclose how frightened she'd been in Parthenia, how shocking it had been to find herself without a single friend but Pippa. Her father's family had competently ruled for centuries, but at the first hint of conflict, she and her siblings had been disavowed by everyone.

That was the most egregious disgrace they'd suffered, the discovery that they had no allies. She had to hope her uncle would be glad to see her, that he'd welcome her and offer to assist. Yet what if he didn't welcome her? What if he wasn't glad?

No, no, I won't think about that. Everything would be fine.

"You're frowning." He turned to study her.

"Was I? I'm sorry."

"What is vexing you? You can confide in me. I'm a good listener and maybe I can help."

"It's nothing," she lied.

"Tell me about your husband."

"My...husband?"

For an instant, she was confused as to whom he referred, and she must have looked like a dunce, because he said, "You claim you're a widow. Are you?"

"Yes...ah...he was a seafaring man." His skepticism was obvious, so she added, "We were married young, and he drowned in a tempest many years ago."

"You don't say."

"But let's not talk about him. Let's talk about you."

He chuckled. "Why am I suddenly supposing you're a woman of many secrets?"

"I have no idea."

"You're a very bad liar."

"I am not. Lying, that is."

"You shouldn't lie to *me*. Your face is an open book, and I can read it clearly. Tell me why you're really here to see Valois."

"I already told you. I have to hire bodyguards and a guide to escort me to my uncle."

"You're bent on reaching him because…"

She glanced away, unable to hold his steady gaze. "He's constantly invited me to visit, and I always wanted to. It was a perfect time to journey to Egypt."

His chuckle grew to a full laugh. "We don't have to chat about your troubles if you don't wish to, but you should work on your story. If you're going to make up facts, you should practice in the mirror so you can figure out how to appear honest and candid."

They were quiet again, and she was bristling with the desire to divulge the particulars as he was urging her to do, but she couldn't. First of all, it was humiliating to announce that she'd been declared a bastard child. And second of all, in the past few months, she'd learned not to trust anyone. Not *anyone*.

"After you've spoken with your uncle," he said, "then what are your plans?"

"I can't guess. It's the reason I'm here. He's my mother's only sibling, and I need his advice on many matters."

"Are you sure he'll give it."

No. "Why wouldn't he?"

He shrugged. "I've met some of the archeologists who are digging. They seem a tad…*obsessed* to me. He might not like to have a gaggle of relatives show up."

"He'll be delighted to see us." She wasn't at all certain he would be.

"Well…good. After you've located him, will you stay in Egypt?"

"I haven't decided. It's a topic we'll discuss."

"If you eventually depart, where will you go? Back to America?"

"I don't know if I would sail the ocean again."

"Is Europe a possibility for you?"

"Maybe."

"If you settle in London, we might cross paths there occasionally."

"That's assuming you can scrape up the funds to leave Cairo."

"I expect it will happen before too long."

"Who is your family in England? Would I have heard of them?"

"No. I'm an orphan—although I've recently found a sister I'd lost as a young boy. We're searching for two of my brothers too. There were four of us, but we were separated when I was five."

"You have stories to tell too."

"Yes, but mine are all true, so I don't have to keep any of them straight when I'm sharing them with strangers."

From his manner, speech, and mode of dress, it was clear he'd been educated and reared appropriately, and she'd presumed he was from a higher echelon of society. She'd been hoping he might have an ancestry that would make an acquaintance between them suitable.

If he was an orphan with a catastrophe in his background, there could be no continuing connection. She desperately needed a friend, and it had been an eternity since notions of amour had been stirred.

Perhaps they could have a wild fling while they were both trapped in Egypt. Perhaps the desert would push them to improper conduct that she'd always deeply regret but fondly recall. She'd read about people who engaged in passionate dalliances during their travels. Evidently when one was away from home and removed from the regular rules about decorum, one was freer in his actions.

Would she ever dare entertain an immoral liaison? She doubted it, but it was humorous to consider. If she ever *was* interested, he would definitely be the man with whom she'd choose to misbehave.

"How do you occupy yourself in London?" she asked.

"Shall I shock you and admit it?"

"Yes."

"I'm a renowned scalawag."

He seemed so stable and well-adjusted. She couldn't imagine him involved in frivolous pursuits. Loyally she declared, "Who says you are? I refuse to believe it."

"No, I'm awful. I gamble—"

"Most gentlemen do."

"And I supplement my income by acting on the stage."

It was the last comment she'd anticipated, and she was so disappointed to hear it. Actors were deemed to be the most depraved scoundrels in the world. There was no worse statement he could have offered to prove how they should never have even the slightest cordiality.

"On the...stage?" she wanly said.

"Yes. I told you I'd shock you."

"I'm not shocked. I'm...I'm...ah...I guess I *am* shocked."

"My mother was a gifted actress and singer. I take after her."

"You sing too?"

"And I play the pianoforte. I'm quite extraordinary, but I like to announce my low habits right up front. It keeps misconceptions from forming."

"Yes, I can see that it would."

"It helps me to discover whether someone is a genuine friend or not."

He studied her, and it was obvious he'd issued a challenge. He'd pegged her as the kind of female who would judge and condemn over his circumstances.

Would she?

Was she the snob he pictured her to be? Would she snub him because he had talents that branded him as being too far beneath her lofty self? Or was she better than he assumed?

She wasn't *lofty* anymore, but she'd had a lifetime of pomposity drilled into her. She was struggling to adapt, and she liked to hope she could befriend a remarkable person despite how he earned his living. She liked to hope she could overlook the vast differences separating them and establish a solid bond. Why couldn't she?

As Pippa constantly reminded her, she was no longer a royal princess. She had to adjust her standards, had to learn how to mingle with and care about all sorts of people. Not only those with blue blood running in their veins.

"I was raised to be a terrible snob," she said.

"I can tell that about you."

"But I'm trying to change."

He nodded. "Change is always good."

"I've never chatted with an actor before."

"Well, I'm not much of an actor these days. I'm changing too, remember? I'm trying to be an adventurer, but I'm not having much luck at it."

"Oh, I don't know. It appears to me that you're having an enormously grand adventure. You'll still be bragging about it when you're old and gray. Your grandchildren will be so weary of your stories about your sojourn in Egypt that they'll refuse to be in the same room with you lest you start in with another tale of your daring-do."

He chuckled. "I'm sure you're correct. When this is all over, I'll likely reflect on it with relish. At the moment, it seems a bit dire."

"You'll get through it."

"Yes, I will."

"Have you asked Valois for funds to pay your passage home?"

"I wouldn't offend him. He's been very gracious, and so far I haven't overstayed my welcome. But I'm certain if I began begging him for money, I'd rapidly find myself shown to the door."

"Maybe you should search for an heiress and marry her. Isn't that what desperate gentlemen usually attempt?"

"An...heiress," he mused as if he'd never previously considered the notion. "Yes, that's precisely what I need. How about you? Are you rich? Should I seduce you to grab hold of your fortune?"

"After that question, if I was wealthy I wouldn't admit it."

"I'll expose all your secrets. Just you wait and see."

"I will never tell them to you, so you shouldn't expect to ever unravel them."

"I'm already making progress."

"How?"

"You just confessed to having secrets. Earlier, didn't you claim you had none?"

"I am merely a widow who's come to Egypt to visit my uncle. That's it."

"Liar."

Before she realized what he intended, he leaned over and kissed her on the mouth. It was quick and brief and very, very dear, and she was so surprised that she didn't try to deflect it.

He hovered an inch away, and she was flummoxed and amazed. They'd been pleasantly conversing, sharing confidences, and she'd been unaware that he was contemplating such a brazen deed. She thought she should probably be irked by his audacity, but she wasn't irked in the least.

She was smiling, wishing he'd do it again.

"You fascinate me, Kat," he said.

"I can't imagine why."

"You're smart and beautiful and mysterious and very alone. How could I not be fascinated?"

"What made you suppose I'd like to be kissed by you?"

"Every woman I've ever met has yearned to be kissed by me. And they all had that opinion even before I became tough and dangerous."

His boasts had her laughing. "Each and every one of them yearned to be kissed?"

"Yes, and you're not so very different from all the rest."

"You're wrong about that. I'm totally different from anyone you've ever encountered."

"I plan to eventually discover exactly what that means."

He kissed her again, his chest crushed to hers, his body pressing her into the bench. His lips were soft and warm, and he felt so good and smelled so good. She was overwhelmed by him, by the night, by the reckless energy that had been surging through her all evening.

There was no predicting what she might have allowed, but apparently he had better sense than she did. He stroked his palms up her arms, over her shoulders and neck, then he wrenched away, almost as if he had to force himself to stop.

"Let's get you inside so you can speak with Valois."

"I'm scheduled to talk with him, aren't I?" But she didn't move, didn't ease him away. "My head is spinning, Bryce. You have me completely discombobulated."

"Of course I have. I just kissed you twice. It's difficult to proceed rationally after such an exciting event has occurred."

She laughed again, which seemed to be her regular condition when she was in his presence. He was vain and funny and charming, and she was so lucky to have met him. Her angels had definitely been guiding her when she'd been tossed into his path.

Her fondness couldn't lead anywhere though. Yet must it lead somewhere? Couldn't she simply welcome his friendship? Couldn't she lean on him during this period when she was so weary and troubled? Where was the harm in that? It wasn't as if a room of Parthenian chaperones was watching her every second.

She was a twenty-five-year-old independent female who'd recently lived through the most trying of times. Why shouldn't she seize a bit of joy? Why shouldn't Bryce Blair grow as close as he liked? She knew all the appropriate boundaries and would never permit him to cross them.

He stood and helped her to her feet, and she was stunned to find that she was sad at having their amorous rendezvous conclude. If he hadn't insisted they return to the villa, she'd have been happy to dawdle all evening.

She'd been kissed in the moonlight! By a handsome, dynamic hero and champion. By an actor! She'd understood that strange incidents would be possible in Egypt, but clearly she'd had no idea.

He bent down and whispered, "I'm going to kiss you again before the night is over."

"Only if I let you," she saucily retorted. My goodness, but she was flirting! She hadn't thought she knew how.

"You'll let me. You won't be able to resist."

She clutched the front of his shirt and rose on tiptoe to place her own kiss on his lovely lips. "You might be correct, Mr. Blair. Perhaps I shall never be the same."

CHAPTER FOUR

"Hello, Mr. Hubbard."

Pippa smiled at Chase Hubbard, and as he smiled back, she decided he was the handsomest fellow to stroll down her road in ages.

He was tall, broad-shouldered, tan and fit. His hair was dark, his eyes blue, and his face was clean shaven, which delighted her. In Parthenia, most men wore beards, partly for fashion and partly to ward off the cold weather. But she always appreciated a man who regularly used his razor.

They were out on Valois's verandah, with the other guests inside chatting, playing cards, or listening to a trio of musicians in the music room.

She'd come out to see where Kat had gone and had arrived to observe her walking into the garden with Mr. Blair. To Pippa's amazement, they shared an attraction that had been so evident it had been blatantly noticeable.

She'd been Kat's best friend for twenty years, and in all that time, Kat had never been smitten. In light of her rank, dalliances weren't possible, so she likely had no idea that she and Mr. Blair were so compatible, and Pippa wouldn't inform her either.

Kat needed to loosen up, to stop being such a prude and a shrew. She was no longer a princess, and she had to climb down off her high horse. Maybe if Mr. Blair flirted with her, she'd start to focus on someone other than herself.

"Pippa is an unusual name," Mr. Hubbard said. "What does it stand for?"

"Phillippa, but I could never pronounce it when I was little. I could only say Pippa, so it stuck. Please don't ever call me Phillippa. It sounds much too old and stuffy."

"Well, I would have called you Miss Clementi, but if you insist, I'm sure I can make it Pippa instead."

"My, my, but aren't you bold. Why would you think I'll let you act so familiarly?"

"I can tell by looking that you're the sort of female who refuses to be trapped by convention."

"You might be wrong about that. I'm certain I'm the most conventional woman who ever lived."

"Shall we bet on it?"

"Are you a gambler, Mr. Hubbard?"

"Yes. I wager on everything."

"Why would you?"

"Because I generally win, so why wouldn't I?" He grinned a cocky grin. "Why are you in Egypt? Bryce mentioned a visit to Miss Webster's uncle."

"Yes, he's a fanatic about all these ancient ruins. He's been here for decades."

"What spurred your journey? You're from America? That's quite a voyage merely to speak with a relative."

"Kat recently had a spot of trouble. She's determined to seek his advice."

"She must want it very badly if she'd come all this way."

"She's a bit mad on the subject actually. I tried to talk her out of it, but she wouldn't listen." Pippa frowned. "Forget I said that. She's always been stubborn. When she gets a wild idea, there's no dissuading her. It won't help matters to have me complaining and second-guessing."

"My lips are sealed."

He leaned against the balustrade and gazed out at the Nile. The moon was up, full and round and glowing an eerie shade of orange. The color, the tropical foliage, the sultry temperature all made her eager to misbehave, and she was no better than she had to be.

She'd nearly wed when she was eighteen. Her dashing, foreign swain had burst into court and swept her off her feet. Unfortunately he'd thought she was a royal cousin, had thought she had a huge dowry.

For the most part, Kat's father had been kind and generous. Pippa had become his ward when she was five and her parents had died of the influenza. Her own father had been a minor Italian composer, not revered or renowned, so there had been no assets when he'd passed on.

Her father and Kat's had been friends when they were boys, with the King not even realizing he'd been appointed her guardian until she'd shown up at court. He'd taken her in and, in many ways, treated her as a daughter.

Yet he'd been obtuse too. It had never occurred to him that she could have used a dowry or that he should supply one. If Kat's mother had survived, she might have pushed him into it, and Pippa hadn't known how to suggest it herself.

Once her elegant beau had learned of her low status, he'd

sneaked away in the middle of the night and she'd never seen him again. Of course by then, she'd been good and truly ruined, and she'd been lucky no babe had caught in her womb.

But she'd enjoyed the physical aspect of romance, so she'd conferred with a local midwife who'd taught her how to avoid a babe. Then she was able to dally occasionally. She picked visitors who were traveling through Parthenia, who would stay a short while, then move on.

She'd participated in many unsavory affairs, and she had no illusions about her character. She was easy and loose, her head always turned by a pretty face. Mr. Hubbard was just her cup of tea, and she was already figuring out how she could trifle with him before Kat dragged her off to the desert.

"Your last name is Clementi," Mr. Hubbard said. "Are you of Italian heritage?"

"Yes."

"How did you get to America? Were you born there?"

Clearly he was about to launch into a lengthy diatribe of questions about the journey, about life on the other side of the sea, and Pippa bristled with frustration. She'd told Kat not to claim they were from Boston. If they'd simply pretended to be from a small village in Italy, no one would have cared about the details, and she wasn't about to tiptoe into Kat's idiotic web of lies.

"It's a long story, Mr. Hubbard. I might tell it to you someday if you're very, very nice to me."

She'd imbued her tone with a hint of the flirtation she hoped to eventually have with him. His brows shot up, his curiosity piqued.

"I can be *very* nice," he said.

"You've brazenly decided to call me Pippa—even though I haven't given you permission."

"I never ask women for their permission on any topic. I typically find females to be too silly to think for themselves."

"You must be acquainted with some annoying specimens of the feminine gender."

"I am."

"I intend to call you Chase."

"Oh, you absolutely may. In fact, I insist on it."

"Even in company? Could I waltz into the parlor and call you Chase in front of the other guests?"

"Why not? I don't usually stand on ceremony."

"I'm delighted to hear it," she said.

"How about you? Do you like to stand on ceremony?"

"If the situation demands it, but I'm guessing our relationship wouldn't be one of those times."

He was growing more intrigued by the second. "How long are

you and Miss Webster planning to remain in Cairo?"

"Not long."

Any minute now, she was expecting to receive a message from Kristof that she'd completed her assigned task and could return to Parthenia. Kat thought she was being discreet and furtive, but from the first moment she'd mentioned fleeing with Nicholas and Isabelle, Pippa had gone straight to Kristof and warned him.

He'd been eager to know where she went, who she saw, and what arrangements she made. He didn't want her contacting supporters who might stir trouble over Nicholas's being deposed.

Pippa was sending him regular reports, and as a reward for keeping him apprised of Kat's location and activities, he'd offered Pippa her own apartment in the palace, an allowance, and an honored place at the king's table during meals. He'd also promised to dower her so she could wed if she wished.

In a few short months, he'd showered her with more boons than Kat's father had in twenty years. The instant Pippa had fulfilled her role, she'd depart for home, but until then she had to tread cautiously.

Kat claimed Kristof was insane, but *she* was insane to have left Parthenia, to have hauled the children with her. She was on a sinking ship, and Pippa wasn't about to sink with her.

She liked Kat well enough, but Kat forgot herself around Pippa. Yes, Kat was royal and Pippa wasn't, but they'd been raised as sisters, and Kat always ignored that pesky detail. She treated Pippa like a servant, and Pippa was tired of bowing and scraping to Kat, especially now when Kat had been stripped of her title and was no one of import.

The day Pippa was recalled to Parthenia, where she'd be lauded and compensated for her service to Kristof, would be the greatest day of her life.

"Since I won't be here for an extended stay," she said, "maybe we should hurry our association."

"I was thinking the same thing. Would you like to walk down by the river?"

"Normally I'd say *yes,* but Kat and Mr. Blair are down there."

"Are they?" He looked vastly humored by the notion.

"I wouldn't like to bump into Kat. She's a tad fussier than I am about how we should comport ourselves."

"Isn't she at the river with Bryce?"

"Yes, but she'd never misbehave." Pippa sidled nearer, approaching so close that her dress brushed his trousers. "I, on the other hand, have no qualms at all about a little misbehavior."

He grinned and clasped her wrist. "Follow me, Miss Pippa. There's another spot that is exactly what we require."

"May I be frank, Miss Webster?"

"Yes, please."

André Valois stared across his desk at the young woman who'd sought his help. They were in his private office, and though Bryce Blair had tried to accompany her for the discussion, André had chased him away. He and Miss Webster were alone.

"I know who you really are," he said.

"What do you mean?"

"I'm honored that you've graced my home, Your Highness."

Princess Morovsky gasped. "You must have me confused with someone else."

"Your father was a friend, so we needn't play games. Tell me what you need, and to the best of my ability, I shall provide it."

She studied him for an eternity, and André held himself very still, watching her, allowing her to decide how they would proceed. Through lengthy experience, he'd learned that most of what he hoped to discover would be revealed after an awkward silence. He had unlimited patience and expressive, coercive features that always succeeded in wearing people down.

Ultimately she asked, "How were you acquainted with my father?"

"I toured extensively before the Great Terror wrenched my beloved France apart. I stopped in Parthenia."

"Have we met?" she inquired.

"No."

"Then how can you be so sure of who I am? I've been incredibly discreet."

"Everyone has secrets," he told her with a sly smile. "I never divulge mine."

He'd lived in Cairo for decades, and local authorities were happy to let him deal with the troubles of visiting Europeans, so he'd personally dispatched her attacker. Just prior to slitting the man's throat, he'd obtained the confession that explained the assault. The bandit hadn't been a robber. A large reward had been posted for her capture, and he'd been hired to kidnap her.

After André had received that startling news, it had been easy to piece together the rest of the story.

Katarina *Webster*? For a woman who thought she was being furtive, she wasn't very good at it. André had once danced with her American mother at a ball in Parthenia, and her mother's maiden name had been Webster.

"If you know who I am," she said, "then you know I've lost my royal position."

"I'm aware of your difficulties."

"I'm no longer a princess so there's no need to exhibit any deference."

"I don't feel that way. Your father was a king. It doesn't matter what your cousin, Kristof, has decreed. You're still your father's daughter."

"Thank you. You're the first person who's spoken kindly to me about it since I was stripped of my title."

"The citizens of Parthenia are idiots."

She was too polite to agree. Instead she said, "You won't disclose my identity to anyone in Cairo, will you?"

"Not if you don't wish it."

"I don't wish it."

"Then *Miss Webster* it is. What assistance do you seek?"

"My mother's brother, Cedric Webster, is digging in the pyramids. I shall travel to his camp and stay with him for a bit."

"I've met Monsieur Webster."

"Are you familiar with his whereabouts?"

"Yes. If you hire a boat and sail on the river, it's a three-day journey from here."

"I'm relieved that it's nearby."

Her anxiety was visible, her nerves at a raw edge. She was brave to have come so far, to have plotted and schemed to protect her brother, and she'd accomplished it with no support from those who should have aided her.

There had been ghastly rumors about the coup in Parthenia. Kristof was an incompetent malingerer with visions of grandeur about his intellect and abilities. If there was any justice in the world—and typically there wasn't—the people of Parthenia would get sick of him quickly enough.

If André had been younger and more reckless, he might have offered to help restore her brother to the throne, but an aristocratic life could be hazardous—as his own kin had learned in a murderous way. All his relatives had had their heads chopped off by the guillotine. Luckily he'd been sightseeing in Egypt when the tragedy had occurred, which was the only reason he was still walking around and breathing the sultry desert air.

"I should like to continue on to my uncle's site," she said, "so I must hire a guide and some bodyguards. I was hoping for recommendations from you."

"I can supply you with the men you need, but I must ask—as an old friend of your father's—what are your plans after you've conferred with your uncle?"

"I have no plans after that. I'm out of options and ideas. If you have advice to share about my predicament, I would love to hear it."

André reflected on the kidnapper who had almost succeeded. Did she realize she was being followed? He didn't suppose she did. Was it his place to apprise her? Should he involve himself in her troubles? He couldn't fix the issues plaguing her, and if he became an ally, he'd have his own issues with Kristof Morovsky who had spies working in Cairo.

Every European André encountered in Egypt was in the midst of a catastrophe. It was the general situation for everyone. They didn't bring enough money, didn't comprehend the dangers, weren't ready for the harsh conditions, the peculiar customs, or problems with the language.

He dealt in information and secrets, but he kept his distance and never grew entangled in any mess. Though Princess Morovsky was a royal, and André had considered her father a friend, she was no different than any other beleaguered traveler who staggered through his door.

He would suggest, he would listen, but he wouldn't actually do much of anything for her.

He said, "You were prudent to remove your brother from Kristof's custody and control."

"I appreciate you telling me. I've been conflicted as to whether it was the right decision."

"It was, but I have no counsel to offer beyond that comment. I haven't a clue how you should carry on. I'm certain your uncle will prove himself wiser than I am."

"You seem quite wise to me, Monsieur Valois."

"You're very kind, and in this circumstance—when you have few viable alternatives—perhaps we should pray that Kristof meets with an early and bad end."

"Monsieur Valois! I would never pray for my cousin's rapid demise."

"I will pray for you."

She smiled. "You're horrid."

"I can be when the occasion calls for it." He smiled too. "Have you worried that there are men following you?"

"Yes, but I was very careful when I fled Parthenia, and I haven't noticed anyone who looks suspicious. I've constantly been on alert."

"I'm afraid your attacker might have been attempting to kidnap you."

She frowned. "You can't be sure of that, can you? Kristof would be the only one who might bother to order it, but I'm positive he was glad to find us gone."

He shrugged. "It was an odd and unprovoked assault."

"I thought it was a robbery. Are you claiming it might not have been?"

"I claim nothing. I simply warn you to be on guard."

"Believe me, I am on guard every second."

"Yet your brother and sister are with servants at the hotel while *you* are here enjoying my entertainment."

"I wouldn't have left them alone if it had occurred to me that they might be in danger."

"I'm not saying they are."

"Then what are you saying?" Appearing frightened and furious, she leapt to her feet. "I hope you'll excuse me, Monsieur, but I must return to my lodging at once."

"But of course." She spun to go, and he added, "I will send a retinue of men to you in the morning. They will provide all the services you require. Can you be prepared to depart by nine?"

"Yes, certainly."

"Have you funds to pay the costs, Princess? Since you've journeyed so far, I'm assuming you do."

"Yes, I have funds."

"They will expect an acceptable wage, and there will be a small fee added for my efforts on your behalf."

"That's fine. I have no idea what would be a suitable amount, so I'll trust you to set it."

"I'll have my clerk contact you about all of it."

"I'll speak with him the minute he arrives."

She nodded so imperiously that he wondered how she'd conceal her identity for long. He rose and tipped his head to her. He probably should have been more deferential, should have performed a bow and remained standing until she'd exited, but she'd insisted she was Miss Webster, so he'd treat her as if she was.

"Good evening," she said.

"Yes, thank you for coming. It has been my pleasure."

She was already in the hall, rushing away and calling for Miss Clementi. He hadn't meant to scare her. Or maybe he had. The blasted woman ought to be more cautious.

He sat in his chair, thinking, pondering. Bryce and Chase needed to keep themselves busy, as well as earn some money so they could book passage to England. They had been sufficiently trained by Valois and would be the perfect choice to watch over the precious cargo of the Morovsky heirs.

Bryce in particular had become lethal and menacing, and with his father's traits surging to the fore, the Princess would be plenty safe in his capable hands. Plus André was a Frenchman, a romantic at heart. He'd noted the passionate spark between the Princess and Bryce.

As a boy, Bryce had been robbed of his own heritage, so in that regard he and the Princess had much in common. Close proximity might be beneficial for both of them. At least the Princess would be protected by a man with aristocratic blood in his veins, and Bryce was very much like his father.

He was loyal, steady, and reliable, and the Princess would be lucky if he'd agree to take the job. She'd never have a better champion.

And as usual, André would have his own spies in the entourage so he would be fully apprised of the Princess's location and conduct. Information in Cairo was like gold, and he could never guess when his knowledge of Princess Morovsky's activities might be valuable.

She'd been stripped of title and rank and presumed she was a person of no consequence, but she was wrong about that. So long as Kristof was perched on her brother's throne, she would never have any peace.

He went to the door and summoned the servant who was outside.

"Find Mr. Blair," he said in French. "Ask him to attend me. I have a proposition that might interest him very much."

"Bring them back! Are you mad?"

King of Parthenia, Kristof Alexis Sebastiano Morovsky, threw his wine goblet against the fireplace, and it shattered quite effectively. He rounded on his chief advisor, Dmitri Romilard.

"There are rumors spreading," Dmitri said. "We must nip them in the bud."

"What rumors?" Kristof demanded.

"People are claiming Katarina, Nicholas, and Isabelle were murdered."

"How ridiculous! They're in Egypt with our spy, Pippa Clementi."

"The gossips insist they're buried in the woods behind the palace. There are stories circulating about a contingent of guards riding out in the middle of the night. Supposedly they were pulling a covered cart that was surrounded by gravediggers."

"Who is saying it?" Kristof bellowed. "Who? Who?"

"It's being whispered in every tavern and shop."

"And who is the purported killer of the Morovskys?"

"You," Dmitri responded without hesitation.

At the reply, Kristof was so incensed that little red dots formed on the edge of his vision, and he wondered if he was about to suffer an apoplexy.

"Name the lying miscreants who have disseminated this tale, and I will cut out their tongues while the rest of this disloyal court observes how my wrath rains down."

For emphasis, he pounded his fist on the table, and Dmitri rolled his eyes.

"We're not cutting out any tongues. Stop acting like a maniac. It will only increase the discontent. If your subjects think you're a lunatic, and you constantly behave like one, you'll simply confirm their low opinion."

They were in his private chambers, having just fled a raucous, rancorous meeting of elder statesmen. It had been a lengthy griping session that had left Kristof exhausted.

Kat's father had been a competent ruler, but lazy and backward. Kristof intended to modernize so Parthenia could stand tall among the other small countries of Europe. Because they were tiny and had no army, they weren't respected. It was the reason he'd seized control from Nicholas.

Nicholas was a child who would never have been able to implement a single improvement that needed to be made. He was too young to have exuded any authority and couldn't have led the country forward as Kristof could.

Kristof understood that people liked things as they were, that they'd be resistant to his ideas, but he hadn't expected such outright defiance. He was *king*, and if they failed to remember that he was, heads would roll—and he didn't care what Dmitri thought. The citizenry would revere him or else!

"Sit down, would you?" Dmitri said. "I'm dizzy from all your pacing."

Kristof was nearing thirty, and Dmitri was fifty. He was older than Kristof, smarter, wiser. Calmer. They were cousins to Katarina and her family, but Dmitri had always hated Kat's father, and he'd helped Kristof plan and execute his coup.

Now he possessed an enormous amount of authority, but he tried to be pragmatic and shrewd when Kristof didn't value either trait. He was more concerned with slyness and devious dealing that would ensure he got his way.

Still though, he plopped into a chair.

"What is it? Speak your piece while I have the patience to listen."

"You must write to Katarina and beg her to come home."

"I'd hang myself first. When she sneaked away, it was the perfect solution to our problem with Nicholas. You said so yourself. It was best to have all three of them gone.

"I've changed my mind."

"So?"

"You have no notion of the agitation that's festering. With you being denounced as a murderer, matters could quickly escalate."

"And I told you I'd cut out the tongue of any idiot who repeats such rancid gossip."

"Will you maim the entire kingdom?"

Kristof gasped. "The rumors are that prevalent?"

"Yes."

He fumed with rage.

He'd been a plump, homely boy, who'd grown to be a plump, homely man. He was never taken seriously, never praised for his accomplishments or hailed for his successes. But he was cunning and crafty, demonstrating his mental agility by how swiftly he'd seized the throne and pushed Nicholas off it.

Not a single person had protested or complained—except Katarina. His assertiveness had galvanized the populace.

Yet he wasn't handsome or regal as Katarina's father had been. He hadn't the effortless charm Nicholas exuded without trying. No, Kristof didn't look like a king or radiate the correct sort of royal deportment. Would he ever receive the admiration that should be his due? Would the crown ever rest easily on his head?

"What would I do with Katarina when she arrived?" he asked.

"I was thinking you could marry her."

"Marry her! We had her declared illegitimate. We yanked away her title and rank. I can't suddenly say it was all a mistake."

"Of course you can. You're the king. People are grumbling that you stole the throne by deceit and treachery, that perhaps spells or witchcraft were involved."

"Witchcraft! Oh, my Lord. This is a nation of imbeciles."

"You could lure her back, show everyone she's alive, then make her your wife. The whole kingdom would breathe a sigh of relief."

"I don't care if they're relieved. I wouldn't have that shrew in my bed if you promised me the keys to Heaven."

Katarina was very beautiful, as beautiful as her glamorous American mother had been, but she was also snooty and rude and horrid.

She'd never been kind to Kristof, had never appreciated him. He'd proposed to her once when she was sixteen, and she'd thought he was jesting, so it had given him particular pleasure to get even with her. If she'd accepted his proposal all those years ago, she'd be his queen now.

He could wed any bride he wanted, could find a princess from a smaller European royal house. He didn't have to settle for a vain, patronizing, half-blood like Katarina, and he wouldn't settle for her.

"Write the letter, Kristof," Dmitri urged.

"I won't," he petulantly replied.

"Then I will, and you shall sign it. We're not playing games. We're bringing her home."

"Why are you so sure she'll come?"

"We'll force her."

"If you assume you can, then you don't know Katarina very

well."

"She's a female, so she doesn't have a man's intellect, and she was much too sheltered. She doesn't understand dishonesty or pretense. We'll cajole her. We'll trick her."

"How?"

"We'll let her believe—if she returns with Nicholas—we'll put him in the line of succession."

"We never would. My own sons will go in that line."

"Yes, they will, but she's a gullible fool. She'll never realize the truth until it's much too late. Now write the damn letter!"

CHAPTER FIVE

Michael Blair rode through the gates of Radcliffe Castle. His twin brother, Matthew, trotted with him.

Radcliffe was just across the English border, on the Scottish side. It was an ancient edifice, so parts of it were in ruins, but much of it had been remodeled with modern amenities. There was a market in progress in the courtyard, so the place was buzzing with activity. Vendors were selling food, clothing, and other items.

As they entered the grounds, they created quite a stir. They were strangers on horseback, and some people took nervous, furtive glances while others brazenly stared, worried as to their purpose, if they were innocent visitors or if they'd come to cause trouble.

He grinned. They'd come to cause trouble.

His father, Julian Blair, had grown up at Radcliffe, had played in this very spot. He'd been a viscount, and as the eldest son, he'd been first in line to be the next earl. The previous despicable, malicious *earl* had been Michael's grandfather.

Supposedly the tyrant was deceased, and Michael's only regret over the ogre's demise was that it meant Michael would have no chance to spit in his face. Perhaps after matters were settled, he'd find out where the fiend was buried and dig up his body. He'd throw his corpse in the woods and let the scavengers pick away at his bones. It would serve him right.

A boy rushed from the stables to tend their horses, and they grudgingly handed them over. They were wondering whether they should keep the animals saddled and ready to depart. There would be no warm welcome from the castle's inhabitants so they might need a quick escape.

"Who is lord here?" Michael asked the boy.

"Lord Radcliffe," the boy replied.

"What's his Christian name?"

"George Blair."

"Is he at home today?"

"Of course, sir. He doesn't travel anymore. Everyone knows that."

"And now I do too," Michael agreed. "What is the countess's name? Susan?"

"Yes, sir."

"Is she here too?"

"She doesn't travel either, sir. She's too ill."

"Good."

Michael was a vindictive, vengeful fellow, and he wished every plague on George Blair and his wife.

People had sidled nearer, studying Michael and Matthew with a combination of fear and alarm, and their trepidation was understandable.

He and his brother were possessed of all their deceased father's best attributes, his tall height and handsome features, his large stature and cunning bravery. They were armed to the hilt too, pistols dangling from their hips, knives in their boots, swords on their belts. They were definitely a sight, looking to be the dangerous intruders they were.

The locals might call George and Susan Blair their lord and lady, but they wouldn't be earl and countess for long.

An older man stepped up and asked, "May I help you gentlemen?"

"We're here to speak with Lord Radcliffe."

"He doesn't keep public hours on Wednesday."

Matthew's glower was malicious. "I'm guessing he'll see us."

There was a woman behind the man, and she peeked around him and shrieked with dismay. "No, no! It can't be! It can't be!"

"Silence yourself!" the man commanded. "What's wrong?"

"It's a ghost! A ghost! He's haunting us from the grave!"

"What are you blathering about?"

"It's Julian Blair! Can't you tell? He's returned from the dead, and there are two of him. Send him away, Angus. Send him away!"

She pulled a crucifix from under the bodice of her dress and held it out as if Michael and Matthew were demons and she could ward off their evil spirits. Others blanched and backed away.

"I'll be damned," Angus muttered, and tentatively he inquired, "Julian?"

Michael and Matthew resembled their father in every way, right down to his penchant for brawling and fights. It didn't surprise Michael that these rural Scots would think he was Julian's ghost. He hoped the image disturbed them for the rest of their miserable lives.

"We're not Julian," Michael said.

"Who are you then?"

"We're his sons." Michael asked Matthew, "Are you ready?"

"As ready as I'll ever be. Let's say hello to the almighty *earl*."

A bigger crowd had gathered, all attention fixed on them as they hurried across the courtyard to the centermost building. The doors were open, people coming and going as part of the market. They entered a spacious receiving hall. There were more booths set along the walls, dining tables arranged in rows with a meal being prepared. Servants were bringing out dishes and cups.

A man and woman—obviously George and Susan Blair—sat on the dais at the front, watching the proceedings as if they were a decrepit king and queen surveying their subjects. They were in their fifties, but they seemed much older, more aged and beaten down. Despair and gloom wafted off them.

George was their uncle, but he bore them no resemblance. He was small and shrunken, and if he'd ever possessed any of his brother's dash and verve, it had faded. Michael suspected it had never been there in the first place. No man could have equaled his dynamic father in looks or temperament.

George appeared feeble, his hair thin and graying, and while his eyes were blue, they weren't the magnificent sapphire shade Michael's father had passed onto his four children. His face was marked by frown lines as if he'd never had a moment's happiness in his life, and Michael was certain he hadn't.

He'd betrayed his brother, stolen his brother's heritage, probably murdered his brother. He'd destroyed his brother's wife, had cast his niece and nephews to the winds of fate.

And he'd done it all simply because Michael's father had married *down*. Michael's mother hadn't been an aristocrat. She'd been a talented actress and singer, and for that paltry sin, Michael's family had paid and paid dearly. They were still paying, with their brother, Bryce, off in Egypt and too weary to seize what was his.

George and Susan Blair could pay now.

Bastard! Michael thought in his mind.

He's as sleazy a character as I could have predicted he'd be, Matthew responded in his own mind. They were completely attuned and didn't need to talk aloud.

Let's introduce ourselves.

I can't wait.

They marched down the middle of the large room, their boots tromping across the stone floor. People observed them—it was impossible not to stop and stare—and noises gradually waned until the hall was silent. A servant dropped a spoon and it echoed off the rafters. It was the only sound.

George Blair was whispering to a priest seated beside him and hadn't noticed Michael's approach, but Susan Blair eased forward in her chair.

As the boy had mentioned in the yard, she was very ill. Her skin was an odd orange color, and she was so thin, she was practically skeletal. Most of her hair had fallen out, and there was an air of disease about her that made Michael suppose she didn't have long to live.

"You there!" she snapped at Michael. "Who are you? Tell me who you are this instant!"

Her sharp tone caused George to whip around and glare at them. He gasped as Susan Blair repeated, "Who are you? Who?"

"Hello, Mrs. Blair," Michael rudely said. "I'd call you countess but you really aren't one, are you?"

"How dare you, sir!" George Blair huffed. "You can't come into my home and insult my wife."

"He already has," Matthew replied, "and we take great issue with you pretending this is your home. It was never yours, and we're here to see that you return it to the rightful owners. That would be us."

"You're mad," George scoffed, but he glanced about anxiously, as if worried over who might be listening.

He waved to a few servants as if they'd run over and accost Michael and Matthew, but none of them moved. They recognized, as George Blair didn't yet, that Michael and Matthew couldn't be intimidated.

"Julian?" Susan Blair suddenly hissed, evidently assuming—as the servants had outside—that Michael was his father, risen from the grave. "Is it you? Julian! Speak up! You're dead. You've been dead for twenty-five years. Don't haunt us. Please! I'm begging you."

"I happen to believe you could do with a little haunting," Michael retorted.

"And quite a bit of revenge," Matthew added.

"Who are you!" Susan demanded again. "You won't say. Why won't you say?"

"I am Michael Blair," Michael coldly announced.

"And I am Matthew Blair," Matthew announced just as coldly.

"What? What?" George Blair chirped like a bird. "You're a Blair? Are you claiming to be kin? For if you are, I call you a liar to your face."

"We would never claim kinship with the likes of you," Michael said. "Our parents are Anne and Julian Blair."

On his mentioning his parents, Michael and Matthew received the precise reaction they'd been hoping to obtain. The names—Anne and Julian—sizzled around the room, as if the universe was marking the declaration.

"No, no, this can't be," Susan wailed. "You're dead! Julian's children are all dead."

"You're wrong. We're all hale and healthy, especially our brother, Bryce, who is the lawful earl. We will retrieve what is ours. You ruined our parents. You killed them, and we've come to finally make you pay for all your crimes."

Susan Blair collapsed to the floor in an unconscious heap.

&ed; &ed; &ed; &ed;

"You're very kind to accompany us, Mr. Blair."

"Thank you, Nicholas, but I'm not working for free. I'm being compensated for my services."

"Of course you are. My sister and I would never accept charity. It's not in our nature."

"Your...sister?" Bryce asked.

Kat had previously informed Bryce that she was a widow and Isabelle and Nicholas were her son and daughter. He wasn't mistaken.

"Yes, Katarina is my sister," Nicholas said. "Who did you think she was?"

"I thought she was your mother."

"Why would you think that?"

"I have no idea," Bryce lied. "I guess I was confused."

"My mother perished while birthing Isabelle."

"You must have been very young when it happened."

"Yes. I was two when she passed away."

"I was five when I lost mine." Bryce sighed with regret.

Yet he wasn't sure she was deceased. Due to his grandfather's perfidy, she'd been transported to the penal colonies as a convicted felon. His sister, Evangeline, refused to believe she was dead.

Evangeline insisted their mother had survived the hazardous ocean voyage to Australia and that she was fine and safe and still living there. She planned to locate her and bring her back to England. It was a grand dream, and when Bryce was with Evangeline, he liked to pretend it could transpire. But he was more inclined to suppose she'd been deceased for many years.

"I don't remember my mother," Nicholas said. "Do you remember yours?"

"Yes, I remember her very clearly."

"You're lucky to recollect."

"I am lucky."

"What was she like?"

"She was beautiful and glamorous. She was a gifted singer so our home was constantly filled with music. She used to invite me to sit with her at her harpsichord and we'd sing songs together."

"What fun that must have been," Nicholas wistfully murmured.

"It was very fun. I miss those times, and I recall them often."

"As you should."

Bryce smiled down at Nicholas. They were standing at the bow of the boat Valois had arranged to deliver them to Cedric Webster's camp.

He'd met Kat at her hotel at nine, and Valois's porters had quickly and efficiently carted the Websters' belongings to the river. Two boats had sailed side by side, with the porters and a cadre of additional guards in one, and Bryce, Chase, Miss Clementi, and the Websters in the other.

They were anchored for the night on the banks of the Nile. The sun had just set, and it was a glorious evening, the hot temperature waning, birds taking their final flights. They cawed and dove into the water, grabbing a last bite of fish. The sky was purple and orange, and off in the distance, he could make out a line of pyramids. It was a magical sight.

Nicholas was an interesting boy. He was only twelve but very mature for his age. Isabelle was ten, and she was very much like him.

Occasionally they were as rambunctious and curious as any other children might be, but they could be very reserved and aloof too, very direct and authoritative in a way Bryce had never witnessed in other children. It seemed that perhaps they'd been trained in decorum and comportment, that they'd been raised to a bigger, more majestic life than the one they were currently leading.

With Bryce having discovered Kat was a sister and not a widowed mother, he suspected there was much more to their story than he'd been told.

Valois had simply asked him to escort Kat to her destination, then stay for as long as Kat required his services. Bryce might have refused, but the stipend Valois negotiated was an outrageous amount, so he hadn't been able to decline.

Chase had signed on too, with his friend needing the money as much as Bryce did. He'd also mentioned Miss Clementi in a fashion that had Bryce assuming there was romance brewing between the pair. He certainly hoped Miss Clementi recognized him for the cad he was. Chase was a handsome devil, but he was completely unreliable.

Quite a bit earlier, Isabelle had gone below, and suddenly she popped up on the deck and called to her brother. "Nicholas, Katarina says it's late and you should come to bed."

"I'm not a baby, Isabelle. Tell her I'll be down when I'm tired."

"She says you're tired now, but you don't realize it."

Nicholas peeked up at Bryce and grinned a grin of conspiracy and an innate male knowledge of women being ridiculous.

"I'm talking to Mr. Blair," Nicholas responded. "We're reminiscing about our mothers. I'm not ready to stop."

"Katarina says we'll be up at dawn so tomorrow will be another very long day. You need your rest."

Nicholas glared at his sister, then sighed. "Fine, Isabelle. I'll come to bed." He peered up at Bryce. "Will you excuse me, Mr. Blair?"

"Yes, of course."

"I can't bear to upset Katarina. She's done so much for me, and I'm very grateful." In a very European manner, he clicked his heels and bowed from the waist. "Goodnight."

"Goodnight," Bryce replied. "I'll see you in the morning."

He watched Nicholas and Isabelle climb down the ladder into the hold to the berths where they would sleep in luxurious comfort. The boat was lavishly furnished with feather mattresses and sheets sewn from the softest Egyptian cotton.

He thought again of what odd children they were. They looked just like Kat, slender and handsome with the same dark hair and green eyes, so when she'd claimed to be their mother, he'd believed her without question. But their close kinship couldn't be denied, so with his learning they were siblings, he'd didn't question that information either.

Nicholas's hair was neatly cut, his clothes expensive and perfectly tailored. Isabelle dressed in the same costly style, and because she was still a girl, she wore her hair plaited in a single braid down her back. Obviously they were rich and had been highly educated, but there was a graciousness and sophistication about them that belied the scant details Kat had provided.

He didn't mind a woman having secrets. He had plenty of his own, but it made his job of guarding her more difficult. If he had no idea what dangers she faced, how was he to guess when danger was approaching?

He went to a chair and sat, lit a cheroot and stared at the fires on the bank. The porters from the two boats were camped on shore, had cooked their supper and rolled out blankets on the sand. He was wondering about their lives and families when he heard footsteps on the deck behind him. He glanced over his shoulder to see Kat. She sat in the chair next to him.

"It's so beautiful, isn't it?" she said.

"Yes, very beautiful."

"The tropical climate is intoxicating. It leaves me so invigorated."

"It's a notorious effect travelers always feel when they're here." He frowned at her, eager to deduce what was going on in her devious head. "Are your children in bed?"

"Yes. I help them, but they're so grown up, they don't need me for much."

"It must be hard being a mother with no husband."

She gazed out at the water and casually said, "Yes, it's been very hard."

"How old were you when Nicholas was born? Ten? Eleven?"

"Ah...ah..."

Her voice trailed off. Evidently she couldn't perform the mathematical equation quickly enough to sound truthful.

Bryce smirked with annoyance. "Give over, Kat. You're not a widow and you're not anyone's mother. At least not Nicholas's or Isabelle's."

"I am too!" she staunchly declared.

"No, you're not. Nicholas spilled the beans."

She looked aghast. "About what?"

"About the fact that you're his sister."

She exhaled a terrified breath. "Oh. Did he...ah...tell you anything else?"

"No, but I'm wishing he would have. I'm trying to ascertain what has you so frightened."

"I'm not frightened."

"Really? If you keep me in the dark, how can I protect you? I'm being paid to watch over you, but if you're concealing important details, you could imperil us both."

"Don't be silly. We're not imperiled."

"Not yet."

She scowled, and he could practically see her struggling to decide how much to reveal. Ultimately she confessed, "Nicholas and Isabelle are my siblings."

"And you're hiding your relationship to them because...?"

"Let's just say Nicholas is a very wealthy boy, and I have relatives who don't have his best interests at heart."

"All right, let's say that."

"If anyone is searching for us—and I'm not claiming anyone is—they'd be hunting for three siblings traveling together. I pretend I'm a widow with two children and that's what people remember about us."

He assessed her, his blue eyes probing, digging deep, until she began to squirm in her chair.

"You're the worst liar, Kat."

"I'm not lying."

"You are, but we'll let it go at that. Will you ever trust me? I'm worried about you."

"You needn't be."

"You don't have to be so tough and independent. Would it kill you to lean on me a bit?"

She was silent for a long while, then she confided, "The past few months have been awful. I learned the hard way that I have no friends."

"I'm sorry to hear it."

"It's not easy for me to trust others. It used to be, but it's not now."

"I can certainly tell. You're not from Boston, are you?"

"No." As if the admission was embarrassing, she peered down at her lap. "We're from Europe, but please don't ask me where."

"I won't."

With how Nicholas had clicked his heels when saying goodnight, Bryce had guessed they were from Europe. But where? Prussia? Switzerland? He'd figure it out eventually.

"If a miscreant was sneaking up on you, what might he look like?"

"He'd likely have a trimmed beard, and he'd have a hat pulled low on his head. He'd be wearing an embroidered wool vest too. It's a common garment in my country."

"You've described the man who assaulted you outside Valois's villa."

"I'm sure that was a coincidence. It was a failed robbery. You said so yourself."

"What if I was wrong?"

"You weren't."

"Well, that fellow has met his Maker, but I'll keep an eye out for his brother or cousin."

"I'm positive there's no need, but I'm relieved by your vigilance."

He stood and went to the railing, and he tossed the butt of his cheroot into the water. It was slowly occurring to him that Valois had put him in an untenable predicament. Bryce hadn't been present when Valois was alone with her attacker. What had the brigand told Valois?

Bryce liked Valois and was grateful for his assistance, but he had secrets and hoarded them like gold. What did he really know about Kat and her siblings? Bryce should have pressed him for more information before he'd sailed off with her.

He studied the porters gathered around their fire pit on the shore. Chase and Miss Clementi had gone ashore too, and he wondered where they were.

He glanced back at Kat. "Is Miss Clementi sensible?"

"Sensible? Yes, I suppose."

"Would she recognize a cad if she saw one?"

"I should hope so. She was engaged to one when she was eighteen, and he jilted her and vanished without a trace. Why?"

"My friend, Chase Hubbard, is a scoundrel and libertine. Caution her, would you?"

"I will, but I can't imagine it's necessary."

Her reply vexed him enormously. She didn't seem to have accumulated much pragmatism or prudence. She was extremely gullible and never thought anything bad could happen, never thought anyone would behave in a way she wasn't expecting. The prior months should have taught her to be wary, but they hadn't, so his job of protecting her would be even more difficult.

If she never noted a person's unsavory traits, a criminal could get much too close before she realized she should be afraid.

He turned to face her, his hips balanced on the railing, his arms crossed over his chest. "I hate that I'm working for you, that you're paying me."

"I'm not having financial trouble. Don't concern yourself over it."

"I wish I could have helped you as a favor without demanding remuneration, but I simply couldn't afford to be altruistic."

"I understand, but I wouldn't be poor if I had ten lifetimes to spend all my money. I won't notice the expenditures."

"So you *are* an heiress after all." He grinned. "Didn't you once suggest I snag an heiress? It sounds as if I'm in the right place."

"I won't precisely admit to being an heiress, but I'm not eager to marry so you'll have to find your rich bride somewhere else."

"Drat it. I figured it would be easy to persuade you." He gestured to her and said, "Come here."

"Why?"

"I'll tell you when you get here."

"I don't like that look in your eye."

"It's dark out. How can you be sure of what *look* is in my eye?"

"I don't require a lantern to see that you're plotting mischief."

"Why, Miss Webster, you already know me so well."

He grabbed her hand and yanked her to her feet, pulling her to him so the front of her body was pressed to the front of his.

"Are you going to kiss me?" she asked.

"Yes."

"We shouldn't."

"So? We'll do it anyway. There's no chaperone to prevent it."

"Just because we don't have a nanny, we can still follow our moral code."

"I have no moral code," he huffed.

"You liar."

"I have a bit of one, but it never precludes me from dallying with a beautiful woman in the moonlight."

"It's not a good idea."

"Again, Kat, let me remind you that there's no one to tell us how to behave."

"I don't care about behaving. I simply wish I was freer."

"Freer to...what?"

"To act however I please."

"You *are* free, you silly goose. We're alone and we're in Egypt and whoever or whatever we were before we arrived, it doesn't matter now."

"If only that were true."

"Trust me, it is," he insisted.

She might have continued, but it was ridiculous to debate the issue.

They shared a potent attraction, and they were two healthy, red-blooded adults. There was no reason to practice restraint, except that she was his employer and he her employee. But he wouldn't think about that. It was a night for romance, and it wasn't as if they would fornicate on the deck. They would merely enjoy a very lush, very satisfying kiss.

Still though, there were porters on the beach and various servants finishing their chores. He couldn't have rumors spread about her character or his intentions, although with how he constantly watched her—like a wolf on the hunt—gossip was probably already circulating.

He pushed away from the rail and stepped into the shadows, tugging her with him. He clasped her wrist, but not very tightly. She could have drawn away, but though she was hesitant, she came without protest.

"You're horrid," she whispered.

"Why? Because I don't want the servants ogling us?"

"No. It's because you make me eager to commit sins with you that I've never considered previously."

"Well then, aren't I lucky?"

He dipped down and kissed her as if he meant it, as if the world was about to end and they'd never be together again, as if he was the last man and she the last woman and no human beings would ever again have the chance.

She joined in with unbridled enthusiasm, her arms snaking around his waist, her shapely breasts crushed to his chest.

Those breasts—the nipples poking into him like shards of glass—were his undoing. A carnal madness swept through him, one that he'd never experienced prior. He wanted her so desperately, wanted to take her and have her and keep her, even though he hadn't the resources to do any of those things.

He couldn't hold her closely enough, couldn't bring her near enough. He ran his palms up and down her back, over her shoulders and bottom. He plucked at the combs in her hair, tossing them away so the brunette tresses tumbled down.

He flicked his tongue on her lips, and instantly she understood what he was seeking. She opened wide and welcomed him inside. He thrust his tongue in and out, in and out, as down below, he worked his hips in the same rhythm.

She was still too far away, and he lifted her onto a pile of ropes. He raised the hem of her skirt so he could wedge himself between her thighs, the bunched fabric providing a soft cushion where he could flex his phallus against her loins.

Very quickly, the escapade spun out of control. He felt feral and untamed, possessed by a wild beast, and at that moment, mating was the primary goal. He craved a rough, angry copulation, and he was a hairsbreadth from ravishment, which frightened him very much.

Somehow he mustered the fortitude to ease himself away, to slow down, then stop.

What must she think? She was sprawled beneath him, gazing with astonishment—and a bit of alarm—and he couldn't blame her. He was a tad alarmed himself. Obviously there were mysterious forces directing them, the universe furnishing a physical chemistry that needed very little spark to ignite. If they weren't careful, they'd burn themselves to death.

"Oh, my," she murmured.

"You're dangerous."

"*I* am dangerous. I was minding my own business when you started in."

"It's your own fault."

"How could it be?"

"Apparently I can't resist you."

"You should try though. This seemed especially shocking."

"Shocking, yes. I agree."

She flashed a smile as old as Eve's, and there was an enormous amount of jeopardy for him in that smile. It was a siren's smile, a vixen's smile, and it called to him in a manner that he was certain would lure him to his doom.

He straightened and stared down at her, wondering if he hadn't been bewitched. He wasn't normally superstitious, but if someone had strolled up and told him she'd cast a spell on him, he wouldn't have doubted it.

She frowned. "What's happening to us?"

"I can't describe it, but it's bizarre."

"I think I like you more than I should."

He tamped down a laugh. "Of course you *like* me. I'm the most likeable fellow in the world."

"But I shouldn't. I can't."

"You're an adult, Kat. You can do what you like."

They were nose to nose, their lips a short inch away from

connection again, and in a thrice, they could be back in the throes of a serious embrace. Yet it was clear when he was around her, he couldn't rein in his worst impulses. He had many carnal encounters under his belt, but he'd never been so thoroughly aroused, and he had no intention of becoming embroiled with a stranger in Egypt.

He planned to earn his salary, then purchase passage on the first ship heading for London. He couldn't waste time in a torrid affair that might entangle him in exhausting ways.

Then and there, he decided it was the last kiss he'd ever share with her. He understood boundaries, understood class distinctions. While supposedly he'd been born an earl's grandson, he'd never felt as if he was, and any aristocratic blood he'd once carried had been drummed out of him during the lonely life he'd led after his parents had vanished.

Whatever Kat's actual identity, he was sure her position was very high. She couldn't entangle herself either. She'd warned him, so it was pointless to consort with her and only heartache would result. And it would probably be on his part.

He liked women too much. He liked *her* too much, and he was positive he'd eventually learn she was untouchable and unattainable. That very second, she likely had an angry father or brother rushing to reclaim her, so he couldn't be caught in a messy scandal.

But as she grabbed his shirt and pulled him near, he couldn't see any reason not to kiss her again, except that someone said, "Kat?"

They froze, and Kat mouthed, "My sister." She called, "Yes, Isabelle, what is it?"

"Where are you?"

"I'm in the shadows, gazing at the stars. What's wrong?"

"I can't sleep. Would you lie down with me? Would you tell me a story about home?"

"Yes, I'd love to. You go down. I'll be there in a minute."

"Do you promise?"

"Yes. I'll be right there."

They waited, listening as her footsteps faded down the ladder. Bryce stepped away, concealing himself so he wasn't observed as Kat walked off.

"You make me happy," she whispered.

Then she left, and he dawdled like a fool, worried over what the hell he'd gotten himself into and how he'd ever get himself out of it. Why would he want to get himself out of it? He had no idea. He'd ride the adventure to the very end and hope he wound up someplace safe and sound.

Where would that be? He couldn't imagine.

CHAPTER SIX

"What are you doing here, Katarina?"

"Hello, Uncle Cedric."

Kat smiled at her uncle, trying to appear calm and composed, but he was staring at her so strangely she wasn't sure what to think.

He'd been digging when they'd arrived, and his servants had made her comfortable while her porters had begun emptying the boats of their belongings. They were unpacking her boxes and trunks and setting up the tents she'd brought.

Cedric had been in Egypt for so many years that she'd thought he'd have built permanent structures by now, that he'd have a villa on the banks of the Nile much like Valois's, but he hadn't.

A bustling village had grown up around his endeavor, his tent large and spacious, the furnishings sturdy and comfortable, but it seemed very temporary as if he'd put down no roots and had to be able to pull up stakes at a moment's notice.

"I wasn't expecting you," he said.

"Didn't you get my letter?"

"Yes. Didn't you get mine?"

"No. When you sent it, we must have already been en route, and I apologize that we're early. We had the wind at our backs when crossing the Mediterranean."

"This is a disaster." His tone was angry and exasperated.

"Why?"

"I don't want you here. What am I to do with you?"

His question was like a slap in the face.

In the weeks they'd been on the run, she'd refused to admit she might not be welcomed by her uncle. If a person was without a friend in the world, and she couldn't turn to her family for help, who could she turn to?

"You don't mean that," she murmured.

"I most certainly do. I wrote and told you to stay in Parthenia. I told you to ride out the storm, that it would blow over."

"It didn't."

"It is your brother's throne, and possession is nine-tenths of the law. So long as he was in the palace, people would see him and remember how he'd been maltreated. It would have been corrected eventually."

"You're totally wrong."

"I'm not, and now you've sneaked away like a thief in the night. How can you hope to recoup what is rightfully his when you're hiding in the desert?"

"How would I have regained the throne for him? With what army would I have accomplished it? Who would have fought for us? Not anyone, that's who."

"There must have been someone," he insisted.

"There wasn't. We were stripped of our titles and rank. My parents' marriage was declared null and void. My siblings and I were labeled illegitimate bastards, and you feel we should have remained there? Is there any other indignity we should have suffered? Is there another humiliation I should have allowed them to level against us?"

They were in his tent, just the two of them sequestered and alone. Bryce had tried to join her, but she'd had to speak with Cedric first, to tell him to keep their identities secret. She hadn't anticipated scolding and disavowal, and his disdain was too much to bear.

She sank down in a nearby chair, and her eyes filled with tears, but she was too proud to let them fall. In her journey to Egypt, he'd been like a beacon on a hill, a lantern shining in the darkness, showing her the direction to travel. To her uncle. To her mother's brother. To her sole relative who was close enough to assist.

"My mother was your only sister," she chided. "What they did to us, they did to *her* memory and legacy. Don't you care?"

"Yes, I suppose I care, but I'm not surprised. I begged her not to wed your father."

"Why not?"

"We weren't royalty. We were merely the American children of a rich textile mill owner, and your mother had no patience for folderol and posturing. She was the least likely female to succeed as a queen. *And* your father didn't love her."

She cut him off. "Don't say that."

"Why shouldn't I? It's true. He married her for her dowry. I thought you knew."

"He married her because she was kind and devoted and beautiful."

Her uncle shrugged. "Believe what you will, but I warned her it would end in disaster. Now it has."

Her temper was sparking. She was weary and aggrieved and

absolutely furious to have her fears discounted yet again. By her own kin no less! "Father's oldest friend whispered in my ear that Nicholas was in danger, that I should whisk him away from Parthenia."

"You're being ridiculously melodramatic."

"What if I'm not? What if Nicholas had been poisoned or *accidently* drowned in a river or perhaps kicked in the head by a horse? Would that have been all right with you?"

"No, of course not."

"Of course not," she muttered back at him.

She glared, showering him with regal derision, and apparently he was capable of some shame.

He flushed and glanced away, going over to a table where there were several liquor decanters, and she watched as he poured himself a tall glass.

He was a short, slender man of sixty, tanned from his years toiling in the hot sun. His skin was peeling and cracked, his blond hair silvered to white. He was bald on top, but he hadn't been barbered so the sides were long and stuck out at odd angles. He looked like a mad scientist about to attempt a hazardous experiment.

She searched his features for a hint of resemblance to her glamorous, stunning mother, but she couldn't find it. And clearly he and her mother had no similar character traits.

Her mother had been considerate and compassionate, a wonderful queen, and Kat didn't care what Cedric said about her. As to her father, he'd adored Kat's mother.

"I'm sorry to have bothered you." She pushed herself to her feet. "It's too late to depart this afternoon, so we'll have to stay tonight. I'm afraid there's no other choice, but we'll leave at dawn."

He noted the contempt in her gaze and, obviously anxious to redeem himself, he grumbled, "No, no, there's no need to go. Not at once anyway."

"I wouldn't want to interrupt your important...*work*."

She imbued the word *work* with all the scorn she could muster. It had been a family joke that he dug and dug and dug and never found anything. Either he was very bad as an archeologist or he had no luck at all.

She'd hit a soft spot, and he declared, "My project is vital."

"Yes, I'm sure it is. Goodbye."

She started out, and he rushed over and stopped her.

"Let's not quarrel," he said.

"Fine, let's not."

"It's just that this place isn't set up for me to entertain you or your siblings. It's quite remote and the conditions can be harsh."

"I understand, but we hardly require entertaining. I simply thought it might be beneficial for Isabelle and Nicholas to get to know their only uncle. And *I* was yearning to receive some guidance from you. But if you don't wish to provide it, I can seek assistance elsewhere."

"No, no, you're correct. I should help you. It's proper that you came to me, and you can remain. How about for two weeks?"

"Don't put yourself out," she sarcastically said.

"We should rent a house for you in Cairo."

"I suppose that would be better."

"We'll spend your visit discussing what path you should take."

She tamped down her aggravation. "I was hoping you'd advise me on that very topic. It's why I've been so desperate to speak with you."

"No matter what happened in Parthenia, Isabelle and Nicholas—especially Nicholas—should live somewhere like London or Paris where they can attend elite schools and interact with other aristocratic children."

"I agree."

"We have to decide the best location." He waved to the door of the tent. "So...why don't you unload your gear, get yourself arranged—the porters will figure it out—and we'll have supper together after the sun has set."

"I'll see you then." She started off again. "Oh, and by the way, we are using the surname of Webster, and I've been telling people we're from Boston."

He smirked. "No one will believe it."

Bryce certainly hadn't. "We'll make them believe it. Who is there to claim we're lying?"

"Who indeed?" He forced a smile. "I'm glad you're here, Katarina."

"I am too."

        ❧   ❧   ❧   ❧

Cedric watched his niece hurry away.

He was very busy, focused on the prospect of huge and amazing discoveries. If he found the tombs for which he was searching, he'd be famous in the annals of Egyptian history. He didn't have time to fuss with Katarina or deal with her brother's problems.

Cedric was merely an archeologist. He wasn't a politician or diplomat, and he was quite sure—wherever Kat ended up—she would experience many difficulties. In Cedric's view, a royal family in one country was never too keen on the royals from another moving in and taking up residence.

What were the ramifications of Nicholas being at Cedric's camp? The local authorities required an enormous amount of bribing and cajoling before Cedric received his permission to dig. He couldn't lose that permission because of the status of his guests.

What if the king in Parthenia demanded Egyptian leaders send Nicholas home? What if Nicholas's presence sparked an international incident between the two nations? It wasn't likely, but Cedric had to plan for the contingencies. He never left any detail to chance. In the rough, hot, Egyptian desert, that's how men ruined themselves. They didn't prepare, and catastrophe struck when they least expected it.

Kat had sneaked off with Nicholas and was traveling under a false identity, so clearly she hadn't shared all the facts about their departure from Parthenia. Obviously someone hadn't wanted them to leave, and if she'd announced her intentions, she might have been prevented.

Nicholas wasn't just *any* child. He was a prince and should have been a crowned king. Katarina had recklessly transported him to a spot where he oughtn't to be. He should probably be somewhere else, but where?

The entire mess was like a complex mental puzzle, but he was too distracted to solve it. He needed advice and answers. For a brief second, he considered contacting Valois, but quickly decided against it. Any counsel from Valois would be watered down by the nuances of how he could profit.

No, Cedric needed an opinion from someone higher, someone who would carefully assess the situation and understand the dilemma Katarina had created by taking Nicholas from Parthenia.

"What was that blasted fellow's name?" Cedric mumbled to himself.

He riffled through a stack of documents and pulled out a piece of paper. Then he dipped a quill in the ink pot and began to write.

To His Majesty, King Kristof Alexander Sebastiano Morovsky...

Bryce studied Kat as she approached, and she looked mad as a hornet. Apparently her meeting with her uncle hadn't gone as she'd expected. Or perhaps it had gone precisely as she'd expected.

He was down by the boats, keeping an eye on the porters, on Nicholas and Isabelle, but positioned so he could observe Cedric Webster's tent too. Kat had introduced Bryce to Mr. Webster, then kicked him out, and he was irked to have been excluded from their conversation.

He was supposed to be guarding her, and he couldn't do a very good job of it if she wandered off on her own and refused to have him near.

Nicholas saw her and rushed over. "Was our uncle happy we're here? Was he surprised?"

She smoothed her features. "Yes, he was very surprised. He hadn't gotten my letter, so he wasn't aware we were coming."

"But he was happy, yes?" Nicholas pressed the issue, as if perceiving his sister's unease.

"Yes, Nicholas. We'll stay for a week or two."

"Then what?"

"Then...I don't know." She shrugged, appearing very young, very alone. "We may rent a house in Cairo while I determine our next move."

"Did you ask Uncle Cedric if I can help him dig?"

"We didn't discuss it, but he's invited us to supper, so you can ask him yourself."

Nicholas was a bright scholar, tutored in the ancient ways of the pharaohs. While they'd waited for Kat to return, he'd regaled Bryce with archeological tidbits. At the news that he might be allowed to hunt for artifacts with his famous uncle, he grinned and dashed away, dragging Isabelle with him as they ran after the porters to watch their tents being erected.

Momentarily the dock was quiet, the boats emptied of their occupants. Bryce went over to her, hating to note the fatigue and worry in her gaze.

"Your brother and sister are gone," he said, "so you can tell me the truth."

"My uncle was surprised. That's the truth."

"He wasn't glad you're here though, was he?"

"What makes you think so?"

"I can see it in your eyes."

She smiled a sad smile. "Perhaps in the future, I shouldn't let you look so closely."

"Where you're concerned, I have a second sense. I can guess your emotions with no hesitation at all."

"I don't know if that's good or bad."

"It's grand. It means we're becoming friends."

"Are we?"

"Yes," he groused, "and don't pretend we're not."

"All right, I won't." She sighed. "Could we sit in the shade on the boat?"

"Certainly."

Cedric Webster might not have built any permanent structures, but he had gravel-strewn walkways, as well as a sturdy wharf where supply boats from Cairo could dock and unload their wares.

Bryce and Kat started down the sloping hill to the river, and about halfway there, she stumbled and he grabbed her arm.

"What the devil...?" he muttered. "Did you trip?"

"No. I'm just so hot. I loathe this accursed land."

"No, you don't," he said as he steadied her. "You find it intoxicating. You told me so."

She was a tad wobbly, so he scooped her up and marched down the path. She was light as a feather, seeming to be skin and bones, the only substantial weight on her the yards of fabric from which her outfit was sewn.

She was attired much as she would have been for an autumn day in Europe, but the desert weather didn't resemble that continent in the slightest. She had on layers of petticoats, shoes and stockings, a jacket and bonnet.

When he'd initially arrived, he'd dressed inappropriately too, but months of heat and wind had taught him to strip to the barest essentials. He wore trousers, boots, a billowy shirt, and a hat with a brim. Always a hat, but he often stared enviously at the local men in their flowing white robes. They always looked so much more comfortable than he was.

Would she be willing to change her style of clothing? Would she be willing to pick different fabrics? Would she dare to live dangerously, to shed her bulky apparel? Her corset ought to be the first item to go, but it probably wasn't his place to inform her.

"Put me down," she insisted but without much force behind the complaint.

"No."

"I can walk."

"No, you can't. You just fell. Be quiet."

"I'm not an invalid."

"You're not? I could swear your legs aren't working very well."

"My legs are fine. I'm simply a bit disoriented."

"And weak and exhausted."

"You can really be a bully when the situation calls for it."

"I can be, and this situation definitely calls for it."

In a few more strides, they were on the dock. The gangplank was firmly secured so it only swayed a little as they crossed it. In a thrice, they were off the burning sand and on the boat. The temperature dropped dramatically.

He thought about sitting her in a chair on the deck, but she had to remove some of her heaviest garments. He proceeded to the ladder, but it would be impossible to maneuver down it while holding onto her, so he stood her on her feet.

"I'll climb down," he said, "then you come after me. I'll catch you."

"I can make it on my own. You don't have to help me."

"Haven't we talked about how independent you are? Haven't I explained that you can lean on me once in awhile?"

"Yes, I believe we have."

"So...I'll catch you. Don't argue about it."

"Yes, sir."

She saluted as if she were a lowly private in the army. He laughed and jumped down into the hull. She descended with no trouble, but he lifted her anyway, just because he could. He carried her to her berth and balanced her on the mattress.

"We have to cool you down," he told her.

"I'm feeling better already."

"You must shuck off some of your clothes."

"Well, I'm not doing it while you're standing here."

"Close your eyes and imagine I'm your favorite lady's maid."

He reached for the bow on her bonnet and yanked it off, and she wasn't irked enough to protest. But when he grabbed her ankles and yanked off her shoes, she yelped with surprise.

"Mr. Blair!" she scolded in a very authoritative tone as if she was a princess lecturing one of her subjects.

"What?" He grinned, sure he looked innocent as hell.

"You're not undressing me."

"Just your shoes and jacket."

"You most certainly will not."

"I'm going to turn my back," he said, "then you'll take off your stockings."

"Absolutely not. My feet will be bare."

"I'm positive I'll survive it."

"It's unseemly."

"It's just your feet, Kat. Now take off your bloody stockings or I will."

He whipped around and waited, listening as she raised the hem of her gown, as she untied one garter, then the other, as she rolled down one stocking, then the other.

His grin widened. He hadn't thought she'd comply. She was so snooty, he hadn't expected he could command her.

"Are you finished?" he asked, and as he spun to face her, she scooted her legs under her skirt.

"Yes."

"Do you paint your toenails?"

"If I did, I wouldn't tell you."

"I had a mistress who used to paint hers red for me. I really liked it."

She gaped at him in astonishment. "I believe that's the most scandalous remark ever uttered in my presence."

"You need to get out more."

"I can't decide if I'm more offended that you keep mistresses or that you'd mention it to me."

"I don't *keep* mistresses. I've never had enough money. I just had the one after a big gambling win. But the money didn't last long so the doxy didn't last long."

She clamped a palm over her eyes. "Oh, my Lord. My ears are burning."

"I like shocking you. I like to drag you down off your high horse."

She jerked her hand away and glared at him. "I don't ride a high horse!"

"You're perched on it all the time, and I'm trying to figure out who you are and where you come by such a puffed-up demeanor."

"I'm perfectly fine, thank you very much."

"Yes, you are."

She studied him and scowled. "You never had a mistress. You said that to discover how I'd react."

He cocked a brow. "Maybe I did. Maybe I didn't. Maybe I'm the worst libertine ever. Or maybe I'm chaste as a nun."

"Men can't be chaste as nuns."

"Then maybe I'm chaste as a priest."

She snorted at that. "I doubt it. Not with you being as handsome as you are."

"You think I'm handsome?"

"You know you are, you vain wretch."

"Well, I can't deny that I've had a few paramours wax on about it."

"I bet they line up to flatter you."

"You could be right." He reached for the row of buttons on her jacket.

She slapped his fingers away. "Behave yourself."

"I won't cease pestering you until I'm sure you can inhale without keeling over in a dead faint."

"I'm not the fainting type. It's simply too hot outside."

"Yes, it is, and you're swaddled in so much wool that you might be on an expedition to the Arctic."

"I don't have any other clothes, and I'm not comfortable with the local attire."

"You have to get comfortable with it, or I'll be picking you up off the ground every two seconds."

"The native women don't seem to wear much in the way of...of..."

She trailed off and she gestured over her body, unable to voice a word like *corset* in front of him.

"They don't wear corsets or petticoats?"

"No, and I'm not discussing those items with you."

"If you'd like, I can tell you what they have on under their dresses. I'm intimately familiar with it."

"Stop it, would you? You're embarrassing me, and you're putting illicit thoughts in my head."

"What sort of illicit thoughts?"

"I'm trying to imagine how you would know such a thing."

"How do you think I know? I'm a scoundrel."

She was fumbling with her buttons, but couldn't manage them herself. Obviously she'd never buttoned her own clothing, and his curiosity spiraled.

He pushed her away, and with a few flicks of his wrist, he had the jacket tugged off. She had a sleeveless gown underneath, so instantly she was freer and less restricted. She breathed a sigh of relief.

"Better?" he asked.

"Much."

There was a pitcher of water on a stand next to her bed. He poured some into a bowl, dipped a cloth and laid it on her neck. He didn't wring it out, but held it there, letting the cool water drip down her back. He dipped it again and swabbed it across her forehead and cheeks, across her throat and the bit of bosom that was exposed. Then he knelt down.

"You should purchase a new wardrobe," he said.

"I had planned on it in Cairo, but we departed so rapidly there wasn't time."

"We can find you garments that are modest enough to suit your European sensibilities. If nothing else, we can get you into other fabrics. If you keep on in these heavy woolens, you'll never survive."

"No, I suppose not."

"I noticed a native woman talking to the porters. She was attired quite fashionably. I'll have her meet with you. We'll see what she recommends."

"When I fled Par..." She halted and began again. "When I left home, I never considered the change of climate."

"And when *I* left home, I was given twenty pages of what to bring and what not."

"Did you follow the list?"

"No. I didn't have the funds for most of it, and I viewed myself as being very manly and tough. I traveled light to prove I could live off the land."

"Could you?"

"With how our boat sank on those rapids, I would have lost it all anyway, so it's just as well I didn't have much."

She laughed, and he liked watching how the merriment climbed into her eyes, how dimples curved her cheeks.

"Oh, you are so good for me," she murmured.

"Of course I am."

"You treat me as if I'm a normal person."

He scowled. "I won't try to figure out what that means."

She waved away her odd comment. "Don't mind me. I'm overwrought."

"And you're not *normal*. Not even close."

He dipped the cloth yet again, laid it on her neck again. She was relaxing, her temper and exasperation fading.

"What did your uncle tell you?" he asked. "From how you were frowning when you stomped out of his tent, I could see you were angry."

"I had written to inform him we were coming, but he wrote back to say we shouldn't. I never received his letter."

"That's too bad."

"Cedric doesn't feel we should stay." "Why not?"

"He claims this camp isn't appropriate for a woman or children."

"Well, perhaps not for you and Isabelle, but Nicholas is very excited to be here."

"Cedric suggested we rent a house in Cairo."

"It's probably best, but then what?"

"I have no idea. I was hoping he'd give me some advice, but he simply barked and scolded."

She looked so dejected, and her woe ignited his masculine instincts so he yearned to protect and shelter and take care of her forever. Yet he had no ability to do any of those things, and even if he had he suspected she wouldn't be interested.

She was a mysterious female who was pursing goals she couldn't admit and chasing endings that would never include him. Yet he was overcome by the worst desire to make her happy. He'd like to march up to Cedric Webster and pound him into the ground for upsetting her.

He wondered if she'd feared deep down that she wouldn't be welcomed by her uncle. Hadn't she confessed to having no friends or support? Mr. Webster had proved himself as being no different than any of her other scurrilous acquaintances.

"Will you remain with me and help me?" she suddenly asked.

"Where? In Cairo?"

"Yes, and my next destination too—once I decide where to go."

He nearly refused, nearly insisted he was heading to England as soon as he could. But he had no emergency luring him back.

His sole genuine tie was to his sister, but she was newly wed and busy with her own life and husband. So there was no rush to leave, and he relished the notion of Kat being a damsel in distress and his having learned the fighting skills to be her knight in shining armor.

"Yes, I'll remain—for as long as you need me." He couldn't guess if that would turn out to be true, but it sounded grand and chivalrous.

"Thank you. You're correct about our becoming friends."

"I'd say I'm your *only* friend these days."

"I have Pippa too."

Pippa was much too busy with Chase for Bryce's liking, but he didn't voice the remark. "In the end, I'll be much higher on the list than Miss Clementi. Just you wait and see."

"You could be right about that."

He took her in his arms and kissed her as he'd been dying to do after their embrace three nights earlier on the boat. Since then, she'd kept her distance, had arranged her schedule so she was never alone with him, so there hadn't been a subsequent chance. But he had a chance now, and again he speculated as to what he was getting himself into with her.

He'd agreed to stay by her side, to be her ally and confidante, but they had a potent physical attraction. If he had his way, and he was sure he would, they'd grow intimately close.

She'd be paying him for his services, but they would gradually comprise more duties than protecting her from miscreants. He'd be her knight and her...what? If he'd been a woman, he'd know precisely what to call himself. There was an unsavory term for a man who was considering what he was considering with his employer, but just that moment he couldn't remember what it was.

Without a doubt, he shouldn't enter into such a seedy alliance. There was no benefit to it, but more and more, he was finding he didn't want to exercise caution. She'd begged him to remain with her and that was exactly what he intended, unless and until fate or circumstances forced him away.

He eased her onto the mattress so she was on her back, and he was kneeling between her legs, her thighs spread, her skirt bunched up so he could press his loins to hers. As had happened when he'd kissed her previously, he was swiftly pitched into a fervor of unruly lust.

He was eager to proceed to acts he had no business attempting, and he drew away.

"Why are you kissing me," she asked, "and why did we stop?"

"I'm kissing you because I can't resist."

"Why do I suppose you say that to every female you encounter?"

"Because it's a cad's favorite lie—but that doesn't mean it's not true."

"*I* am irresistible?"

"Yes, and you make me ponder all sorts of conduct I shouldn't be pondering."

"Which indicates we should go up on the deck."

"Not just yet."

"Why not?"

"We're not finished."

"Someone might come on board. They might see us."

"We'll hear them in plenty of time."

"Plenty of time to what?"

"To pretend we're not misbehaving."

He crushed his lips to hers again, moaning with pleasure at how sweet it was, how arousing it was. He stroked his hands over her shapely hips, up her belly, to her lush breasts, and he massaged them in slow circles. Her nipples responded, growing taut and poking at the front of her dress, and he nibbled a trail down her neck, her bosom, to bite and nuzzle them through the fabric of her bodice.

She was laced into her corset, but in the hot, sultry air, how could she breathe? He'd like to yank off the blasted garment, but he didn't imagine she was ready for such a drastic move.

He slid a palm under the material, for an instant caressing bare skin. She frowned and grabbed his wrist, and she skittered across the mattress. The space was very small though, so she couldn't go far.

"What was that?" she said. "You were touching my...my..."

"Yes, I was kissing you and touching you. It's what men and women do when they're together. It's enjoyable."

"My heart is pounding so fiercely, I feel as if it might burst out of my chest."

"Your pulse will decrease. Just relax."

"I don't have much experience with amour."

"I can tell that about you."

"When you start in on me, I don't want to stop.""Good."

"I didn't know passion could be like this. I didn't realize it could be so exhilarating."

"It can quickly spin out of control though. It's the reason maidens have chaperones. So they can't have too much fun."

She snorted with amusement. "But it can't lead anywhere. You understand that, don't you? If you were expecting we might court or woo or wed, I must inform you that I—"

"Hush, Katarina. It's not courting, it's not wooing. It's just kissing."

"More than that too."

"I'd like it to be more, but we'll never do what you don't wish to do."

"I like kissing you." She looked shocked, as if she'd admitted to a great and unforgiveable sin.

"I believe I've told you that you *should* like it. We're adults, and we're alone in Egypt. Live a little."

"I'm predicting—with scant effort—you'll convince me to see things your way."

"I should hope so, or we have some very boring months ahead of us."

"Will you entertain me with kissing?"

"Whenever you desire it, my lady."

"You can obviously provide services beyond being a bodyguard."

He grinned his devil's grin. "Some very interesting services."

"I'm glad I was smart enough to hire you."

"I am too."

She smiled, and the most potent wave of affection swirled between them. It felt as if they were connected, as if they belonged together, as if they'd always been meant to find each another. Fate had brought them down the Nile at the same moment.

Any wild deed might have occurred, but the boat rocked slightly, someone coming on board up on the deck. Ultimately her sister called, "Katarina? Where are you?"

Bryce chuckled. "It seems your sister is to be your moral compass."

"A good thing too. If she hadn't arrived, I can't guess what I might have done with you."

"Seriously?"

"Yes."

"Well then, next time I'll push harder to get what I want."

He stood and went to the ladder. "We're down here, Miss Isabelle."

"Mr. Blair?"

"Yes. Your sister was overheated, so she's resting where it's cooler."

Isabelle appeared and stared down at him. "Is she all right?"

"She's perfect," Bryce said. "Absolutely perfect."

CHAPTER SEVEN

"You are so naughty, Chase Hubbard."

"I try to be."

"You succeed at it spectacularly."

Chase grinned at Pippa and linked their fingers, hurrying her toward the bathing ponds.

Cedric Webster might be dodgy and mad as a hatter, but he'd had the good sense to build a series of pools that brought drinking water into his small tent village but also provided a fine means for washing. Considering the heat, grit, and sweat that accumulated during the day, it was a welcome relief.

Palm trees and ferns had been planted, paths graveled and groomed, and benches discreetly arranged. It was the perfect spot for an assignation, and once he'd pointed it out, they'd decided to use it as often as they could.

It was late, any sane person asleep. Mr. Webster ran the place like an army camp, everyone up at dawn and working like slaves—actually there were slaves on the property—until the sun set in the west. Mr. Webster claimed the slaves weren't his, but who else could be their owner?

They weren't treated badly, being fed, clothed, and housed. They simply had to toil away like…well…slaves. If he'd have been one of them, he'd have stolen away long ago, although that was probably harder than it sounded.

On one side, they were surrounded by thousands of miles of desert. On the other, there was the river, which should have been an escape route, but the poor creatures had inked tattoos that marked them, so even if they'd made it to Cairo, they'd have been captured and dragged back.

Chase didn't have moral qualms about many things, but he liked to suppose acceptance of slavery was beyond the pale—even for someone of his low character. Yet apparently it wasn't. The females were very beautiful. They did his laundry and cooked his food and, while he hadn't requested more unsavory services, he'd certainly received the impression that they'd be delighted to supply those too.

How had he stumbled into such a bizarre situation? He definitely understood why Cedric Webster stayed year after year with no archeological triumphs to show for his efforts. If Chase could have created the ideal life for himself, he'd have selected one similar to Webster's.

Chase thought it must be grand to be so wealthy. Webster loafed and pursued his hobby, but never had to worry about money.

Pippa stopped and maneuvered him over to a pond. There were seven or eight of them, and she'd snooped about earlier in the afternoon and chosen her favorite.

They'd sneaked off twice since they'd met, but he was beginning to wonder if she was worth the bother. She talked a good story and pretended to be loose, but she really wasn't, and Chase never wasted energy on women who teased him. There were too many willing doxies who were happy to deliver what he sought, and doxies were more fun anyway. They didn't require wooing or cajoling.

With her blond hair and blue eyes, her plump figure and feminine curves, Pippa would be accustomed to men panting after her. The idiots in her country probably tagged after her like dogs on a leash, but Chase wouldn't much longer. Not unless something interesting happened.

She halted at the pool's edge. "Isn't this lovely?"

"It's very nice."

"Let's take off our shoes and wade in the water."

"Forget your bloody shoes. Let's get naked and swim."

"Naked! Are you mad?"

"No. Why shouldn't we? It's late and there's no one to see."

"I'm not taking off my clothes."

"Then why are we here?"

The question flummoxed her. Obviously she expected they'd have another evening where kissing and caressing were all she'd allow. He didn't mind kissing, and she was proficient at it, but a fellow could only continue for so long before his poor cock couldn't abide the torment.

They either had to get down to business, or he had to find a partner who knew her way around a mattress.

He plopped down on the sand and kicked off his boots. His stockings were next, then his sword, pistol, and the knives he carried at all times. Since arriving in Egypt, he'd suffered so many disasters and had encountered so many dangerous characters that he never went anywhere without an arsenal of weapons.

She was still standing, glaring at him as if she was angry. Whatever her plan by coming with him, he wasn't acting as she'd hoped. She ordered men about and they obeyed, so clearly he was at the wrong party.

Usually he was easy-going and tolerant with females, but he'd been anticipating a torrid tryst ever since she'd whispered in his ear at supper.

He tugged his shirt over his head and tossed it on the ground so, in a thrice, he was wearing just his trousers. In London, he'd always been neatly barbered, but during his sojourn in Egypt, he'd let his hair grow, and it hung down his back, currently tied into a tidy ponytail. He yanked at the ribbon, his hair sweeping across his shoulders.

"What are you thinking?" she hissed. "You've removed most of your clothes."

"I told you I'm taking a swim. I've been hot and sweaty all day. I need a bath. No offense, but you could use one too."

"But...but...what if a servant walks by? What if he tells Katarina?"

"First of all, we're away from the main path, and everyone is in bed. Who is there to see us? And second of all, what could they tell Miss Webster? You're fully clothed, I'm mostly clothed—"

"Your chest, arms, calves, and feet are bare!"

"Yes, they are, and I don't give two figs for Katarina Webster's opinion. She's not my wife, mother, or sister, and she has no authority over me."

"What if she fired you for moral turpitude?"

"Turpitude? Really?" He scoffed with derision. "She doesn't have a replacement for me as a bodyguard, so I'm not worried. But if she did send me packing, I'd return to Cairo in no worse shape than when I joined this pointless expedition. I was penniless then, and I'm penniless now."

On his mentioning Miss Webster, he experienced a minor twinge of guilt. He was being paid to protect her, not to trifle with her traveling companion. At that moment, if mischief erupted, he was away from the camp and would be completely ineffective as a sentinel. He wasn't doing much to earn his wages, but then again he didn't understand why Miss Webster was so afraid.

They were at a secluded village in the desert. No one appeared to be following or watching them. The chance of a brigand creeping in by riding across the sand was nil, and while an outlaw could stealthily sail up in a boat, why would anyone?

"Sit down and take off your shoes," he told her. "Don't behave like a prude. I hate persnickety women."

"I'm not persnickety."

"You couldn't prove it by me. You prance around like a mare in heat, but so far I haven't seen much evidence that you have any idea how to tempt a man like me."

"A man like *you*?" She was practically sneering. "What would that be? A scoundrel and scalawag?"

"Yes, that describes me perfectly. I gamble, cheat, lie, and steal too. My friend, Bryce, is the gentleman. If you're yearning for flowers and poetry, you're flirting with the wrong fellow."

He thought they were fighting, though he couldn't figure out why, and he wouldn't fuss with a grumpy shrew.

She stared down her pert nose, then seemed to reconsider her foul mood. She was so peculiar. One minute, she acted loose and available. The next, she might have just stepped out of a cloistered abbey. She dropped down beside him.

"You constantly surprise me," she said. "I never know what might happen."

"In my book, that's a good thing. Who would like to dabble with a stuffy boor?"

"I agree." She flashed her prettiest smile. "I'm sorry to be such a grouch. I get so exasperated with Katarina, and I have no confidante to whom I can complain. I guess I'm taking it out on you."

"I guess you are too, and I don't like it. We don't have to have a fling. We can simply be friends."

"No, I don't want that. If I didn't have you to entertain me, I'd go mad."

"The desert can be overwhelming."

"Kat's talking about renting a house in Cairo. It will be better there. We won't be so isolated."

"It's not so bad here, is it? The tents are spacious and comfortable and the slaves courteous and competent."

"Slaves!"

"Who did you think all those dark-skinned people were?"

"Well...servants."

"Yes, servants. *Slave* servants."

"Oh," she murmured.

"Since I arrived in this ghastly country, I've stayed in much worse places. In my view, this camp is actually quite pleasant."

"Monsieur Valois's villa was nice," she said. "I wish we could live somewhere like that."

"He's rich as Croesus."

"As is Katarina, so hopefully once we're in Cairo, she'll select a property that will suit my expensive tastes."

"You have expensive tastes?"

"I grew up with Kat, so I was showered with fine things. Why would I lower my standards?"

He chuckled. "What a mercenary little trollop you are. Is that the only reason you're traveling with her? Because she's rich?"

She pondered, then admitted, "I suppose."

"You don't like her? I thought you were her best friend."

"I am, but I have my own wants and needs. I'm happy to revel in the largesse she tosses my way, but I'd like to possess some of my own."

"Gad, you're greedier than I am. At least I like Bryce for who he *is*. Not for what he can give me. Of course he's poor as a church mouse so he couldn't give me a farthing even if I begged him."

"Katarina is all right."

"High praise indeed, Pippa."

She genuinely perplexed him. What sort of person despised her best friend? What sort of person hung on simply for the lofty style of living that was provided? Tons of sycophants did it, and Chase probably would too if he had the chance, but he liked to believe he was true and steady in his relationships with the people who mattered.

He had many faults, but for the most part, his friendships were valid ones. He and Bryce had met at school as boys. Bryce had been an orphan and charity case, and Chase no better than that. His father had been a French count, his mother the man's notorious mistress, and Chase their scandalous love child.

They both died when he was very young, his French kin paying for his education but no more than that, and it was the very devil struggling to survive with no parents, family, or means of support.

Yet he was clever and tenacious and had become quite successful. Well, other than being stranded in Egypt without the resources to leave. The salary he'd earn from Miss Webster would rectify that situation very soon. He really ought to take more pride in his position, ought to *try* to keep her safe.

If he'd had a conscience—his was very small and very quiet—he'd have felt guilty about his behavior. But he rarely felt guilty about anything.

"How will you get your own *largesse* dumped on you?" he asked. "What is your plan? Will you marry a wealthy man? Will you rob a bank? What?"

"I already have a scheme in the works."

"What is it?"

Her smile was sly and devious. "If I explain it to you, you have to promise not to tell anyone. Not *anyone*."

"I won't."

"Not Mr. Blair. Especially not him."

"All right. What is it?"

She studied him, then confided, "I'm about to receive a reward."

"For what service?"

"I'm watching Katarina for someone."

He scowled. "Who?"

"Her...family. She has relatives who were upset when she left."

"Why would they care?"

"She's rich, and with rich people, it's always about the money, isn't it?"

"Yes, it is."

"Her brother, Nicholas, is heir to a great fortune too. There are several powerful cousins who'd like him to return so they can be in charge of him."

"And you're...*what*? Just watching her? How will that garner you a reward?"

"I'm sending reports about where she is and what she's doing."

"These cousins of hers must be very, very interested."

"They are."

"The reports are worth a lot of money?" he asked.

"Not the reports precisely. Her kin might grow tired of her antics and decide they want her home. I can help make it happen."

He frowned. "Meaning what? Would you tie her up and kidnap her?"

She shrugged. "I can't predict what might transpire, but if I needed assistance with a certain task, and I had a fellow willing to aid me, there'd be remuneration for him too."

"You don't say?"

"*If* I found the right fellow."

He let the subject drop.

He was never concerned about rich people and their problems. Nor could he deduce if she was actually plotting or simply boasting. Would there be money at the end of it for a betrayal? At that moment, he was content to piddle along behind Miss Webster, doing nothing and being compensated when he was finished.

But what if there was a possibility of earning more than he'd expected? What if he could earn quite a bit more?

He had no connection to Miss Webster and owed her no loyalty, but if he engaged in unsavory conduct, Bryce would be furious. He always hated to disappoint his friend, but Bryce wouldn't necessarily have to ever learn of it, would he?

"Take off your shoes," he said. "And your stockings. Don't make me beg."

After all their talk of conniving and schemes, she was in a much better mood. "I am awfully hot."

She bent over and fussed with buckles and laces, and eventually the shoes were off.

"Turn around," she said.

"Why?"

"I'm going to remove my stockings. I don't want you to see my legs."

"Heaven forbid."

He scooted away from her and waded into the water. It was the perfect temperature, cool and pleasant on his heated skin. The pool was only three or four yards across, and it was part of a string of pools that funneled the water from one to the other.

He went out to the middle where it was just above his waist, and he dunked down until he was fully submerged. Then he leapt up, causing a huge splash, as if he were an ancient god, rising out of the Nile.

She was still sitting in the sand, although her feet were finally bare. Her hair was down, the combs pulled away so the curly blond locks had tumbled down her back.

"That's more like it," he murmured.

"I'm trying to be more like you."

"Good. I detest prudes."

"So you've said, and I heard you every time."

"In light of our circumstances, there's no need to be morally correct. We're alone and no one knows what were about."

"*I* know, but I'm forcing myself not to care."

"Aren't you flirtatious and loose? You pretend to be."

"I guess I'm not as decadent as you. I'd like to be, but I'm not."

"After you spend a few more hours with me, my bad habits will rub off."

"Here's hoping."

She came to the edge, but didn't dip in her toes, and he wondered if perhaps she couldn't swim. He walked over to her, spun her, and started unbuttoning her gown.

"What are you doing?" she asked.

"I'm undressing you. It's easier to move in the water without so many layers of clothing."

"I hadn't thought of that."

"And we should keep your gown dry. You'll want to put it on when we're finished and we head to our tents. It would be difficult to explain why it was damp."

"I hadn't thought of that either."

He yanked the garment down and off, not giving her a chance to balk or complain. Her petticoat and corset were next, and very quickly, he'd stripped her to chemise and drawers. She didn't protest, which was a relief. With how skittish she'd been, he'd been wondering if she was a virgin and that would have been the most horrid conclusion imaginable.

He never wasted time with innocents. It was too dangerous. He might wind up with a ring on his finger, and he was determined to remain a bachelor unless his bride was rich as a queen.

"That's better, isn't it?" he asked.

"Much better."

He took her hand and led her in. Initially she was hesitant, and ultimately she admitted, "I don't know how to swim."

Just as he'd suspected. "Don't worry about it. It's not deep. You can stand on the bottom."

She grinned. "Lovely."

He guided her out to the middle, and finally—finally!—they began kissing. Gradually he eased her to her knees, wanting to cool her down, wanting them both wet and slippery, and with her learning the water wasn't deep, her trepidation had vanished.

They were chest to chest, thigh to thigh, her full, round breasts riveting his attention. Her bosom was covered only by the thin fabric of her chemise so she might have been wearing nothing at all.

Their kiss went on and on until she reached down and cupped him between his legs. Apparently she had a bit of amorous skill, had been taught a few tricks that a man might enjoy. Thank goodness!

To his great delight, she unbuttoned the front of his trousers.

"It occurred to me," she said, "that you might assume I was trifling with you."

"It had crossed my mind."

"I'm not a flirt or a tease."

"I certainly hope not."

"I've simply been fretting over Katarina, and it's distracting me from what's important." She tugged at his waistband. "I think these have to come off."

"Now we're getting somewhere."

"Yes, we are."

She slid in a hand and took hold of his cock, giving it several proficient caresses that nearly had him shooting his wad like a green boy. He was that aroused. He tried to pull down his pants, but they were stuck to his skin.

He stood, and she was still kneeling so his crotch was directly in her face. Would she dare to provide a salacious treat? Was she that brazen?

With how she'd just stroked his phallus, it was clear she'd been schooled in all the appropriate tasks. He jerked his trousers down to his flanks, his erect rod perfectly positioned. She didn't bat an eye, but studied him with unbridled curiosity.

"You're built like a stallion, Mr. Hubbard."

"So I've been told."

"You a fine specimen of a man."

"I trust I meet your high standards, your ladyship."

He pronounced the word *ladyship* sarcastically, but she nodded, liking the sound of it. "You can call me a lady, if you like. If matters work out as I'm expecting, you'll be surprised by how far I'll rise."

"Speaking of *rising*," he said. "Let's keep our focus where it needs to be."

"Oh, I'm focused, Chase Hubbard. I'm very, very focused."

She flicked her tongue over the tip, then opened wide and sucked him inside.

Luckily he'd been wrong about her. She wasn't innocent after all. He rested a palm on the back of her head and started to enjoy himself much more than he'd imagined possible when the evening had begun.

CHAPTER EIGHT

Susan Blair stood in her bedchamber at Radcliffe Castle and gazed out the window toward the village. Usually she could see the church's steeple and be comforted by the sight, but the morning was cool and foggy so it wasn't visible. She was disturbed that she couldn't see it. She didn't want a single detail altered, wanted to stare out as she always had at the familiar view.

She was growing weaker by the day, the tumor in her abdomen pressing on her other organs, making it hard to breath, to sit, to sleep. A traveling doctor visited occasionally, and though he kept telling her to be optimistic, that she'd get better, she knew it wasn't true. He simply couldn't bear to inform the lady of the manor she was dying.

His sole remedy had been to bleed her over and over until she'd begun to worry she had no blood left in her veins. After his last visit, she'd told him not to stop by again, and instead the local healer came.

She was more of a comfort. She talked bluntly about death, about how to muddle through with a modicum of dignity. That was the worst part for Susan. In her time as a debutante, then a young wife, she'd been a great beauty, and despite birthing three children, her splendor hadn't faded for decades.

Now she was skin and bones and looked more like a skeleton than a human being.

She fingered her pocket, touching the pouch of lethal herbs the healer had given her. Susan was extremely pious so she would never consider taking her own life, but she received enormous satisfaction from having the herbs, from being aware they were in her pocket should she change her mind.

She scowled at the fog, wishing she had magical eyes so she could peer into the surrounding countryside to discover what was happening, what gossip was spreading.

Michael and Matthew Blair were out there, chatting with the neighbors, asking questions that Susan didn't dare have answered. What would the villagers and tenant farmers say about the incidents that had occurred those many years ago? What secrets would they reveal?

She had no idea what people suspected, what they could prove, and she'd never wanted to know.

At age eighteen, she'd been engaged to the twins' father, Julian Blair. His father had arranged the match without consulting him, and he'd been adamantly opposed.

He'd been a viscount, the oldest son and heir, so it was madness for him to have assumed he could reject his father's choice of bride. But he had, and it was a humiliation she'd never forgotten or forgiven. In the end though, the snub had been irrelevant. He'd perished in a hunting accident, and George had become the heir. She'd married George instead.

With the union, she'd stepped in line to be a countess. Everyone—including herself—had pretended that one fiancé was the same as another, that the objective was to wed a viscount and eventually be a countess. When assessed in that light, how could it matter which man was standing at the altar?

Yet she'd never admitted how upset she'd been. Julian Blair had been a dashing, flamboyant explorer and adventurer. He'd been tall, dark, and handsome, like a hero out of a romantic novel, and every girl in the kingdom had fantasized about having him as her husband.

In comparison, George had been...nothing much at all. He was average in stature, in intellect, in demeanor. He had a temper though, and it was the only trait that stood out in any noticeable fashion. He was stubborn too, bone-headed and inflexible and always positive he was in the right. Since he normally *wasn't* right, it was a huge character flaw.

He'd been a shrewd son though, fawning and obsequious and able to flatter his wretched, unlikable father. George was perfectly obedient, while Julian was obstinate and independent and never cowed by anyone.

When the two were held up side by side, George came up lacking. Susan figured that was why he'd hated Julian. Julian was the better *man* in every way, and no one—most especially George—could deny that fact.

A knock sounded on the outer door to her suite, and she pushed away from the window and slid into a nearby chair. She nodded to her cousin, Katherine, who was her companion and confidante.

Katherine was pretty and pleasant, but at age twenty-four, she was a spinster with no options. As the dreaded poor relative, she had no dowry, no home, and no family save for Susan.

Dear, pathetic Katherine. She'd been reduced to caring for an invalid, to waiting on Susan hand and foot as Susan grew weaker and more infirm. What a dismal role!

"Answer that, would you?" Susan said.

"Yes, certainly."

"It will be my husband. Let him in, then you can leave me for a bit so he and I may speak in private."

"I'll watch for him to depart, then I'll be back."

"Fine, thank you."

Susan listened as Katherine greeted George, as they exchanged a few words, then George appeared in the doorway. He pulled up a chair, his dour expression not surprising.

They'd never gotten along, even in the early years when esteem might have been expected. There marriage was an unpalatable sham. Julian's ghost had hovered between them, and despite how hard they'd tried, they'd never shoved him away.

She'd done her duty by her husband, had birthed him three boys, but they hadn't been lucky enough to raise any of them to manhood. George had schemed and plotted and rid himself of his brother so he could seat himself on the throne of the earldom, but none of his machinations had brought him what he'd sought. None of his dreams had come true.

They were old now, Susan dying, and George impotent and incapable of siring more children.

"You wanted to see me?" he asked.

"Yes. We have to talk about the Blair twins."

"Honestly, Susan, we have no evidence their surname is Blair. Don't imbue them with an importance they don't deserve."

"They claim to be Julian's sons."

"So?"

"Don't lie about it. At least not to me. You know they're his."

"I know nothing of the sort," he huffed.

"What shall we do about them?"

"What do you mean?"

"They don't seem the type who will simply go away."

"They can stay. They can go. Their movements don't concern me in the slightest and they shouldn't concern you either."

He was cruel and petty as his father had always been cruel and petty, and often she'd suspected they enjoyed being malicious just for maliciousness's sake. Because they could. Because they were rich and powerful and they liked proving they were.

"You told me Julian's children were dead," she said.

"How could I have told you that? He was a cad who sired a thousand bastards. It wouldn't have been possible to keep track."

"He wasn't a cad, and I wish you would stop insisting he was. It's embarrassing."

"Yes, Saint Julian. Allow me to praise him for you."

"He was a devoted husband and father."

"Don't defend him to me."

"It's his four children, George! His children with Anne. It's three sons and a daughter."

"Was it four?"

"You know it was. Why must you pretend they never existed?"

"Why would I care if he had bastard offspring running around on the streets of London? Why would I care if he left four waifs or a hundred?"

"They're your niece and nephews," she tersely reminded him.

"They're yours too, but I don't recall you shedding any tears over their plight. Perhaps you'd rather I'd brought them to Radcliffe. Perhaps you'd rather I'd put them ahead of your own sons."

They glared, a thousand comments bubbling up that were never voiced aloud, but maybe they ought to finally discuss them.

When Julian had disavowed Susan, he'd stated he couldn't wed her because he was *already* married. Susan's father-in-law had refused to accept the union, had refused to acknowledge it or declare it valid. He'd never wavered.

Susan had been spoiled and horrid, incensed by Julian's rejection and offended by Anne's intransience.

Anne could have stepped aside, could have admitted she'd up-jumped into a role she never should have had, but Anne wouldn't. Or Julian could have agreed that the marriage had never transpired, could have had it annulled. It would have meant bastardizing his children and denouncing his beloved wife, but Julian had never been the sort of man George was.

At the time and for many years after, Susan had viewed his decision as a personal affront, and she'd wanted him punished. So...when Julian had been killed and her father-in-law had set Anne's downfall in motion, Susan had kept her mouth shut.

Very soon, she would be standing at Heaven's gate and eager to be invited in. Before she could enter the Lord's kingdom, her life would be laid bare, and she'd be asked to explain and justify her worldly sins.

How would she?

"Anne cursed us, remember?" she said.

"Yes, and I have always told you that I don't believe in curses. She had no special power or ability. She was simply blowing smoke, hoping to scare us."

"Well, she succeeded with me. I'm still afraid of her."

"I don't know why you would be. She's dead and gone. Where she's currently located—which is in a deep, dark grave with a doorway that leads straight to Hell—she can't hurt anyone."

"She warned us that Julian's death would be avenged, that *she* would have vengeance against us."

"I shouldn't have had her shipped to the penal colonies. I should have had her dragged to Scotland and hanged as a witch."

"She threatened any sons we might have. She said they wouldn't reach manhood, that they'd be destroyed as hers had been destroyed. Our sons all died at seventeen."

"It was a coincidence, Susan."

"It wasn't!"

"Why must you remind me of that hideous curse? You've constantly demanded I lift it for you, but how could I *lift* something that doesn't exist?"

"She harmed our boys and you did naught to prevent her."

"I had her deported to Australia, didn't I?"

"It wasn't far enough," she hissed.

"I swear your illness is affecting your mental capacities, and I won't tolerate this absurd ranting. Get control of yourself."

"I am in firm control."

"You couldn't prove it by me."

He pushed himself to his feet, ready to storm out, but she couldn't let him go. If he left in a temper, she wouldn't be able to coax him back for weeks, and she had no time to waste.

"I want to make amends to Anne and Julian," she said.

"Amends?" "Yes, I want to fix what we did to them."

"Fix it! How would we?"

"It's easy. You'll simply designate the oldest boy as your heir."

He studied her with distaste. "You're mad."

"What was his name? Bryce?"

"Don't mention him to me. Besides, I'm sure he's deceased, despite what those miserable twins are claiming."

"You can't continue to conceal the truth. Not with their showing up and telling people who they are."

"I'll never admit they're Julian's children."

"They are, George! Stop pretending."

"I'm not pretending. I sent their father to Hell, and I can send them too."

"Listen to yourself! Still posturing! Still threatening! Stop it!"

"Don't order me about. I won't stand for it."

She should have dropped the issue, but she couldn't. Her immortal soul hung in the balance.

"There's no one else to inherit the estate," she said. "The property will revert to the Crown."

"Yes, strangers can have the whole wretched place."

"Strangers! Rather than your own flesh and blood? And you say *I* am mad."

"Good day, Susan. Don't summon me again until you've regained your wits."

He stomped out, and she might have called him back, but their quarrel had drained her.

She was haunted by what she'd done to Anne Blair, consumed by guilt and terrified over how she'd be received in the next life. Anne and Julian were both on the other side, waiting for her to arrive, waiting to get even. Susan could feel it in her bones.

She'd been conferring with her priest, hinting at a great sin in her past, anxious for absolution, but she was too ashamed to clarify the details. The priest urged her to confess, but she wasn't that brave.

Though Julian had supposedly been killed in a hunting accident, she knew that wasn't the case. Her own husband had pulled the trigger, and she'd remained silent. He'd falsely prosecuted Anne Blair, and again she'd remained silent. They'd cast Anne's four children to the winds of fate, and yet again she'd remained silent. But she was finally at a spot where she was choking on all her secrets.

It was a supreme irony that she'd kept those secrets for her husband, but he had never deserved her loyalty. She'd kept those secrets for herself because she'd wanted to be a countess so badly.

Yet it had all been futile. She had no sons, and she was dying with the weight of this dreadful transgression on her shoulders.

Was it too late to atone?

"Will we ever go home?"

"You shouldn't count on it."

Kat flashed a tremulous smile at Isabelle. She was only ten, and she'd been such a good sport about sneaking away with Kat. She never complained, never cried, never begged to turn around. Even at such a young age, she was a wonderful princess, and it broke Kat's heart that her little sister would never marry according to her station.

She'd have been a marvelous wife for an aristocrat. No king was likely, but certainly a duke or prince. Kat had had her hopes that high. It would never occur now, and all because of Kristof. How could one cousin be so cruel to another?

Kat's father had been kind to Kristof, but they'd all been repaid with perfidy. If Kat had been a rugged, burly male, she'd have gladly murdered him for the insults leveled on her family.

"Will we stay in Cairo?" Isabelle asked. "Nicholas said you might rent a house."

"Would you like that?"

"I'd rather live somewhere that isn't so...different from what we're used to."

"Cairo is definitely different."

Kat sighed, yearning to be brilliantly wise and have all the answers. She'd left Parthenia, desperate for advice from her uncle, but he wasn't inclined to give any, and she wasn't having any luck picking a path on her own. She was too beaten down, too worried that any choice would be wrong.

The sun had set, the temperature dropping. They were in the children's tent, and Kat had just tucked Isabelle into her cot. Nicholas had been at the bathing pools to wash off the sweat and dirt. He was having the time of his life, tagging after Cedric, peppering him with questions and learning the ropes of archeology.

Cedric was actually being civil to Nicholas, and Kat was relieved by that small gesture. He seemed charmed by his nephew, but then Nicholas was a very charming boy. It was difficult not to like him. She'd never met anyone who didn't.

"Would you be disappointed if we remained in Cairo?" she asked her sister.

"I will carry out any task required of me." Isabelle's pretty green eyes were serious and concerned.

"I know you will. You've been so supportive throughout our ordeal."

"I wish all the bad things hadn't happened."

"So do I, Isabelle. So do I."

Nicholas bustled in. He was dressed in his drawers, his hair wet and curling over his shoulders.

"Are you cooled down?" she asked.

"Yes."

He came over to his cot, riffled in his traveling trunk and pulled out his comb. He was growing up, becoming so independent. He'd gone to the pools without protest, had agreed to bathe without a quarrel. Everything was changing.

"Isabelle and I were talking about Cairo," she told him.

"Have you decided to rent a house?"

"Probably."

"Could I stay with Uncle Cedric? He thinks I'd be a grand archeologist. I really have a knack for it."

"We'll discuss it after it's an issue. I'm not sure we'll tarry in Egypt for long."

"I wouldn't mind," he said, "but whatever you choose, Kat, I'm happy."

"You're a wonderful boy, Nicholas. You're such an enormous help to me."

He grinned as Isabelle said, "What about me, Kat? Am I a wonderful girl?"

"Yes, you're a very wonderful girl."

They both giggled, although Nicholas didn't sound much like a child anymore. Soon she'd have to buy him a razor and have someone teach him to shave.

Her spirits flagged.

Was this all she could offer her brother? A camp in the desert? Would he live out his life digging in the dirt like a common laborer? He should have been a king, should have been sitting on the throne in Parthenia.

Oh, she should have fought for what was rightfully his! Why hadn't she?

With what army, Kat?

"You two get to sleep," she said. "No laughing or talking."

"I worked hard today." Nicholas looked very proud. "I'm too tired to laugh or talk."

"There are guards outside. I believe it's Mr. Hubbard's turn at the door. I'll bathe, then I'll be in my tent."

"Yes, *Mother,*" they replied in unison, and they giggled again.

"I'm serious." Her tone was scolding. "If you have any trouble—even if you hear a noise you don't like—call for Mr. Hubbard."

"Stop worrying, Katarina," Nicholas said. "We're safe here. You found a good place for us."

Dear Lord, have it always be true...

She hesitated, and Isabelle said, "Take your bath, Kat. Nicholas is correct. We're fine."

Kat smiled and departed. She was being a ninny to continually fret, but she simply couldn't help it. They were her world, and she'd let them down so dreadfully.

She went to her tent to fetch a towel, robe, soap, and other items. Bryce was there, waiting to escort her. As she moved by him to slip under the tent flap, he winked and squeezed her hand.

She wagged a finger, warning him to be careful. She couldn't have gossip spreading. He grinned and shrugged, apparently not able to resist, which was exhilarating and terrifying. She had no business encouraging him, but more and more, she couldn't ignore her reckless impulses.

Over the years, she'd known women who ruined themselves for passion, and she'd never understood that sort of temptation. She'd certainly never experienced it. She'd told herself she was more sensible than other females, that she'd never be so foolish or irresponsible.

But when he gazed at her, all her good intentions flew out the window.

Was she smitten? She appeared to be, and she couldn't figure out how to handle her burgeoning affection.

She was on her own, with no one to advise her on her conduct, no one to counsel caution. She could do as she liked, with the danger being that she thought she might *like* to do quite a bit with him. So far they'd kissed and touched and caressed, but hadn't accomplished much more than that. Yet those simple pleasures had left her restless and raw.

She noticed her body all the time now, pondered him all the time now. She wanted things she couldn't describe or explain, and the very fact she was considering scandalous behavior was shocking. It underscored how she liked him much more than was wise, but she couldn't persuade herself to desist.

She emerged from the tent, carrying a basket filled with her toiletries. He took it from her, and they walked down the path, her arm and leg constantly brushing his. The slight contact had her pulse racing.

She chuckled and shook her head.

"Why are you smiling?" he asked.

"You make me feel like an adolescent girl with her first crush."

"You have a crush on me?"

"Well, something more than a crush actually."

"I'm glad to hear it. I'd hate to think I was naught more than a passing fancy."

"You're more than that."

"How much more?"

She scoffed with disgust, at herself and at him. "Never mind, you bounder. A woman has to have a few secrets."

"Why? What fun is that?"

They arrived at the pool she'd chosen, and he set down her basket.

"This is lovely, isn't it?" she murmured.

"Yes. The minute I learned of them, I jumped in and rinsed off. I come over twice a day."

"Why didn't you tell me they were here?"

"I didn't suppose I should discuss your bathing habits with you. It's a tad too familiar."

She snorted at that. There was a bubbling sound at the other end, and she pointed to it. "Is that a waterfall?"

"A small one. The pools are linked so fresh water flows through them."

"That's clever."

"Yes, very clever."

She beamed with delight. "It's magical, isn't it? It doesn't seem real."

"No, it doesn't. I'm definitely a long way from London."

There was a hesitation where he expected her to agree that she was a long way from somewhere too. It would have been easy to mention Parthenia, to apprise him of her identity, but if she did she'd wreck their connection.

She didn't know who he assumed she was, probably the wealthy heiress they'd joked about her being. He was happy to fraternize with an heiress, but would he feel the same about a royal princess? She didn't imagine so. She suspected it would drive a wedge between them that would force him to keep his distance.

They were friends, and she couldn't push him away. He treated her like a normal person, and she'd never previously enjoyed the anonymity of being a commoner.

Every relationship in her life had been colored by the knowledge that she was a princess. It set automatic barriers, and she didn't want any of those barriers to arise with him.

"Will you wait for me?"

"Of course." He grinned his wickedest grin. "Unless you'd like me to join you."

She was stunned by the suggestion. "In the pool?"

"Yes. We could swim and try a few other...things."

"Adults behave so outrageously?"

"Yes, and with their clothes off too."

Her jaw dropped. "Their clothes off?"

"Don't look so shocked."

"I can't help it. I'm astonished."

But she glanced out at the pond, and she could practically see the two of them in it together. They'd be wet and slippery, and he was so dashing without a shirt. She'd be able to run her hands all over his sculpted chest, would be able to press her nude flesh to his own, and just from thinking about it, she grew so excited she felt dizzy.

"You know so little about real life," he said. "Were you raised in a convent?"

"Something very close to that."

"If you won't let me swim with you, will you let me act as your lady's maid?"

"To perform what task?"

"To undress you, what would you suppose?"

"Undress me! You actually ponder such indecent conduct?"

"Yes—all the time. Don't you? Wouldn't you like to strip naked and have your wicked way with me?"

"If I did, I wouldn't admit it."

"I'm a male so fantasizing is allowed. You females pretend to be chaste and innocent, as if you never have an impure thought."

"I never do," she claimed which was a bald-faced lie. Since she'd met him, she'd suffered nothing *but* impure thoughts.

As if he could read her mind, he said, "I'm certain—until you met me—you tamped down your worst urges. I'm guessing these days you're rippling with pent-up lust."

She laughed. "Why would you guess that?"

"I told you women love me. They always have. I'm too charming."

"I'm sure it's a gift. Was it inherited from your father?"

"Probably, but I have much of my mother's charisma too. She was extremely dynamic, and I possess all her best traits. I employ them in my amorous pursuits. I'd hate to waste them."

"You're not humble. I'll say that for you."

"Who wants to be humble? Besides, no matter how hard I work at it, I can never rein in all my splendidness. It's simply impossible." He cocked a naughty brow. "Now then, will you let me play lady's maid or not?"

"Not," she firmly replied before her treacherous anatomy could force out a different answer. She shoved him toward the main path. "Wait out there. And *no* peeking."

"I wouldn't dream of it."

"I'm serious."

"So am I."

"Oh, you're horrid," she scolded. "I don't know why I put up with you."

"You can't resist, remember? Women never can. You might as well stop trying." He pointed to her clothes. "Can you manage to disrobe without my assistance?"

"Yes." She'd removed her corset in the tent, and it was the most difficult piece to discard on her own. Without it, she was scandalously unclad, but she'd left it behind anyway. "Go, would you? If you keep pestering me, I'll never finish."

"I'm in no hurry."

"Go!"

She smiled up at him, and he smiled back, and a wonderful intimacy flared. She didn't understand how it happened, but he made her so happy. Just by his being near, she felt better and less afraid, and she had no idea why she'd permitted him to escort her to the bathing pool.

She should have brought Pippa or one of the slaves, but she hadn't. She was desperate to spend time with him, so she was growing loose and free in her habits. The simple fact was that she'd wanted to be alone with him in the moonlight, and she'd gotten her wish. But there were limits to what she'd allow, to what she'd attempt.

He bent down and stole a quick kiss. "Call if you need me. I'll come running."

"I'll be fine."

"Or call if you decide you'd like me to join you after all."

"I won't call you."

He took another quick kiss. "Think about it, would you? I'm right here."

He marched off, and she almost told him to stay, but she didn't. Instead she suffered a depraved thrill, picturing him close by and spying on her through the palm fronds.

She dawdled until he disappeared, then she started in on her buttons, gradually stripping to chemise and drawers. She tugged at the combs in her hair, and it swung down her back.

For a wild, reckless instant, she considered shedding her undergarments too so she'd be naked, but there were some boundaries she wouldn't cross. She dipped in her toe, finding the water pleasantly warm, and she waded out to the middle and dropped to her knees. The moon was up, the air balmy, and Bryce Blair was keeping watch on the other side of the foliage.

It was the most exotic, perfect moment of her life.

CHAPTER NINE

Bryce stood on the dark path, struggling to behave himself.

It was very quiet, the camp settling down for the night, and he could hear Kat undressing, could hear her wade in, could hear a splash as she immersed herself in the pool. He'd always had a vivid imagination, and it was working at a frantic speed. He pictured her naked, the water sluicing over her smooth skin, her pretty hair flowing out behind.

He groaned and rubbed a palm on his cock. The unruly rod had grown so hard that it nearly doubled him over.

He shouldn't have accompanied her. Not on his own anyway. He should have forced Miss Clementi to come, although she'd been conspicuously absent when he'd tried to locate her. So he should have had a slave woman attend Kat, but he hadn't. He'd wanted to sneak off with her.

As he'd reminded her several times now, they were adventuring in Egypt and away from all that was familiar. In the hot, sultry, foreign country, it seemed that any misconduct might be allowed. The rules guiding morality no longer applied.

Was that his cock talking?

It probably was, so he paced, anxious to focus on a topic besides the fact that Kat was a few feet away and bathing.

He turned and paced the other direction, and to his dismay—or was it his delight?—he could see the pool through the foliage. Moonlight shone on the water, giving him a perfect view of her.

She was over at the far end, sitting on a rock bench. She was wearing her undergarments, not having had the temerity to remove them.

Had he planned this very situation? Had he brought her to the isolated spot, hoping a salacious encounter would occur?

Typically he liked to envision himself as being a gentleman, liked to comport himself in a manner that let him remember he was nothing like Chase. Yet maybe Egypt had changed him in ways he hadn't realized, or perhaps deep down, he possessed the heart of a cad.

They were both lonely and alone in the world. Why couldn't they enjoy each other's company? Why couldn't they reach beyond friendship and cordial conversation?

"*Carpe diem,*" he muttered to himself. Seize the day. Or the night, as the case might be.

He blustered over to the pond. She saw him immediately, and he'd expected her to either scold him or shriek with alarm. But she simply stared at him and asked, "What are you thinking?"

"I'm going to swim with you."

"I really don't believe you should."

"I don't care. I'm not giving you a choice."

He kicked off his boots and yanked off his stockings. Then he pulled his shirt over his head, pulled knives from various pockets and sheaths.

She watched him disrobing, but didn't lurch away in maidenly disgust, which he took as a very good sign.

Clad in just his trousers, he waded into the pool, and he walked straight to her. She remained perched on the rock bench, and he knelt down and drew her to him, instigating a passionate, thrilling kiss.

Without telling her what he intended, he dragged her onto his lap, her legs wrapped around his waist, her bottom pressed to his loins. He pushed himself into the pond so they bobbed in the center, the water lapping at their shoulders and chins.

All the while, he was kissing her and kissing her. She eagerly participated, her tongue in his mouth, her fingers riffling his hair. It was tied into a ponytail, and she grabbed the ribbon that held it in place and tossed it away.

"Do you think people tryst here occasionally?" she asked.

"I'm guessing they tryst frequently."

"Would you imagine my uncle built it specifically for this purpose?"

"No. I'm sure he built it for bathing, but humans have interesting ways of using water."

"You're right about that, and you're horrid to have joined me without permission."

"I couldn't help it. I caught a glimpse of you through the trees, and I couldn't resist."

"You were spying on me."

"Not deliberately, but once I saw you I wasn't about to look away."

"Oh, what am I to do with you?"

It was a rhetorical question that required no reply.

She initiated another series of kisses, clutching him tightly, as if she couldn't get him near enough. He was happy to let her nestle and snuggle. Each move of her body rubbed her perfect breasts against his chest until his agony was so pronounced he had no idea how he'd stumble through the evening without committing a few reckless and forbidden acts.

He broke off and nibbled a trail down her neck, to her bosom. He found a pert nipple and sucked it into his mouth. She gasped with surprise but didn't tell him to stop, and even if she had he probably wouldn't have listened.

They shared such a hot, potent attraction. Why deny it? Why ignore it?

"Why are you doing that?" she asked him.

"Because it feels wonderful, to me *and* to you. Doesn't it feel wonderful?"

"Yes, but I'm certain it's a sin."

"I'm certain it is too, but there's no vicar lurking so there's no one keeping count."

"Bryce, this can't mean anything."

"Hush, Kat."

"I must be leading you on, but I'm not sure how I'm enticing you."

"Seriously? You don't know?"

"No." She appeared confused and very young, and he chuckled.

"It's your beauty, you little fool. I simply gaze at you, and I'm overcome."

"You're so sweet."

"Yes, I am, and you spend too much time worrying. Relax, would you?"

"I'm trying."

"Try harder."

He lifted the hem of her chemise, worked it up and over her head so her breasts were bare. For a second, she squealed with distress and attempted to cover herself, but he wouldn't let her.

He pinned her arms and tipped her away so he could study her. The moon shone on them, painting her smooth skin a silvery color. With her brunette hair down, she might have been a mermaid, and he was positive she was singing a siren's song aimed directly at him. No doubt he would crash on the rocks before she was finished with him.

He leaned in and sucked on her nipple again, and he kept on and on, shifting from one to the other, going back and forth, back and forth. Gradually he carried her to the rear of the pond and sat her on the stone bench. He was still on his knees and wedged between her thighs.

He slipped his hand into her drawers, quickly finding her lush center. He slid a finger inside, then another, and she was such a sexual creature, and so incredibly titillated, that he didn't need to stroke them in and out.

He'd scarcely touched her, and she was pitched into a violent orgasm. Her body tensed, and she moaned with dismay and astonishment, being so loud that anyone who'd heard her would definitely assume misbehavior was in progress. They wouldn't have to speculate.

Laughing, merry, joyous, he clamped a palm over her mouth to stifle the sound. She spiraled up and up the ladder of desire, then she reached the top and tumbled down. She was laughing too, sputtering with amazement.

"What did you do to me?" she asked when she could speak again.

"Quiet down or you'll rouse the whole camp. They'll rush in to see what we're about."

"What happened to me?"

"It's carnal pleasure, Kat. Didn't you know?"

"No." She scowled. "Am I still a...a..."

"Yes, you're chaste as the day is long. Well, mostly chaste."

"I'm not with...child, am I? There's no chance of that?"

"No, no. Don't fret. We've just had a spot of fun."

Her frantic queries made him feel awful. She was twenty-five, and he'd been wondering if she was a virgin, or if some young man in her past had pushed the issue with her. But she was naïve and innocent, and clearly he was much too experienced for her.

At the same time, he was delighted to realize she was untried and untrained. If he was shrewd and clever, he might win the ultimate prize she would ever bestow.

Yet it wouldn't be here, in a pond in her uncle's desert camp. No, if Bryce was ever lucky enough to have her for his own, it would be in a grand bedchamber, on a feather mattress with sheets covered in rose petals. He wasn't typically a romantic fellow, but she inspired that sort of devotion.

"You are so wicked," she whispered.

"Not usually, but you draw out my worst impulses."

"Can that occur more than once?"

"Yes, it can occur over and over. It's a secret of the marital bed, but we don't inform you females in advance. If you learned how exciting it is, you'd be ruining yourselves all over the place."

She giggled like a schoolgirl. "We're not married though, so how can we engage in marital conduct?"

"It's just physical behavior. All of it is physical, and people don't have to be wed to enjoy it."

"Obviously not," she murmured. "Have I told you that it's dangerous for me to fraternize with you?" "I believe you might have."

"I want to do it again. I want to do it all night."

"We can't. Someone is certain to stroll by, and if I don't get you back soon, the guards will notice how long we've been gone—and who you were with."

"Drat it. I imagine you're correct."

"I could sneak into your tent later."

She looked scandalized, but intrigued too. "You wouldn't."

"I would—if you ask me nicely."

She snorted and assessed him with a keen eye, but in the end—as he might have predicted—she couldn't take the leap.

"I'm not ready to have you sneaking into my tent."

"Are you sure?"

"Fairly sure."

"No, you must declare that you're absolutely sure. Otherwise I'll convince myself to barge in and surprise you."

"I am by and large absolutely sure," she said.

"I'll keep that in mind."

"If you came to my tent, would we...would we..."

He nodded. "We'd do things we probably shouldn't."

"That's what I figured you'd tell me."

"It would be thrilling though. You'd like it. I promise."

"You're a man so you would promise that."

"True, but I'm not lying. You would love it. But..."

"We shouldn't."

"I can't control myself around you."

"And *I* can't control myself around you."

"Yes, you Jezebel. At heart you're loose as a doxy."

"If that's supposed to render me more amenable, you've misplayed your hand."

"I never misplay my hand, because I never bet more than I can afford to lose."

"Could you afford to lose me?"

She asked the question in a flirtatious manner, as if she was teasing or jesting, but he thought, deep down, she might be seriously inquiring.

He smiled, letting all his affection shine through. "I could never afford to lose you."

She sighed with pleasure. "It's why you make me happy. You always say just the right thing."

"Of course I do." He pulled away and pointed to her basket. "Let's dry you off, put some clothes on you, and get you back before the guards deduce who was moaning and groaning."

Her blanched with horror. "They wouldn't suspect it was me, would they?"

"Maybe."

"I'll never be able to show my face among them again."

"Then they'll really know it was you."

"You're so hazardous to my moral character. I have no idea why I'm spending time with you."

"You're crazy about me. You can admit it."

"I might be crazy about you. But just a little."

She pushed off the bench and brushed by him, grabbing her drenched chemise out of the water and walking to the sandy beach. He followed her, liking how relaxed she was, her limbs rubbery and languid. She didn't try to conceal her breasts, but wrung out her chemise and tugged it over her head while he watched. Her dress was next, and she spun and let him help her with the buttons.

"I want us to come here often," she said.

"All right."

"We have to be careful though."

"Certainly."

He doubted caution was possible, but he pretended it was. She didn't realize how rapidly passion could spiral out of control, and he wouldn't explain the risks. He would ride out the affair and see where they landed at the end.

She rose on tiptoe and kissed him.

"Thank you," she said.

"For what?"

"For being you. For forcing me to become someone else. I *need* to become someone else."

"I will try my best, Katarina, to make you into someone entirely new."

"I hope so, for I hate the person I have been."

"We'll work on her together."

He yanked on his boots, picked up his shirt and drew it on too. He found his knives and stuck them in the various spots where they were always hidden. Then he linked their fingers and they started off.

They'd reached the main path when a scream rent the air. Isabelle shouted, "Nicholas! Nicholas!"

"Oh, my Lord," Kat murmured. "What's happened?"

They sucked in a shocked breath and raced for the tents.

Nicholas wasn't quite asleep when his kidnapper snuck in.

He'd been lying quietly, thinking about the marvelous day he'd had, tagging after his Uncle Cedric. He was an odd duck, but Nicholas liked him anyway. While Kat yearned to be welcomed back to Parthenia, his country was beginning to seem very far away. He couldn't imagine how they'd ever return.

In the meantime, he was twelve years old, and it was wrong to have Kat supporting him. A female shouldn't have to support a male. Since Nicholas wouldn't be a king, he had to consider the type of life he'd like to live instead. Digging for antiquities would suit him.

As he'd been worrying about the future, he'd heard a peculiar tearing sound, and he'd glanced over, astonished to see a knife slicing through the canvas. Very quickly a man slipped in the opening and proceeded straight to Nicholas.

Nicholas called to his sister, managing only a simple, "Isabelle!" before a palm was clapped over his mouth. He was rudely jerked out of his bed and carried off. Isabelle jumped up and clasped hold of the man's arm, but he was very large and very strong, and she couldn't stop him.

Nicholas was stunned by the violence of the assault, by the swiftness of it, so he was outside before he remembered that he had to fight his attacker. He kicked and struggled, as behind them, Isabelle was screaming, her voice exploding in the dark.

"*Mon dieu*," the man cursed in French.

It was the main language of Parthenia, and the bandit was wearing the wool trousers and embroidered vest favored by the citizenry. Nicholas's mind was awhirl with questions as he tried to figure out why one of his own subjects would steal him away.

What was transpiring? Who had ordered it? Where would he be taken? If the destination was Parthenia, he wondered if he shouldn't offer to go along peacefully. He'd be glad to go home, but he'd never depart without Kat and Isabelle.

Nicholas bit the man's hand very hard, and the criminal yelped and nearly dropped him.

"Put me down!" Nicholas spoke in French too. "As your king, I command it."

But his decree had no effect. The man firmed his grip and continued on.

They were headed toward the Nile. Was there a boat? Would he be whisked away? If the sails were raised, the oars at the ready, he might never see his sisters again.

"Kat! Kat!" he cried. "Mr. Blair! I need you! Where are you?"

He reached up and jabbed his thumb in the kidnapper's eye. The man bellowed with outrage. Nicholas poked him again and wiggled away, and he ran—only to be seized by two others who'd been lurking in the shadows. They hurried him toward the river.

The camp was coming to life, Isabelle still screaming, people yelling. He kicked and wrestled, but couldn't halt their forward progress.

Suddenly Mr. Blair appeared in front of them, blocking their route. The kidnappers pulled up short, glared at him, glared at each other. For a moment, all of them were frozen in place.

"Going somewhere gentlemen?" Mr. Blair casually asked. They didn't reply, and he said, "You have something of mine. Release the boy."

"Merde!" one of the brigands cursed. In heavily-accented English he added, "If you would be so kind as to move out of the way, Monsieur? We are leaving and taking him with us."

"I don't think so," Mr. Blair responded.

Seemingly from out of nowhere, he produced a pistol and a sword. He looked very calm, but very dangerous too, as if he wasn't afraid of any hazard in the world. Nicholas realized he'd spent entirely too much time around his sisters, and females never understood the importance of knowing how to brawl.

He decided—after the incident was over—he would have Mr. Blair instruct him in battle skills. If Nicholas ever expected to protect himself and his sisters, he had to learn how to fight and win. He had to learn how to stand as Mr. Blair was standing and face down murderous adversaries without blinking an eye.

"I'm not scared of them, Mr. Blair." He proudly exuded the same calm audacity.

"You shouldn't be scared," he agreed.

"I believe they're trying to kidnap me."

"Well, we won't let them, will we?"

"No. I have no desire for them to succeed."

"They haven't a chance of succeeding," Mr. Blair said, "and they won't bother you much longer."

Nicholas stared at Mr. Blair, wanting him to remember that Nicholas had been very brave, very steady in a crisis as his beloved father had trained him to be. His body weight went slack, the abrupt motion throwing the criminals off balance. As they struggled to subdue him, he raced away.

Behind him, he heard shouting and the crack of a pistol shot. Then swords clanged together. Nicholas flitted into the trees, recollecting that there was at least one other miscreant lurking, and he had no intention of being captured again.

He peeked down the path, and one of his attackers was lying on the ground, while the other was skirmishing with Mr. Blair. Nicholas wished he was courageous enough to barge into the middle of the fracas, but he had no weapon.

Mr. Blair didn't need any assistance though. He dispatched the second brigand with very little trouble. The oaf emitted a loud woof, then joined his unconscious friend in the dirt.

Nicholas crept from his hiding place and called to Mr. Blair, "Are they dead?"

"I hope so," he replied. "Are you all right?"

"Yes."

Nicholas walked over, and though his knees were knocking, he feigned composure, as if he hadn't been unnerved in the slightest. It was another lesson imparted by his father. A royal person never showed fear or alarm, and it was actually the first time Nicholas had had to practice the skill.

Mr. Blair leaned down and riffled through the men's vests, but didn't find anything.

"Do you know them?" he asked Nicholas.

"No. I've never seen them before. There was a third man too. He cut his way into the tent with a knife. We were headed to the river. They might have planned to abscond with me in a boat."

Mr. Blair whipped around, and they peered out at the water. There had been a boat. It was skimming away, the sails just visible, so whoever had captained it, whoever the crew, they'd escaped.

Mr. Blair put his arm across Nicholas's shoulders. No one was supposed to touch him so there had been few occasions when he'd been hugged in his life, and it felt very grand. At the moment, with his heart thundering like mad, he was safe and protected and very, very glad that Kat had hired Mr. Blair.

"You did really well, Nicholas."

"Thank you." He grinned. "So did you."

"You were very tough, very calm in an emergency."

Nicholas beamed at the praise. "My father always told me I need to be."

"He was correct."

"Will you teach me to fight?"

Mr. Blair snorted. "I doubt your sister would like it."

"Yes, but she's a female so I wouldn't expect her to understand."

"True."

"When they carried me off, I hated being so helpless."

"I know the sentiment. It's the reason I developed my ability with a sword. I've been accosted numerous times in this dreadful country, and I don't like it."

"I don't either."

Mr. Blair studied him, then nodded. "We'll begin tomorrow. Even if she disapproves, we'll proceed anyway."

"If she complains too much, I'll simply order her to be silent."

Mr. Blair seemed shocked by the admission. "Can you make her stop talking?"

"Oh yes," Nicholas said. "She has to obey me."

Nicholas had revealed a bit more than he should have about his station, about Kat's station in regard to his. He spun, forcing himself to look at the men on the ground, forcing himself not to be sorry for them. And he most especially refused to fret over their fate like a silly, trembling child.

He'd been raised to be a king, and they had tried to harm him. The penalty had ended up being death, which meant they'd received the appropriate punishment.

Others rushed up then, servants and slaves, and more of the guards Monsieur Valois had sent with Mr. Blair and Mr. Hubbard.

"Take them away," Mr. Blair said to a guard and to a servant, "Wake Mr. Webster. Inform him of what's occurred. Ask what should be done with them. They have to be buried and probably the authorities notified, but I'm not certain of the protocols."

The servant bowed and hustled off as others picked up the bodies and lugged them away. Again, Nicholas forced himself to watch, to stoically accept their violent demise. Then and there, he resolved—should he ever regain his throne—he would knight Mr. Blair for his brave daring on Nicholas's behalf.

As the last man passed by them, Mr. Hubbard hastened over.

"I heard there was trouble," he said to Mr. Blair. "What happened?"

Instead of answering, Mr. Blair asked, "Where were you? I thought you were guarding the tent."

"Well...ah..."

Mr. Blair's angry, disappointed glare had Mr. Hubbard stumbling to a halt.

"Don't bother explaining," Mr. Blair snapped. "I can't listen to your excuses."

"I just slipped away for a few minutes," Mr. Hubbard claimed. "I never imagined there'd be mischief. You said yourself that it was unlikely."

"Be silent, Chase! We'll discuss it in the morning."

Mr. Blair sounded regal and imperious, like the man Nicholas hoped to become someday. He put his arm across Nicholas's shoulders again. "Let's get you back to your sisters. I bet they're worried sick."

"Are they all right? Isabelle wasn't hurt, was she?"

"They're fine," Mr. Blair told him.

They walked off, leaving a disgraced, inept Mr. Hubbard alone on the dark path.

CHAPTER TEN

"You can't stay. Not another second."

Kat glared at her uncle. She understood his fury, but couldn't bear it. She was being kicked out by her only kin in the world. It was galling and depressing.

They were in Cedric's tent, with her sitting and him pacing. He was livid, venting at Kat, and she was trying to remember that she was an unwanted guest, that he was an elder male relative, and she owed him deference and courtesy.

She was *trying* to remember, but was failing miserably.

"You're making too much of this," she claimed.

"In my view, I'm not making nearly enough," Cedric huffed. "I told you not to leave Parthenia."

"I never received your letter!"

"Someone obviously wants Nicholas back, and they're so determined that they'd kidnap him."

"There's no proof they were specifically looking for him. They might have been slavers and not set on any particular boy."

At voicing the comment, she shuddered with dread. Was it better to imagine they'd been slavers? Was it better to imagine it had been random rather than targeted?

Cedric scoffed. "Don't talk to me as if I'm a fool, Katarina."

"What do you mean?"

"I saw the bodies of the two brigands. If they're not from Parthenia, I'll eat my hat."

"But it's insane to assume they're from Parthenia. We were stripped of our titles and lands. We were cast out like vagabonds. Why force our return?"

"How would I know? Why don't you save everyone an enormous amount of trouble and head home?"

"We don't belong there," she caustically retorted. "Not anymore."

"Well, if you don't belong there, you don't belong anywhere."

"No. That's the problem."

She peered down at her lap, exhausted that life had to be so hard. One day in her recent past, she'd been a rich, contented princess. The next, she'd been tossed away like garbage. Where was a princess supposed to go when she wasn't a princess anymore? Where was a king supposed to go?

"I've written to Valois," Cedric said.

"On what topic?"

"I've asked him to find you lodging in Cairo."

"Thank you for consulting me first," she tersely stated.

Cedric ignored the jibe. "I requested a property with gates and walls so you can be safer there than you were here."

She recalled that the initial attack in Cairo had occurred directly outside Valois's villa. No doubt she wouldn't be safe, no matter where she put down roots, and she simply couldn't fathom why they were having difficulties.

They hadn't been welcome in Parthenia, so they'd left. It's what the citizenry had appeared to want. Kat had accepted their fate, hadn't fought or chastised. Why couldn't people just let them be?

"When are we to leave?" she inquired.

"As soon as you're packed."

"You're kicking us out. Is it what you truly desire? For I must tell you—if we depart—you'll probably never see us again."

"I certainly hope not."

At his heartless reply, she gasped, and he recognized how cruel he'd sounded.

"I just mean—" "I know what you *mean*, Uncle Cedric. You were very clear when we arrived. We are your nieces and your nephew. We are facing many obstacles, but you can't be bothered to aid us."

"It's not that!" he hotly responded. "It's dangerous for you here! There was a shooting in my camp! Two criminals were killed."

"I realize that fact."

"I've had Valois bribe the authorities so they don't investigate, but we're lucky Mr. Blair wasn't arrested."

She scowled. "He was defending my brother from kidnappers. Why would he have been detained for such a heroic act?"

"We're foreigners, Katarina, in a foreign land. We don't have any status or privileges. I shouldn't have to explain our precarious situation to you."

"He was protecting us!"

Cedric slammed his fist on his desk. "I won't argue the point!"

Bryce must have heard them quarreling. He'd been waiting outside, and he poked his head in.

"Is everything all right?" he asked.

"Everything is fine," Cedric said.

Bryce flicked his cool gaze to Kat. "What is your opinion, Miss Webster? Is everything fine?"

"Yes, Mr. Blair, and we're almost finished. I'll be out in a minute."

"Katarina and the children will be sailing shortly for Cairo," Cedric told him. "Monsieur Valois is renting lodging for them in the city."

Bryce looked at Kat, a thousand comments flitting between them, but they would never have a conversation in front of Cedric.

"I'm sure that's wise," Bryce ultimately said.

"I'm sure it is too," Cedric agreed, "for she's not safe in the desert with me."

"Is that what you want, Miss Webster?" Bryce asked her.

She wondered how to answer. He was such a marvelous champion. If she demanded to stay, would he refuse to let Cedric throw her out?

But she wouldn't push the issue. Her uncle was eager to evict her, and she'd learned a bitter lesson in Parthenia. When her presence was blatantly unpalatable, she wouldn't beg to remain.

"It's best if we leave," she murmured. "I'll fill you in on the details in a moment."

He slipped out, and she knew he'd be close by. Nicholas and Isabelle were with him too, playing where he could observe them. He was determined to keep them in his sight at all times. It was obvious the other guards—most especially Chase Hubbard—couldn't be trusted.

Cedric riffled through a stack of papers and pulled out an envelope.

"You received a letter," he informed her.

She blanched with shock. "*I* received a letter? Who knows I am here?"

"From the markings on the front, it's easy to see who's written."

He handed it to her, and her shock intensified. It was from the royal court, the King's seal stamped on it.

She ripped it open and, on reading Kristof's signature, she nearly fell out of her chair. He was ordering her home, ordering her to bring Nicholas and Isabelle too.

She was furious and aggrieved. During her frantic journey south, he must have had spies following her. They must have been tracking her movements and filing reports.

The attacks on Kat and Nicholas must have been orchestrated by Kristof. Evidently his minions were desperate to retrieve them by any method necessary, and considering the force they'd employed, Kristof must have told them rough treatment would be allowed without consequence.

Kat was humiliated all over again, but frightened too. The threat to Nicholas suddenly reared up. She remembered the whispered warning from her father's friend, the man's insistence that she take Nicholas and go.

Why would Kristof order them back unless Nicholas *wasn't* safe?"What does he say?" Cedric asked.

"He's commanded me to return Nicholas to Parthenia."

"Will you?"

"Absolutely not."

They were the last words she ever spoke to her uncle. She stood and swept out.

ॐ ॐ ॐ ॐ

"We have to talk."

"I was wondering when you'd get around to it."

Chase peered over at Bryce and sighed with regret. He and Bryce had been friends since they were boys. They'd both staggered into their boarding school as homeless orphans, waifs who had no one to worry about them, no one to care.

Chase had arrived, having lost his parents and having been separated from his only sister, and he'd been bewildered and forlorn. The students had mostly been from lofty families. Many had had noble parents, while others like Chase were the natural born sons of aristocrats. A few were like Bryce who'd seemed to have come from an elevated background, though his antecedents were uncertain.

He'd claimed his father had been a prince and he'd grow up to be a king, but no one had believed him. His lies had spawned many fistfights, so he'd learned how to defend himself.

By the time Chase had been enrolled, Bryce had become the unofficial protector of those students who were picked on or bullied. At the ripe old age of eight, Bryce had been Chase's hero. As a result, Chase had never had any problems at school. He'd merely mention that he was being harassed, and Bryce resolved any difficulty.

Bryce was magnificent that way. He couldn't tolerate an injustice, couldn't bear to see a person tormented or harmed, and Chase had always deemed himself incredibly lucky that Bryce had bothered to take Chase under his wing.

Bryce had constantly proved himself to be loyal and true, but Chase had rarely reciprocated those stellar traits. He simply didn't have it in him to be trustworthy or dependable. Had he finally squandered Bryce's goodwill?

They were on a boat and sailing for Cairo. It was one of those perfect Egyptian evenings, the sun setting in the west, the Nile stretching on forever. A row of pyramids dotted the horizon, the stones glowing an eerie purple color as the sky darkened.

The crew had anchored for the night, but Bryce had refused to have them stop by the river's banks. They liked to cook their supper and sleep on the sand, but Bryce wouldn't permit it. They would bob about in the middle so it would be hard for a brigand to approach.

Chase wasn't overly concerned about Miss Webster or her siblings. Yes, he'd agreed to guard them, but only so he could pay his fare to England. It had never occurred to him that he'd actually have to work to earn the money.

Not for a single second had he expected a violent incident to transpire, and he wasn't about to endanger himself on their behalves. Once they reached Cairo, he would request his wages, then leave Miss Webster to her own devices. He hoped he could convince Bryce to leave too, but he was apprehensive about Bryce.

While neither Bryce nor Miss Webster had provided the smallest indication of a developing fondness, Chase knew Bryce really well. To his dismay, Bryce seemed smitten.

"Let me have it," Chase grumbled. "You're fairly bursting with indignation. Go ahead and scold me. I'm ready."

"Don't be flippant. I'm not in the mood."

"I've said I was sorry a dozen times. How can I give you a pound of flesh if you won't accept it?"

When Nicholas was nearly kidnapped, Chase should have been watching the tent, but he'd sneaked off with Pippa. In the brawl that had ensued, Bryce had killed two men, and even though they'd deserved their fate, Bryce took that sort of thing very seriously.

He was angry with Chase for shirking his duty, but in Chase's defense, he hadn't felt disaster would ever strike. He'd dubbed Miss Webster a trembling worrier, but apparently her fears were justified, which meant Chase had signed onto the wrong convoy.

"You were in charge of Nicholas," Bryce chided as if Chase were ten.

"I know, I know."

"That's our job. It's what we are being paid to do."

"We haven't received a farthing yet, have we?"

"We'll be paid, although after what happened, if Miss Webster decides to reduce what we were promised, I wouldn't be surprised. I have no desire to be trapped here because you screwed up and lost us the money we were owed."

"Gad, that would be the limit, wouldn't it? We get roped into a predicament that ultimately requires swordplay, and when we step up, we're slapped on the wrist."

"*We* weren't involved in swordplay, Chase. I didn't see you anywhere during the entire fiasco. If I remember correctly, it all fell on my shoulders."

"Yes, it did."

"You didn't have to accept this position," Bryce reminded him.

"I'm aware of that fact."

"Where were you when the trouble started? It would be nice if I could hear the truth for once."

Chase smiled a sly smile. "A gentleman never tells."

"No he doesn't, and since you're *not* a gentleman and we both know it, the prohibition doesn't apply. What were you doing?"

"I was dallying. What would you suppose?"

"Was it by any chance with Miss Clementi?"

Chase shrugged. "Perhaps."

"What are your plans with regard to her?"

"Must I have plans?"

"Is she expecting decent behavior from you? Might she be expecting a marriage proposal when you're through?"

"No," Chase scoffed. "She has even less scruples than I do."

"I find that hard to believe."

"She doesn't anticipate or want a commitment from me. Besides, she has big ideas back in her home country that don't include me."

"So I don't need to have a word with her about you?"

"No. Why would you? I'm not a child, Bryce. Don't fuss over me as if you're my father."

"With the way you act, Chase, sometimes I feel like I'm your father. Nicholas might have been murdered. Does that possibility resonate with you?"

"I like the boy, but you're braver than I am. We both understand that you are. I wouldn't have jumped in front of a line of brigands to protect him, but you were happy to imperil yourself."

"I'm not happy about it at all. I killed two men, and even if they were criminals, it's extremely disturbing to me."

"Better them than you."

Bryce threw up his hands. "Why am I wasting my breath?"

"What would you have me say, Bryce? I'm glad Nicholas is all right. I'm glad no harm was inflicted on either of you. And I'm *sorry* for the whole bloody debacle. Are you satisfied now? I think I'm done apologizing."

They glared, on the brink of a quarrel, but it would never begin. Bryce wasn't the type to shout or argue, and Chase couldn't be goaded into a lather on any topic.

"When we arrive in Cairo," Bryce eventually said, "you shouldn't continue working for Miss Webster."

Chase chuckled. "Are you firing me? Because if you are, I should probably inform you that I'll quit as soon as I can."

"How soon?"

"If I can convince Miss Webster to give me my wages, I'll book passage to England immediately. What about you? Will you come with me or will you stay behind?"

"I haven't decided."

"Why haven't you? Are you sweet on pretty, mysterious Miss Webster?"

"No," Bryce insisted.

"Are you sure? You were with her down at the bathing pools when the brouhaha started with Nicholas."

"I was guarding her, Chase. That's why we were employed, remember?"

"I remember. You're not involved with her? You're not sneaking off in the dark to misbehave?"

"No," Bryce insisted again. "As opposed to Miss Clementi, Miss Webster has high moral standards."

"Meaning what? She won't lower herself to consort with you?"

"Yes, that's precisely what I mean."

"Then why would you remain?"

"She's all alone in the world, and she's in trouble. I don't mind helping her."

"And that's all it will be? You helping a damsel in distress?"

"Yes."

"You're so chivalrous, Bryce. I wish I could be more like you." "No, you don't. You're happy being your usual corrupt self."

Chase considered, then grinned. "You could be right."

Chase studied Bryce, wondering as to his claims about Miss Webster.

Pippa was pushing Chase to aid her in a scheme she was hatching against Miss Webster. Pippa had adamantly and repeatedly declared it wouldn't be horrid or awful. It would just be a way for Pippa to earn a ton of money and head home wealthy.

If Bryce had an emotional attachment to Miss Webster, Chase wouldn't entangle himself in Pippa's plot. But if Bryce didn't care about Miss Webster, if he wasn't fond, then Chase had no qualms about participating.

Pippa had offered him an exorbitant reward for his assistance, and he was a scoundrel. He'd be the first to admit it. Even so, he wouldn't deliberately hurt a female. Did he trust Pippa? No, and he'd definitely pressure her to provide more details. If nothing sounded dodgy, he'd be delighted to pocket the extra funds.

Still though, he frowned at Bryce. "Are you positive you're not lusting after Miss Webster?"

"I said *no*. Why keep asking me about her?"

"You're together constantly. You seem very friendly."

"It's because I'm a friendly person, Chase, and at the moment, she doesn't have any friends."

"There's no chance of an amour developing?"

"Are you joking? I have no idea who she really is, but whoever she turns out to be, she'll be much too lofty for a man of my station."

"You're a bloody earl, Bryce."

"Only in fairytales."

"You could make it come true."

"Never in a thousand years."

From Bryce's stoic expression, Chase understood the issue was closed. He couldn't comprehend Bryce's decision not to fight for his heritage and had given up pleading with him about it.

It was likely jumbled up in those hard times at school when he'd tell people he was a prince and he hadn't been believed.

Yet if he'd proclaim himself and seize what was lawfully his, he'd be Earl of Radcliffe. No matter Miss Webster's actual rank, Bryce would be a suitable match for her. Even if she was a princess—and with how she acted, he wouldn't be surprised to learn she was—Bryce would be a good match for her. A bit low, but still good.

Chase shucked off the dilemma. Bryce wasn't interested in her, and she was too far above him. With that being Bryce's opinion, he would never reach for her.

So...Chase wasn't bound by any loyalty to Bryce over Miss Webster. Pippa needed his help and would pay him handsomely for whatever that dubious, unexplained help wound up being.

Why not? Chase mused.

It couldn't be any worse than many of the other sordid deeds he'd done in his sorry life. He grabbed the liquor decanter and refilled his glass.

CHAPTER ELEVEN

"It was your father's."

"Seriously?"

"I thought you'd like to have it."

Bryce gaped at Valois. They were back where they'd started, in Cairo at his villa, all of them his guests until a rental property was arranged for Kat and her siblings.

Supper was over, the weary travelers off to their rooms, but Valois had asked Bryce to join him in his private quarters. He'd just opened a locked safe and pulled out a glorious weapon, and Bryce studied it in amazement.

It was too long to be called a knife, but too short to be a sword. It was what a Bedouin might have wielded in olden times, swinging it to lop off heads as he rode past his enemies on a camel.

It looked ancient and exquisitely crafted, the hilt made of gold and inlaid with gemstones, mostly emeralds and rubies. A leather sheath had been designed for it too, the leather tooled with odd scrolling and even more gems pounded into it.

It was magnificent and deadly and Valois was claiming it had belonged to Bryce's father.

Before Bryce had trotted off to the desert with Kat, he'd stayed with Valois for several weeks, and while Valois had admitted to having been friends with Bryce's father many years earlier, he hadn't mentioned being in possession of any of his father's things. Why would his father have left behind such a beautiful item?

Bryce was dubious, and Valois noted his skepticism.

"When you were here before, I couldn't find it, and I didn't want to get your hopes up."

"It's superb." Bryce ran his thumb over the sharp blade. "Why did he give it to you?"

"I did him a favor once."

"It must have been quite a favor."

"It was."

Valois's expression was stoic and bemused, informing Bryce that he wouldn't confess any details. He was always reserved and cautious, and apparently a secret could be safe with him even three decades later.

"Your father was a fine man, Bryce."

"I'm proud to hear you say it."

"I'm aware of how he passed on, as well as how your grandfather harmed your mother."

Bryce shrugged, not eager to discuss it. The topic was painful, and it stirred horrific memories of that day at the dock when his mother had been taken away. If he talked about it, he'd have nightmares for a month.

"It was a long time ago, Valois," he said. "It's water under the bridge."

"Mr. Hubbard tells me you found your sister, Annie."

"Yes, but her name was changed when she was little. It's Evangeline now. She married very high, into Lord Sidwell's family. Her husband is Aaron Drake, Lord Run. Do you know him?"

"No, I don't know any of them. What about your brothers, the twins? What were their names?"

"Michael and Matthew."

"Yes. Have they been located?"

"Evangeline is searching for them, and she's hunting for my mother too. She's the ultimate optimist, and she has this wild idea that Mother might still be alive."

"It would be a splendid ending, wouldn't it? But not likely. The voyage around the globe is treacherous."

"I realize that fact. It's why my sister is the optimist, but I am not."

"Let's pray it turns out to be true. If she's alive, your grandfather will roll in his grave."

"He should never rest easy."

Valois assessed Bryce, his gaze probing and astute, and Bryce felt ten years old again and about to be paddled by the headmaster for a rules infraction.

"Mr. Hubbard also tells me you will not fight for your legacy."

Bryce smiled a tight smile. "Mr. Hubbard should keep his mouth shut and stay out of my business."

"I believed you and your siblings were dead. Everyone thought so."

"I survived just to spite my relatives, I guess."

"And now, as an adult you've learned your heritage."

"Yes, but it doesn't mean much to me." "It should."

"It doesn't," Bryce said with a grim finality.

"Your grandfather and your uncle stole it from you! Aren't you enraged? Have you none of your father's grit and determination?"

"I'm finding out if I have any. It's why I traveled to Egypt."

"You are your father's son, Bryce. I see it in you more and more every day. You have his bravery and daring, his sense of justice and fairness. You have inherited his very best traits."

"You're kind to mention it."

"He would want you to fight for what is yours. He would want you to right this horrible wrong."

"I suppose."

Bryce was extremely uncomfortable to be conferring about his family's tragedy.

When he'd originally discovered his actual rank, he'd told Evangeline he would attempt to reclaim what was theirs. But the fantasy was much simpler to contemplate than the reality.

How precisely was he to wrest Radcliffe from his wicked kin? He wasn't the sort to ride into Radcliffe Castle and kill in revenge. Nor had he the funds to hire lawyers and institute legal proceedings. Even if he had the money, how could he prove the truth?

He had an old birth certificate and his parents' marriage license. So what? How could he establish they weren't forgeries? He could stand up in a court of law and shout to the heavens that he was Bryce Blair, son of Julian Blair, that he ought to be Earl of Radcliffe. Who would listen? Who would care?

The entire, sad saga was too agonizing to recollect. He never talked about it. What was the point?

Yet as he stared at Valois, as he tried to devise a polite way of telling him to drop it, someone laid a hand on his shoulder. It was a gesture that imbued encouragement and strength, that reminded him he was powerful and tough, that he wasn't alone.

He glanced around, wondering who had snuck up behind him, but no one was there.

"What is it?" Valois asked. "What are you looking at?"

"Someone laid a hand on my shoulder."

"How curious. Maybe it was your father's spirit, stopping by to inform you that he agrees with me."

"If my father is haunting any spot, it would be Radcliffe Castle in Scotland."

"Or your mother's grave in Australia," Valois said. "He loved her very much."

Suddenly the air was filled with the scent of red roses, and Bryce glanced around again, figuring someone had entered the room with a bouquet of flowers. But no. They were still very much alone.

"Do you smell that?" he asked Valois.

"The scent of roses?"

"Yes."

Valois chuckled and raised a brow. "You have many ghosts,

Bryce. They're following you."

"Just my luck," Bryce muttered.

"I have many of my own ghosts, as you know. Typically when they are restless, they want something from me. What could your father want from you? Vengeance, perhaps?"

As Valois voiced the word *vengeance*, the hand was placed on Bryce's shoulder again. He held himself very still, and a calm sense of purpose flowed through him. Was it his father? Could it be?

Why not...

He liked to imagine his parents were hovering, and he wouldn't discount any possibility. He'd been distressed all his life by how he'd lost them, by how his family had been ripped apart. Even though he'd been a little boy when it had happened, his mother had commanded him to protect his siblings, but he hadn't been able to.

He'd always felt guilty and at fault, as if he could have arranged a better path for all of them. He was still enormously troubled by how Sissy had been wrenched from his arms after he'd given her the ivory statue that had been on their mother's harpsichord.

He'd promised to come for her, to find her someday, but he'd only been five. His father's friend, Mr. Etherton, had separated them, had sent Bryce to school, then never visited. Bryce hadn't had the means to search for Sissy.

Did his parents forgive him? Did his mother understand the obstacles he'd faced? He'd failed his mother and his siblings, and the fact tormented him.

Am I forgiven, Mother?

The scent of roses was gradually fading, and he inhaled deeply as a memory from his youth was stirred.

"Why are you smiling?" Valois asked.

"I just recalled that my mother always smelled like roses. I suppose it was her perfume."

"Then I'm sure she's with us too, along with your father. They must be together on the other side."

"Do you think she's forgiven me?"

"For what transgression?"

"She told me to watch over my siblings, but I couldn't."

"You were *five*, Bryce."

"I know, but it seemed that I should have been able to...to..." He stopped and waved away a huge surge of melancholy. "Never mind me. It's late. I should be off to my bed."

"As should I."

He picked up the sword or knife or whatever it was. "Thank you for this wonderful gift. I will always cherish it."

"You're welcome, and it appears I've upset you with this discussion of your past."

"Well, it's an upsetting subject."

"I won't apologize for raising it though, and I'd like to continue our conversation tomorrow."

"To what end?"

"I'm older and wiser than you are, Bryce, and I was your father's friend. I'd like to offer you my advice."

Bryce could imagine nothing more painful or distressing. "We'll see how I feel in the morning."

He bowed and departed, and while he'd assumed he'd proceed to his bedchamber, their chat had been too vexing. It had left him anxious and angry and confused.

What was the best path? How was he to know? Perhaps he should contact a clairvoyant and have her look into his future.

He roamed the dark courtyards of the villa, and for a moment he nearly went to the dock to stare at the Nile and be soothed by its soft currents. But he didn't want to be by himself. Instead he turned and headed for Kat's suite.

Since the kidnapping attempt on Nicholas, he'd barely had a private minute with her. Was she lonely? Was she missing him? He'd knock, and if she wasn't interested in having a visitor, she was fully capable of telling him to go away.

He approached her room, and once he arrived, he decided not to knock. He wouldn't give her a chance to order him out. He spun the knob and slipped inside.

The sitting room was empty and quiet, but a candle burned in the bedchamber beyond. He could see her bed, and she wasn't in it. He walked over and peeked in. There was a small alcove behind the bed that led onto a balcony, and she was standing in the moonlight and gazing out at the Nile.

He tossed his father's sword onto a chair, and she must have heard him, because she asked, "Pippa, is that you?"

She glanced at him, and he tried to read her expression, but she was too far away.

"You shouldn't be in here," she murmured. "It's not proper."

"I know."

"But I'm very, very glad you came."

She flew toward him and practically leapt into his arms. Then he was kissing her and kissing her. He lifted her off her feet and turned them in circles until they were dizzy and breathless with laughter.

"I've been dying to talk to you," she said.

"I was hoping that was the case."

"That stupid boat was so tiny. There was no spot where I could have you all to myself."

"My thought exactly."

"The entire trip to Cairo, I was so upset. I'm still upset. I needed you."

"I'm here now."

He began kissing her again, and he swept her around, then tumbled her onto the mattress. They landed in a tangle, bouncing together, giggling like schoolchildren.

She was dressed for bed, wearing a nightgown and robe, so there were no petticoats, no skirt or corset in the way. He rolled on top of her, every curvaceous inch of her body pressed to his, and they moaned with pleasure.

"It seems as if we've been separated for years," she said.

"I agree. I feel as if I've been wandering in the desert and finally found you."

"Was I mad for leaving my uncle's camp?"

"No. After how he insulted you, I wouldn't have let you stay even if you'd begged."

"It wasn't safe there, was it? Not for Nicholas. Probably not for Isabelle. It's better that we're in Cairo."

"Yes, and Valois has feather mattresses." Bryce grinned his devil's grin. "There's not a camping cot in sight."

"Thank heavens." She blew out a heavy breath. "I'm so relieved you're with me. If I'd had to face the past few days on my own, I wouldn't have survived."

"You'd have been fine, Kat. You're tough as nails."

He stared into her pretty green eyes, and he was overcome by the most potent wave of affection.

Somehow during their Egyptian sojourn, he'd started to think she belonged to him, that she was his and could never be anyone else's. It wasn't a passing fancy, wasn't a fleeting holiday amour.

He recalled his discussion with Chase, how Chase wanted to draw his wages and head for England. Bryce had briefly speculated over whether he shouldn't do the same, but the notion of abandoning her was too heart-wrenching to contemplate.

Would she come with him to England? Should he ask her?

He had no money or prospects, but she was very rich, and he wasn't too proud to have her support him. Should he propose? Would she scoff and assume he was jesting?

What if she accepted? She was an heiress, and he was extremely aware of that fact. If she traveled to London and was confronted by his pathetic situation, would she grow to resent him?

There were too many impossible questions to be answered, and he couldn't figure them out. He'd much rather focus on her, on how beautiful she was, how warm and fragrant and lovely.

He let his hands roam freely, caressing her hair, her shoulders, her arms. He spent an eternity massaging her breasts, playing with her nipples. She was an eager participant, urging him on with plenty of oohs and aahs whenever he touched a particularly sensitive spot.

He yanked at her robe, pulling it off so she was wearing only her nightgown. It was held up by two tiny straps, the bodice cut very low, which surprised him. It seemed too risqué for the female she exhibited to the world.

He eased the straps down, gradually baring her bosom so he could suck a taut nipple into his mouth. He'd done it before, at the bathing pool at Cedric's camp, so she knew what was happening, what bliss was hovering out on the horizon.

He was working the hem of her nightgown up her legs, her thighs. He slipped his fingers under the fabric, jabbed at her soft center, once, twice, and she was pitched into a wild, delicious orgasm.

He laughed with joy, happy as he hadn't been in ages. She was such a treasure, such a gem, and he wondered what it would be like to have her as his wife, to have her in his bed and in his life every day until he drew his last breath.

For a man who'd always been a confirmed bachelor, it was a shocking realization, but he couldn't put it aside. Was he in love with her? Could that be it?

He'd never been in love, so he had no idea if that was the sentiment rocking him. He constantly pondered her, worried about where she was, if she was all right. Did she suffer similar thoughts about him? Did she pine and mope and fret?

They'd never spoken a word about heightened affection. If he broached the subject, would she be offended? He didn't think so.

As her orgasm spiraled to an end, she was gazing at him as if he hung the moon, and he'd never felt more powerful or alive. He was the only man to ever know her like this, and if he had his way, he was the only man who ever would.

"You're so good for me," she said.

"I'm trying."

"I'm safe and contented around you."

"I'm the male in this dashing duo. It's my job to make you feel safe."

"You're succeeding, my dearest champion."

He kissed her again, keeping on forever, until his ardor grew so unruly that he couldn't control it. He slowed and pulled away, tugged up the straps of her nightgown to cover her pretty breasts.

"Why did we stop?" she asked.

"You arouse me to such a high degree, I can't continue. If we're not cautious, we'll go places we shouldn't. You have that effect on me." "I never viewed myself as a coquette, but maybe I am."

He chuckled. "Trust me, you have a coquette's heart and manner. You're a natural at these sexual games, and I can't resist you. You are dangerous to my equilibrium."

They were silent, pensive, and he was overcome by a pressing urgency, as if these were their final minutes together and if he didn't tell her certain things, he'd never get another chance.

"Sit up, would you?" he said. "I want to talk to you about something."

"You look so serious all of a sudden. It's not horrid, is it?"

"No, it's not horrid. I promise."

He helped her up, her hips on the edge of the mattress, while he grabbed a chair and positioned it directly in front of her. They were knee to knee, toe to toe.

"What is it?" she asked. "With all the trouble I've had recently, you're making me awfully nervous."

"Don't be nervous. I'm simply wondering if you'd come to London with me."

"To...London?"

She pronounced *London* as if she'd never heard of the city before, as if it was an exotic location unknown to mere mortals.

"Yes. You travelled to Egypt because your uncle was here, but he didn't seem interested in having you visit."

"That's putting it mildly."

"We don't belong in this unforgiving country. I've had enough excitement and catastrophe to last ten lifetimes. I'm eager to go home."

"But to England..."

"Why not?" he asked. "Where else is there for you? You told me yourself that you have no friends. Let me be your friend. Let me be more than that."

"What do you mean?"

"Marry me. Be my wife."

He couldn't believe he'd blurted it out as he had, without thinking, without easing her into the idea. Yet once voiced, the prospect sounded very grand.

"Marry you?" She laughed as if the notion was hilarious. "I barely know you."

"And I barely know you, but we're both very alone, and we share a potent physical attraction."

She blushed. "I can't deny it."

"Most couples start with much less." He clasped her hands in his own. "Marry me! Say *yes*."

"This is so unexpected," she killed him by replying.

"I realize it is, but I've been ruminating over what I want in my life, and it occurred to me that I want *you*. I can't imagine departing for England and leaving you behind."

"You're leaving? I thought you had decided to stay in Egypt with me."

"Not forever. I'd like to head home, and I'd like you to come with me."

"What would we do in England? How would we live? Where would we reside?"

"We could live wherever and however you choose. We'd be so happy."

"Is that why I should consent? Because we'd be *happy*?"

"There are worse reasons to wed."

"Who would base a marriage on whether the parties will be happy or not? It seems a flimsy way to begin."

"In my book, it seems a marvelous way."

"People should marry for stability, for children."

"We'll get there eventually. London is a very boring, very stable place. We'll be the most boring, stable couple on earth. We'll try our best to have a dozen children."

Her blush deepened. "I always secretly yearned to wed for love."

"Ah, so you're a romantic at heart."

"I guess I am."

"I won't lie and say I'm in love with you."

"Thank goodness."

"But don't you suppose it could grow between us? I'm so fond of you, and we're so compatible."

"Are we compatible? With our acquaintance being so new, I'm not sure."

"How would you define *compatible* then?"

She shook her head. "I'm being ridiculous. It's pointless to talk about love and fondness. When I wed, sentiment will have naught to do with it."

"Why must it be that way? Your parents are deceased, and you're an adult. You can pick whoever you want for a spouse. Who is there to tell you that you can't?"

"No one, but..."

"But...what?" he pressed when she couldn't finish her sentence.

"You're making this so hard. I wish you hadn't raised the issue."

"Why shouldn't I have? It would solve so many of your problems. You'd have a husband, which is always better for a woman. You'd have a father for Nicholas and Isabelle." Why couldn't she understand how fantastic it would be? "Take a chance on me, Kat. Take a chance."

She groaned with dismay. "I can't."

"Why not?"

"You're confusing me."

"How am I confusing you?"

"This seems too...convenient."

"Convenient?"

"You're aware that I'm very rich."

"So?"

"We joked about it, and now here you are proposing marriage when neither of us had ever previously considered it."

"Are you accusing me of being a fortune hunter?"

"No, but it's not unheard of for a poor man like you to chase after a wealthy woman like me. You can't blame me for being wary."

"Yes, I can. Don't you know what kind of person I am? Haven't you been paying attention?"

"I hope I know, but our association has been so brief. How can I be positive I've witnessed your true character?"

"I killed to protect your brother," he tersely stated. "I risked life and limb for him—and for you. Didn't you notice? While I was dispatching those miscreants, didn't it occur to you that I might have been exhibiting a few of my genuine traits?"

"You're a fine man, Bryce. I realize that you are." She pulled away. "There are other issues too that make it impossible."

"Name one." She didn't reply, and he said, "Are you already married?"

"No, it's not that."

"What then?"

She scooted off the bed, going over to the window to stare outside. For a long while, she gazed out at the stars. He watched her, feeling glum and morose, and he refused to break the awkward interval.

He was incredibly wounded by her rejection, and it surprised him. Apparently he was much fonder of her than he'd recognized himself to be.

What was he to do now? With her opinion revealed, how would they carry on? He'd assumed he would loiter in Egypt, would tarry by her side as a confidante, lover, or defender as needed, but clearly in her view none of those roles was imperative.

She had Miss Clementi to give her advice, and she could hire more guards. His position as lover was the only one for which he was currently irreplaceable, but with her being so beautiful, she could lure another fool into her bed. So...there was actually no part for him to play at all.

He was an idiot, a dunce. What had possessed him?

Temporary insanity...

She spun around, her green eyes tormented and sad. "Don't be angry with me."

"I'm not angry. I'm disappointed."

"Don't be disappointed either. You've been so kind to me, and I've hurt you."

"You haven't hurt me. I'm a grown man. I took a gamble. I tossed the dice, but I held a losing hand. I'll get over it."

"Oh, Bryce..."

"Is it because I'm too far beneath you?"

Just the slightest instant, she hesitated, and it told him what he'd been anxious to know. She lied and claimed, "No. You could never be *beneath* me by any measure."

He snorted at that, even as he wondered if he should declare his true station and rank. For the first time ever, he yearned to crow the news to the world, yearned to throw it in her face so she'd realize who she'd snubbed. But since he'd declined to acknowledge his title to his sister and friends, why would he suddenly announce it to the likes of Katarina Webster?

He picked up his father's knife and stuck it under his arm.

"What is that?" she inquired. "I didn't have an opportunity to ask you."

"It was a gift from Valois."

He could have apprised her of its significance, that Valois had been keeping it all these years, that it was the sole item Bryce had that had belonged to his father.

Yet he said none of that.

"It's quite stunning," she said.

"It is."

"Are we quarreling?"

She took a step toward him, but he took a step back, bluntly signaling she should stay where she was.

"Chase Hubbard and I are heading to England."

"When?"

"As soon as we can. We'd like to consider our employment terminated and collect our wages tomorrow, if that's all right with you. We need the money so we can book passage."

Her jaw dropped, but she collected herself. "Well, yes of course that would be all right. But...but...I was expecting you to remain in Cairo with me."

"I've been in Cairo for months, and I'm ready to depart. You've only just arrived, so you haven't yet reached that conclusion."

"I understand."

"You can speak to Valois about replacing me. In light of how rich you are, he'll be able to retain as many guards as you require."

It was rude to mention her money, but he was irked that she'd accused him of being a fortune hunter.

"I don't want you to quit," she said. "I don't want you to leave."

"I have to, and I think it's time."

He walked to the door, and she chased after him but kept her distance.

"I hate that we're fighting," she said.

"We're not fighting, Kat."

"Yes, we are. You proposed and I refused you, and now you're eager to flee both me and Cairo. Let's not make a hasty decision."

"It's not *hasty* for me. I've been searching for months for the funds to go home. I originally hired on with you for the money."

"I wasn't talking about your decision to depart. I meant your staying here with me, helping and protecting me."

"I'm not inclined to do that anymore."

"I need you with me."

He'd like to shake her, to snap at her. "Answer one question for me."

"If I can."

"If I agreed to remain, would you ever change your mind about being my wife? Or would you always assume you were too far above me?"

"I have *never* assumed that," she fumed.

"I don't believe you, and just so you know, I haven't learned a single thing about you except that you're wealthy. While you're fussing and fretting and deeming yourself too good for me, I have no information about your past or your family or your secrets or the source of your difficulties."

"It's hard to discuss it, and it would cause so much trouble."

"That might be true, but I was willing to have you anyway—despite what I don't know. I hope you'll reflect on that after I'm gone. Who was your one real friend, Kat? Who was your only friend in the entire world?"

He felt petty and snide, but rejected and ill-used too. He'd claimed they weren't fighting, but they absolutely were and he couldn't bear it.

"I'll have Valois calculate my wages," he said. "I'd appreciate it if I could be paid immediately so I can begin making plans."

He marched out, closing the door with a determined click. He thought she called to him, but he ignored her and continued on.

CHAPTER TWELVE

"What's wrong with you these days?"

Pippa glared at Kat, aggravated as she usually was by her friend. Kat was rich and beautiful. So what if she'd lost her crown and no one could refer to her as Your Royal Highness anymore? It was just some silly words. She was still rich and beautiful.

As far as Pippa was concerned, things were going swimmingly. They'd left Cedric Webster's filthy desert camp. They were in Cairo and had been welcomed by Monsieur Valois. He was French, charming, and elegantly stylish. If he hadn't been so old, she'd have commenced a flirtation.

Matters were intensifying with Kristof. He wanted Nicholas back in Parthenia and was willing to take drastic action to ensure it happened. Pippa was ready to do her part, then rush home to wallow in the boons Kristof had promised.

She was fairly certain Kristof had sent Kat a letter, and she'd been biting her tongue, waiting for Kat to mention it, but she'd been mum as a corpse.

They were out on Valois's dock, sitting on a shaded bench and watching ships sail by on the river.

"What's wrong with you?" Pippa repeated. "Your mood is so dour you could turn the sky gray."

"I'm unhappy, Pippa. Why must you nag about it?"

"What have you to be unhappy about? I can't understand it. Yes, you've had a few bumps in your road, but you're very wealthy. With money to provide a cushion, you can never truly have any difficulty."

"Yes, yes, money makes my life perfect, doesn't it?" Kat pulled her troubled gaze from the water and scowled at Pippa. "Should I give it to you? Would that make *you* happy?"

"What do you mean? I'm a happy person, but I won't deny if I was affluent like you, I'd be a lot happier."

"Ever since we fled Parthenia, you constantly whine and complain. It's annoying."

"Well, excuse me, Your Majesty."

"Don't be flippant. Just be silent. I have a headache."

"I'm not your servant, Kat. There's no need for you to speak to me so abominably."

Pippa rose to march off in a huff, but Kat grabbed her wrist and drew her down.

"I'm sorry," Kat said. "I'm being a shrew."

"Yes, you are."

"I have so much on my mind."

"Perhaps if you'd confide in me once in awhile, I could ease your woe."

Kat smiled a tight smile. "I doubt it."

"Try me. Let's see how I fare at offering advice. You used to share your problems with me."

"Yes, I did, didn't I?" Kat pondered for an eternity, then ultimately admitted, "I received a letter from Kristof."

Pippa was very good at feigning surprise. "When?"

"When we were still at Cedric's camp."

"How could he have known you were there? He must have had people following you."

"Yes." Kat laughed wearily. "All this time, we believed we were so furtive, but he's been aware of our location from the very beginning."

Of course he has.

Pippa bit down the remark. She regularly met with Kristof's spies to deliver her reports. Riders raced away to convey the dispatches to Parthenia. Parthenian men were skilled equestrians, so the link between Kristof and Pippa was a short, fast one.

"What did he say?" Pippa asked.

"He ordered me to return to Parthenia, to bring Nicholas and Isabelle with me."

"Why would he want that?"

"Kristof is insane, Pippa. I couldn't guess why."

"His command makes no sense. You'd think he'd be glad to have all of you gone."

"I agree. It's madness, but then he's deranged."

"So...will you return?"

"No," Kat scoffed. "He has no authority over me or my siblings. He insulted our parents, robbed us, and deposed Nicholas. We owe him no fealty."

"But he's our king, Kat. You can't disobey."

"Yes, he is currently King of Parthenia," Kat countered, "but we were stripped of our titles. He claimed our parents had never been married, and he can't have it both ways. He can't declare us no longer citizens but then assume he has control over us. Especially when we're not even in the country."

"No, I suppose not."

"I'm trying to figure out his ploy. There has to be a reason."

"With Kristof, there always is," Pippa said.

"What do you imagine it is?"

"I have no idea."

"I don't either, but it can't be to my benefit."

"I'm sure you're right."

Kat stared out at the water again, and she was lost in thought, miserable in her contemplation, and Pippa yearned to shake her. Kat sulked and moped relentlessly, and Pippa was exhausted with attempting to cheer her.

"I need to tell you something," Kat eventually said, "but you have to swear you'll keep it a secret."

"My lips are sealed. You know that. I've always stood as your friend."

"Yes, you have, Pippa."

She reached over and patted Pippa's hand.

"What is it?" Pippa inquired. "What is your secret?"

"Mr. Blair asked me to marry him."

"Mr....Blair?" Pippa nearly shrieked the name.

"Yes."

"He's quite set on himself, isn't he? I didn't realize you two were cordial."

"He's been a great help to me these past few weeks."

"Yes, but honestly. Marriage! Isn't he an actor?" She pronounced the word *actor* like the epithet it was.

"Yes, acting is one of his many talents."

"How dare he propose to you," Pippa huffed. "What gall."

"He doesn't know who I am, Pippa."

"Maybe not your true station, but he has to recognize you're a woman of consequence."

"I'm certain he does." Kat smiled a wistful smile. "He was willing to have me anyway."

Pippa frowned. "You're not considering it. If you are, admit it so I can box your ears."

"I'm not considering it precisely," Kat claimed. "I was curious as to your opinion."

"The man is a brazen libertine who's trying to up-jump to a level of society he should never attain in a thousand years."

Kat couldn't let it go. "If I wed him though, we could move to England. We could reside in London. I'd have a husband and a father for Nicholas and Isabelle. We might stumble on some Parthenians who were loyal to my father, who might ultimately be loyal to Nicholas."

"I wouldn't count on it. They're all cowards. The entire lot of them. Haven't they proved their spinelessness to you over and over again?"

"Yes, but I can't stop hoping."

She and Pippa glared as if they were fighting, and finally Pippa said, "You can't be serious about Mr. Blair."

Kat shrugged. "It's sweet of him to want to protect me."

"But you told him *no*?"

"I told him *no,* but I'm not sure I should have. What are my options, Pippa? I came to Uncle Cedric for assistance, but he was worthless. What should I do instead?"

"I'm not the best person to advise you, but you need to be wary of a cad like Bryce Blair."

"He's not a cad. Cease your denigration."

"You're off on your own for the very first time, and you haven't had much experience with men. The handsome ones can be smooth-talking devils."

"Mr. Blair isn't like that."

"Isn't he? He and Mr. Hubbard are both wishing they could snag an heiress. Mr. Hubbard bluntly brags about it. What makes you think Mr. Blair is any different? He's after your money. That's all it is, but he's pretending affection so you won't guess his motives."

"I wondered about that, but he's not a fortune hunter. I believe he's genuinely fond of me."

"Are you fond of him?"

"I might be very fond. If he left me and went back to England, I'd be crushed."

Pippa took a deep breath and slowly let it out.

Kat had to return to Parthenia as Kristof was demanding. She couldn't become involved with an English nobody. She had to go home. If she didn't, Pippa would never get the reward Kristof had dangled in order to persuade her to betray Kat. The whole idiotic journey to Egypt would have been a complete waste.

Pippa had worked so hard on Kristof's behalf, and at this late date she wasn't about to forfeit the gifts she'd been offered.

Pippa needed to file a report immediately, and she faked a yawn. "This heat is making me sleepy. I'm off to my room for a nap."

"I'll stay out here. I like to watch the traffic on the river. It soothes me."

Pippa stood and stared down at her old friend, perplexed over how she could be so smart, but so stupid too. Bryce Blair! Of all the inappropriate, unsuitable men in the world! How could such a low-born fellow have enticed her?

When and how had the romance flourished? How could it have progressed so far and Pippa hadn't noticed? Gad, what if Kat had eloped? Kristof would have blamed Pippa. Why, he might have had her arrested for incompetence!

"Don't do anything foolish, Kat," she murmured.

"I won't."

"You can't run off with Mr. Blair."

"I'm not planning on it. I refused him, didn't I?"

"Just don't act rashly. Promise me you won't. Come to me if you find yourself having second thoughts." "I won't have second thoughts. Now take your nap. Don't worry about me."

Pippa studied her another moment, then hurried away. Kat couldn't be permitted to flit about any longer. Kristof had to be informed and action implemented. Pippa knew what Kristof wanted, and she'd sworn to him that it would be accomplished.

"I don't have much time left."

"Nonsense, Lady Radcliffe. You're looking healthier every day."

As Katherine listened to Father Macgregor gush and pretend Susan was fine, she struggled to keep her temper in check. They were in Susan's bedchamber, with a very ill, drained Susan still in bed and attired in her nightgown and robe.

The obsequious priest always filled her head with drivel, always told her that her condition would improve if she prayed frequently enough.

Katherine would like to shake him. It would give her great satisfaction.

At age twenty-five, she'd cared for several people all the way to their demise, including her parents and a younger sister. It served no purpose to lie and claim it wasn't happening. Denial simply made matters more awkward.

She'd like to have the authority to bar him from the premises, but when he visited, his presence gave Susan some comfort. Katherine preferred the healer from the village who was truthful and blunt in her assessments. There was no wondering with her. She stated the facts right out loud.

Susan glanced at Katherine and said, "Bring my quill and inkpot."

Father Macgregor sighed. "Must we do this, milady?"

"Yes, we must." Susan was displaying an unusual amount of vigor. "I won't be condemned to Hell over this secret. I've kept my mouth shut much too long."

"You've confessed your sins," the priest insisted. "You're forgiven."

"Pardon me, Father, but my sins are grave and monumental. I don't believe you have sufficient power to forgive them on your own, and I can't risk that I might arrive at Heaven's gates and not be allowed in."

"You're being ridiculous," the priest grumbled.

Katherine frowned, about to tell him to stuff it, but it wasn't her place to chastise him. She whipped away to retrieve the items Susan had requested. Then she approached the bed, balancing a writing tray on Susan's lap.

Katherine didn't know what Susan intended so she was surprised when Susan pulled out a sheath of papers from under the blankets. She shifted to the final page and signed her name, then she gestured for Father Macgregor to sign too.

He hesitated, his expression so wrinkled he might have been sucking on sour pickles. "Really, Lady Radcliffe, I wish you'd forget this mad scheme."

"It's my last chance to fix it."

"I must encourage you to discuss the subject with your husband."

"I'm fully aware of George's opinion. And *he* is not the one who is dying."

"Everyone is dying, Lady Radcliffe," the priest intoned as if he was in the middle of a sermon.

"Sign it or leave me be!"

Ultimately he did as she'd demanded, and as Katherine was fussing to remove the tray, Susan snapped at the priest.

"Where are you going with those?"

"Oh, I was just holding them for you."

Katherine whirled to see that—whatever the documents—he'd tried to stick them in his robe so he could sneak out while Susan was distracted.

"Give them to Katherine," Susan fumed, and she stared him down until he relented and slapped them into Katherine's hand.

"This is a terrible mistake," the priest said to Susan. "Your husband has to be informed."

"You would break the privacy of the confessional?"

"If we've put it all in writing, it's not private any longer."

"I will do what I must do."

"As will I," the priest muttered like a threat.

"Go away," Susan said, "and don't come back."

"What?" Macgregor huffed. "I must return. I'm cognizant of how much solace I bring you. I refuse to stay away."

"Since you won't support me in this vital issue, you bring me no solace at all. Go!"

He appeared eager to argue, to harangue at her, and Katherine wasn't about to let him. She deftly clasped his arm, and as she was escorting him out, he leaned in and hissed, "She's insane. The illness is affecting her wits." "Her reasoning is sound," Katherine loyally declared.

"If you care for her, you must get those papers away from her. You must burn them, or if you don't dare, take them to her husband. He must be warned."

"I serve her, not you. You're in no position to order me about."

She pushed him into the hall and shut the door in his face. There was a latch to bar it, and she laid it across the wood.

"Good riddance, you pious old grouch," she murmured loudly enough that he'd hear.

She hurried to the bedchamber, and Susan was over by her desk, searching through the drawers.

"Is he gone?" she asked.

"Yes, and I locked the door so he can't slither back in."

"You're a smart girl."

Susan pulled out a leather satchel and handed it to Katherine.

"I need you to do me the greatest favor you ever will," Susan said.

"Of course I'll do it."

"There are two Englishmen in the area. At least I think they're still here. I haven't been notified they've left."

"The twins? Michael and Matthew Blair?"

"Yes. Rumor has it that they've rented rooms at the coaching inn in the village."

"Yes, they have."

"Put on your cloak—with your hood up to conceal yourself."

"My hood *up*? Honestly, Cousin, why all the melodrama?"

"Then you must sneak down the rear stairs and walk to the inn to speak with them."

"On what topic?"

"Give them this pouch. Tell them the papers in it are from me, and I...I..." Susan's voice broke off, and for a moment, she nearly collapsed. But she took a deep breath and finished her sentence. "Tell them I'm very, very sorry for my part in what was done to their parents. I will be eternally ashamed, and I hope this will help them to attain the justice they seek."

Katherine stared at the satchel, wishing she could peer through the leather to the documents inside. What could Susan be sending to them? Katherine couldn't imagine.

Since the Blair twins had arrived, there had been a thousand stories circulating. They were boasting that their father was murdered by George, that their older brother, Bryce, was the rightful earl. They insisted George and Susan were usurpers, that they'd stolen what belonged to the twins' brother.

People were grumbling about George, who was generally despised. They were spreading tales hither and yon, starting to agree that they'd suspected he wasn't the heir, that Julian had children who should have inherited. It was a small fire of gossip and innuendo that was growing bigger by the day.

Katherine didn't know why George hadn't had the twins run off or jailed, but they looked dangerous and tough. He probably couldn't find any men courageous enough to confront them.

"You must leave at once." Susan's urgent tone yanked Katherine out of her reverie.

"To the coaching inn?" Katherine asked.

"Yes. I'm positive Father Macgregor went directly to my husband. George is likely already on his way to stop me."

"From doing what, Susan? You're scaring me."

"Don't be frightened. I am simply trying to correct a very hideous and immoral wrong I perpetrated many years ago."

Katherine scrutinized her cousin, wondering if she should assist in the stealthy endeavor. After Susan passed away, Katherine's role in delivering the satchel would eventually come to light. George would be furious. In punishment, he'd kick Katherine out of Radcliffe and she was truly a poor relative with nowhere to go. Dare she risk it?

Yes. Susan had brought her to Radcliffe when she'd been alone and without a friend. She would always be grateful.

God will provide...

She wasn't certain she believed the adage. But if George evicted her, surely there would be some divine compensation for carrying out Susan's final wishes.

"What is in here, Susan? Will you confide in me?"

"It's my Last Will and Testament. I had a new one drafted recently."

"And what else? I saw you add the document Father Macgregor signed."

"It's a confession of my perfidy. Because of my pride and vanity, I committed a horrendous sin against an innocent woman and her children. I've listed all of my transgressions so—after I perish—there will be a written record. I can't let the facts die with me."

"No, no you shouldn't."

"I made Father Macgregor sign too so he'd bear witness to what I told him in the confessional."

Susan's strength was fading, and she staggered to the bed, being nearly too weak to climb up on her own. Katherine dashed over to aid her, but Susan waved her away.

"I'll be fine, Katherine. Please go now. You must be away from the castle before George arrives."

Someone pounded on the door. Father Macgregor called, "Lady Radcliffe, may I come in? May I explain myself? You've placed me in an untenable position with regard to your husband. I have to speak with him about what you're planning!"

Susan called back, "Do what you must, Father."

She motioned Katherine to the rear stairs. Katherine grabbed her cloak and scooted out. She exited into the side yard without encountering a single soul. There was an ancient gate that wasn't locked anymore, and she slipped through it without being observed.

Within a matter of seconds, she was in the woods. She didn't use the main trail, but took a circuitous route that skirted her past the village. In a quick half hour of walking, she was at the coaching inn.

She entered the building to ask after the twins at the front desk, but when she glanced into the taproom, she saw one of them sitting at a table by himself. He was drinking a glass of ale, his back to the wall, as if worried an assailant might creep up on him from behind.

Feeling furtive and reckless, she marched over to him, and he raised a curious brow as she approached. He didn't stand but gestured to the chair across from him. She seated herself, and he studied her, waiting for her to clarify her purpose, but she wasn't sure how to start.

"If you're offering your delectable services," he said, "I'm very happily married. I'm not interested."

As she realized what sort of *services* he meant, she blushed so fiercely, she was glad her cloak hood was still up.

"I'm not here for salacious reasons," she replied.

"Then why are you here?"

"I have something for you from Lady Radcliffe."

"Susan Blair," he corrected. "She was never the true countess. My mother should have been, and her name was Anne."

Katherine wasn't about to be drawn into an argument over the succession. She simply laid the satchel on the table.

"What's this?" he asked.

"It's some documents for you."

"What kind of documents?"

"You'll see. Keep them safe. It took an enormous amount of effort for her to give them to you, and they're very valuable."

"What the devil...?" He lifted the flap and peeked inside, then whipped his blue gaze to hers. "She wanted me to have these? You're positive?"

"Yes, and she said to tell you she was sorry. She said to tell you exactly this: She will be eternally ashamed, and she hopes this will help you to attain the justice you seek."

"Thank you, Miss...?"

Katherine didn't supply her identity. "Please don't ever reveal how you came by this information. It would cause me harm that I'd rather not suffer."

"I won't breathe a word. I swear it."

"Goodbye, and good luck to you."

She stood and hastened out, sneaking into the woods to the trail that led to the castle. It appeared no one had noticed her swift trip, but then that's the person she tried to be, the most ordinary, unexceptional woman in the world.

CHAPTER THIRTEEN

"May I drag you away from the party, Miss Webster?"
"Of course, Monsieur Valois."
"This shouldn't take long."

Valois led Kat out of the main parlor. It was crammed with people, but no one noticed her departure.

To celebrate her return to Cairo—which she wasn't certain ought to be celebrated—he'd hosted a large supper in her honor, complete with fourteen courses and four dozen guests.

She'd protested the extravagance, but he'd insisted if she was staying in the city for an extended period, she needed to meet other expatriates so she could begin building a social circle. She knew he was correct, but she was extremely upset over her quarrel with Bryce the previous night and in no mood to mingle with strangers.

After intense deliberation, she was positive she'd given him the wrong reply. On initially hearing his proposal, she'd viewed it through a royal lens, had evaluated it as if she was a princess who had to promote her family and country.

But as he'd bluntly reminded her, she was an adult who could choose any ending that tempted her. Why shouldn't she wed Bryce Blair? Why shouldn't she move to England with him? What was stopping her?

She'd looked for him all day, being sufficiently desperate that she'd even snuck into his bedchamber and peeked in his wardrobe to be sure his clothing was still there, that he hadn't packed and left.

Neither he nor Mr. Hubbard had attended Valois's supper, and she was terrified they'd book passage to England, then slip into the villa, grab their bags, and leave without her learning they had.

If it occurred before she had a chance to speak with him, she truly thought she might book her own passage and chase after him. Yet she was so self-centered that she hadn't bothered to discover any personal details about him. If she showed up in London, how would she find him?

The only genuine fact she possessed was his being an occasional actor and gambler. Would she tarry at the theaters on Drury Lane, hoping to espy him? Would she lurk in the shadows outside White's gambling club, praying he was a member?

"Mr. Blair and Mr. Hubbard seem to have vanished," she casually mentioned.

"Oh, I forgot. They asked me to calculate their wages so they can be paid."

To her great aggravation, his comment didn't reveal their current situation.

"Yes, Mr. Blair requested it of me."

"Your offer of employment was a godsend for them."

"I'm glad I could be of assistance."

Valois was whisking her down the hall toward his private quarters. Even though she was a guest, there were areas of the house that were off limits, so she hadn't been in this section.

They halted at a closed door, and he murmured, "You have visitors."

"*I* have visitors? Who is it?"

"They're from Parthenia." She blanched with astonishment, and he said, "I had them wait in here. With you shielding your identity, I didn't suppose you'd want them paraded into the dining room."

"Thank you." She scowled. "Why have they come? Did they say?"

"No, and I didn't feel I should pry. Let's go in, shall we?"

"All right."

"I'll stay with you—if you like."

"Yes, please stay."

He nodded that he would and guided her into an ornate parlor.

There were four men from home, all dressed in formal court regalia displaying honorary sashes and swords. They were standing two on each side of the door, forming a sort of honor guard for her. When they saw her, they snapped to attention and bowed very low.

They were acting as if she was a princess, and she couldn't decide how to interpret their behavior. Valois raised a curious brow as Kat shrugged and walked by them.

As she spun around, their leader, Captain Romilard stepped forward. He was Dmitri's brother, a treacherous fiend whom she loathed, and she carefully shielded her exorbitant dislike. Why would Kristof send a Romilard to her? He had to realize she'd rather cut out her tongue than converse with him.

"Your Royal Highness," he started, but she interrupted him.

"I'm sorry, Captain Romilard, but as you're aware, I no longer claim the title."

"Yes, but I am happy to inform you that your rank has been reinstated."

"By who?"

"By his most gracious and benevolent majesty, King Kristof the First."

The pronouncement was so strange, he might have been babbling in a foreign language. She frowned. "I have been reinstated?"

"Yes, and your brother and sister too."

"Well..."

Kat was struck dumb. She wanted to spit in his face, wanted to tell him to take his benevolent King Kristof and jump off a cliff. But she had to tread cautiously. There was mischief afoot, and until she fully grasped what it was, she didn't dare say or do the wrong thing.

"Miss Webster is my guest," Valois said.

"*Her Royal Highness* is your guest," Romilard corrected him.

"Yes, and I am her friend. May I inquire as to why you are here?"

"No, you may not," Romilard curtly retorted. He spoke to Kat. "I bring tidings from the King."

"How nice." She kept her smile firmly in place.

"He begs your pardon for the past misunderstanding."

"I'm delighted to hear it."

"And he requests you read this letter and respond at once. I am to convey your answer to Parthenia with all due speed."

He opened a pouch and pulled out an envelope. It was an official correspondence, the edges rimmed with gold, the King's seal in the center. Romilard handed it to her with a great flourish.

Kat glared at all of them, then flicked at the seal and perused the missive. The words Kristof had penned were so outrageous that she nearly laughed aloud. Yet every move she made would be reported back to him.

"What is it?" Valois asked. "What does he say?"

"It is a proposal of marriage," Kat told him.

"From whom, to whom?"

"It appears His Majesty, Kristof, wishes to marry *me*."

Valois tried to tamp down his shock, but couldn't quite manage it. "He has proposed?"

"Yes."

"My, my," Valois mused, "that's interesting."

"Very interesting," she agreed. She looked at Romilard. "I'll need some time to draft my reply."

"There is no need for a reply," Romilard said. "We are here to escort you and your siblings to Parthenia for the royal wedding."

"Are you? That's very kind."

She stealthily reached over and squeezed Valois's fingers so hard she was surprised he didn't cringe. He was very shrewd and instantly recognized she was silently screaming for help.

"Your escort will be acceptable to all parties," he blithely said. "Now then, if you'll excuse me, I have guests. Captain, you may stop by tomorrow at three, and we will discuss the Princess's departure."

Romilard blinked, then shook his head. "My orders are to leave at dawn with the Princess and her siblings. The King is most eager."

Valois snorted with derision. "It will take the Princess at least two weeks to prepare for such a lengthy journey."

"But...these are my orders, Monsieur, and I cannot disobey. We go at dawn."

"No, you don't." Valois was very regal, very grand, his centuries of aristocratic blood clearly evident. "The Princess will write a letter to the King to explain the delay. I'll have it ready for you tomorrow afternoon."

"It cannot be as you have said, Monsieur," Romilard complained.

"The matter is out of your hands," Valois countered.

He went to the door and yanked it open, indicating the appointment was over. There was a brief standoff where Kat was afraid that they would grab her and drag her out, but just as Valois had centuries of aristocratic blood in his veins, Romilard had had centuries of learning deference.

He clicked his heels and motioned to his men. They bowed and sidled out, not showing their backs to Kat, so apparently Romilard hadn't been lying. She was really and truly a princess again.

Valois's butler arrived and hustled them to an exit where they wouldn't be observed by anyone. Once the sound of their boots had faded, Valois proceeded to his sideboard, poured two glasses of brandy, and brought them over.

As he gave one to Kat, he said, "Pardon my rough language, Your Grace, but what the hell is going on?"

"I have no idea."

"What would you predict is happening?"

"For some reason, Kristof suddenly needs me as his wife."

"I'm trying to imagine a scenario where that would arise, but I can't devise any. Perhaps his crown is not resting easily on his fat head, and the citizenry is clamoring for your brother's reinstatement."

She scoffed. "I doubt it very much. We were forced to accept Kristof's rule. We couldn't muster a single supporter to our cause."

"No offense, Your Grace, but your people were idiots to pick Kristof over you and your brother."

Kat had always thought so. "Have you heard any news from Parthenia?"

"No. Have you?"

"None, although before I left Cedric's camp, I received a very brusque letter from Kristof commanding me home."

"Your siblings too?"

"Yes."

"So first you were commanded, and now you are cajoled." Valois smiled a sly smile. "He must want you back very badly."

"But...why?"

Valois shrugged. "With Kristof, who can guess?"

"The man is deranged."

Valois sipped his drink. "Will you marry him?"

"No. After what he did to my brother and how he insulted my parents, I never would. Not in a thousand years."

"You'll be ruining any chance for your brother to sit on the throne."

"There is no benefit to my delivering Nicholas to him. Kristof would never step down or put him in the line of succession."

"It might be best to take him home though. His subjects might eventually demand he be crowned."

"Yes, but then I'd have to be Kristof's bride while I waited for this miracle to occur. I'd rather slit my wrists."

He chuckled. "I understand."

She staggered to a chair and plopped down. For a long while, she stared at the floor. Ultimately she peered up at Valois. "Am I being selfish to refuse Kristof? Am I throwing away my brother's future? Maybe I should go. Is that what you would advise?"

"I can't give you an opinion."

"Why not?"

"It is a political matter that is beyond my purview. And whatever you choose, it's probably the wrong option. You must either return to Parthenia and wed an oaf you despise or wander the courts of Europe with your deposed brother. As I said, there are no good options."

"Your reply does not make me feel any better." She rubbed her temples where a fierce headache was suddenly forming. "I'm so confused."

"Shall I call you Princess? Or should I still call you Miss Webster?"

"Let's stick with *Miss Webster* for the moment."

"Well, Miss Webster, Captain Romilard seemed determined to abscond with you, so I believe I can counsel you on this one topic. If you don't journey to Parthenia with him as he's requested, he won't cease pestering you."

"No, I don't suppose he will."

"We're in agreement on that point anyway. So...if you don't wish to accompany him, you'll have to hide from him and steal away again, and it's clear your last furtive flight wasn't so furtive after all."

"I see that now."

"I can stall him and keep him thinking you need a fortnight to prepare. When the deadline arrives, we can claim you're still not ready. But he won't let you delay forever."

"Perhaps I should depart Cairo while he's cooling his heels."

"Perhaps you should." Valois grinned a conspiratorial grin. "I know two gentlemen who are leaving Egypt very soon. They would be excellent bodyguards to escort you safely to England."

"Are you saying I should settle there?"

"I'm saying nothing of the sort. I'm simply saying there are two gentlemen headed in that direction."

❧ ❧ ❧ ❧

Bryce was in his bedchamber. It was very late, and the house had finally quieted. Valois had hosted a large supper party, but Bryce had skipped it. The excuse for his absence was that he'd been running errands to arrange his trip.

In reality, he wouldn't sit across the table from Katarina Webster and moon over her like a smitten boy. It was his specific intent to never see or speak with her ever again.

Evidently he'd had his heart broken, and he didn't like the feeling.

She was a mystery woman, full of secrets. She had dangerous brigands following her, a family that was fighting, and she was obscenely rich, but he'd never cared much for rich people. They were callous and clueless and never appreciated all that they had.

There were many reasons for him *not* to have fallen for her, but he had and he wouldn't try to figure it out. It had happened. Cupid's arrow had struck without warning, and the only route forward was to slink out of Cairo before he made an even bigger fool of himself.

He had his traveling trunk open, and he was tossing clothes into it. He didn't have much to put in. When he'd first trekked to Egypt, he'd been equipped for a protracted expedition, but after their disaster on the rapids, most of his belongings had been lost. The items he possessed now had been accumulated since then, and it was barely enough to bother with a trunk. He ought to find a portmanteau and use that.

He was in a temper and restless as a caged bear. After having quit his job as Kat's bodyguard, he was anxious to leave immediately.

He and Chase had spent the day inquiring about the journey home. In the morning, they would retrieve their wages, then sail to

Alexandria where it would be easier to book passage to London. They'd already hired the boat that would take them up the river.

At this sad juncture, he wasn't concerned over how he got to England. He just wanted to go.

In the outer parlor, someone entered his suite. He sighed, hoping it wasn't Chase. With Bryce's low disposition, he wasn't in any mood to deal with his friend.

But as he listened to footsteps crossing the tiled floor, he realized it was a female, and he scowled, not eager for it to be a servant. He wasn't the type to tumble the hired help, and he was too grouchy to abide an awkward scene.

"Bryce?"

He whipped around, stunned to see Kat. To his consternation, she'd dressed for bed. Her hair was down and brushed out, the lengthy locks curling to her bottom. She was attired in a negligee and robe, both garments sewn from an intriguing material that shimmered when she moved.

He glanced down and noted that her toenails were painted red. Had she painted them just for him? Was she trying to entice him? To goad him? Into what conduct? Why would she?

He pointed at her, his irate finger quaking with wrath. "Turn around and get your ass out of here, Miss Webster."

"Don't be angry with me."

"I'd have to care about you to be angry. Go away."

"I have to talk to you."

"Go away!"

"Please?"

Her green eyes were poignant and beseeching, and he couldn't stand to gaze into them. He spun away and pitched a shirt into his trunk.

"We've said everything that ever needs to be discussed."

She stated the obvious. "You're packing."

"Yes, I am."

"When are you leaving?"

"If I thought it was any of your business, I'd tell you."

"Will it be tomorrow?"

"Miss Webster! Your presence is extremely disconcerting, and I don't wish to be further upset by you."

He whipped around again, ready to scold, ready to bark and bite, but she'd sneaked over when he wasn't paying attention, so she was right beside him.

"My answer is *yes*," she said.

"To what question?"

"You asked me to marry you, and I refused. I've changed my mind. I want to be your bride. I accept."

"You're laboring under the mistaken impression that there is still a proposal on the table. There isn't."

"You can't propose one day, then renege the next."

"I can and I have."

"No. You took me by surprise, and I gave you the wrong answer. I'm giving you the correct one now."

"And the *correct* answer is what, that you'll lower yourself to have me?"

She clutched his shirt and shook him. "Will you stop claiming I feel I'm too far above you?"

"I'll stop claiming it when you stop acting as if you are."

He flicked her hands away, not able to bear being touched by her. It was torture to have her so near, barely dressed, and supplying the response he'd been desperate to receive.

"What happened between yesterday and today?" he asked. "Yesterday, you were adamantly opposed. Yet today, you're eager as pie. Pardon me if I seem a tad skeptical."

"I'm all alone in the world, Bryce."

"So am I, but then I've always been alone. My parents passed away when I was five, so I've lived this way for decades. How about you? You've had a bad couple of months. Boo-hoo," he hissed like a child. "I'm having difficulty mustering any sympathy."

"I only mention it to explain my behavior. I was confused and couldn't decide what was best. It's since become obvious that I want you more than I've ever wanted anything."

"Don't flatter or sweet-talk me. It won't change my opinion."

"I love you," she blurted out.

He banged a palm on his ear as if it was plugged. "My hearing must be affected. I could have sworn you just announced that you love me."

"Yes, I said it, and I say it again. I love you."

"You don't mean that," he scoffed. "You can't mean it."

"I do. It occurred to me in the wee hours when it was dark and quiet, and I couldn't figure out why I was so miserably glum. What will you do about it? I'm brave enough to declare my feelings. Will you pout and mope and depart Cairo without me?"

She'd thoroughly perplexed him. He was very proud and had an enormous ego. He'd never previously proposed to a woman, and when she'd rebuffed him, he'd been devastated. Yet now...she was singing a totally different tune.

His head was spinning. What was true? What was false? Why would she abruptly be excited to proceed? It made no sense.

"You seriously expect me to believe you're anxious to be my bride."

"Yes."

"You expect me to believe you're delighted to wed an actor, to be a humble actor's wife."

"Yes, and there's nothing *humble* about you, Bryce Blair. Don't you dare denigrate yourself to me. I don't know who your father was, but blood will tell. It's clear your veins pulse with the blood of a king and the heart of a lion."

It was the perfect moment to admit his failed ancestry, but he couldn't bring himself to enlighten her. He wouldn't raise himself up in her esteem. She insisted she wanted him—even though he was simply an actor. He wouldn't provide her with a reason to suppose he might be *more* than an actor.

To hell with her and her conceited views!

"I had some news from home," she told him.

"What was it?"

"My relatives are ordering me to return."

"As you've kept your past a complete secret, I have no idea whether to congratulate you or commiserate."

"If I take Nicholas back, they'll get their greedy hands on his fortune."

"That's too bad." He liked Nicholas very much and wouldn't pretend he didn't.

"And...they'll make me marry a man I hate, the man who destroyed my family."

Bryce frowned. The revelation was terribly distressing. His Katarina wed to another? His Kat, shackled to a fiend she loathed?

All his anger and upset flew out the window. Could he stand idly by and lose her? Could he allow her despicable kin to hurt her brother? Hurt her?

They'd already sent her reeling to the desert in search of her uncle, and if Cedric Webster was any indication of the type of swine who were commanding her now, she was in extreme danger. He would never deliver her to their custody and control.

"Will you go as they've decreed?" he inquired.

"No, and when I realized I could say *no* to them, it dawned on me that I can say *yes* to you. I need no one's advice or permission. So ask me again, Bryce. Ask me to marry you."

"This seems so bizarre, Kat. I'm no longer convinced we should proceed."

"I'm not playing games, and I'm not jesting. I'll have you and no other."

Suddenly she shucked off her robe so she was attired in just her negligee. It hugged every curvaceous inch of her body, and his cock sprang to attention.

"Tell me you don't love me," she said.

"I don't think I do," he stubbornly replied.

"Tell me you won't have me."

"Kat! Stop it."

"Let's find out what you really want and what you don't, shall we?"

She grabbed the straps of her negligee, tugged them off her shoulders, and the slippery garment slid down to pool at her feet. In an instant, she was naked.

"Your move, Mr. Blair, and this might be checkmate."

CHAPTER FOURTEEN

Kat stood before Bryce, naked as the day she'd been born. Her pulse was racing, but she kept her head high and summoned all her royal training not to display a single hint of nerves.

She'd stripped off her clothes as a dare, as a challenge, but from how he was glaring at her, she wasn't sure it was the right move.

He looked angry and disgusted, as if she'd proved herself a whore—or worse. Was there something worse than a whore? She was so naïve in the ways of the world that she had no idea.

If she'd been more experienced at amour, she'd have known how to flirt and cajole, but she didn't know how, and she didn't have time to waste figuring them out.

He was a lusty man who reveled in carnal behavior, and she'd been positive, if she could coax him into a physical encounter, all would be forgiven. But what if she was wrong?

If so, she'd made the biggest blunder ever, but just as she was about to admit defeat, he grabbed her and tossed her onto his bed. He fell on her as if he was possessed, like a wild beast stalking its prey.

"Be careful what you wish for, Katarina."

"Why?"

"Because you might get it."

"That's what I'm hoping. Why do you suppose I took off my negligee?"

"I can't guess why, but it was likely a moment of temporary insanity. What precisely are you expecting to accomplish?"

"I'm expecting you to put your proposal back on the table."

"You think a bit of nudity will bring you what you desire?"

"It seems to work for other women. Why not me?"

He snorted with disgust. "Are you yearning to fornicate? Is that your ploy?"

"I don't know what that word means. I've never known."

"It's also called *mating*. It's how a babe is created. If I decide to try it with you, I'd have to wed you when we were finished. I wouldn't have a choice."

"Good."

"I *want* to have a choice. I won't be commanded. Most especially by a female."

"Then choose to fornicate." She flung her arms to the side, like a virgin about to be sacrificed on an altar. "Have your way with me, then marry me when we're through."

"I don't want to marry you. I thought I did, but I've changed my mind."

"Liar," she said. "You're too honorable, Bryce. You would never have proposed unless you craved it very, very much."

"Tell me what's really happening. Why are you suddenly so eager?"

"I already told you. I don't have to have my relatives picking my husband. That's how it's always been handled in my country, but my parents are deceased, and I would never allow my cousin to pick for me."

"Your cousin is the one you loathe? The one you'd have to wed if you went home?"

"Yes."

"So you'd shackle yourself to me instead, merely to avoid it?"

"No, I'd do it because I love you, and there's no one to prevent me."

He stared down her body, and it was clear he enjoyed what he was seeing. Why was he hesitating? Why was he so reluctant? She was so unschooled in passion. She wished she knew a coquette's tricks so she could spur him to the ending she sought.

"What if I proceeded," he said, "but refused to marry you afterward?"

"You're too decent to act like that."

"You can't be sure of that. What if—deep down—I'm as much a cad as any other man? What if I ravished you, then walked away?"

"Go ahead," she defiantly replied. "Let's discover what kind of man you are *deep down.*"

He was perched on some sort of personal ledge and about to jump off. Would he? Could she push him? Would it help? Or would it simply make him more opposed?

She brushed her mouth to his. He froze, but didn't respond, which was so exasperating.

"I'm rich and beautiful," she said, "and I'm begging you to have me. Take me, you bloody fool."

He was trembling with restraint then, as if a dam burst, he pulled her to him and initiated his own kiss. It was nothing like the tepid peck she'd just given him. It was the type of heat and hunger she'd always imagined two people could share together, but in her stilted world, she'd never witnessed it.

His tongue was in her mouth, his questing hands everywhere. He caressed and massaged, pitching her into a heightened state of ecstasy.

Why had she waited to the ripe old age of twenty-five to wallow in carnality? Then again with a different man, she probably wouldn't have been so enticed. From the moment she'd espied him in Valois's courtyard, practicing his fencing, she'd been intrigued.

She was so lucky to have met him! She was so glad!

He blazed a trail to her breasts, to her nipples. He tormented them, sucking and playing, pinching and biting. She knew what was coming, and when he touched her between her legs, she exploded, her anatomy shattering into a thousand pieces.

As she reached the peak, as she floated down, he was glaring at her. How could she bring a smile to his handsome face? How could she convince him to love her?

"Oh, Bryce, stop scowling." She traced a finger across his creased brow, easing away the worry lines. "You claim you'd like to wed me. When would we do it?" The question seemed to be yanked from his very soul.

"How about first thing in the morning?"

Apparently it was the correct answer, the answer he needed to hear. He sat on his haunches and tugged off his shirt.

"How can I be certain you mean it?" he asked. "I've learned since yesterday that you're very fickle."

"I'm not. Not really. You simply overwhelmed my better sense."

"I've started to believe you have no *sense,* so it's not possible to overwhelm it."

She chuckled. "Make me yours, Bryce. That way, we can never be torn apart."

"You're sure about that, are you?"

"Yes, very sure."

"I have a boat reserved tomorrow. It's leaving at three for Alexandria."

"I can be ready."

"I haven't said I'd book passage for you."

"I'll buy my own ticket. I'll stalk you."

"A ship's captain can perform a marriage ceremony," he pointed out.

"So he can."

"We could marry once we set sail."

"Is that a new proposal? If it is, I accept."

He frowned. "It might be a new proposal."

"Let's have our wedding night right now. There's no reason to delay, is there? Not if we'll wed tomorrow."

He didn't reply to her suggestion, but studied her as if she was a stranger, as if he couldn't figure out how she'd wound up in his bed.

He stretched out and began kissing her again, his bare chest pressed to her own. As their skin connected, sparks seemed to ignite, the room sizzling as if they were about to light it on fire with their ardor.

He wasn't so wildly driven, but more focused, more determined. Down below, he slid two fingers into her womanly sheath. He shoved them in and out, in and out, until she was wet and relaxed.

"Have you any idea what's about to happen?" he asked.

"No."

"Has no one explained it?"

"No. My mother died before I was old enough to have that conversation, and I've never had another person with whom to discuss it."

"Men and women are built differently in our private parts." "I know." She'd seen Nicholas when she'd bathed him as a baby. "But why are we different?"

He was fumbling with his trousers, undoing the buttons. "I'm going to join my body to yours."

"What does that mean?"

He didn't clarify any details. "At first, it might feel awkward, and it might hurt."

"Hurt!"

"Only the first time and only for a moment. After that it will always be grand."

She smiled tremulously, suddenly wondering what she'd set in motion. It was likely a virgin's jitters, the fear of the unknown, and she wasn't actually afraid. She wanted Bryce to be the one, wanted to bind him so he'd have to wed her, so he'd have to keep her.

"Show me how it can be," she said.

"Don't worry."

"I'm trying not to."

"It will be over in a minute."

"You make it sound like an execution."

He shrugged. "Well, it is an execution after a fashion. We're ridding ourselves of the woman you used to be, and when we're through, we'll have someone else in her place."

"I suppose that's true. Is it difficult to accomplish?"

"No. It's just physical conduct."

"Can you explain it? I'm nervous."

"Every maiden is, and *no,* I can't explain. It's easier if I simply forge ahead."

"Then please proceed."

He scowled. "You have to promise me something."

"Anything."

"You can't be sorry later on. I'm just me, Bryce Blair, the son of an adventurer and an actress. I don't have a penny to my name, but for the wages you owe me."

"I understand."

"No, I don't think you do. For some reason, you've decided you'd like to be my bride. I don't know if it's because you're frightened for the future or if you feel you're out of options."

"I don't feel that way."

"You claim you love me and that's why you want to be my wife. So...I'm telling myself to believe you. But I'll only ever be the man who is lying here with you. If you grow to wish you hadn't wed me, that's too bad. We can't change it."

She studied him, recalling the times he'd saved her, protected her, befriended her, advised her. She thought of how kind he was to her sister, what a fine mentor he was to her brother.

He was acting as if she was a great prize, as if she was lowering herself in order to marry him. Yet he was remarkable and decent, and he would be her husband forevermore. She was so very, very lucky. And blessed. And happy.

All of the horrid events of the past year, all the humiliations and slights, the snubs and heartbreaks, none of it mattered now. She was starting over. She was starting over as Bryce Blair's wife, and there would never be a role she would rather play.

"Listen to me, Bryce."

"I'm listening."

"I will never be sorry. I will never regret my choice. I will *never* regret it. I swear to you."

"I intend to hold you to your vow. There's no going back with me."

"There's no going back with me either," she agreed.

"You and me. Kat and Bryce. 'Til death do us part." "I like the sound of that."

He nodded and began kissing her yet again, driving her up and up the spiral of desire. Her passion was rising, her body tensing. While she was racing to the edge, racing to ecstasy, she kept being distracted by how he was touching her.

He'd gripped her thighs and widened them, and he was pushing something into her. It was long and hard, and he was flexing with his hips. It felt very odd and very scary, but very thrilling too.

"What are you doing?" she paused to ask.

"I'm joining myself to you, remember?"

"Yes, but I told you I don't know what that means."

"We're almost there. Relax."

His expression was severe, as if he was struggling toward a goal. Their kissing became more raucous, more unruly, his thrusting more determined and rhythmic. A wave of pleasure ignited, sweeping over her, and as she cried out, he gave a particularly fierce shove with his hips.

There was a sting of pain, a rush of blood, then he was fully impaled. Tears flooded her eyes, but they weren't tears of distress. She was overwhelmed, the moment incredibly intimate, like nothing she could have imagined or described.

"Are you all right?" His voice was strained.

"Yes. I'm fine."

"It'll be over in a second."

And in fact, it was over just that quickly. He thrust once, again, and he moaned and collapsed onto her. Then he laughed and pulled away. He flopped onto his back, an arm flung over his face.

"Why are you laughing?" she demanded.

Had she done it wrong? How could she have? She'd had no idea what was happening. She'd simply lain there and let him do all the work.

"I'm laughing," he said, "because I performed as if I'm a callow boy of fourteen. It's embarrassing"

"Why?"

"I like to think of myself as a manly fellow, but you arouse me so completely I can't control myself."

"Oh."

She grinned and rolled toward him. He rolled too so they were nose to nose. They were staring, giggling like naughty schoolchildren.

"Did you survive?" he asked.

"All in one piece."

"Usually it lasts a little longer."

"Why did it end so rapidly then?"

"I have been dying to fornicate with you since the instant we met."

"This is called fornication?" "Yes."

"You've been anxious to do it with me? Is that normal for a male?"

"Is what? To want to fornicate with *you*? Or to want to fornicate in general? Men constantly ponder fornication. It's on our mind a hundred percent of the time."

"Really?"

"Yes, but I'm guessing every man who's ever seen you has wanted to fornicate with you specifically. *I* was the one lucky enough to persuade you."

"I picked you, don't forget."

"I won't forget. Not ever."

"I'm predicting this will turn out to be the best decision I ever make."

"I'll try very hard throughout my life to be certain it is."

To her dismay, she burst out crying, and he looked horrified.

"What is it?" he frantically asked. "Are you sad? Didn't you like it? What?"

"I loved it, and I'm not sad. I'm very, very happy."

"Are you sure?"

"Yes."

"Hush, then. There's no reason to be distraught. Everything will be perfect now."

He drew her to him so her cheek rested on his chest, her ear over his heart where she could hear its steady beating. Eventually her tears slowed, and he grabbed a corner of the sheet and dried her eyes.

"Better?" he asked.

"Yes, but I feel silly. You must think I'm a watering pot. I never cry."

"We'll let it be our secret that occasionally you do."

"Don't tell anyone."

"I won't."

They were nose to nose again, and he was smiling. So was she.

She was no longer a maiden! She'd given him her most valuable possession, and shortly she would be his bride, and he would be her husband. They would settle in England and never have to worry about Kristof or Parthenia ever again.

"What now?" she asked.

"Now we rest for a bit, then we'll awaken and do it again."

He spun her onto her side, and he spooned himself to her back. She found it to be the most spectacular part yet, the emotional intimacy after the passion had ebbed. She was desperate to memorize every detail so she'd never forget.

"Are we still leaving tomorrow?" she inquired.

"Yes."

"We'll marry on the boat?"

"Yes."

"When we get to London, could we wed again? Could we have a grand ceremony in a cathedral with my brother and sister in attendance and all your friends watching?"

"That would be splendid. I would like it very much."

Lethargy was creeping in, and she yawned. "I'm sleepy all of a sudden."

"Sexual play can be exhausting."

"I can't doze off in here. I would hate to have Valois's maids find me. It seems rude to misbehave like this under his roof."

"I doubt he would care, but I'll kick you out so you can sneak to your own bed before the servants are up."

With that assurance, she quickly faded into a deep, dreamless slumber.

"Love you, Bryce," was the last thing she recalled saying.

She might have imagined it, but she thought he replied, "Love you too, Kat, and I always will."

&c&D; &c&D; &c&D; &c&D;

Pippa straddled Chase, her knees digging into the mattress as he thrust into her. He was a very proficient lover, probably the most skilled she'd ever had.

She felt her orgasm rising, felt Chase's too, and she yanked away just as he began to spill himself. He knew better than to come so close to the edge, but he liked to live dangerously.

She collapsed onto the mattress, and they were giggling, breathing hard, struggling to slow their respiration.

Teasingly she slapped him on the shoulder. "You're horrid. What if I hadn't pulled away?"

"If you hadn't moved, I would have. I like to see your ire flare when I don't act as you wish I would."

"You are a vain beast, and I can't figure out why I put up with you."

"It's because we're in Egypt—where the rules don't seem to apply. You're bored and you haven't met anyone else who tickles your fancy."

"You'll never get me to admit it."

They were quiet for a bit. Chase wasn't big on snuggling or cooing. He stared at the ceiling, then rose to light a cheroot. He smoked it over by the window, gazing out at the Nile, letting the air cool his heated skin.

"What time is it?" she asked.

"I'm guessing dawn is about to break."

They'd been fornicating for hours, and she stretched her legs, relishing the feel of how roughly her feminine parts had been used.

"Could you do me a favor tomorrow?" she inquired.

"It depends on what it is. It can't be a difficult task. I've been up all night, so I'll be groggy and grumpy and not good for much of anything."

"It will be easy. I'll simply need you to lure Nicholas and Isabelle out of the villa."

He scowled at her. "Why?"

"I have to coax them out on the street where it's a tad less...safe. I'd like them to be away so I can convince Kat to hunt for them with me."

"Then *she* will be out of the villa too and a tad less safe." "Yes."

Pippa rolled to face him, and she was grinning like a cat that had gotten into the cream.

"What's happening?" he asked.

"It's time for her to go home. She doesn't want to, but she doesn't realize she has no choice in the matter."

"You'll force her?"

"No, she'll go on her own."

"How, Miss Pippa, will you accomplish that?"

"Nicholas and Isabelle will be heading home too. Once she learns they've departed, she'll depart too and without a fuss."

"Where are you from? You've never said."

"I'm not supposed to."

"Tell me or I won't help you."

"I'll provide all the details tomorrow, after we're successful."

"Tell me now." He looked doggedly intent on knowing.

"No. You'll run straight to Mr. Blair and blab all my secrets."

"I won't blab to Bryce. You have to give me some hint of what's occurring. I'm happy to assist you, but I won't place Miss Webster in harm's way. Nor will I take action that would be detrimental to her brother and sister. I'm a cad and a ne'er-do-well, but I won't deliberately injure them."

Pippa slid off the bed and tugged on her negligee and robe. She was conflicted and weighing whether to confide in him.

The royal courtiers had arrived, and the marriage proposal had been tendered, but Kat hadn't mentioned it. She should have left with Captain Romilard, but she hadn't, and Pippa was afraid of what Kat's refusal portended. Pippa had to get Nicholas and Isabelle out of the villa, and Chase was the only person who might aid her.

"I'll tell you," she ultimately decided, "but if you breathe a word to anyone, I'll have you killed."

He laughed. "Seriously? You think you could?"

"There are soldiers here from my country. They'd find you."

"My lips are sealed then." He was definitely sarcastic. "I wouldn't want a soldier to sneak up and murder me in a Cairo alley. I'm extremely determined to make it to London in one piece."

"I'm from Parthenia," she announced, proud to proclaim it.

"Do you mean that tiny country, where is it? In the Alps or some such spot?"

"Yes, more toward the Spanish border though."

"Fine, you're from Parthenia. Why all the covert plotting?"

"Kat is really Her Royal Highness, Katarina Morovsky."

He didn't appear to believe her, and he wasn't impressed. "Never heard of her."

"She's *Princess* Morovsky."

"I get it, Pippa. She's a princess, but why the hell is she in Cairo and calling herself Kat Webster?"

"Her father was the king, but he died so her brother, Nicholas, should have been king. But there was a coup."

"I vaguely remember reading about it."

"Kat's cousin, Kristof, and his advisors thought Nicholas was too young, so Kristof seized the crown instead."

"And Miss Webster came to Cairo because...?"

"It's Princess Morovsky, Chase. Try to keep up."

"All right. Why is the Princess here?"

"When Nicholas was passed over, she left in a fit of pique, but he's in the line of succession directly after Kristof. People are furious that she absconded with him."

It was mostly the truth, with a little fibbing, and Pippa didn't feel guilty for voicing it. Very soon, she would leave for home where great riches awaited her. She could practically smell the money that would be deposited in her bank account.

Chase studied her, his skepticism obvious and annoying. "So...they won't cut off Nicholas's head or anything like that."

"Of course not. For pity's sake, Chase, it's not the Middle Ages. He's heir to the throne, and Kat ran off with him."

"Swear it to me. Swear he won't be hurt."

"Gad, no. Kat is insane. She has been ever since her father perished. She assumed *she* would be put on the throne, and when she wasn't, she fled and took the heir with her."

Her falsehoods were growing bigger and bolder, and Chase was very astute. In a quick instant, he'd recognize a tall tale, so she couldn't have him note her sly expression. She leaned down and picked her hair combs off the floor, and when she stood again, she was calm and serene. She walked over and kissed him.

"I have to get back to my room," she said. "Yes, you should."

"Will you help me or not?"

"What's in it for me? That's what I keep asking myself."

"I'll tell King Kristof of your assistance, and you'll be rewarded."

He scoffed. "Yes, I just bet I will."

"You can travel with me to Parthenia and speak to him yourself. I guarantee he'll give you financial compensation. Why, if you play your cards right—and you're very shrewd that way—he might grant you some land or let you wed a royal cousin with a fat dowry."

He chuckled snidely. "A royal cousin?"

"The King is very generous so there's no predicting how you might benefit."

"You're leaving tomorrow, is that what I should take from all of this?"

"Yes, I'll be leaving."

He feigned a pout. "You weren't even planning to say goodbye."

"It doesn't have to be goodbye. You can come along. We could be lovers the entire trip."

He didn't answer with the positive reply she'd expected. With her being so close to the royal family, men always wanted her more than she wanted them. She'd finally stumbled on a fellow who wasn't agog over her regal connections.

"You'd better hurry." He pointed to a sliver of light on the eastern horizon.

"What about Nicholas and Isabelle? Even if you're not interested in accompanying us to Parthenia, there's a captain here from the palace guard. He can pay you."

"Talk to me in the morning."

"I will, and don't forget, Chase. You can't tell anyone."

"I won't, Pippa. Now go before a servant sees you. I like Valois, and I won't insult him by having him know I trifled with a guest."

"Valois has no authority over me," she boasted. "I am my own woman."

She whipped away and headed off without a word of farewell. She tiptoed down the hall, racing against the brightening sky. Her suite was next to Kat's and as she turned toward it, she was stunned to find Kat sneaking in from the other direction.

There was no question as to how they'd both misbehaved during the hot, sultry Egyptian night. They were attired in their bedclothes, their hair down, their feet bare.

For a brief instant, Pippa thought about hiding from Kat. But Pippa wasn't just anybody. The King of Parthenia had charged her with watching over Kat, making sure she did nothing reckless or ridiculous.

Kat had a royal husband waiting for her in Parthenia, and if she had ruined herself, if she wound up with a bastard in her belly, the blame would fall on Pippa. She was so near to the end of her journey, and she would never forgive Kat if she'd wrecked Pippa's future.

Just as Kat would have passed on by, Pippa stepped out of the shadows. Kat blanched, but bit down a yelp of alarm when she recognized Pippa.

"Where have you been?" Pippa hissed.

"I've been...nowhere."

Kat straightened and moved as if she'd march on by, but Pippa grabbed her arm to stop her.

"I ask you again, Kat. Where have you been?"

"Unhand me." Kat tried to yank away, but Pippa dug in her nails.

"Have you been out shaming yourself?"

"You have no right to interrogate me."

Kat's tone was haughty and imperious, and her snotty attitude aggravated Pippa as naught had in ages.

"Yes, Your Highness, heaven forbid that I demand an explanation. You're creeping in as dawn is breaking. Tell me where you've been!"

Kat noticed that Pippa was dressed in the same dissolute condition, and she sneered with irritation. "I could ask you the same. Why are *you* roaming about in your nightclothes?"

Pippa lied with aplomb. "I heard a noise, and I came to check on you. Imagine my surprise when I discovered you weren't in your bed where you were supposed to be."

"I'm twenty-five years old, Pippa, and I have no parents or brothers to command me. I am making my own choices."

"What *choice* have you made, Kat? Are you a slut who's hoping to scratch an itch?"

"I won't stand here and be castigated by you."

"Let me guess the name of the lucky fellow. Was Bryce Blair worth it?"

Pippa assumed Kat would deny her tryst, but she grinned and said, "Yes, he was absolutely worth it."

Pippa gasped with affront. "What have you done?"

"Nothing that's any of your business at all." She jerked very hard and pulled away. "Don't ever touch me again. Not unless you'd like to lose an appendage."

She walked on, entered her room, and locked the door with a determined click.

CHAPTER FIFTEEN

"We should probably sneak away."

"Is that wise, Mr. Hubbard?"

Chase gazed at Nicholas and grinned his friendliest grin. "We don't have to *sneak,* but I'm betting if we ask your sister for permission, she won't give it."

"I'm sure that's true," Nicholas agreed.

"I'll have the servants tell her where we are after we've left."

Nicholas glanced at his sister. "What say you, Isabelle?"

"I would like to see the camel races, but I don't believe we ought to disobey Katarina."

Chase had promised to take them to a famous, but completely fabricated camel race, and they were eager to attend, but they were both so well-behaved. He would need a shovel to dig them out of the villa without Miss Webster's consent.

Valois's property was a fortress, and they were safe inside it. Outside on the streets of Cairo, there was no predicting what might happen.

Chase hadn't meant to assist Pippa, but she'd shown up in his room and handed him an enormous amount of money that he'd been desperate to receive. From there, matters had gone downhill quite fast. Apparently he would betray anyone, even a pair of innocent children, if the price was right.

His conscience was trying to pipe up, but he wouldn't let it. He had no connection to the Webster family, and if they had royal lineage, he certainly had no dog in that fight. His only worry was about Bryce and whether Bryce would be irate, but Chase had discussed Katarina Webster with Bryce, and he'd most emphatically claimed he wasn't sweet on her.

Besides, if Chase could get the children out without being seen, no one would know he'd played any part in their disappearance.

At least no one would know if Pippa could keep her mouth shut when the stakes were high. The risk was huge, but then if it crashed down, he had the money she'd paid him to smooth over any hard feelings.

"We'll be back in two hours, Miss Isabelle," Chase lied. He doubted they'd ever be back to the villa.

"Let's do it, Isabelle," Nicholas begged. "Please?"

She was as charmed as everyone by her brother, and she couldn't refuse him. "Fine, but if Kat is angry when she finds out, you have to take the blame. I hate to upset her."

"I'll take all of the blame," Nicholas gallantly said.

Chase added, "And I'll take the rest."

He led them down an empty hallway, and he motioned with his finger that they should be silent and furtive. They crept away, swallowing down giggles as they acted precisely as they shouldn't.

Chase had hired a chair and had it waiting by a rear door. He hurried them into it and had them squat down on the floor, then he covered them with a rug. They thought it was a grand lark, and he sighed and shook his head at his folly.

All of it felt sordid and seedy, but evidently he would press on. He summoned the porters, then seated himself and stretched out. They lifted the chair and carried it off, the guard at the gate waving them through once he saw Chase.

They proceeded to the location Chase had been given, and the porters deposited him on the cobbles. He pulled off the rug and helped Nicholas and Isabelle to the ground. If the porters had an opinion about his conduct, they didn't mention it.

They rushed off to their next fare.

"We didn't go far." Nicholas studied the busy city street. "I assumed we'd be out in the desert."

"Where are the camels?" Isabelle inquired.

Chase was saved from having to answer as several stern-looking foreign soldiers marched around the corner to meet them. The man in the front greeted Nicholas with a gushing, "Your Majesty."

The soldiers bowed low, exhibiting incredible deference. So...perhaps they were royals after all. About that one aspect, Pippa seemed to have been telling the truth.

"Hello, Captain Romilard," Nicholas said, "but you're not supposed to address me that way."

"I couldn't stop myself, Sire. We have missed you at home."

"We've missed home too."

Nicholas was cordial, while Isabelle was dubious. She glared up at Chase. "Why are they here, Mr. Hubbard? We shouldn't be speaking to them."

"They wanted to talk to you," he said. "I told them I'd bring you to them."

"There's no camel race?" she asked.

"No."

The men spun to her, and they bowed again, with the Captain

saying, "Your Grace, how lovely to see you. If you'll come with me?"

An ornate carriage rolled up, and Romilard gestured to it. He was a stocky, muscled fellow, with an ugly face, as if he was a pugilist who'd had his nose broken too many times.

"No, I won't come with you," Isabelle scoffed.

Nicholas asked, "What is the meaning of this, Captain? What's happening?"

"Your cousin, Kristof, begs you to return to Parthenia."

"I would be most pleased to return," Nicholas replied, "but I must confer with my sister, Katarina, first."

"She will be joining us shortly."

"You liar," Isabelle said. "Katarina would never go anywhere with you."

Captain Romilard's smile slipped, and for a moment, he looked as if he might strike the girl, but he quickly smoothed his expression.

"Your sister has been making plans for days, Your Grace, but she has simply not shared them with you."

Isabelle was visibly frightened, and she clasped her brother's hand.

"Let's go, Nicholas. We shouldn't be here with them."

"But they're from *home,* Isabelle."

"They're not our friends! Remember yourself." She gazed up at Chase. "Would you take us to the villa, Mr. Hubbard? My sister will be very upset when she hears about this." "It's all right, Isabelle," he said. "Your family wants you back. That's all."

"Our *family* will chop off Nicholas's head once we arrive."

The soldiers stiffened, and trepidation surged through Chase. Did monarchs still murder rivals? Maybe in ancient times, but this was a modern era. No one beheaded anyone anymore.

"You're wrong, Miss Isabelle," he said.

"I'm not," she insisted.

Nicholas seemed more wary too, and he told Romilard, "Katarina is my guardian, and I simply must ask her if I may leave with you. If she gives me permission, I will be happy to accompany you, but until then I'm afraid I can't."

As if they had practiced a secret signal, they whirled and ran, but the soldiers dashed after them as Chase hollered, "Hey! Hey! There's no need for any physical violence."

His protest was ignored, and in an instant they were surrounded. Two soldiers grabbed Nicholas and two grabbed Isabelle. The rest of the group mustered around, then they started off in lock-step, the children enclosed in a tight circle of large, burly men. Isabelle was screaming for Chase to save them, while Nicholas was scolding Chase for his perfidy.

There were many local people on the street, but they weren't inclined to intervene. Obviously a substantial event was occurring, but passersby weren't sure what it was, and they weren't willing to be harmed for an inane reason. Chase couldn't blame them.

He was aghast and felt he should attempt a rescue, but there were twenty soldiers in the contingent, all of them armed as he was himself. Clearly Pippa had been less than candid about her motives as well as the repercussions for Nicholas and Isabelle.

They marched by Chase where he dawdled like a statue, too impotent to fight or even object.

Isabelle scowled at him and spat, "You dog! You cur! You swine! I curse you and your kin for all time."

Chase blanched at her vehemence, at her fury. He wasn't superstitious and didn't believe in curses, but she was so passionately intense that he worried she might have the power to bewitch him.

Nicholas was more circumspect, but no less fervent in his comments. "Mr. Hubbard, get my sister. Tell her Romilard has kidnapped us. She'll know what to do."

"Hush!" a soldier growled, and he clapped a palm over Nicholas's mouth to silence him.

Nicholas bit him and raged, "I am your rightful king. You don't have leave to touch me. When we are home again in my kingdom, you will learn your manners."

Isabelle added a remark in Italian that Chase couldn't translate, but it must have been another curse, because the men holding Nicholas blanched with dismay.

The group was almost to the carriage, and Chase decided he had to make a stand. He raced in front of them and blocked their path.

"Stop it, Captain Romilard," he commanded. "I was told that I was assisting with a reunion, but it appears I've been misled."

"Move, Mr. Hubbard," the Captain ordered.

"No. We'll convey the children to their sister. If she says you may have them, then I will gladly step aside."

"Move," Romilard repeated.

"No."

"I won't tell you again, Mr. Hubbard," Romilard fumed. "You dawdle at your own peril."

Chase wasn't much of a brawler simply because there was never much that mattered to him that was worth brawling over. But he'd been endangered too often in Egypt, and he'd trained hard with Valois.

For once, he felt very tough, very brave. He shouldn't have listened to that lying bitch, Pippa Clementi. He braced his feet. "You'll take them over my dead body."

"That can certainly be arranged," Romilard said.

Chase didn't see the blow coming. Someone hit him—very hard—from the side. Isabelle shrieked with horror, then his knees buckled and he collapsed to the ground in an unconscious heap.

He had no idea how long he laid there, but when he awoke, he was prostrate on the dirty cobbles, people swarming by him as if he was dung in the gutter. His head pounding with agony, he peered around, not surprised in the least to find that the carriage was gone, the soldiers were gone, the children were gone.

How would he ever confess his treachery to their sister? And how many more hours would he be allowed to live before Bryce murdered him?

&c& &c& &c& &c&

Pippa entered Kat's room without knocking. Kat was in the bedchamber, merrily humming to herself as if she hadn't a care in the world. Why shouldn't she be happy? Apparently she was in love for the very first time.

Pippa suffered a moment of regret for her friend that her affair would have to be abandoned. No doubt Kat had an entire fantasy life built up in her mind about Mr. Blair, but Kat knew better. She had a destiny that could never include him, and she had to remember who he was and who *she* was.

Pippa walked over to see Kat twirling in circles, lost in thought, smiling and more content than she'd ever been. As she noticed Pippa, she stumbled to a halt.

"Pippa, I didn't hear you come in. Please go away."

"I have to speak to you. It can't wait."

"After your behavior last night, I'm not in the mood to converse with you."

"You have to, Your Grace."

"Oh, shut up, Pippa. I won't have you spewing absurd titles at me. When you call me *Your Grace,* I can tell you're angry, and I don't wish to deal with you."

"You can't deny your true station."

"Kristof revoked my title, and I've decided he can have it. I don't need it any longer, and I refuse to miss it." She pointed to the door. "Now go!"

"I'm sorry, but I can't."

On returning from Cedric's camp, their trunks had been put in storage. Pippa had retrieved the one filled with court regalia, the robes, jewels, and crown that indicated Kat's imperial condition.

Pippa had it with her, and she gestured to two servants who were loitering behind her.

"Place it on the bed," she told them, "then you're excused."

Kat observed, frowning, as they wrestled in the heavy trunk and set it where Pippa had requested. They hustled out, their footsteps fading down the hall.

"What's happening?" Kat inquired.

"We're leaving for Parthenia."

"We most certainly are not."

"I've brought some of your official clothes. There is a royal escort outside. You'll dress and we'll meet with them."

"Pippa, aren't you listening? I'm not departing. Especially not for Parthenia. If you think you can command me in this, you are stark raving mad."

"I don't have to command you."

"You don't? Well, it definitely sounds to me as if you are."

Pippa stared at Kat, wondering what would be left of their relationship after the facts were revealed. She didn't suppose there would be any trace remaining, and again she suffered a twinge of regret at what would be forfeit. But Kat had always treated her like a servant and never as an equal, and Pippa was loyal to king and country.

She had no loyalty to Katarina at all. From the instant she'd reported Kat's escape plan to Kristof, their association had been severed.

And really, this wasn't a betrayal, was it? Kat should be in Parthenia. Their family had ruled there for centuries. What other choice was there but to return?

In an odd and convoluted way, Pippa was doing Kat a favor, helping her get back to where she belonged. If Kat didn't like it, so what? Pippa shrugged off any remorse. She never felt guilty about anything.

"Have you seen Nicholas and Isabelle this morning?" Pippa asked.

"No, why?"

"Mr. Hubbard lured them out of the villa."

Kat gasped. "He what?"

"I bribed him, and for a great amount of money, he smuggled them out and delivered them to Captain Romilard."

"You're lying."

"No, I'm not. They are being whisked to Parthenia with all due speed. You'll never catch them."

Kat looked so pale that Pippa worried she might faint, but she recovered herself and marched by Pippa as if she were invisible.

"Isabelle!" Kat called. "Nicholas! Where are you? I need you!"

Pippa grabbed Kat's arm, and Kat shoved her away, appearing so furious that Pippa thought Kat might physically attack her. Pippa hoped she wouldn't. They shouldn't brawl on the floor like a pair of tavern wenches. Even if Kat won the fight, even if she beat

Pippa to a pulp, she couldn't prevent what was transpiring.

"Here is the offer King Kristof makes to you," Pippa said.

Kat yanked away. "Don't mention his despicable name to me."

"He has proposed marriage, but from your behavior yesterday, he perceived that you were opposed. So he forces your hand."

"Kristof can jump off a cliff."

Pippa continued as if Kat hadn't spoken. "If you come without a fuss, he will put Nicholas in the line of succession so your brother will take the throne after Kristof passes away from what should be a long and fruitful life."

"He's a liar. He never would."

"But if you refuse to obey as he has ordered..."

Pippa stopped and swallowed twice. The next part was a threat, but she was sure Kristof wasn't serious. He wouldn't hurt anyone, but Kat could be so stubborn.

"But what, Pippa? What can he do to me that he hasn't already done?"

"If you don't comply, he will have Nicholas thrown into the dungeons."

"He wouldn't dare."

"Nicholas will never be released. He'll die without food or water."

"You tell me this, Pippa? To my face, you share this shameful news? After all the kindness my family showered on you, you would act in this disgraceful manner? Do you detest us so much?"

Pippa steeled herself against Kat's rage. "Then he will marry Isabelle."

"He'll...what?"

"He'll marry your little sister."

"She's ten years old!"

"He doesn't care. His advisors are clamoring for a Morovsky princess to be his queen. He will have you or he will have your sister. It is your choice."

She went to the trunk and opened it. She pulled out the purple robe of state, the tiara Kat used to wear every day, the gold rings for her fingers and jewel-encrusted belt for her waist. She arranged it all on the bed and pointed to the clothes.

"The King commands that you attire yourself and travel as befits your station. He will have no more hiding and conducting yourself as a person of no consequence. You will present yourself at all times as a royal princess who is about to wed the King of Parthenia."

They stared and stared, Kat's hatred wafting out. There was no denying it, no pretending it wasn't there. Pippa had known Kat would be very angry, but she hadn't expected such virulence so soon. She'd expected concern, questions, grief. Not immediate, unmitigated ire. Not malice that was frightening to witness. But then Kat was her father's daughter, and she'd been imbued with all the imperious traits for which he'd been renowned.

"What is it to be, Your Grace?" Pippa asked. "Captain Romilard's men are waiting. They are eager to depart."

"Leave me," Kat hissed. "I need to reflect."

"There is no time. I will help you dress, then we must go."

"Leave me!" Kat said more spitefully.

"No. You are not to be alone a single second until you have been safely delivered to Kristof."

Kat studied Pippa as if she were vermin, as if she were a rat or a maggot. She sneered, "Were you the one who informed Kristof I was sneaking away? Is that how I've been followed?"

"Of course I told."

"You're a spy. You're a betrayer."

"Not to my country. Not to my king."

"Nicholas is your king."

"Not anymore," Pippa retorted with a grim finality, and she gestured to the clothes. "Will you submit to your betrothed? Or shall I send word to Captain Romilard that you decline to obey? Shall I send congratulations to your sister on the high marriage she is about to make?"

Kat glared, glowering, pondering. Ultimately she vowed, "I will get even with you, Phillippa Clementi. I'll get even if it takes the rest of my life."

She pushed Pippa away and stomped to the bed to prepare herself without Pippa's assistance. Pippa watched, wanting to feel something, regret or guilt or sadness, but all she could think about was the glory that would be showered on her once she was home.

CHAPTER SIXTEEN

"What happened to you?"

Bryce glowered at Chase who was slouched in a chair in the corner of his bedchamber. His eye was black and swollen, his clothes dirty, the sleeve of his jacket torn. He was holding a kerchief to his cheekbone, staunching blood that oozed from a cut.

Had he been in a brawl? He must have been.

Bryce had been in his own room packing. He was excited to leave Cairo with Kat, and he wanted no delay. When he'd realized he hadn't seen Chase all morning, he'd rushed over, expecting he'd still be in bed and sleeping off a hangover. What he hadn't expected was to find him battered, injured, and not having made any preparations to depart.

"You won't believe it," Chase muttered.

"Yes, I will. From the looks of it, you've involved yourself in a huge mess that will ultimately bite us in the ass. What did you do?"

"Why must you always immediately assume I *did* something?"

"Because I've known you for over two decades, and you never surprise me. If there's mischief afoot, you're in the center of it. So I repeat, what happened? Don't lie and don't whitewash it. And don't you dare tell me it will prevent our sailing this afternoon."

"A problem has bubbled up."

"What sort of *problem*?"

"Has Miss Webster ever confided in you?"

"On what topic?"

"Well, for instance, has she ever mentioned where she's from? Or maybe has she talked about her true position there?"

"No, why?"

Chase scowled. "We're in the soup now, Bryce. It's my fault, and I take full responsibility."

"For what? Spit it out, Chase. Your dithering is aggravating me."

"You're aware of how my head can be turned by a pretty face."

Bryce blanched. "By...Miss Webster?"

"No, no, by Miss Clementi. She's very sly, very clever, and I shouldn't have listened to her."

"About what?"

"I guess Miss Webster's family ordered her to bring her brother home, and Miss Webster refused."

"Yes, he's very rich, and they've been after his fortune."

"Are you certain that's why she's on the run?"

"Yes."

"Miss Clementi claimed it was a different issue entirely. She claimed Miss Webster is deranged and her relatives feared for the boy's safety."

"Which is utter nonsense."

"Miss Clementi said it wasn't. She was...ah...very adamant and...ah..."

"And...?" Bryce pressed when Chase couldn't finish.

"She agreed to help them retrieve Nicholas."

Chase flinched as if Bryce might hit him, and Bryce gasped with dismay. "Oh, my Lord, Chase, what have you done?"

"She made it sound so noble, and she paid me a fortune for my assistance."

He held out a pouch, and Bryce heard metal clinking. He grabbed it and opened it, seeing too many gold coins to count.

"She paid you," Bryce repeated like a dunce.

"Blood money." Chase looked ashamed for once. "I didn't have to do much to earn it. I just took Nicholas for a ride out of the villa. Isabelle too."

"What is your middle name? Chase Judas Iscariot Hubbard?"

"It was reprehensible behavior. I admit it."

"So...you lured them out of the villa. Then what?"

"There were soldiers waiting for them, and they whisked the children away." Chase gestured to the kerchief. "I tried to stop them."

"How gallant of you," Bryce sarcastically spat.

"I'm sorry," Chase said.

"Where are they? Have you any idea?"

"Supposedly they're on their way to Parthenia."

"Parthenia? Where the hell is that?"

"It's that little country north of Italy."

"Parthenia? That's where they're from?"

"Yes, and they're royalty or some such."

Bryce frowned. "Why would you think that?"

"Nicholas was the king, but he was deposed, and then Miss Webster sneaked him away and—"

"Whoa!" Bryce snapped. "Nicholas is King of Parthenia?"

"*Was* the king, Bryce. He's not anymore."

"What about Isabelle and Miss Webster? If Nicholas was a king, are you saying they're...what? Princesses?"

"Miss Webster is actually Her Royal Highness, Princess Katarina Morovsky."

Bryce studied his friend, wondering if he'd ever really known him. Yes, he was unreliable and untrustworthy. Yes, he could be flighty and flippant and capricious. But he'd never been deliberately cruel. What had possessed him?

"You abetted the kidnapping of Miss Webster's siblings?"

"Princess Morovsky's siblings," Chase corrected.

Bryce smacked his palm on a nearby dresser. "I don't care what name we use to speak of her. You helped Miss Clementi kidnap Nicholas and Isabelle."

Chase huffed with offense, almost as if *he* was the injured party. "Pippa acted as if Princess Morovsky was an unhinged criminal who was endangering them."

"You should have talked to me. You should have asked my advice."

"I'm sorry," Chase mumbled again.

"Where is Kat? Have you told her?"

"No, I just returned myself. I haven't had a chance."

Bryce bristled with fury. "How long were you intending to sit in here without breathing a word to anyone?"

"I was about to find you. In case you haven't noticed, I was roughed up."

"I noticed, but I have no sympathy." Bryce pointed to the door. "Come."

"To where?"

"To confess your sins to Miss Webster."

"Me! I can't."

"Grow a spine, Chase. You were brazen enough to harm two innocent children. Surely you can face their sister to confess your diabolical conduct."

"Would you tell her for me, Bryce? Please? I can't bear to."

Bryce remembered their years together as boys at school. Bryce had befriended Chase when he'd been a bullied runt. Bryce had fought for Chase and defended Chase. Gradually it was dawning on him that Chase probably hadn't been worth all that effort.

"I'll tell her, you pathetic coward," Bryce fumed and he stormed out.

He burst into the hall and hurried to the other wing where the women's bedchambers were located. His pulse was racing, his hands shaking. He was terrified about Nicholas and Isabelle and vividly recalled the prior attacks on Kat and Nicholas. The brigands who'd initiated both assaults had been violent fiends.

But he was also alarmed over the discovery that Kat was a

royal. He and Kat were planning to marry and start a new life in England. Yet if Kat was from a royal family, she couldn't have been serious. Could she? The previous night had been splendid, like no evening Bryce had ever spent with a female. Ever since she'd crept out of his room at dawn, he'd been walking on air, elated and excited and astonished by his decision to proceed.

He'd been a man in love, a man on the precipice of a future that could only be amazing and remarkable. What was he now?

He was awhirl with frantic emotion. He wanted to bellow her name, to demand answers, to demand the truth. He had to apprise her of what Chase had perpetrated. Had she learned her siblings were missing? He had to be strong for her, had to be calm and rational, and he took a deep breath and slowed his pace.

He'd just managed to compose himself as he entered the villa's central courtyard. A contingent of soldiers was marching toward him, approaching from the direction of Kat's suite.

Pippa Clementi was leading the way, and she looked very grand, thrilled with herself and what she'd wrought. There was no evidence to indicate that she'd once been a lowly traveling companion.

She was dressed in a blue velvet gown with heavy petticoats and jewels on her fingers and neck. The outfit was stunning, but it was much too weighty for the hot climate. He hoped the disloyal shrew sweltered to death before she was able to depart Egypt.

The others followed behind her, ten in all, and they were more ceremonial than protective. They were flashily attired, with sashes, gold braid, and plenty of medals, but while they had sabers on their hips, the weapons were more the sort for decoration at balls and weddings.

There was a woman in the middle, wearing a purple cloak and tiara. She was bedecked in gold and diamonds, a jeweled choker around her throat, a belt embedded with rubies and emeralds around her waist.

It took him several seconds to realize it was Kat, and his heart sank. Currently there was nothing about her that resembled the lonely spinster who'd charmed him, who'd made him yearn to be a husband rather than a bachelor.

She was still very beautiful, but there was a regal aura about her, as if the purple cloak shielded the person underneath. She appeared untouchable, unknowable, unlovable. She was a stranger, an exotic, foreign dignitary who probably wouldn't bother to glance at him as she passed by.

Yet as the group neared, he said, "Kat."

The men kept on, nary a one so much as peeking over to see who had called out.

"Kat!" he said again, and he stepped in front of them.

Pippa Clementi pulled up short and scowled. "Mr. Blair, you have rudely interrupted a royal procession. Please move or I will have you moved."

"You think you could, Miss Clementi? Go ahead and try, you deceitful, lying doxy."

At the taunt, her cheeks flushed bright red, and Bryce thought she might slap him. She was clearly considering it, but in the end she peered over her shoulder and spoke to the soldiers.

"We shall continue to the carriage. There will be no delay." She whipped her furious glare to Bryce. "We are on important business of state."

Bryce didn't budge, and the only way she could get past him was to knock him over or walk around him. Her enormous pride wouldn't let her walk around, and she wasn't strong enough to knock him down.

She gestured to the soldier with the most medals on his chest. "Captain Romilard, rid the Princess of this uncouth boor at once."

The burly, thuggish fellow huffed up to Bryce. He looked cruel and stupid, and Bryce was sizing him up, taking his measure, preparing to throw the first punch as Valois had taught him to do.

In heavily-accented English, the Captain said, "I dispatched your pathetic friend with one blow. I'm happy to show you the same discourtesy."

"You must mean Chase Hubbard, the man for whom Miss Clementi has been spreading her thighs with reckless abandon."

Miss Clementi hissed with outrage and ludicrously seethed, "Kill him, Romilard. I command you."

"We are guests in this country, Miss Clementi," Romilard told her, "so we will not engage in conflict with him. But he *will* move. Now."

"I'll gladly comply," Bryce replied, "after I have spoken to the Princess."

"I'm afraid that won't be possible," Romilard said.

Bryce would have leveled him then and there, but Valois strolled into the courtyard. He was his usual, affable self, but he was accompanied by three men who had studied fencing with Bryce. They were armed, and as opposed to the ceremonial sabers worn by the soldiers, Valois's pistols and swords were very real.

"Ah, Miss Clementi," Valois smoothly said, "how delighted I am that I was able to catch you before the Princess departed. I so wanted to make my goodbyes to her."

"We're late," Miss Clementi insisted. "There's no time."

Valois ignored her. "And of course Mr. Blair has been a great friend to the Princess during her sojourn in Egypt. I am sure he will wish to say goodbye to her as well."

Romilard was a bully and an idiot, but apparently he wasn't keen on starting a fight with Valois. He stepped away, and Bryce stomped forward, causing the soldiers to stumble aside so he could approach Katarina.

He stopped directly in front of her, and she extended her hand as if he was one of her subjects, as if he should fall to his knees and kiss it.

He'd be damned if he would!

He peered into her eyes, but the glow of merriment he'd always seen there had been drummed out of her. The Miss Webster whom he'd loved so fiercely had vanished.

"What are you doing?" he asked.

"I'm leaving for Parthenia. My king has sent an honor guard to escort me."

"Really?" he sneered. "It appears to me they're taking you by force."

She laughed, but it was a brittle, cold sound. "By force? Why would they have to? I'm eager to return to my country. There is no force involved."

"This witch"—he pointed at Pippa Clementi—"had Nicholas and Isabelle kidnapped. Were you aware of that fact?"

Princess Morovsky blandly stared at Miss Clementi then shifted her gaze to Bryce. "She has simply obeyed her sovereign."

Bryce felt as if he was speaking to an automaton. If there was a tiny piece of Kat Webster lurking inside, he couldn't connect with it.

He reached out and laid a hand on her arm. The soldiers gasped and spun as if they'd attack, and the Princess frowned and leaned away.

"Let's go to your room, Kat. I need to talk with you in private."

"That wouldn't be appropriate, Mr. Blair, and I can't believe you suggested it."

"Tell me what's happening. Why are you letting Miss Clementi lead you about like a puppet on a string?"

"My marriage has been arranged, Mr. Blair. I am traveling home for my wedding."

Bryce might have been punched in the stomach. "Who are you marrying?"

"My cousin, Kristof."

"And who is he?"

"He is King of Parthenia."

"So you'll be a queen. Is that your heart's desire? Is that how all your dreams will be fulfilled?"

She didn't answer his question, but said, "Yes, I will be Queen of Parthenia—as my mother was queen."

"The way I hear the story, the actual king is your brother, Nicholas. The way I hear it, this Kristof fellow staged a coup and seized your brother's throne. When he has done you such a wrong, why would you wed him?"

"Mr. Blair," Miss Clementi snapped, "that's quite enough."

The Princess ignored her and callously stated, "It's all arranged, Mr. Blair, and you have no right to pester me about any of my choices."

"What about me?" he bleakly asked.

"What about you?" She was focused on a spot over his shoulder.

"We would have been so happy together, Kat."

"I have no idea what you mean."

"You let me assume you were a lonely, friendless nobody. You let me think I had a chance."

"Again, Mr. Blair, I have no idea what you mean."

He searched her face, trying to get her to look at him, but she wouldn't.

"What about last night?" he whispered. "What about the promises and plans we made?"

She flinched imperceptibly, and if he hadn't been standing so close, he wouldn't have noted it. A single arrow had finally hit its mark, but she glanced away and cruelly whispered, "There were no promises between us."

"I see." He dithered, confused and angry and at a loss. "Are you leaving because they have your sister and brother? Is that why? Because previously you told me you would never return, no matter what. Pardon me if I find this sudden decision to be a tad peculiar."

"Why would I care as to your opinion? Goodbye."

Her voice cracked on *goodbye*, but it was the only sign that she was affected in the slightest.

She swept by him and said to Romilard, "Let's be off. I'm ready to depart, and I don't wish to delay another second."

As she reached the door, Bryce caustically hurled, "I guess it's because of my being an actor after all, isn't it, Your Highness? You claimed it wasn't an issue, but it's obvious a mere actor could never have been sufficient for you."

She lurched to a halt, as if he'd stabbed her in the back. The group behind her froze, and Bryce thought she'd reply to his horrid taunt, but she squared her shoulders and commanded, "Romilard, let's go!"

Though it was petty and pointless, Bryce was determined to have the final word. "Just so you know, Your Highness, along with my being an actor, I am Earl of Radcliffe." He announced the title aloud for the very first time ever. "So even with my true status revealed, I'm still much too low for you. An exalted person such as yourself could never have stooped to having an earl, I suppose. For a woman of your rank, it's a king or no one."

She whirled around, and he sensed there were a thousand comments roiling her, but she could never mention them. She yanked her gaze from Bryce to Valois and said, "Thank you for your hospitality, Monsieur Valois."

"You're welcome, Your Grace. I am honored to have had you as a guest."

"I shall recall my visit to Cairo with great...fondness."

It sounded as if she'd swallowed down a sob, and Bryce couldn't imagine who she might be crying for. She was headed home, with a royal fortune in her pocket, to wed a king and become a queen. To hell with her.

"It wounds me that you must depart so precipitously," Valois said.

"Well, Monsieur, there are some things in this world that are out of my hands."

Then she was gone. The soldiers marched out behind her, but Miss Clementi lingered, looking sly, looking smug. "Goodbye, gentlemen. Monsieur Valois, I also thank you for your hospitality."

She sashayed out, and Bryce couldn't resist muttering, "Lazy, deceitful whore."

It was an awful remark, but he didn't regret it. She glared back, her expression even more cunning. "Yes, but certain whores are very significantly rewarded for their efforts. I happen to be one of them."

"Slut," Bryce fumed. "Betrayer. Shrew." He imbued the insults with all the scorn he could muster.

She might have added a snotty aside, but she noted Valois's disparaging glower. Her snide grin faltered, and she huffed out.

Bryce stood, listening as Princess Morovsky climbed into her carriage, as doors were slammed and horses mounted. A command was called, whips were cracked, spurs jingled, and the entourage rattled away.

In another minute, it was eerily quiet, as if none of them had been there.

Bryce frowned at Valois. "Did you know who she was all along?"

Valois simply shrugged.

"Couldn't you have warned me?"

"It wasn't my secret to tell, Bryce."

"I hate that I made such a fool of myself over her. I believed she and I had an understanding, that we were marrying."

"I'm sorry, my friend."

Chase took that moment to stagger in. He was still disheveled, a kerchief still pressed to the cut on his cheek. His eye had continued to puff up and was now swollen completely shut.

"They left?" Chase asked.

"Yes," Valois responded when Bryce didn't.

"What about Nicholas and Isabelle?"

"Apparently they're bound for Parthenia," Valois said.

"But...but...they were kidnapped! They were terrified of those men. Isabelle screamed and cried. We have to help them." Chase turned to Bryce, accusation in his tone. "Why didn't you stop Pippa?"

Bryce studied Chase, a wave of dislike and disdain bubbling up.

"Prick," he spat. "Rude, stupid prick."

He pushed by Chase and proceeded to his room where he could lock himself in and figure out what to do next.

CHAPTER SEVENTEEN

George Blair, Earl of Radcliffe, hovered behind a tree in the woods outside Radcliffe village. The Blair twins rode out every day, and George was waiting for them to pass by.

The coaching inn was just up the road. They'd taken rooms there, bold as brass, as if they had every right to flaunt their paternity. They were talking to whoever would listen, telling stories that were circulating like wildfire.

George could barely leave his bedchamber. Whenever he did, he was met with insolent stares of condemnation. So far no one had dared to mention the gossip to his face, but he could sense the festering derision, the hope that change was coming.

Well, change wasn't coming.

From the moment the twins had blustered into the castle, George had known he had to get rid of them, but he couldn't figure out how. It had never occurred to him that Julian's children might live and thrive, that they might have the audacity to show up where they weren't wanted.

He'd devised no contingency plans, had prepared no counter offensive against their lies and smears. Of course they weren't lying. That was the problem. Their every comment had a ring of truth. People believed whatever they said. They had their father's charisma, their father's gift for making others like them.

George had considered having them arrested and immediately executed, but apparently their sister was alive too and married to a British aristocrat. If George had had them jailed, no magistrate would have dared to hang them, and he'd have stirred an aristocratic incident between the two countries besides.

His next idea had been to hire a murderer, a tenant or perhaps an employee at the inn who could enter their room in the middle of the night. But with how they were starting to be worshipped wherever they went, George didn't trust anyone. Any paid assassin would likely tattle.

No, there was just one way to handle it. He had to dispatch the twins himself. He could do it too. He had the gall, the nerve. He'd dealt with their father easily enough. Without a word of warning, he'd shot Julian in the chest, and he'd never regretted it.

George and his father had never understood Julian, had never liked him, had always been embarrassed by him. He'd been wild and carefree and independent, had never worried about conventions or morals.

George's father had yearned to be free of the constant humiliations Julian had inflicted on the family. His marriage to an actress had been the final straw. Like a plot out of a Shakespearean tragedy, his father had begged to be rid of his rebellious son.

George had acted on his father's plea, and it remained the only remarkable deed he'd ever committed. He'd killed Julian for his father, then he'd been allowed to wed Julian's rich, pretty fiancée.

If he could shoot his own brother and not regret it, he could certainly kill his brother's sons. He merely wished he was younger, his hands steadier, his vision clearer.

Suddenly he heard horses approaching, but they were traveling very fast. If it was the twins, he'd get just one chance and didn't dare miss.

He eased out from his hiding place and glanced down the road. It was the twins! Their horses were cantering, and in the blink of an instant, they'd hurried on by. He slumped against the trunk of the tree, railing over his fate, his lot.

It was desperate business, attempting homicide, and he dawdled for a few minutes, letting his pulse slow, his nerves calm. Then he spun to sneak into the woods and return to the castle. As he did, he was gazing down the barrel of a pistol held by one of his nephews.

"Hello, Uncle George. Fancy meeting you here."

"What the devil...?" George muttered, his fear acute, his rage boiling over.

Why couldn't his plans ever succeed? He was old now, and none of his dreams for Radcliffe had ever come to fruition. He'd been cursed the day he'd murdered his brother, cursed again when Anne Blair had been convicted, then transported. It wasn't fair for the twins to demand justice after so many years.

He might have raised his own pistol, but before he could move a muscle, his nephew grabbed it and tossed it away. He was tall and imposing, and with his dark hair and blue, blue eyes, George might have been staring at Julian all over again.

"I'm Matthew, in case you were wondering," the man said.

"I wasn't wondering," George grumbled.

"Were you hoping to shoot me in the back?"

"Bugger off."

"I have a problem with people shooting at me unaware, and ever since we arrived, I've been expecting you to try something stupid.

Were you supposing I wouldn't observe you lurking in the trees?"

"You have no right to question me, and I won't stand for it on my own land."

"There's the rub, Uncle. It's not *your* land, is it?"

The other twin blustered through the forest. He noticed George's gun lying in the grass, and he snatched it up and stuck it in his belt.

"What have we here?" Michael Blair asked.

"I told you I saw him," Matthew said.

"Your eyesight must be better than mine."

"No, I simply don't intend to be shot ever again. I'm a little more vigilant than you."

Michael sneered at George. "You scurry around like a rat in a sewer, don't you? I wouldn't put it past you to attack on the sly."

"It's the coward's way," Matthew said.

"We'll see who's a coward in the end," George fumed.

"Shut up, Uncle," Michael said. "A great benefit of being *me* is that I don't have to listen to anyone who annoys me."

He marched over and stood shoulder to shoulder with his brother. They towered over George, their imperious expressions snide and condemning.

Fate was so cruel. It seemed as if Julian had returned to Radcliffe, except there were two of him instead of one. Two exact copies. Two replicas who looked the same and talked the same and acted the same. They'd already disarmed George, and he felt so helpless he might have been castrated.

"We have your wife's confession," Michael said.

"I have no idea what you mean," George replied.

"We've sent all the papers to our solicitor in London."

"Why would I care about that?" George asked.

Michael chuckled, and it was an eerie, dangerous sound. "We've commenced legal proceedings to retrieve what belongs to our brother, Bryce."

"It'll be a cold day in Hell when you best me," George said.

"You don't believe we can?" Matthew mused. "Michael is disgustingly wealthy, and we've heard you're not."

Michael said, "We've heard you're a lousy landlord, that you've wrecked the farms and the fields and the flocks. You're land rich, but money poor."

Matthew continued, "Michael can keep our claim locked up in the courts for the rest of your miserable life, and he won't miss a penny of the lawyer's fees. We can have your bank accounts seized and your crops garnished. We can have you evicted while we're adjudicating. We can have you arrested for murdering our father and held without bail until the case is resolved."

"You could make it easy on yourself and go away." Michael smiled his deadly smile. "That way, we won't have to torment you to the bitter end."

"Go away?" George said. "You're mad if you think I'd leave my rightful place."

"You always call Radcliffe your *rightful* place," Matthew said. "It's not yours, you scurvy dog, and it never was."

"I won't be insulted by you," George huffed.

He pushed them, but it was like shoving a brick wall. Neither of them moved, and the only thing George accomplished was to feel his palms throbbing where he'd smacked those two massive chests.

"Tell me something, Uncle," Matthew said.

"What?"

"Did you enjoy killing our father?"

"Sod off, Matthew Blair. I don't answer to the likes of you."

But the idiot wouldn't be deterred. "Did you creep up on him from behind? Or did you have the balls to shoot him in the face so he'd die knowing it was you?"

George was so incensed, it was on the tip of his tongue to crow about his supreme triumph. He'd never been able to admit the deed, how quickly it had happened, how unsuspecting Julian had been. They'd been hunting, with Julian being his usual confident, posh self. He'd been bragging about his wife, about his children, about how silly their father was to demand he set his wife aside.

Julian had been beloved by everyone, so he'd never understood the level of George's dislike, had never understood George's jealousy or envy. Julian had had the courage to flee Radcliffe, to travel to distant lands and see fascinating sights and people. He'd wed without permission, to the most extraordinary, beautiful woman in the world. He'd done it unabashedly, without shame or remorse, and George had seethed through all of it.

He'd yearned—just once—to exhibit the same sort of brash aplomb, but he'd been stuck at Radcliffe, too meek to shuck off their father's heavy hand, too timid to reach for things he'd craved. So he'd taken what Julian hadn't wanted. He'd taken Radcliffe and Susan and never looked back.

But standing here in the forest, with Julian's sons glaring at him, he didn't dare confess any of it.

He grinned maliciously. "I guess you'll have to go to your grave wondering how he perished. For if I knew—which I don't—I wouldn't give you the satisfaction of apprising you."

"You stole everything he had," Matthew taunted, "but we hear you've received no pleasure from any of it."

"Let's tabulate your sorry list of accomplishments," Michael said. "Tenants who loathe you. A bitter, disloyal wife. A failed estate.

Three sons who were never hale."

"Doesn't it gall you," Matthew said, "that you struggled so diligently to ensure Julian's children died. Yet we're all thriving, while your children didn't make it. You have the worst luck."

They smirked, and George should have kept his mouth shut, should have let the taunt go unchallenged, but he couldn't help blurting out, "None of it was my fault. I was cursed by your mother."

"Good," Matthew said. "It appears to have worked."

"Your mother was a whore," George spat.

Both twins gasped, and Michael hissed, "What did you say, you prick?"

"She was a whore, a mercenary leech, a money-grubbing fortune hunter who viewed your father as naught but a fat bank account."

He was surprised he managed to spew the entire string of insults. Michael Blair seized him by the throat and lifted him off the ground, and he was squeezing tight, choking the life out of George. George pried at his fingers, but couldn't pull them away, and he was rapidly losing consciousness.

Before matters could escalate to a dire level, Matthew stopped his sibling.

"Whoa! Whoa!" Matthew counseled. "Steady, Michael, steady on. We agreed not to kill him, remember?"

"I've changed my mind," Michael said.

"No, you haven't," Matthew insisted. "We're shaming him to death. That's the plan. We'll expose him for the brother-murdering dog he is. We'll pilfer what he has and leave him with nothing—as he left out mother with nothing. It's a better punishment by far."

Michael tossed George away, and he collapsed in a heap. He was too terrified to get up, and he peeked at Michael, alarmed over what he might do next. From the bloodthirsty gleam in his eye, George wasn't certain he'd been calmed sufficiently to prevent further mayhem.

"I want him dead," Michael tersely said.

"Not now. Not yet," Matthew replied. "He's still an earl. We'll finish it when he's not."

They gazed at one another, and they appeared to be carrying on a conversation in their heads. Ultimately Michael whipped away and started into the trees to where his horse was chomping on the grass.

"I'll join you shortly," Matthew called.

Michael waved but didn't glance around. He jumped on the animal and galloped away.

George heaved out a desperate sigh. "Where is he going?"

"To the coaching inn. We're waiting on an arrest warrant."

George blanched. "An arrest warrant for who?"

"For you, Uncle. For killing our father."

Matthew leaned down and dragged him to his feet. He was wobbly, off balance, dizzy and disoriented. His throat throbbed where he'd been throttled, and he felt sick to his stomach.

"You have no evidence," he murmured.

"We have your wife's written confession. We weren't joking."

George scowled, anxious to conceal his panic. "You couldn't possibly have."

"Yes, we have it so we're aware of every sordid crime you committed."

How had it been delivered into their possession? Who had done it? Susan was too ill. Had it been Katherine? Would she have betrayed him? Or was it someone else?

He'd learn the identity of the culprit and that person would be hanged. Until he was carted off in chains, he was still lord and master at Radcliffe. He would be happy to impart a bit of swift justice. Even if it was to pretty, quiet Katherine.

"You can't prove any of it," he declared. "It's the words of a dying woman who's mad as a hatter."

"We don't have to prove it. As I said, my brother is very wealthy. We can torment you over it for the remainder of your days. You'll have failed in your quest to steal our father's legacy. Julian and Anne Blair will be avenged—by their children."

Matthew pushed him toward the road, but George wasn't sure he could make it to the castle on his own. He wished he could ask Matthew to give him a ride, but he'd rather be boiled in hot oil than ask the man for any favor.

Still though, he tried to look regal and in charge. He straightened and glared at his nephew. "The minute I'm inside the castle gates, I'm sending the law for both of you. Best prepare yourself, for you're about to be arrested too."

"I'm trembling in my boots, Uncle."

"You keep forgetting that I am an earl, a peer of the realm, and I will not be assaulted as if I'm a commoner. I shall have Michael Blair executed for putting his filthy paws on me."

"Didn't you know?" Matthew grinned his father's grin. "We've bribed everyone who matters in this country. No one will help you, and you have no friends."

George stood in the middle of the road, afraid, belittled, offended. He nearly burst into tears. How had it all gone so wrong?

Julian was dead. Anne was most likely dead too. Their children had been scattered to the four winds. But two of them had returned, like righteous angels. They seemed omnipotent, as if they'd been imbued with Julian's strength and steady character.

It was so unfair! They were supposed to have perished too. They were supposed to have starved on London's mean streets. They weren't supposed to show up without warning and prove themselves rich, powerful, and invincible.

All those years ago, when he'd moved against Anne, if he'd thought for a single second that any of her horrid brats might survive, he'd have killed them too.

To his father, they'd been a nuisance, a non-issue. What could they do on their own but falter and fail? Yet they'd not only lived through the disaster, they'd flourished. How was it possible? How had it happened? It was almost as if Julian was staring down from Heaven, laughing at George, letting him know he'd always been inept.

"Get going, Uncle," Matthew said.

"I'm not well. I don't think I can make it without assistance."

"Maybe someone will come by and take you in their wagon."

"What if they don't?"

"After how you disparaged my mother, are you expecting me to be sympathetic?"

"You should be kinder to me. I'm old, and I've been physically attacked."

"You're an unrepentant, evil ass, and it's about time you were attacked. And you're not *old*. You're lucky I stopped Michael. If you aggravate him in the future, I won't intervene. Now get walking."

Matthew braced his feet, his hands clasped behind his back, as if he was standing at attention, as if he might have once been a soldier. Julian used to stand the same way, and for just a moment, Matthew melded into George's memories of his brother until George might actually have been looking at Julian.

A voice whispered in his head. *You shouldn't have murdered me, George. My sons are here to make you pay...*

Julian's words were loud and clear, spoken next to his ear, so close he could feel his brother's breath brushing across his skin. He yearned to glance over to see if Julian's ghost was there, but he was too terrified to know for certain.

He whirled away and staggered off.

CHAPTER EIGHTEEN

Princess Morovsky stood at the ship's rail, staring down the wharf.

Alexandria was a busy port, and there was a swarm of people as far as the eye could see. Ships lined the dock in both directions. Cargo was being loaded and unloaded. Passengers boarded and debarked. Men were hawking food, supplies, offering taxis and carriages, seemingly in a thousand different languages.

The tide had turned, and they were ready to sail. Behind her, sailors ran about, calling orders and questions to one another. The captain had assured her of good weather, that their crossing of the Mediterranean would be fast, smooth, and uneventful.

She hoped so. She'd agreed to go back to Parthenia, and she would brook no delays. Briefly she worried about her sister and brother. She wondered where they were, if they were safe, and she supposed they were.

If she arrived in Parthenia only to find that they weren't there, she would shoot Kristof right in the center of his cold, black heart. She should have murdered him the day he'd seized the throne. She should have killed him then. She still could, and if her siblings had been mistreated, his end would come much sooner than he'd expected.

Under her purple robe, her diamond tiara, Kat Webster struggled to emerge. For a fleeting, nostalgic minute, the Princess allowed Kat to bubble up.

She studied the throng, searching for Bryce, praying he was out there somewhere. In case he was, she wanted him to note which vessel was taking her away, which one to follow.

It was simply beyond her ability to imagine that he wouldn't chase after her. Yes, she'd been horrid to him that last morning at Valois's villa, but he would have seen through Princess Morovsky's cruel words.

He would have recognized Kat's fear and alarm, would have understood Kat would never forsake him, that she'd had to protect her siblings. With Pippa pressuring her so unmercifully, she'd been confused and frantic and not thinking clearly. She was certain he'd have forgiven her and made plans to rescue her once again.

But during the entire trip to Alexandria, there had been no sign of him. She kept looking though, and couldn't seem to stop. She'd been so sure of him, of his devotion and loyalty. He would never let Pippa get away with her blackmail, would never let Kat be forced into marrying Kristof.

Yet as each mile passed, her optimism had waned. What if he didn't realize how desperately she needed him? What if she never saw him again?

No, no, he'll come after me. He will!

She rubbed a hand over her belly and smiled a secret smile. Had he planted a babe in her womb? Was she already increasing? She knew some of the signs a woman experienced, but was there a way to tell so early?

She yearned to be carrying his child. She craved it with a vehemence that shocked and surprised her.

Thoughts of Parthenia, of Kristof, pushed into her head. For some reason, he was intent on wedding her, so there had to be a dire situation spurring the bizarre decision. What would he do to Kat if she was with child? More importantly, what might he do to Nicholas or Isabelle?

Princess Morovsky had had enough of Kat's fretting. There was no purpose to wistfulness, and she wouldn't suffer it. She smoothed her expression and gazed down the wharf again.

Miss Clementi had left to purchase a few items for their journey across the sea. The ship's captain was pacing, anxious to leave, but with her elevated status as Kristof's spy, she felt free to be late. Off in the distance, her carriage was gradually meandering through the crowd. A footman was out in front, maneuvering the horses around various impediments, but he wasn't having much luck.

It might take them forever to reach the ship, and the Princess couldn't figure out why Miss Clementi didn't climb out and walk the rest of the way. Didn't she grasp how her slow speed was causing a problem?

Of course, since the Princess had initially fled Parthenia, Miss Clementi's star had risen quite high. She was very set on herself, and it would never occur to her that her behavior might be an issue.

Kat bubbled to the surface once more, remembering all the years she'd been kind to Pippa, all the years she'd treated her like a sister. They'd shared every dream, every secret, every heartache.

Had Pippa ever cared about Kat? Had she ever cared about Nicholas or Isabelle? Had she ever been grateful for the many boons showered on her by the Morovskys? Kat had to accept that she probably hadn't been.

She couldn't bear to travel with Pippa another second. She'd have to see her every morning, watch her coo with the crew, and scheme with Captain Romilard. Most of all Kat would have to constantly recollect how Pippa had betrayed her.

Kat retreated into the shadows, and Princess Morovsky spun to the ship's captain. "We needn't wait for my companion."

He scowled. "What?"

"We needn't wait."

"Are you…ah…positive, Your Grace?"

"Absolutely. Raise the gangplank. I'm eager to be away."

"What of your friend? I'm worried about leaving her behind."

"I'm not."

"Alexandria is a dangerous place for a woman."

"She'll be fine. She loves to remind me that she's very wealthy now, so she can use her own money to pay her expenses. I hardly need to spend more of mine."

The comment was cold and harsh, but Princess Morovsky didn't blink as she voiced it. The captain studied her, studied the wharf, but he didn't know which carriage belonged to Miss Clementi, didn't know how close she was.

"If you're positive?" he asked again.

"Please get moving. Her dallying has tried my patience to the limit."

She stared him down, pelting him with all her imperial grandeur, and apparently he understood how to obey a royal command.

He began barking orders to his sailors. As she'd demanded, the gangplank was raised, ropes untied, the anchor pulled up. A raft manned by slaves rowed them away from the pilings, and very quickly a breeze caught the sails. They drifted into deeper water.

Feet pounded on the deck, and momentarily Captain Romilard appeared at her side. Evidently he'd been napping. His coat was off, his shirt untucked. Several of his men blustered up with him.

"What have you done?" he wheezed.

The Princess whirled on him, and her furious glower caused him to step back. "Were you addressing me, Captain Romilard?"

"Ah…yes, Your Highness." He was a stupid little bully who was cowed by royalty too. She only had to act the part, and he trembled in his boots.

"So far on this unpleasant journey," the Princess fumed, "I have been much too lenient with you. Speak to me with the deference I am due or be silent."

"Yes, yes, Your Grace." The obsequious toad nodded. "It's just that the captain tells me you've forced him to depart."

"Yes, I'm tired of Egypt. If we'd missed the tide, I would have had to spend an extra day here."

"Where is Miss Clementi? My men inform me she's not yet on board."

The Princess pointed to the dock where the hapless shrew had finally bothered to glance out the window of her stalled carriage. She had realized the ship was being tugged away, that no one was waiting for her. She might have had many friends in Parthenia, but in this tiny corner of Egypt, she suddenly had no friends at all.

"I believe Miss Clementi is there," the Princess said. "Isn't that her waving to us? I'm quite sure it is."

"Your Highness, we can't go without Miss Clementi."

"We already have, Captain."

"But...but..."

Miss Clementi was flagging them with a kerchief, trying to get their attention. She was swearing, calling to Captain Romilard to stop, to fetch her.

"Really, Your Grace, we can't abandon her."

"Are you deaf, Captain Romilard? I am the affianced bride of your king and very soon I will be your queen. I have commanded that we leave her, and we have. I will not suffer Miss Clementi's annoying presence for the rest of the trip."

"We can't desert her in this country of infidels. What will happen to her?"

"Her fate does not concern me." The Princess smiled a cruel smile. "Now then, Captain, your company here at the rail is neither wanted nor necessary. Go below."

"I have to confer with the captain about this," he blustered. "We have to turn around."

She glared at his soldiers. "Captain Romilard seems to feel it is appropriate to argue with me and countermand my direct order. Remove him from my sight."

The soldiers shuffled about, uncertain whether to obey their future queen or their leader. Ultimately they nudged Romilard, a remark was whispered in his ear, and they dragged him away and climbed the ladder into the hold.

The Princess was free to gaze at the wharf without interruption, to watch Phillippa Clementi growing smaller and smaller as the ship picked up speed. While Miss Clementi had been confident of her authority and power, she was swiftly losing her poise and cunning attitude. She was crying, begging not to be left behind.

Over and over, she beseeched her old friend Kat Webster, but only Princess Morovsky stared back.

&xo; &xo; &xo; &xo;

"I thought we'd travel to England together."

"Seriously?" Bryce glared at Chase in disgust. "After your part in this debacle, I wouldn't travel across the street with you."

"I realize you're angry," Chase said.

"You have no idea, Chase, and I suggest you drop the subject."

"If it's a question of funds, I'm happy to pay your fare."

"You'd pay my fare? With what? Your blood money from Pippa Clementi?"

"Why shouldn't I offer? You need to get home so we'd be putting it to good use. My purse is full of gold coins for once, and while I regret what I did to receive them, I'm not about to pretend I don't have them. That would be ridiculous."

Bryce scoffed. "I wish I had your ability to make excuses for my worst traits."

"What would you rather I do? Should I head to the market and toss them to the beggars? I won't. Nor will I continue to apologize for what occurred. The fiasco is over, so there's no point in hashing it out."

"No, there's not. Goodbye."

They were in Valois's courtyard where he'd confronted the Parthenian soldiers the previous day. Since then he'd hidden in his room so as to avoid any conversation with Chase.

He tried to walk on, and Chase said, "Where are you going?"

"To speak with Valois, to thank him for his assistance these past months, then I'm leaving."

"For England?"

"Yes, but not with you."

Chase sighed with exasperation. "You're being an ass, Bryce."

Bryce whipped around. "*I* am being an ass? Look in the mirror, Chase. Look in the mirror."

"What about the Princess and her siblings?" Chase asked.

"What about them?"

"Won't you follow after them?"

"To do what? Tell me that."

"To...to...rescue them?"

"Princess Morovsky was very clear. She has no desire to be rescued. She's marrying as her family has been demanding for ages. When the ceremony is over, she'll be a queen. What woman would hope to evade that fate? Not her, that's for certain."

"Oh." Chase fiddled with a button on his shirt. "Isabelle and Nicholas didn't want to go with those men. They fought quite vehemently. I think *they* would probably appreciate a rescue."

"Perhaps you should have considered that before you sold them for your thirty pieces of silver. Or was it gold? Yes, it was gold."

"So...just like that, we're splitting up?"

"Yes, Chase, just like that."

"Our Egyptian adventure is ending with a whimper."

"It definitely is," Bryce agreed.

"It started with such a bang. Remember how excited we were when we left London? Shouldn't we celebrate the conclusion? Shouldn't we toast or reminisce?"

"I'm busy, Chase, and you need to move out of this villa. After how you conspired with Miss Clementi, I can't believe Valois hasn't thrown you out."

Chase huffed with indignation. "You can't storm off in a snit. This entire mess involves naught more than some foreign females and their internal squabbling. You know better than to let a woman come between us."

"If that is what you presume this is about, you're more of an idiot than I ever suspected."

"You don't have to insult me."

"Then don't act like a dunce." Bryce's temper flared. He was struggling to tamp down his emotions, but he was hurt and livid and couldn't keep his frustration bottled up inside. "Kat and I were planning to wed!"

"You and the Princess?" Chase snorted with derision. "She never could have married you. Not if she's a royal. She wouldn't have stooped so low."

"Exactly, Chase. I assumed her affection was real, so I've been played for a fool by everyone. Including you, and you're supposed to be my best friend."

"Sorry."

"You're not, Chase. That's the problem. You've never been sorry for anything. Stop saying that you are."

"I hate that we're quarreling. Let me buy your ticket home, and we'll work it out on the way."

"I'm not interested. For now I'm too furious with you, but I expect I'll eventually calm down. You head for London, and I'll show up someday. We'll talk then."

Chase stared at Bryce, and he must have noted Bryce's irritation and resolve.

"I'm already packed," Chase said. "I'm leaving in an hour to catch a ferry to Alexandria. If you change your mind about accompanying me, I'll be in my room."

"I won't change my mind."

Bryce marched off, and thankfully Chase didn't call out a final time.

He wondered if he'd ever see Chase again. It was always dangerous to travel, dangerous to be on the high seas, crashing through the waves. No passenger could ever be sure he'd reach his destination. He probably should have glanced back, should have taken a last look just in case, but he didn't. He was too aggravated.

He went in search of the butler and was led to Valois. He was in his private garden, sitting at a table, drinking a glass of wine. He appeared cool and composed as ever, and if he was suffering any upset over the incident in his courtyard, there was no sign of it.

"Ah, my dear Bryce," he said as Bryce sat across from him, "the Earl of Radcliffe. How delighted I was to hear you proclaim your heritage yesterday. Your father would have been very glad."

"Fat lot of good it did me," Bryce grumbled.

"Your heart is broken," Valois commiserated like the Frenchman he was.

"I'll get over it."

"But she was worth it, wouldn't you agree?"

Bryce's feelings over his failed engagement were still too raw to explore. He wouldn't discuss Kat. And he definitely wouldn't parley over Princess Morovsky. It would be pointless.

"I'd rather not dither about what transpired."

Valois gave an elegant shrug of his shoulder, but he couldn't let it go. "It had to be hard to learn she would wed her cousin."

"It wasn't one of my better moments."

"I've met her cousin."

"Have you?"

"He's a pompous, incompetent dolt. I doubt his countrymen will allow him to have the throne for long."

"Really, Valois, I don't care about any of this."

"Yes, but might you be curious about some servant gossip?"

Bryce didn't want to ask, but he couldn't stop himself. "What gossip?"

"It seems our Princess was coerced into the marriage."

"She didn't seem all that coerced to me."

"No, you're wrong. Miss Clementi had the children kidnapped, and she told the Princess that—should she decline to come home—her brother would be killed."

"Killed!"

"Yes, and Kristof would marry her little sister instead."

"Isabelle is only ten. That's disgusting."

"Yes, isn't it? Princess Morovsky felt she had no choice but to comply."

"Everyone has choices. She could have refused."

"You saw her with her siblings. Can you actually suppose she would have abandoned them? Over the past year, she gave up everything in order to keep them safe from just this sort of eventuality."

Bryce squirmed in his chair. He was furious with Kat and wouldn't listen to any details that might excuse her behavior. She was an adult. She could have confided in him, and he would have helped her.

But no. She'd acceded to her cousin's demands, had let Miss Clementi torment and blackmail her, and she'd prepared to leave without a goodbye. If he hadn't stumbled on her when she was scurrying out, she'd have gone without his being apprised.

How could she justify such conduct? How could Bryce forgive her for it?

"I don't want to talk about it," he glumly stated.

"I realize that, but I hate to have you thinking badly of her. I knew her mother. She was a fine woman, trapped in awful circumstances."

"What awful circumstances?"

"She was an American and not cut out for life as a royal. She tried her best, but she was miserably unhappy. I imagine Katarina will be the same."

"She appeared eager to be a queen."

"No, she was putting on a brave front. It's what royals are taught to do, and don't forget I've met her cousin. No woman in the world would willingly marry him—even to be a queen."

"Don't try to make me feel sorry for her. It won't work."

"I'm sure it won't. You're much too level-headed to be swayed by romantic sentiment."

"Yes, and I'm too exhausted to be a knight in shining armor."

"I understand completely. I simply thought it would be wonderful if *someone* cared about what happens to her and her siblings. Not you of course but someone."

"Stop it, Valois. I'm departing for England, and I won't be traveling anywhere near Parthenia."

"Not if you sail, but if you rode cross country, it's an easy detour. Have you seen much of Europe? The Alps are beautiful this time of year."

"Stop it!" Bryce said more vehemently. "I won't be anyone's savior, and I most especially won't rescue a reluctant princess from her ivory tower. No matter how you harangue, you'll never convince me. It would be a fool's errand."

Yet even as he verbally refused to consider it, a small voice nagged, *Why not ride through Parthenia? Why not speak to her?*

What if Valois was correct? What if she was in desperate need of a rescue? What if she was looking over her shoulder, watching for Bryce and certain he would arrive? What if she kept watching, but he never did?

The questions fired in his mind, but he shoved them away.

He wouldn't be goaded into actions he didn't wish to take. He wouldn't let maudlin emotion spur him to recklessness. Even if he could help her, even if he could snatch her away from Parthenian, she could never wed him. She was a princess, which meant she was like an angel in Heaven. She could be adored and worshipped from afar, but that was it.

"I have a letter for you," Valois said, yanking him out of his despicable reverie.

"A letter? My goodness. What a marvelous surprise."

"I'm predicting it's from your sister."

"Evangeline! Finally."

While he'd been away from England, mail service had been sporadic and unreliable. In total he'd received exactly three letters, and none of them had been from people with whom he'd truly wanted to correspond.

Valois handed it over, waiting silently as Bryce broke the seal.

"Was I right?" Valois asked. "Is it from your sister?"

"Yes." Bryce skimmed the words, knowing he'd pour over it a thousand times in the coming days. As he reached the third paragraph, he paused and murmured, "Oh, my Lord."

He must have appeared stricken, because Valois frowned. "It's not bad news, I hope."

"No, no. I can't believe it. I just can't believe it."

"You're scaring me, Bryce. What has happened?"

Feeling pole-axed, Bryce stared up at Valois. "She's found my lost brothers. She's found the twins, Michael and Matthew."

"Both of them?"

"Yes."

"Oh, my Lord," Valois muttered too. "How? Where?"

"They've been hiding in plain sight. One is the owner of a notorious gambling club in London. He's something of a brigand, with a reputation for violence and deceit."

"A criminal? It should make for some interesting family suppers. Which one is this?"

"Michael."

"And the other?"

"Matthew is a captain in the King's army."

"How on earth would he have afforded it? He must have had a stable upbringing. Who provided it? Does she explain how he managed to climb so high?"

"No, she says she'll write more in subsequent letters, but she was excited for me to know immediately." He scanned down to the bottom. "She says she still has no information about Mother's current condition, but she learned Mother's ship arrived safely in Australia and she survived the journey."

"That's splendid, Bryce. I'm glad for you."

"So...she could be alive, as Evangeline always insisted."

Valois flashed an enigmatic smile. "Yes, she could definitely be alive."

Bryce sat back in his chair, and he sighed heavily as if a great weight had been lifted off his shoulders. "Matthew and Michael," he mused, as if trying out the names. "I've crossed paths with Michael once or twice. I've wagered in that gambling club he owns. He's a dark-haired, blue-eyed devil, renowned for his cunning, bravery, and obsessive drive to succeed."

"Just as your father was." Valois sighed too, as if charmed by the revelations. "This is all too impossible."

"Yes, and with how I stumbled on Evangeline last year, it's as if it was all meant to be. I told Evangeline to search for the twins, but I never actually thought she'd find them."

"I'm convinced your parents are watching over all of you."

"Yes, and if our luck continues, we'll locate Mother too."

Bryce rippled with an odd swell of emotions. He was impatient to be home so he could meet his brothers, but sad too that he couldn't tell Kat what had occurred. Over the past few weeks, they'd spent every second together. He'd gotten in the habit of discussing everything with her.

But Kat had never existed. She'd been a figment of Bryce's imagination, and while he hadn't been looking, Princess Morovsky had swooped in and taken Kat's place. Princess Morovsky was a stranger, an exotic foreigner, who had nothing in common with Bryce and who could never understand the simple pleasures of his small world.

Yet even as he tried to persuade himself that he and the Princess were too different, that little voice was back, reminding him it was a lie. Kat might have been a royal princess, but in the period he'd been with her, they'd been very close.

A terrifying prospect rattled him, one he'd conveniently forgotten in the hours since Kat had turned into the Princess.

They had rushed their wedding night, had made love several times, with Bryce expecting to wed her the next day. Had it dawned on her that she might arrive in Parthenia, deflowered and with someone else's child growing in her belly?

If she was increasing, she wouldn't be able to conceal it for long. When her condition was discovered, what would happen to her? By all accounts, her cousin was a fiend. If she couldn't marry him, what might he do to her? The answers to that question were frightening and vexing.

"I'm leaving for England, Valois. I have the wages I earned from protecting Princess Morovsky, so I'm in financial shape to travel."

"I know. My servants are very good at apprising me of every detail."

"You've helped me in incalculable ways."

Valois waved a dismissive hand. "It was no trouble."

"I'm very grateful to you."

"I'm honored I could be of service to Julian's son."

"I will always call you my friend," Bryce told him. "If you ever need anything, contact me. If I can provide it, I will."

"You're a fine man, Bryce. You father would be proud."

"Yes, I think he would be."

"On your journey home, will you reflect on reclaiming your title from your kin?"

"I probably will forge ahead. I'm starting to want it very much."

He was tired of being scorned for his lowly birth, of being viewed as an ordinary person, when in fact he was extraordinary. His parents were Anne and Julian Blair, his blue blood the best he could have received. He'd been born to be an earl, and it was an insult to his father's memory to deny it.

When he hid his status, he was complicit in his grandfather's dastardly sins. When he kept the truth from being revealed, he kept the man's crimes from being exposed.

In Bryce's opinion, one of his Scottish relatives could declare himself Earl of Radcliffe, but from here on out, Bryce would declare it too. If his cousins had a problem with that choice, they could tell him to be silent. And Bryce would tell them exactly what he thought too. He would tell them what he *knew*.

As if his father was suddenly present, he felt that comforting hand on his shoulder again, and for just a moment he shut his eyes and relished the sensation.

A vision stirred from when he was a tiny boy. His father had burst into their house after being so long away. He'd grabbed Bryce and thrown him up in the air.

"How's my little lord?" his father had asked. "Look how you've grown while I was away. You weren't supposed to grow!"

Bryce had laughed with joy, and the twins had been in the corner, laughing too. They were all Julian Blair's sons. The three of them would always make him proud.

His father's aura faded away, and Bryce gazed at Valois.

"I miss my Father," he said.

"Of course you do."

"When I was in school, many of my classmates were sons of aristocrats, and I wanted to be one too. I used to lie and insist my father was a prince."

Valois shrugged. "In many ways, he was. He certainly had all the required traits. You have them too."

"I know, and my thieving, duplicitous Scottish relatives had better watch out. The next time I visit Scotland, I'll have my brothers with me. We'll be unstoppable."

"I'm sure you will be. Will you write to me of your adventures? Will you inform me of how your story ends?"

"Yes, absolutely."

"And I hope you'll reconsider your route to England. A man can go by land or by sea, and I'm worried about Katarina. It would mean so much to me if you could check on her."

"Ooh, Valois, you don't play fair. With how gracious you've been, it's impossible to refuse you."

"You shouldn't refuse me. Whatever else Princess Morovsky is, she was also your friend, Kat Webster." Valois's smile was very sly. "What can it hurt, hmm? If you arrive and she is still Princess Morovsky, then you have done nothing but waste a few weeks in a beautiful part of Europe. But if she is Kat Webster, if she is the girl we knew here in Cairo..."

Bryce finished the sentence for him. "Then she'll need my help."

"Yes, and no matter what, her brother and sister need a champion. Why not you?"

Bryce hesitated, pondered, then threw up his hands. "Why not? Why the hell not?"

He penned a letter to his sister, advising her he was headed home, that he'd be traveling by horseback across Italy, with a quick trip into Parthenia, and coming the remainder of the way through France.

After settling on his itinerary, he borrowed a satchel from Valois, and it didn't take him long to pack. He strapped on his father's sword, then mounted one of Valois's horses to proceed into the city to the docks to hire a boat bound for Alexandria.

He probably should have stayed the night, should have left in the morning, but with his deciding to go, he couldn't bear a minute of delay.

He rode out of the villa, a servant trotting with him who would return to the villa with both horses once Bryce booked his passage.

He studied the hectic street, absorbing the sights and smells, eager to imprint the busy details into his memory so he'd never forget. He'd trekked to Egypt because he'd been adrift and depressed. He'd wanted to follow in his father's footsteps, to find some of the man in himself. With Valois's assistance, he'd achieved that and much more.

He grinned, finally feeling—now that he was about to depart the country—that he was glad he'd come, glad he'd dared.

Suddenly there was a loud bang. His horse shied, its hooves slipping on the cobbles. Valois's other horse raced by, its rider unseated.

Bryce peered back, figuring the servant must have fallen, but the man was lying on the ground, blood pouring from his chest.

People had gathered, and they were shouting and pointing.

"What happened?" Bryce called in English, then he repeated the question in Arabic, but over the raucous noise, they couldn't hear him.

It looked as if the servant had been shot or stabbed, and as Bryce pulled his horse around to nudge the crowd out of the way, he was hit very hard from behind.

He tried to shift in the saddle to learn who had assaulted him, but before he could react, he was struck again. His arms went limp, and he dropped the reins. A third blow knocked him out of the saddle, and he couldn't stop his descent.

He landed with a painful thud, and though he ordered himself to rise, to protect himself, he simply couldn't move. Was he dead? He didn't believe so. He could still see the surging horde of passersby, could still hear their strident voices.

Soon a man was hovered over him, and he was wearing the vest and trousers favored by the Parthenians.

He leaned in very close and spoke in French. "Dirty dog, we have been waiting for you to exit the villa so we could kill you."

Bryce answered in French. "I'm too tough to die. I'm the son of Julian Blair. A cur like you could never harm me."

"We'll see what we can do," the man threatened. "I'm thinking death would be too easy for you. I have a better plan. We'll see how you like it. We'll see if you are too tough to die."

Again Bryce ordered himself to stand, to fight, but he seemed paralyzed, his body unable to obey a single command.

Rough hands lifted him, and his wrists and ankles were trussed. Then he was tossed into the bed of a cart. His attacker jumped in after him, and it took a moment for Bryce to realize the villain had his eyes on Bryce's sword, that he intended to steal it. He withdrew a large knife and sliced through the leather, claiming the remarkable weapon for his own.

"I have admired this for many days," the brigand crowed. "It will rest more comfortably on my hip than yours. Thank you, Monsieur, for this very fine gift."

"You can't have it, you filthy swine," Bryce managed to spit out. "It was my father's."

"Well, it is mine now, and you needn't fret. I will always cherish it."

He laughed and leapt to the ground. He marched to the front, the vehicle swaying as he climbed onto the seat and grabbed the reins. The animal pulled away, and Bryce vanished as quickly and quietly as if he'd never been there at all.

CHAPTER NINETEEN

"I'm delighted by your return."

Kristof smiled at Katarina, but she didn't smile back.

"I didn't have a choice," she curtly said. "Let's not pretend."

"Of course you had a choice," Kristof smoothly replied. "You're Katarina Morovsky. There's no one to tell you what you can and can't do."

"Yes, all right. Pretend if you wish."

Dmitri piped up from the corner. "The whole country is glad."

She leveled a glare at Dmitri that was so cutting Kristof was taken aback by it. He'd never seen her glower that way. She possessed a new aura of power and authority he didn't recall witnessing before. What could have occurred during her time away to render such a change?

Kristof was suddenly half-afraid of her, and Dmitri appeared stunned.

She whipped her gaze to Kristof and hissed, "I will not converse with you when that traitor is in here with us."

"I can't leave," Dmitri insisted. "There are too many matters we must discuss."

She continued to stare at Kristof. "You are king, and I am soon to be queen. Must we suffer the rude interruptions of a servant I can't abide?"

Dmitri sputtered with affront, but tamped down whatever comment he'd planned. He scowled at Katarina, obviously wondering—as Kristof was—how she'd become a fuming virago.

"Dmitri," Kristof said, "why don't you step out for a bit? Katarina has only just arrived. I'm sure she's exhausted from her trip."

"I'm not tired," she declared. "I simply will not bother to address your low-born cousin. Nor has he my permission to talk to me."

Dmitri was too confident of his position with Kristof to depart. "The men who escorted you from Cairo inform me that you abandoned Miss Clementi in Egypt. She was in service to the Crown while bringing you home, and the situation can't go unremarked."

Katarina cocked her head as if Dmitri was a gnat buzzing by her ear. She rose to her feet, looking furious and omnipotent, as if she were an ancient Olympian goddess and destroyer of worlds.

"Were you speaking to me, Dmitri Romilard?" she asked in a snide voice. "How dare you, sir! I am certain I just demanded you excuse yourself from my presence."

Dmitri glanced helplessly at Kristof, visually begging for him to intervene, but Kristof was disturbed by her display of temper. In all the years he'd known Katarina, she'd been kind and cordial. Nothing had ever ruffled her. Nothing had ever enraged her. She was a mediator and problem-solver who hated to bicker.

Her calm, composed nature was the reason it had been so easy to shove her brother off the throne. She was so damned *nice*. She hadn't understood how to wage a battle, let alone win it.

"Dmitri," Kristof said, "give us a few minutes, would you?"

"I won't," Dmitri huffed. "Am I your chief advisor or not? She can't stroll in here and treat me this way."

Katarina advanced on him, approaching until they were toe to toe. Dmitri was several inches taller than she was, but somehow she seemed larger.

"I will count to ten," she seethed. "If you are not gone from my sight, I shall call for the guards and have you dragged away."

Dmitri bristled with dislike, but wisely shut his mouth. He likely realized there would be plenty of opportunities in the future to get even with her, to get and keep the upper hand, but this moment wasn't one of them.

He marched out, his anger barely in check. Katarina was frozen in place until he'd exited, then she went to her chair and sat as if naught had happened.

She stared innocently at Kristof, her burst of indignation completely concealed. The abrupt alteration in her character was so disorienting he felt dizzy.

He'd expected meek, compliant Katarina to return from Egypt. He'd expected to deal with the same woman who'd left so many months earlier. But this was a stranger he had no idea how to coerce or bully.

They were in his private solar, with Katarina and her escort of guards having just ridden through the palace gates. They'd brought her to him immediately, with Kristof wanting to confer with her before anyone else had a chance.

She had to grasp how vital it was that she be viewed as widely as possible. He had parades, suppers, and festivals arranged in her honor. The rumors that she'd been murdered, that Kristof was her killer, had never died down, and he had to explain the gossip, had to convince her to agree it was silly, that the stories had to be quelled for the good of the nation.

She had to appear happy to be back, happy to be marrying Kristof, and she couldn't exhibit the slightest hint that there was any duress on Kristof's part.

He would make all sorts of promises, but she had to remember that the safety of her brother and sister was her responsibility. Should she betray him in even the tiniest fashion, her siblings would pay the price.

"I apologize for that unpleasantness." He pulled up a chair and sat directly across from her. "Dmitri can be exasperating."

She ignored his amiable overture, pushing him off balance again.

"I'm weary from my journey," she said, "and I was not permitted to wash or change before I was delivered to you." "That's because I was so eager to see you. I had you conveyed to my chambers at once."

"What is it you are so anxious to tell me?"

"I'm glad you're back."

"Fine. May I be excused?"

"In a minute."

He frowned. She wasn't normally rude, wasn't a grouch or a grumbler. Yet she was oozing blatant disdain. Perhaps she was as weary as she claimed. He couldn't imagine what else would be creating such an alteration of her personality.

He walked over and poured himself a goblet of wine. Without asking if she'd like one, he poured one for her too. She took it and gulped down the entire contents. It was another new trait. She'd always sipped wine like the noblewoman she was, a few dainty swallows and no more than that. Had she become a drunkard while she was away?

"When is our wedding scheduled to be held?" she inquired.

"Three months from today."

"Why must we delay? I'd rather get it over with." "It's a royal event, Katarina, the first in the palace in thirty years. There are plans to be made, food to be ordered, invitations to be sent, and I couldn't begin until you arrived."

"It's autumn already. In three months, it will be winter, and the mountain passes will be closed. Maybe we should put it off until spring."

A muscle ticked in Kristof's cheek. He couldn't abide any postponement for he couldn't give this snide, powerful Katarina too many chances to evade his marital noose. There would be a constant risk she might vanish again or that she'd change her mind or muster supporters.

He would be delighted to proceed immediately, but he'd been waiting his whole life to be king. He'd dared to seize the throne, to take what he'd always dreamed of having, and he wanted the royal wedding that was his due. He wanted nobles from other countries to attend, wanted to establish himself as a monarch to be esteemed.

If he had a hasty, secret ceremony, there would be no pomp, no grandeur. He'd remain the overlooked, pathetic king of a tiny principality no one cared about and no one respected.

He'd received letters from some other monarchs, and they weren't letters of congratulations. They were angry with Kristof, and the world was an unstable place. None of them liked to have a ruler deposed. It made them nervous. It made them worry the same thing could happen to them.

But Nicholas was a boy, and Kristof would be a much better king. He had to host an impressive spectacle so he'd be observed in all his regal splendor. It was the only way to ensure he was recognized as having been right to stage the coup.

"Let me think on this." He tried to sound magnanimous, but with how she was glaring, it was difficult to project much supremacy. "I will notify you tomorrow whether it will be in three months or whether we will wait until spring."

"I will be on pins and needles until then." Was that sarcasm? "There is one other matter we must address."

"What is it?"

"I've arranged a series of honorary gatherings."

"For what purpose."

"To welcome you back. You and your siblings of course." "Oh, of course."

"We'll ride out together every morning."

"To do what?"

"To allow the public to see the three of you." "Why? Don't claim the citizenry has been missing us. I'll never believe you."

Kristof's cheeks flushed bright red. "Well, there has been some gossip since you left."

"Gossip about what?"

"People were a tad concerned over your condition."

"Over my condition?"

"Yes."

"It was no great mystery. I can't stand that we have no friends in this country where my family has ruled for centuries. Why would we have stayed?"

"No one knew your reasoning, so your disappearance seemed odd."

Katarina scowled, then she laughed maliciously. "They thought you killed us?"

"As I said, there was gossip."

"That *you* killed us specifically? I was wondering why you were so desperate to get us back."

He smiled a tight smile. "I wasn't desperate. My advisors simply decided it might be best if you and I wed. They felt it would generate a sense of stability."

"*And* show you hadn't murdered me." She laughed again, then stood to go. "I'll play your game, Kristof. I'll let you parade me around, and I'll grin and wave and pretend I'm glad to be home."

He rose too, irked that she would sashay out before he gave her permission. She'd always been too independent, but she was about to have a husband, and suddenly he was exhausted at the prospect of how much training he would have to provide so she would be a proper wife.

"All I ask, Katarina, is that you comport yourself as the royal consort you were born to be."

"I can do that, but the instant my brother or sister is imperiled, I will murder you in your sleep."

He sucked in a sharp breath. "I will tell myself you're tired so you didn't realize your comment might be viewed as a threat."

"Yes, I'm tired. Where are my brother and sister? Are they here?"

"Yes, they're here."

"I'll be in my rooms. Have them sent to me at once."

"I'll inform the servants."

She sidled over to the door and opened it herself. The servants on the other side snapped to attention.

She glanced back at him. "Don't forget what I said about Nicholas and Isabelle. If I'm ever worried about them..."

There were dozens of courtiers in the outer chamber, so she didn't finish her sentence. Instead she furtively motioned with her finger, indicating she'd slit his throat if he wasn't careful.

She whipped away and left, and he gestured to the servants to shut the doors, to conceal him from all those prying eyes.

He was watched every second, and where in the beginning it had been thrilling, with all of them agog over his daring, now they simply whined about his missteps and mistakes, about how he wasn't as fearsome or awe-inspiring as they'd assumed.

He sank down in his chair, his head in his hands, fretting over how he'd control Katarina, how he'd keep her sufficiently frightened so she'd act as was required.

Dmitri stomped in, and he marched over, nagging, "How could you let her speak to me that way?"

"How could I stop her?"

"You're her king, and you'll soon be her husband."

If she doesn't kill me in my sleep first.

"What happened to her while she was away?" Kristof asked.

"What do you mean?"

"She's powerful and angry. She seems very different. I'm alarmed by her."

"Don't be," Dmitri said. "She'll settle in and remember her place. If she doesn't behave herself, I'll deal with her."

Kristof wasn't sure any of them knew how anymore. Katarina had abandoned Pippa on the dock in Alexandria, and there'd been no word from her. Once they'd landed in Italy, Captain Romilard had sent two men back to Egypt to search for her, but there'd been no trace.

Katarina and Pippa had been friends practically since their days in the cradle. If Katarina would be so cruel to Pippa, if she would revenge herself in such a dastardly manner, were any of them safe from her wrath?

He was almost trembling with concern, but he refused to have Dmitri notice. He went to the sideboard and poured himself another glass of wine. He drank it down, then drank another too, continuing until the shaking in his hands wasn't visible.

      ⊰⊱   ⊰⊱   ⊰⊱   ⊰⊱

Bryce held very still, the noose around his neck cutting into his skin. The slavers to whom he'd been delivered had grown weary of fighting him, and he was completely restrained. There were shackles on his wrists and ankles, his body wrapped in chains, his arms pinned to his side so he couldn't lash out as they walked by.

But it was the noose that was most vexing. If he moved the slightest inch, it had a special knot that tightened imperceptibly. Gradually it was strangling him, and he had to give them credit for the crafty device. It had definitely curbed his more violent impulses.

He didn't know where he was, but he was fairly certain he wasn't in Cairo. He'd been beaten nearly to death by the Parthenians who'd attacked him, had been unconscious for a lengthy period, though he wasn't positive how long. When he'd awakened, he'd been dumped into the sludge in the hull of a boat with rats nibbling at his toes.

He was unwell, sweltering with fever, likely from drinking fetid water. If he eventually discovered he was dying of typhus, he wouldn't be surprised. His arm was probably broken, a couple of ribs too. One of his eyes was swelled shut, and there were oozing gashes on his back where he'd been flogged.

After being dragged to a slave market, he was on the block and about to be sold to the highest bidder. Yet he hadn't gone quietly to his fate. He'd battled to the last, which had simply left him injured and starved.

Who would dare to purchase him? He had to be a ferocious sight, wounded, aggrieved, fettered, and eager to commit mayhem.

Standing out in the open as he was, the tropical sun beating down, it was harder and harder to focus. He kept drifting in and out of consciousness, but each time he faded away, his body would slump and the garrote on his neck would constrict and yank him awake.

He didn't think he could survive much more, didn't think it was possible for a person to endure all that he'd endured. Vaguely he thought about Chase, curious if he'd departed for England. Bryce recalled his beautiful country, the cool, rainy weather, the vibrant greens of the fields and trees, and he wondered if that was what Heaven would be like.

Had Valois learned what had happened to Bryce? Bryce, himself, wasn't too clear. He'd been riding down a street, headed for the docks to leave Cairo, but disaster had struck. Was Valois looking for Bryce? Was anyone aware that Bryce was missing? Or would Valois assume he'd perished?

Why search for a dead man?

Mostly he reminisced about Kat Webster. Where was she? How was she? He didn't spend a single second pondering Princess Morovsky. No, he reflected on the Kat he'd known and loved for such a brief interlude. He reflected on the lonely woman who'd been trying to protect her siblings from her horrid family.

Occasionally during his tormented dreams, he'd fantasize about the wedding they might have had. He pictured them in the cathedral in London, his sister, brothers, and friends applauding as the organ blared.

He pictured them at Radcliffe Castle, with Bryce as earl and Kat his countess. He liked to envision himself traveling the Scottish countryside, meeting the tenants, proving that he was Julian Blair's son, that he belonged at Radcliffe.

In his mind, it was such an idyllic portrait, and it supplied enormous succor when he was rambling and delirious. Did Kat ever wish she'd made a different choice? Did she ever think of him?

He scoffed. Of course she didn't ever think of him. Everyone in the world made choices, and she'd made hers. It hadn't included him.

He snorted with disgust, the tiny move tightening the noose, jerking him to reality. The bidding had just ended on a group of females who appeared to be a trio of sisters. They were urged off the dais, sticks slapping to hurry them away.

Then it was Bryce's turn.

The noose was tugged away, but not the chains. An auctioneer called out to the crowd, but he spoke in a language Bryce didn't understand. He wasn't exactly sure what was being said, but he figured his strong torso and large physique were mentioned.

A slaver circled Bryce, poking at him with a cane as if he was a bear at a baiting. Each jab on his hot, fevered skin was like a lightning bolt striking his temper, and it dawned on him he might not survive until morning.

He grew angrier and angrier, and his fury must have been evident to the spectators. They were whispering, shaking their heads, and fleetingly he wondered—if no one bought him—would he be killed when the auction was over?

He hoped so. He really and truly could not continue. It would be such a blessing to close his eyes and never open them again.

The auctioneer uttered a remark that had people snickering, and the slaver prodded Bryce's genitals so they must have been discussing another sort of ability. Would they mate him with slave women? Would he be purchased as a stud for someone's slave stables?

A man stepped forward and entered the bidding, and from his clothes and mannerisms, it was clear he had designs on Bryce that were perverted in nature. Two others, who also looked debauched, started driving up the price.

A woman began to bid, and she seemed determined to acquire him. The cost went up and up, but since Bryce didn't know the language, he couldn't guess how much was being offered. He yanked on the chains, straining, trying to break free. The crowd gestured and shouted as if they were at a zoo and the lion about to jump the fence.

The slaver beat him, and several others rushed over to join in. They whipped and yelled, people throwing objects. At some point, he was knocked out, and what transpired after that he couldn't imagine.

When he awoke, he was on a boat again, but not in the hull with the rats. He was lying on a bed, on a feather mattress with crisp, clean sheets that had a lovely scent he'd never smelled prior. He was floating in a white beam of sunshine, and everything was bright white: the air, the blankets, the walls and rugs and curtains. Out the window, he could see he was on a river, but he had no idea which river it might be. It too was white, as was the foliage on the white banks.

It was very quiet, very peaceful, and he was so content. Was he in Heaven? Had he died? If so, it was safe, calm, and beautiful. He recalled that his body had been wrecked by much brutal battering, but he felt no pain. He felt nothing at all except an abiding happiness.

He glanced over, and his father was sitting in a chair, silently observing Bryce. He was dressed in tan trousers and a flowing white shirt, knee-high black boots, a jaunty red kerchief tied around his throat. He was young, handsome, physically commanding. His black hair was pulled into a ponytail, his blue, blue eyes studying Bryce, missing no detail.

"There you are," his father said. "I was hoping you'd rouse before I had to go."

"Am I dead?"

"No, it's not time yet. Not for many, many years."

"Where am I?" Bryce asked. "How did I get here?"

His father didn't answer, and he seemed to be fading away, his form not as distinct as it had been.

"I'm sorry I couldn't be with you when you were a boy," his father said, "but I always watched over you as best I could."

"I know."

"I'll keep watching over you. Don't ever be afraid."

His shape was becoming fainter by the second, and Bryce panicked. "Don't leave."

"I have to. I can't stay."

"Take me with you," Bryce begged, wanting to be with his father forever, to walk off with him into the serene white light.

"You can't come." His father's smile was kind, reassuring. "You still have an important task to complete."

"What is it? What must I do?"

"Tell your mother I'm waiting for her on the other side. I'll be the first one to greet her when she arrives."

Then he vanished, and Bryce drifted off. As he revived, his mother was there, tending him. She was leaned over him, swabbing his face with a cool cloth.

"Mother?" he gasped.

"Yes, Bryce."

"Father was here." "I know."

"Where have you been?"

"In Australia, you silly boy."

"Are you alive? Am I? Are we in Heaven?"

"No."

"Father is waiting for you there."

"I know," she said again.

"Am I dying?" he asked. "Do you think I will?"

"Not if I can help it. Rest now. Don't talk. Just rest."

He smelled her perfume, the delicious scent of roses filling the air as he drifted off yet again. He suffered in fevered dreams, seeing deceased relatives and friends, seeing strange and frightening sights. Often he was hovering outside his body, trying to join his father in the light, but something kept pulling him back.

Kat...

The name slithered by.

When he opened his eyes, his head was pounding, his throat parched. He moved his arm the slightest inch, and he groaned with pain, agony shooting through his whole torso down to the smallest pore.

So...he wasn't in Heaven anymore. He wasn't hovering between Heaven and Earth. He was alive and injured and ill. But...he sensed he was better than he had been, that he'd turned a corner or had stumbled out of a very dark forest.

He was in a different bed, the white light gone, the white décor replaced with very typical Cairo cottons and silks. He glanced over, yearning with all his heart for his father to still be there, but instead Valois was sitting in the chair.

"Hello, my friend." Valois's crisp French accent was a welcome sound.

"Where am I?" Bryce inquired.

"In my villa. Where would you suppose?"

"How did that happen?"

"My men and I rescued you, with some fine assistance from Mr. Hubbard."

Bryce scowled, struggling in a weary fog to recollect what had occurred. "I was sold as a slave."

"Yes." Valois grinned. "I own you now. You cost me an exorbitant price too, but I'm happy to sign papers setting you free. You won't have to work as my houseboy."

Chase suddenly appeared, and he took Bryce's hand in his own.

"You scared the devil out of us," Chase said.

"Why?"

"Because we thought you'd passed away a half-dozen times."

"I always told you I'm too tough to die."

"Well, you didn't have to stroll out to the edge of mortality and prove it to me."

Chase eased away, and Bryce gazed over at Valois again.

"Am I better? Will I survive?"

"My Moorish healer tells me your infections are mending and your fever vanquished. But you will be weak and tired for a very long while."

Bryce frowned, a memory creeping in. "I have to do something important."

Valois laughed. "Not for a bit, I'm afraid. You'll be too frail for anything but rest and recuperation."

Bryce was quiet, the short burst of conversation exhausting him. He dozed, and when he roused again, Chase was gone, but Valois was still there, seated in his chair, watching over Bryce like a devoted nanny.

"I saw my father," Bryce said.

"When?"

"When I was ill."

"Then you were close to death's door indeed."

"And my mother..." Bryce stopped, pondered. "Was she here? Was she nursing me?"

"No, but I have frequently smelled her perfume as I visited your sickroom."

"I'll live? You're sure?"

"Very sure."

Bryce slept and didn't awaken again for days.

CHAPTER TWENTY

"It's like something out of a fairy tale."

Evangeline sighed. She was on her horse outside Radcliffe Castle. It was a castle, a real castle with turrets and ivy and battlements.

Michael and Matthew were with her, mounted too, flanking her, letting her take the lead as they rode through the gates.

She'd tried to remain in England, to have the twins handle the situation. But once she heard about Susan Blair giving them a copy of her Last Will and Testament, it had been impossible to continue twiddling her thumbs in London.

Lady Susan was Evangeline's aunt, and to Evangeline's astonishment, Susan was bequeathing all her jewels to Evangeline. They were family pieces that should have ultimately belonged to Evangeline's mother if she'd ever become countess.

Evangeline was extremely shocked by the gesture. The twins said their Aunt Susan was dying, that she was remorseful for her part in what had been done to Evangeline's parents.

The twins were dubious about human nature, skeptical about human motives, so they weren't the optimists Evangeline had grown up to be. They insisted Susan was a devout Catholic and terrified of being condemned to Hell. They saw her change of heart as a cheap and convenient ploy to worm her way through the Pearly Gates, and they were disgusted by it.

Evangeline didn't care why Susan had finally declared her misdeeds. She was just glad it had transpired before the woman had taken her secrets to the grave.

"Shall we go in?" she asked her brothers.

"Absolutely," they said in unison, and Michael added, "They're expecting you. I don't know that you're welcome, but they were informed you'd be here."

"Will we shout out parents' names?" she inquired.

"We already have," Matthew said, "but you can too if it makes you feel better."

She kicked her horse into a trot and entered the yard. As she reined in, she didn't shout the names but whispered, "My parents were Anne and Julian Blair. I have come to reclaim what was stolen from them."

It was a juvenile announcement, but she grinned, delighted to have uttered it.

The twins were correct that she'd been expected. People rushed out to get a look at her, and they gawked as if she was visiting royalty. They nervously studied her, but she had a knack for putting others at ease.

She'd always been able to, and she'd learned lately that it was a trait inherited from her mother, who'd been dynamic and charismatic.

She smiled as if she *was* royalty, as if she was a princess arriving, and the crowd smiled in return, waved, curtsied, and doffed their caps. Boys dashed from the stable, tussling to tend her horse, to help her dismount. But her brothers dismounted first, and they assisted her.

They'd been in Scotland for over a month, telling everyone the tragic tale of Anne and Julian Blair. The locals had accepted the truth, and Susan Blair had publically confessed. Only George Blair was holding out, refusing to admit his sins and crimes, but Evangeline wasn't surprised.

He'd wanted to be Earl of Radcliffe so badly that he'd likely committed murder so it would happen. A man that obsessed would never willingly relinquish what he'd pilfered. It would have to be pried from his greedy, cloying grasp.

Evangeline swept into the castle, and the servants were lined up on both sides of the hall. The butler and housekeeper introduced themselves, pointing out the other high level servants. Then the twins escorted her to the end where a woman waited. She was about Evangeline's age, pretty and kind-looking.

"Greetings, Lady Run," she said to Evangeline.

"Hello." Evangeline smiled her most charming smile.

"I'm Katherine Blair. I believe we're distant cousins."

"Lovely," Evangeline responded. "I'm always thrilled to stumble upon another member of my family." "Your Uncle George won't meet with you, but your Aunt Susan has asked that I bring you to her at once."

"I'm so glad she's agreed to see me."

"She was very gratified that you decided to make the trip."

Katherine guided Evangeline to a winding staircase. They climbed quickly and quietly, with Evangeline trying to take in the details. There would be time later for a slower viewing, but the walls were covered with ancient tapestries, paintings of ancestors, and even a few sets of armor discreetly tucked into corners.

HEART'S DEMAND

They walked down a hall and stopped at a closed door.

"She's failing rapidly," Katherine murmured, "and she tires easily."

"I understand. Will she be awake, do you suppose?"

"Yes, she's actually having one of her better days. She's excited that you wanted to speak with her."

They entered, tiptoeing, and the twins stayed outside, two stern, stoic sentries guarding her, keeping her uncle away while Evangeline talked to her aunt.

The room was dark, the windows shuttered, a candle burning on the table. Katherine led her over to the bed.

"Susan," Katherine said, "Lady Run is here." When she received no reply, she added, "It's Anne's daughter. She's finally arrived."

There was still no answer, and for a fraught moment, Evangeline worried the poor woman had died, but no, the blankets rose with her staggered breathing.

There were chairs by the bed, evidence of a lengthy vigil, and Katherine gestured to them. They sat, comfortable in each other's company, and eventually Susan opened her eyes. She was skin and bone, most of her hair having fallen out. She'd once been affianced to Evangeline's father, had once been a beauty, but there was no hint of beauty now.

"Katherine, how long was I asleep?"

"Not long."

Susan noticed Evangeline, and she gasped. "I'm sorry, Anne. I'm so sorry. Will you lift the curse? Will you let me pass away in peace?"

Katherine reached over and patted Susan's hand. "You're confused, Susan. This isn't Anne Blair. Anne is deceased, remember? This is her daughter, Evangeline Drake, Lady Run."

Susan's vision was cloudy, focused on Evangeline but peering right through her. "I was young and foolish, vain and proud. My father-in-law harmed you and your children, and I was silent during your entire ordeal. I shouldn't have been silent! It was wrong of me."

"Susan," Katherine tried again. "This isn't Anne. It's her daughter."

Evangeline pulled her chair nearer. "Aunt Susan, I'm Evangeline. I am your niece."

Susan scowled, assessed Evangeline. "You're not...Anne? Are you sure?"

"I'm very sure."

"You look just like her. There's not a shred of difference." "I'll take that as a great compliment."

"She cursed me in London after her trial. She said none of my dreams would come true, and none of them have."

Evangeline had no idea how to respond so she mumbled, "That's too bad."

"I planned to speak with her in Heaven, but I couldn't find her."

The comment made no sense, and Katherine whispered to Evangeline, "She floats in and out. She talks to people who aren't really there."

"I saw Julian—off in the distance," Susan claimed. "I tried to catch him, to apologize, but he was moving too fast. Anne wasn't with him. Is she still alive? Is she still here on Earth? George always insisted she was dead."

"I don't know if she's alive, Aunt Susan," Evangeline said. "I'm hoping she is. I'm searching for her."

"If you see her, tell her she has to lift the curse. Please tell her!"

"I will."

"Tell her I'm sorry and that I've confessed my sins."

"I will," Evangeline said again.

Susan seemed to deflate, and she relaxed. She was quiet, staring at nothing, observing sights Evangeline couldn't imagine. Ultimately she turned and studied Evangeline very meticulously.

"I thought you were named after your mother. I thought your name was Anne too."

"It was, but it was changed when I was little."

"Were you all right when you were growing up? Were you warm? Did you have enough to eat? Were people kind to you?"

"People were very kind." For the most part it was true. "I'm married now, Aunt, to a marvelous man."

"Who is it?"

"Aaron Drake, of the Sidwell Drakes. His father is Lord Sidwell, and my husband is Viscount Run. Are you acquainted with them?"

"No, but you married very high."

"Yes, I did."

"You deserved to marry high."

"I'm glad you think so."

Susan sighed. "I didn't wreck everything."

"No, not at all. My brothers are all fine too. We all survived. We all thrived in our own ways."

"I was jealous of your mother, and I was so angry with your father that he wouldn't wed me. I was eager to hurt him. I committed some horrible sins because of it, but I've admitted my complicity."

"I wanted to thank you for that," Evangeline said. "It's why I traveled to Scotland. I wanted to meet you and thank you in person."

"Your brother should inherit Radcliffe. It should have been his all along."

"Yes, I know."

"Make it happen." Susan sounded desperate and distressed. "Make sure it passes to him."

"I'm determined to make sure."

Susan drifted off, and they waited many minutes, but she didn't awaken, and Evangeline wondered how many more times her aunt would open her eyes before they closed forever.

Katherine gestured to the door, and Evangeline slipped out, saddened by all that had been lost.

Susan Blair was Evangeline's aunt, and Evangeline had such a tiny family. Her husband. Her father-in-law and brother-in-law. Bryce and the twins.

What would it have been like if Susan and George Blair had never destroyed her parents? What if Anne and Julian had ruled at Radcliffe? What if there had been weddings and anniversaries and christenings and holidays spent playing with cousins?

Instead it had been treachery and malice that brought about the most vindictive conduct imaginable. It was all such a waste, such a ridiculous, pointless, heart-breaking waste. Could there be justice? Could there be happiness in the end?

Evangeline vowed to obtain both.

&c&&c&&c&&c&

"Why tell them? What possessed you?"

George glared down at Susan where she lay dying in her bed. If she'd kept her mouth shut a few more days, a few more hours, no one would have ever discovered what George and his father had perpetrated.

Anne had brashly intended to file a claim against Radcliffe on behalf of her oldest son, Bryce. George's father had warned her not to, had bullied and pressured her to butt out, but she'd demanded her children receive what George and his father would never have let them receive.

If she'd behaved as she'd been commanded, if she'd accepted the bribe she'd been offered, she wouldn't have had to suffer a single moment of difficulty. But no. She'd threatened to go to the newspapers, to hire lawyers, to speak with peers who'd known Julian and who might have assisted her in fighting the Blair family.

She hadn't understood the tidal wave of hatred bearing down on her until it was much too late for her to move out of the way.

He asked his question to Susan again. "Why tell them? Why couldn't you leave it alone?"

Susan roused and flinched with alarm. Since she'd delivered her declaration to Michael and Matthew Blair, she'd kept her door locked so he couldn't come in and beat her for her betrayal. For once Katherine was out of the room, Susan unattended, and George had snuck up the rear stairs without being observed.

"How did you get in?" Susan inquired.

"It's my property, and it will be mine until the day I die. If I decide to enter your room, or any room, I shall."

"Katherine!" she called, but she had no vigor to muster any volume.

"She can't help you now."

"I'm not scared of you," she blustered.

"You're not? In your weakened state, I could wrap my fingers around your throat for a few seconds and I'd be shed of you." "I've confessed my sins. I'm not afraid of death. How about you, George? Aren't you afraid? I'll be in Heaven. Where will you be?"

"Shut up."

"I won't. Can't you feel the Devil licking at your heels? Or is it Julian's ghost, here for revenge? I see him whenever I close my eyes. He's nearby, George, and he's waiting for a chance to strike. You'd better watch out."

"Shut up!" he said more vehemently. Cruelly he added, "I never wanted to marry you."

It wasn't precisely true. As a young bachelor, he'd been ecstatic to wed her, to bind himself to the beautiful heiress Julian had refused. But in his current aggrieved condition, he was keen to hurt her.

"I never wanted to marry you either," she replied.

"You swore to love, honor, and obey." "And I always have. Years ago, you ordered me to be silent, and I *was* silent until I began choking on all your lies."

"You told Julian's sons what we did."

"I made a clean breast of it, and I'll go to my grave with a clear conscience."

"That's awfully convenient for you, isn't it?"

"Why would you say so?"

"You eagerly and enthusiastically participated in my ruining Anne Blair, then for three decades, you enjoyed all the fruits of our conspiracy. Each and every day, you were rich and pampered, sitting in the seat that should have been hers, flaunting the jewels and title and status that should have been hers. You put your sons in the positions her sons should have held. I never heard you complaining."

"I was wrong to harm Anne. *We* were wrong. At least I have had the courage to admit it. What about you, brother-killer? How will you explain yourself when you meet your Maker?"

He whipped away and went to the window to stare down into the yard. He was on the opposite side of the building so he couldn't see what he was anxious to see.

Several official-looking men had ridden in with the twins. George had gotten only a quick glimpse of the visitors, but he thought it was the sheriff and the magistrate. The twins had insisted they'd sought an arrest warrant for George, but he hadn't believed them. He'd assumed they were trying to rattle him, but they didn't understand his resolve.

They weren't even Scots, and George was a peer. How could they move against him? Why would anyone listen to them?

Since his encounter with them in the forest a few days earlier, he'd been in hiding, mailing fretful letters, begging for support to fight the twins' allegations, but George had never had many friends and hadn't received a single reply. Even his lawyer in Edinburgh had failed to respond.

"You're terribly jumpy, George," Susan snidely said. "Why? Is Julian's ghost breathing down your neck?"

He whirled around and marched to the bed. "Some men have arrived."

"Oh, good. I've been waiting for them."

"Who are they?"

"I don't know who all is coming, but I'm giving sworn testimony."

"About what?"

"About you. What would you suppose? It's only fitting that Julian's oldest son recoup the title you stole from him. I plan to tell them everything—under oath."

"You witch," he fumed. "How can you consider it? You, who pretends to be so pious. You, who promised in our wedding vows to obey me."

"I guess I've reached the limit of what I can abide."

"I'll be charged with murder! I'll be hanged! I'm your husband, and you'll be condemning me to the gallows!"

"I'm sorry, George, but I'm dying, and I really don't care what happens to you after I'm gone."

A strand of rage snapped inside him. He grabbed a pillow and crushed it over her face, being perfectly happy to send her on her way a bit sooner than the Lord intended. He pressed down, elation surging through him that he was finally taking action, finally reversing the futile course he'd been on since the twins had brazenly entered his castle and asserted it was their own.

Though gravely ill, she was stronger than he'd suspected she'd be. She fought back like a madwoman, clawing with her fingers, her nails raking the skin on his wrists and hands. He was so swept up in the moment that at first he didn't detect Katherine behind him, but she sounded very shocked.

"George! What are you doing?"

He was in a manic state and couldn't desist. Susan's wrestling was slowing. He just needed another minute or two, and it would be over. He'd be safe from her slander.

"George!" Katherine ran over. "George! Stop it!"

She gripped him around the waist, struggling to drag him away, her determination to prevent him as powerful as his determination to continue to the end.

She was shouting, calling for help, and after a fierce yank, he was wrenched away. Susan shoved the pillow off, and she was gasping, crying.

"He tried to kill me," she moaned. "He tried to kill me—as he killed Julian all those years ago."

"George," Katherine scolded, "what are you thinking? This is lunacy."

There were boots on the stairs, stomping toward them. Was it those dastardly twins? He felt trapped. He had nowhere to go, nowhere to stay where he wouldn't be found.

He was alone, with no sons, no heirs, and a wife who was disloyal and unfaithful. Had any man in history ever been so appallingly abused? Had any man ever been so wrongly treated?

He pushed by Katherine and as he raced out the rear of the suite, she said, "George, where are you going? Where can you hide after this...this...infamy?"

Then he heard no more. He tromped down the stairwell and burst into the courtyard.

Before sneaking to Susan's bedchamber, he'd had a horse saddled, had packed his bags so he could ride like the wind to Edinburgh. There had to be someone who would support him against the twins, someone they hadn't bribed, someone who would listen to George, who would believe George's version of events.

He leapt onto the animal and kicked it into a canter. He headed for the castle gates, people scurrying out of his path. In a matter of seconds, he was speeding down a long stretch of empty road. There were tall, ancient trees on either side. He was leaned over his horse's neck, urging it to run as if its hooves were on fire.

He glanced to the horizon, and to his consternation, there was a man some distance away, standing in the center of the road. His feet were spread, his hands clasped behind his back.

Though it was a cool afternoon, he wasn't wearing a coat or hat. He was clean-shaven, his hair pulled into a tidy ponytail. He was attired in a flowing white shirt, tan breeches, his boots polished to a shine. A jaunty red kerchief was tied around his throat.

He stared intently at George, and the idiot didn't move a muscle, didn't show any sign he was worried that a horse was barreling down on him.

George sat up and began waving, yelling, but the fellow didn't react. Was he blind?

George neared, getting closer, closer, and he blanched in horror as he saw that it was Julian. It was his brother standing there!

"You can't be here!" he bellowed, wondering if he'd gone mad. "You're dead! You're dead! You can't be here! You're *not* here!"

Julian grinned his devil's grin, then his form became indistinct, and he started to disappear. As the apparition faded, another gradually oozed into its place. It grew bigger and murkier until the Grim Reaper was standing where Julian had been. A black hood was draped over his face, but his glowing red eyes were visible. They were eerie, bottomless, the color of spurting blood.

There was a rumbling laugh, and George smelled a strong odor of sulfur. The horse smelled it too, and it finally seemed to notice the gruesome specter that was lurking, blocking their way.

The animal screeched with alarm, desperate to stop, but it couldn't. George grappled with the reins but lost his seat. He flew through the air and landed very hard, his breath whooshing out of his body.

The last sounds he heard were his neck breaking, the bones in his back shattering, then he was floating in a dark void. He tried to shift about, tried to see where he was, but he was paralyzed. Suddenly the lethal phantom was hovering over him, his red eyes glowing even brighter, a sense of menace and hellfire wafting over George.

There were flames billowing from his cape, the stench of sulfur even more potent.

"We've been waiting for you, George," the evil spirit hissed with a grimace that promised eternal damnation. "What took you so long to arrive?"

CHAPTER TWENTY-ONE

"Monsieur Valois, a pleasure to meet you."

"Mr. Drummond." André nodded in welcome. "What may I do for you?"

"We are advised that you are the man to talk to in Cairo when a traveler has questions about continuing on to Europe."

"Yes, I am. And I'm happy to assist with other tasks that are within my purview while you are in the city." He smiled a tight smile. "For a small fee of course."

"Of course," Mr. Drummond said.

They were in André's receiving parlor, with André seated at his desk, and Mr. Drummond seated across. Drummond wasn't very old, perhaps twenty-two or twenty-three, but he seemed much older. He spoke English, but had an accent André couldn't quite place.

There was a woman with him that André supposed was his mother, although she hadn't been introduced. She was probably in her fifties, slender, slight of stature. He suspected she'd once been very beautiful. There was still an ambiance about her that appealed to his male sensibilities.

She'd previously had magnificent golden blond hair, but it had faded with age so it was a vibrant silver color. Even though they were inside his villa, the cool walls and gardens shading the room, she wore spectacles with dark lenses, so he couldn't see her eyes, but he imagined they would be blue.

Her most intriguing aspect was her throat. She had a huge scar on her neck as if someone had tried to execute her or as if she'd tried to commit suicide by hanging herself. She did nothing to hide the scar and was attired in a gown with the bodice cut low so the repugnant mark was clearly observable. It was almost as if she was daring people to look, daring people to note what had happened to her.

She hadn't commented yet, and André wondered if she could. Maybe the injury to her neck had rendered her mute.

"How may I help you?" he asked Mr. Drummond.

"We have been traveling for almost two years, gradually working our way to England. We are getting closer by the day."

"How far have you come?"

"From Botany Bay."

"Isn't that in Australia?"

"Yes."

"My goodness. That's halfway around the globe."

"Yes, it is."

"May I be introduced to your companion?" André inquired.

Mr. Drummond peered over at her, and though no visible sign passed between them, he replied, "I'm sorry, but no you may not."

André was incredibly fascinated by her. Because of his position in Cairo, his connection to his aristocratic family, and his accumulated wealth, people fawned over him. They begged to be his friend, to do him favors.

André never refused any overture, and he was definitely used to groveling and flattery. He couldn't remember when he'd last been snubbed. His vanity nearly goaded him to toss them out, but he wouldn't give her the satisfaction.

"What route brought you to Egypt?" he asked Drummond.

"We sailed much of the distance, stopping in India and other places. Recently we landed in Africa, and we came across the desert to the Nile."

"I'm extremely impressed. You must wish to get to England very badly."

"I've never been," Drummond said. "I'm going there to complete an important task."

"It must be *very* important."

"It is."

André studied Mr. Drummond, waiting for him to explain, but he didn't, and it was so aggravating. André traded in information, and he didn't like anyone who could keep a secret. They always ended up confiding in him, but not Mr. Drummond.

He appeared dangerous and deadly, like a cobra that was coiled and ready to strike. He had black hair, and he was dressed in stark black clothes and boots, the dark garments adding to his sense of menace.

He reminded André of the Arabian assassins he met occasionally. They were raised from the cradle to kill. They could sneak up on a man and slice out his heart before he realized it was no longer beating. Drummond had that sort of lethal quality.

"What is it you seek from me?" André asked.

"We are on our way to Alexandria where we will book passage to London. We would like to employ the fastest ship we can. We have no desire to dally or delay, so we'd like some advice as to which captain would best suit our purposes."

"Speed and skill will cost you."

"Cost is no object," Drummond claimed.

"In that case, Egypt is the perfect spot for you. Everything can be purchased here if the price is right."

"It's what we have been told."

"I shall make inquiries. In the meantime I have a clerk who can aid you in buying your supplies for the journey. He'll keep you from being cheated."

"His assistance would be most welcome."

"I have many acquaintances in London," André apprised them. "Will you require letters of introduction?"

Drummond peered at his companion again, then said, "My mother is from London. She needs no introduction."

"I see."

So...it was mother and son, but they were a strange pair and they looked nothing alike. He doubted they were as they'd portrayed themselves to be, but they had stories they didn't choose to share, and for once André hadn't the ability to draw them out.

"How long were you in Australia?" he asked the woman, hoping she might answer, but she didn't.

Mr. Drummond said, "Almost thirty years now. She was transported as a criminal."

"I'm very sorry to hear that," André said to the woman, "and I'm glad you survived. There have always been terrible tales about the wretched conditions and unfair treatment."

"It was horrid," Mr. Drummond agreed, "and *unfair* does not begin to describe it."

The woman watched André through her tinted spectacles, and though it was peculiar, she seemed to be daring him or challenging him, but he couldn't precisely figure out what it was she was trying to accomplish.

For a fleeting instant, he wondered if he was staring at Anne Blair. Could it be?

André had never been to England, had never met her, but she'd been renowned as a great beauty, a dynamic singer and actress. If any of those talents remained, none of them were discernible, and as quickly as the curious question had occurred to him, he shoved it away.

Thousands of women had been transported to the British penal colonies. What were the chances that Anne Blair might pop in for a visit? It was too preposterous to consider. Besides, she had to be dead, and André had never stumbled on a shred of evidence to prove she wasn't.

Yet he couldn't help mentioning, "I recently had an acquaintance from London staying with me. His name is Bryce Blair. He's heir to the Radcliffe Blairs in Scotland. His parents were Anne and Julian. Might your mother remember the family from her former time in England?"

Mr. Drummond and his mother held themselves very still. If she was Anne Blair, if André had pricked at an old wound, he'd missed the mark.

Yet he couldn't resist adding, "Bryce is a good friend and has grown to be a very fine man. If you would like his address in London, I would be happy to provide it. You'd have at least one contact there when you arrive."

"Yes," Mr. Drummond said, "we would like to have Mr. Blair's address."

André motioned to his clerk who was seated in the rear of the room, making discreet notes about the discussion so they could be referred to later on. The notes were useful should there ever be a quarrel about monies owed. André might have been descended from aristocrats, but he counted pennies like the most miserly merchant.

The clerk brought Bryce's information and handed it to Mr. Drummond.

"Will there be anything else?" André asked.

"No."

"I'll notify you when I've arranged your ship."

"Thank you."

"And I'll have my clerk stop by your hotel to take you shopping for the correct and necessary supplies. The trip can be especially grueling, particularly when you sail around Gibraltar."

"It can't be any more rigorous than it's already been."

"I'm certain that's true," André concurred.

Drummond and his mother rose, and they started out. André escorted them, which he normally wouldn't have, but they were such an odd pair and he knew very little more about them than he'd known when they'd entered.

He hated for someone to venture into Cairo with secrets he couldn't unravel. It bothered him. It didn't seem fair that his curiosity hadn't been assuaged. He had so few interesting events happen in his life. He enjoyed living vicariously through others.

They walked to the courtyard, and André was surprised to see Drummond and his mother were on horseback rather than utilizing a carriage or renting a chair. It was another odd quirk. Women in Cairo didn't go about on horses.

Drummond's mother mounted without any assistance, and as Drummond swung into the saddle too, André said, "You never did tell me why you're traveling to England. It's such a great distance. What is the important task you must complete?"

"We intend to kill an old enemy—but he deserves it."

André was shocked by the response, but he kept his expression carefully blank. "I'm sure he does. *Au revoir* and *bon chance* with your killing."

"We won't need any luck," Mr. Drummond replied, "but I appreciate the sentiment."

In unison, they tugged on the reins and left.

André watched them go, and he suffered a ridiculous wave of nostalgia. Everyone was always leaving, passing through, never coming back.

The Princess and her siblings were gone. Mr. Hubbard had sailed for England. Bryce had eventually recovered and departed too. Fortunately André had convinced him to ride to Parthenia on the way home. Perhaps amour would blossom there as it hadn't been able to in Cairo.

He was frustrated that he might never learn what became of the young couple. He wondered if Bryce would write as he'd promised, if André would ever hear the details.

For just a moment, he nearly called to Mr. Drummond, nearly asked him to correspond in the future, to apprise André if they managed to commit the murder that had propelled them around the globe. But André didn't involve himself in other people's troubles, so the ending would have to remain a mystery.

&&&&

Evangeline strolled down the main hall at Radcliffe Castle. Servants bowed and curtsied to her, looking pleased as punch to have her roaming about. She was delighted too. She smiled and climbed the winding stairs to Susan's old suite.

The twins weren't inclined to domestic chores, so they were outside, checking on the stables, the farm, the animals and crops.

She had taken charge of things inside the castle, but there weren't many who mourned the deaths of Susan and George Blair. Yet even though they were generally reviled, Evangeline thought it appropriate to maintain the correct rituals. There wasn't any other kin to assume the burden, and the property belonged to her family now, so she didn't mind.

Mr. Thumberton was her attorney in England, and he'd referred her to a colleague in Scotland who was handling the legal wrangling, which would conclude with an investiture ceremony once Bryce returned from Egypt.

The twins had arranged for the lawyer, with several other officials, to record Susan's deathbed statement. It had been her last act. After she'd confessed her crimes and moral transgressions, she'd been able to die in peace.

George's demise had been more appalling, with two days passing before anyone had realized he was deceased. A traveling peddler had stumbled on his body, crumpled in the trees in the mud. Apparently he'd been thrown from his horse and had broken his neck.

There had been some fussing over the funerals and the burials, and Evangeline had taken charge of that fiasco too. Considering how George had tried to murder Susan, Evangeline didn't think Susan would want to lie next to him in her grave.

Evangeline had ordered separate services. Then Susan was buried in the Catholic cemetery up the road, and George was buried at the church in the village. Some had complained that he shouldn't be lowered into hallowed ground, that he should be interred with the heretics and suicides, but she'd told the vicar to allow it, and thankfully he hadn't argued the point.

She didn't know if it was the best decision, but it was over and she wouldn't second guess.

"It's Bryce's now, Father," she murmured, "as it should have been from the start."

She paused, wishing she'd sense his presence, but she didn't so she continued on.

The door to Susan's suite was open, and Katherine was seated on a chair in the corner. She was dressed in black mourning clothes, appearing forlorn and afraid, and Evangeline couldn't blame her for being scared. A woman's lot was difficult, but a woman with no money and no husband was particularly vulnerable.

Katherine had defied George and bravely delivered the documents to the twins that had proved his perfidy. She'd performed such a great service for the Blair siblings. Did she suppose they weren't grateful? Did she suppose they wouldn't reward her?

Well, probably. Her only experience with the Blairs had been with Susan and George, and they hadn't exactly been a stellar example of kindness or generosity.

"Hello, Miss Blair," Evangeline said.

"Hello, Lady Run."

Evangeline went over and laid a palm on Katherine's shoulder. "Since we're cousins, would you call me Evangeline?"

"I would like that very much. And you must call me Katherine."

"I will. Why are you sitting up here by yourself?"

"I've been tending Susan for so long, and I'm feeling lost."

"I understand."

"She suffered so much at the end, so I'm glad it's over, but it will take time for me to adapt. It's strange for the room to be empty." Katherine fiddled with her skirt, ran a kerchief through her nervous fingers. "Might I ask you a question?"

"Of course."

"Could I stay at Radcliffe for a bit?" She seemed to fear Evangeline was about to kick her out the door for she hurriedly added, "Just until I can find another situation for myself."

"You can stay forever if you wish." Evangeline pulled up a chair, and she grinned, hoping to put her cousin at ease. "Actually I probably shouldn't say *forever*. The castle is my brother's now, so once he returns from Egypt, he might have a different opinion. But for now, you can stay."

"Thank you."

"If he comes back with a bride in tow, or has some wild plans for the place that don't include you, we'll make other arrangements."

"Truly?" She looked so relieved that Evangeline wondered if she might slide to the floor in a heap.

"Yes," Evangeline assured her. "We have several grand estates in the family, and there will always be a spot for you at one of them."

"I'm so glad."

Katherine had tears in her eyes, and Evangeline reached out and patted her knee.

"You've been fretting, haven't you?"

"Yes."

"I should have spoken up sooner. I hate that you've been worrying."

"I'm happy to search for a position, perhaps as a nurse or a lady's companion. You and your brothers don't have to support me."

Evangeline waved away her concerns. "You needn't work—unless you want to. In fact, I own a girl's academy in England. It's where I went to school when I was growing up. My husband bought it for me as a wedding gift. You could teach there if you like."

Katherine's jaw dropped in amazement. "I'll definitely ponder it. It would be better than tending another dying relative. I've done it four times in a row."

"You poor thing. A school of giggling, cheery girls might be just the ticket for you. But you don't *have* to seek employment. Would you like to marry? Is that an option you'd enjoy?"

Women usually married, but occasionally there were some who liked to buck the trend, who thought they could be modern and independent, but they were few and far between. And they were mostly shunned as being too eccentric and unfeminine.

"I would like to wed," Katherine admitted, "but I haven't had the means."

"Then we'll get you the means. I'll talk to my brother, Michael, to see if he'll dower you."

"Oh, Lady Run—Evangeline—that's not necessary. I wouldn't

dream of asking him for such a favor."

"Well, I would. Michael is rich as Croesus. He wouldn't miss a penny. He'd likely earn the whole amount from one night of gambling income at his London club."

She couldn't imagine Michael would refuse, but if he did Matthew might agree instead. He was very rich too and so was his stepbrother, Rafe Harlow. Surely among all of them they could scrape together a few farthings to secure their cousin's future.

Katherine was very fetching, and with her even temperament and loyal character, she was a marvelous matrimonial catch. Briefly it occurred to her that Bryce might be interested. With Katherine already being ensconced at Radcliffe, she could help him settle in once he arrived to take possession.

At the notion, Evangeline chuckled to herself. Her family was expanding so rapidly that she was having a chance to play matchmaker. It was a far cry from the lonely period when she was an orphan and charity case.

"You're so kind," Katherine said.

"Not too long ago, I was in a spot similar to yours. I nearly wed a vicar who was completely wrong for me, but I managed to pitch myself into my husband's path. I'll never forget how adrift I was before that happened. It was scary to have no options."

"I've been scared too."

"Those days are gone. From here on out, you're part of our family. You're our cousin, and I've spent my entire life wishing I had cousins, so I'll hardly abandon you."

"I can't tell you how grateful I am."

"Now then, I'd like to clean out this suite and remove all the reminders that it was a sickroom. It feels like bad luck to me."

"Susan's fate was one of bad luck, but it was of her own making."

"I thought I'd send up the maids, and you can direct them. Or is it too soon? I realize Susan just perished, and I would hate to insult anybody."

"No one will be insulted."

"I want to open the windows and let in some fresh air."

"Maybe then her spirit will depart," Katherine said. "It seems to be haunting the bedchamber."

"Have you sensed her lingering?"

"Yes."

"Gad, then we must be rid of her. My father seems to be dawdling too. We can't have ghosts feuding."

They both laughed, and as they quieted they heard boots on the stairs. Momentarily the twins blustered in. It was a beautiful autumn afternoon, and they looked healthy and full of mischief. Their cheeks were rosy from the cold, the smell of leaves and horses wafting from their clothes.

"Why are you up here?" Michael asked Evangeline.

"Katherine and I are having this suite cleared out. I'm eager to wipe away any trace of it being a sickroom."

"While you're at it," Matthew said, "clean George's too. It couldn't hurt to make a new start in there as well."

"I agree," Evangeline said.

Katherine promised to find servants to handle both tasks, then she excused herself so Evangeline was alone with her brothers.

Once her strides faded, Evangeline said, "I like her."

"What's not to like?" Michael said. "She's courteous and pretty, and she helped us obtain all that we sought. I can't believe it was so easy."

"It's odd having a cousin, isn't it?" Matthew said.

"Odd, but nice," Evangeline replied and she stared at Michael. "I want you to dower her. Would you consider it?"

"You're not supposed to gaze at me with those big blue eyes of yours. You know I can't tell you *no*."

Matthew added, "How does your husband stand living with you? He must never be able to put his foot down and mean it."

"He's very generous," Evangeline said, "and it doesn't have anything to do with my eyes."

"He's a complete idiot for you." Michael sighed with exasperation. "How much of a dowry are we talking about?"

"I'll think about it and apprise you of how much would be appropriate. She is cousin to the new Earl of Radcliffe. That should propel her to a higher level in the marriage market so she'll need a few extra pounds."

"This is already sounding expensive and you haven't even provided a number."

"I like to keep you in suspense."

"I hate to interrupt," Matthew said, "but this room gives me the willies. Could we return to the main hall? Would you mind?"

"Are you afraid of ghosts?" Michael taunted.

"You know I am," Matthew responded, "and I'm not too manly to admit it. If a ghost decides to haunt me, I only want it to be my mother or father. I don't care to have any others patting me on the back."

"Come on, you poor boy." Evangeline stood and led them down the stairs.

They arrived in the hall, and the butler brought over the mailbag, and it was crammed with letters from England. Evangeline grinned and dug into them as if she'd stumbled on a secret stash of Christmas presents. She had a dozen from Aaron, and Matthew and Michael had nearly the same amount from their own spouses.

The most precious one was at the bottom of the bag. It was from Bryce, and Aaron had jotted a note on the front. *I didn't open this because I figured you'd want to read it first. But please reply immediately to tell me what he says.*

She held it up and waved it at the twins. "It's from Bryce."

They had moved over by the massive fireplace, had pulled up chairs and were sorting through their own letters, arranging them by date so they were in the correct sequence.

"Where is he?" Michael inquired as Evangeline sat next to him.

"He's still in Egypt, but...he's had enough of adventuring and he's about to start for home."

"About time," Matthew grumbled.

"I've been so worried about him," she said.

"When did he write it?" Matthew asked. "Is there a date? He must be on his way."

"Yes, but he's riding horseback. He decided not to sail."

"Riding rather than sailing? Why?"

"He plans to see a bit of Europe, and he's included a detailed itinerary. I'll have to locate a map so I can track where he'll be."

She handed the letter to Michael, and he read the list of cities. "If he left Cairo right after he posted this, he must be halfway to England by now. He'll be here before we know it."

"We have some great news for him when he arrives," she said.

"I hope he's happy," Matthew said. "Wasn't he opposed to the whole idea of retrieving title to this rotting pile of stones?"

"He simply couldn't bear to fight about it," Evangeline said. "He felt no one would believe us."

"Yet it was so easy to get it all back." Michael snorted with amusement. "Like taking candy from a baby."

Matthew chuckled at his brother. "It was only easy because you terrify everybody. You walk by, and they tremble and pray you won't cause too much trouble."

Michael raised a cocky brow. "It's my best trait."

Evangeline stared around the hall, wondering about her ancestors. The butler had mentioned that a portion of the building was six-hundred years old, so some version of the Blairs had been in residence a long time. Or had the Blairs swooped in during a border war and stolen it from a Scottish family?

She couldn't guess, but she would learn her entire history. As a girl, she'd assumed she had no history. Now, with the truth revealed, she was keen to know every fact.

"I was thinking..." she mused.

"Uh-oh," the twins said together, and Michael teased, "Don't hurt yourself."

"Very funny," she muttered.

"What are you thinking about?" Matthew asked.

"It would be lovely to spend Christmas here, wouldn't it? We could bring Aaron and Maggie and Clarissa. I bet Aaron's brother, Lucas, and his wife, Amelia, would come too. We could have a full house. Or I should probably say a full castle."

"I'm not spending Christmas with Aaron's brother," Michael griped. "The man's a scoundrel who's addicted to wagering."

"You earn your money from dolts like him," Matthew groused. "Don't complain."

"And don't bicker," she scolded. "We're creating something grand here, aren't we? We mean to honor our parents." The more she considered it, the more excited she became. "Let's do it. Let's spend Christmas. We'll have our first real family holiday."

"December is an awful time to travel," Matthew pointed out.

"We'll do it anyway," she said. "We'll be reckless and wild and journey to Scotland when we shouldn't."

The twins gazed at each other, and it was obvious they were carrying on a conversation in their heads. They were very good at it, but when she couldn't read their minds too, it could be annoying.

"It would be marvelous to have Christmas here," Michael ultimately said.

And Matthew said, "We were calculating whether Bryce would be back by then. We thought this castle would be a fine Christmas gift for him to receive."

"He'll be stunned," she agreed. "I wish we had some type of machine that could indicate his precise whereabouts. Or some way to magically contact him and advise him to hurry. I imagine he's lollygagging in Europe, not realizing how impatient we are."

The twins looked at each other again, a silent discussion ensuing that she couldn't decipher. Eventually Matthew shrugged and said to Michael, "Why not? Clarissa will kill me, but she'll get over it."

"Why will Clarissa kill you?" Evangeline asked.

"We'll ride to meet Bryce," Michael said, "and fetch him to Radcliffe."

"Across the continent of Europe? How would you locate him?"

"He's told us his exact route. How difficult could it be? We'll travel hard and fast to find him, then we'll bring him home."

"It'll be a piece of cake," Matthew said.

"What if you miss him on the road?"

"We'll go as far as that little country. What's it called? Parthenia? If we haven't stumbled on him by then, we'll turn around."

She studied them, recognizing they were serious. "You're both mad, and you're correct, Matthew. Clarissa will kill you."

Michael frowned at him. "Are you henpecked already? Will you let your wife prevent you?"

Matthew scoffed. "No chance of that, and we'll only be away for a few weeks."

As Evangeline saw their plot hatching, she felt as if she should quash it or slow it down. Her sisters-in-law wouldn't like it, of that fact she was certain. If it grew into a disaster, she didn't want any of the blame.

"Are you sure you should?" she asked.

"Absolutely," Michael said, and Matthew added, "I'm suddenly dying to meet my older brother. I'm dying to tell him Father has been avenged."

"It all sort of fell in our laps," Michael said. "We didn't actually distribute much vengeance."

"Are you joking?" Matthew said. "Our idiotic, murderous uncle broke his neck in a hideous accident and left this mortal coil. His crimes were exposed, his name ruined, no one is mourning him, and Bryce has the title that always should have been his. I call that vengeance served on a very hot plate."

"Bryce gets a castle too," Michael said. "He'll be anxious to hear that news."

"So...you've decided?" she tentatively inquired.

"Yes, we're going," they replied together. "We're going right away."

CHAPTER TWENTY-TWO

Three months later...

"People are talking."

"About what?"

"They're saying I should have been king. Not Kristof."

Nicholas stared at Katarina. They were in her bedchamber in her private rooms in the palace, so he felt he could voice the statement without being overheard. Apparently she didn't agree.

She scowled and hurried over so they could murmur rather than speak aloud.

"Who is saying that to you?"

"No one in particular," he lied.

Several different men had whispered the sentiment to Nicholas. They were older men who'd been his father's advisors and friends. They were men who should have stood with Nicholas at the outset, but they'd been too cowardly to act in his defense.

So he didn't necessarily trust any of them, but he was viewed as a child, so he could listen and spy without being noticed. He'd become an expert at it. Everyone was complaining about Kristof, from the richest merchants to the lowest scullery maids.

"You have to be careful in repeating gossip about Kristof," Kat warned.

"I know that."

"He could have you arrested."

"I know that too."

"He'd consider it treason, and I wouldn't be surprised if he shut you away in the dungeons."

"He wouldn't dare," Nicholas huffed.

"He threatened it when we were in Egypt. It's why I came back, so he wouldn't lock you in there."

This was a part of the story she hadn't told him before, but then he'd just turned thirteen. Perhaps she thought he could better handle bad news.

"How can it be treason when I'm the rightful king and he's not?"

Nicholas asked.

Kat sighed. "It's a difficult world, Nicholas. If I had an army, don't you think I'd raise it for you? Don't you think I'd shove him off the throne and put you on it instead?"

"But Kat, he's expecting you to marry him."

"Well, it hasn't occurred yet, has it?"

"No."

"I'm being very clever. I'm delaying and questioning his plans. I'll keep on delaying too, and maybe something will...happen."

"What could happen?"

She shrugged. "I have no idea, but I'm trying to devise a strategy."

"I won't let you wed him," Nicholas said. "You don't have to. Not to save me. Isabelle feels the same. We won't allow you to sacrifice yourself for us."

"I can't figure out what else to do except constantly hinder him and hope an alternative arises."

"Why don't we leave again? I won't remain and have him force you."

"First of all, we don't have anywhere to go. That fact was evident after our failed trip to Egypt."

"It wasn't a failed trip. Why don't we go back? We don't have to camp with Uncle Cedric. I'm sure we could stay with Valois."

She didn't answer, but said, "And second of all, if we depart, you'll never have a chance to recapture the throne. If we're here, it could transpire someday, but if you're not, I can guarantee it will *never* transpire."

"I don't care if I have to relinquish it. I'd be happy to run away for you, to keep you safe from him."

"You say that now, Nicholas, but you're not mature enough to fully grasp the consequences."

"I'm thirteen, Katarina."

"I realize that, but I am still your guardian. *I* will decide what's best for you."

"I wish Mr. Blair was here," he said.

She smiled a sad smile. "Why would you wish that?"

"He'd help us, and he'd succeed too."

"Yes, I imagine he would."

"Why don't you write to him? Why don't you ask him to come? I'm certain he would."

"Oh, Nicholas, I can't begin to explain."

"He seemed to like you so much, and he was a grand fellow. He was teaching me to fence and fight." "He was? You didn't tell me."

"You don't have to know everything, do you?"

"Where it concerns you? Yes."

"I must learn how to fight so I can protect you and Isabelle."

"You don't have to protect me, Nicholas. I can look after myself."

But that wasn't true.

She'd returned to Parthenia because Nicholas and Isabelle had been used to compel her obedience. Kristof and Dmitri had been shrewd in choosing that route. It was the only way they could coerce Katarina.

Nicholas was angry at how they treated his sisters, and he hated feeling powerless. He needed an ally, someone tough and smart and brave who could assist him. No matter what, he wouldn't let Kristof push her into marriage. If she wouldn't leave prior to it happening, then Nicholas would make her leave. He and Isabelle would steal her away even if she didn't wish to go.

They'd fled before, and they could do it again, and this time they wouldn't have a traitor like Pippa Clementi in their midst. It occurred to him that he should write to Monsieur Valois to inquire about Mr. Blair and how he might be contacted.

Despite what Katarina thought, Nicholas was positive Mr. Blair would help them, and he didn't understand why Mr. Blair hadn't shown up in Parthenia already. He lived in England, and maybe they could seek him out in London. He wouldn't turn them away, would he?

Nicholas was determined to discover the answer to that question, and he'd just decided to head to his own room, to write to Valois, but he was halted by a loud knocking on the outer doors to Katarina's suite.

They left her bedchamber and went out to the sitting room. Dmitri was there, Katarina's women having admitted him. He was flanked by a phalanx of guards.

"Dmitri." Katarina nodded, barely able to conceal the scorn in her voice. "To what do I owe the pleasure?"

"The King commands me to inform you that—after lengthy consultations with his advisors—he can no longer delay the wedding."

"Is that so?"

"Yes, so it will be held in three days." "Three days?" Katarina scoffed. "That's not possible. We agreed to have it in the spring when the weather clears so we can invite foreign guests. It's to be a national celebration."

"He's changed his mind."

"He can't expect dignitaries to travel this time of year. If an early blizzard hit in the mountain passes, they'd be trapped."

"He will not wait."

"Is he prepared to miss out on his royal wedding? He was counting on it."

"He has more pressing issues to deal with than the size and spectacle of the ceremony."

"He must be so disappointed." She oozed sarcasm.

Nicholas slipped his hand into hers, and he could feel she was trembling.

"I am my sister's only male relative," Nicholas said. "No one has asked me if I approve of this union, and I suggest Kristof find a moment to confer with me about it."

Dmitri's disdain was obvious and insulting. "His Majesty is too busy to parley with a child, but he must speak with you immediately on another subject."

Nicholas loathed Dmitri more than Katarina did, and he wouldn't walk across the street with the vile oaf, let alone accompany him to a meeting with Kristof.

"I'm completing my school lessons," Nicholas fibbed. "My sister is assisting me with some difficult mathematical problems. I'll come as soon as we're finished."

For some reason, Dmitri didn't argue. "Yes, come at once. The King has an important topic to discuss with you." He shifted his glare to Katarina. "Three days to your wedding, Your Grace. Make ready."

He clicked his heels but didn't bow or display any deference. He turned his back on them and marched out as if he was better than them or above them in rank. But he was simply Kristof's lowly, distant cousin, so his behavior was particularly galling.

Katarina's women shut the door after him. Several of her servants were spies for Kristof and Dmitri, so she kept her smile firmly in place, not giving them the satisfaction of witnessing a reaction. She'd assumed they had all winter to formulate a plan. She'd assumed they could delay into the spring and perhaps the summer.

Nicholas was still holding her hand, and he led her into her bedchamber. One of her women tried to enter with them, but Nicholas flashed such a furious glower that she didn't dare. She slinked out, and he and his sister had some privacy.

"You can't do it, Katarina," he insisted.

"What is my choice, Nicholas? I didn't tell you this before either, but I suppose you're old enough now. If I don't marry him, he'll marry Isabelle."

"Over my dead body," Nicholas fumed.

"It's why I would force myself through it—so I don't have to worry about him harming you or her."

"I hate him!"

"It's pointless to be angry," she counseled. "We have to buck up and carry on."

"No, Katarina, we have to *do* something. I won't let you proceed. It's madness, and you'll regret it your entire life."

"What is our option? We're being watched every second. I can't sneeze without it being reported to Dmitri."

"I can move more freely than you. They think I'm a child, so they don't pay attention to me."

"So what? You can wander about the palace, but if we tried to escape, he'd capture us, imprison us, then he'd wed Isabelle. We can't take a risk."

"We can run away again. We can hide. I know it! We must have some friends somewhere in the world."

"Who?" she bleakly inquired. "Who is our friend? Name one person."

"Mr. Blair."

She shook her head. "If he cared about us at all, Nicholas, don't you expect he'd have shown up by now?"

"Maybe he suffered a mishap and couldn't come."

Looking pained, she admitted, "We quarreled, Nicholas. Before I left Cairo, he and I fought bitterly. He won't come. He believes I wouldn't want him to."

"Oh." It was the most distressing news yet.

For months, Nicholas had been scanning the faces in the markets, on the streets, hoping he'd see Mr. Blair. The prospect that he wouldn't arrive, that he didn't care, seemed the worst blow of all.

"I'll think of a plan," he firmly stated. "We have three more days."

"I won't have you scheming with traitors. Kristof would hear about it, and you'd get yourself in trouble over me."

"I don't understand your reasoning, Kat. You'd shackle yourself to that usurping swine to help *me*, but you won't permit me to help *you*. How is it different?"

"I am your staunchest ally, and I will always do what I feel is best to protect you. Of course I would wed him if it will keep you safe."

"Well, I would do anything to keep you safe too." He scowled. "How can you suppose I wouldn't?"

"Let it go, Nicholas."

"I absolutely won't, Katarina. If I have to kill him in order to prevent this, then I shall."

He stormed out, and though she called to him, he didn't stop. There were guards waiting for him in the hall, which was odd. They claimed they were to escort him to Kristof, but their keen focus unnerved him. He never had guards following him and couldn't imagine why they suddenly would.

As they marched in lock-step behind him, he groused and complained, telling them he wasn't a little boy and didn't need a nanny. Ultimately they backed away so he could continue on his own. He ambled along, pretending he was headed to Kristof, but once he was out of their sight, he went in the exact opposite direction.

Clearly mischief was brewing. Dmitri had demanded he meet with Kristof immediately, and he'd been so intent on it that he'd positioned sentries at Katarina's door. Without a doubt Nicholas had to figure out what was occurring.

He had to locate Isabelle too, had to be certain she was safe, then they'd find a place to hide until they could unravel the danger confronting them.

He wasn't sure where she'd be, but it was market day so there were hundreds of merchants selling their wares outside the palace gates. Isabelle liked to converse with the vendors, liked to chat with people from faraway lands so she could practice the languages she knew.

He walked out and started up and down the rows, searching for her at the various stalls. It was very busy, and she could be anywhere, so it was a great surprise when a merchant said, "Young Mr. Webster, might I interest you in some items from Egypt?"

Nicholas whipped around. A man was there, dressed in traveling clothes and seated by himself. He'd laid a blanket on the ground and had pieces of brightly-colored silk fabric arranged on top of it.

He was wearing a knitted cap, a wool cape over his shoulders. He'd grown a bit of a beard, and his hair was darker, but it was his blue, blue eyes that gave him away.

"Mr. Blair?" He mouthed the name to conceal it from passersby.

"Yes," Mr. Blair murmured. "I was hoping you'd stroll by. I didn't dare come into the palace looking for you."

Nicholas sidled over so he was standing slightly behind Mr. Blair and shielded by his body. He whispered, "I'm so glad to see you."

Mr. Blair whispered too. "I can definitely say the same."

"I've been waiting for you. I'd begun to suppose you'd never arrive."

"I had a spot of trouble when I was leaving Cairo, or I'd have been here much sooner."

Nicholas frowned. There was a scar on his cheek and a brace on his wrist. Not his sword arm, thank goodness. "What happened to you?"

"Some of Captain Romilard's men tried to kill me after you left."

Nicholas's fury soared. "Did they?"

"Yes, but they didn't succeed."

"I'm delighted to hear it. While you're visiting, we'll have to give Captain Romilard a chance to decide he's sorry."

"I was thinking the same."

They both grinned, and Mr. Blair said, "There's gossip swirling that a royal wedding will be held in three days. I guess the sudden date is a shock. Everyone's talking about it."

"It's a huge shock. My sister is quite vexed. She thought she'd have until spring to devise a scheme to avoid it."

"But she's not married yet, is she?"

"No, and if I have my way, she won't be. Not to Kristof. *Never* to Kristof."

Nicholas had observed Mr. Blair with Katarina. They'd been very friendly, but it had been Isabelle who'd pointed out they were in love. It would take a girl to notice such a thing, but after she'd explained the situation, he'd noted their affection too.

If Katarina married anyone, she should marry Mr. Blair. And Nicholas didn't care that Mr. Blair wasn't royal. He wanted his sister to be happy. He wanted all of them to be happy.

There was a bit of a commotion in the crowd, and Nicholas glanced up to see guards approaching. Four of them marched by, with Isabelle in the center. She didn't appear to be having any difficulty, but obviously they were escorting her somewhere.

He nearly called out to her, but Mr. Blair squeezed his leg, urging him to silence.

The group kept on and vanished into the throng, so very quickly there was no sign that Isabelle had passed by.

"Where are they taking her?" Mr. Blair asked, lowering his voice even more.

"I don't know, but they just tried to force me to go with them too. I snuck away."

"That doesn't sound good."

"I need to get away from the palace. Could you help me?"

"Of course." Mr. Blair didn't turn around. "I have a room at an inn in the village. We'll pretend you're my son. No one will question it."

Very discreetly, he slid off his knitted cap, and he handed it to Nicholas. Nicholas pulled it on, covering much of his face. Mr. Blair riffled through a satchel and found a wool sweater, and he handed that back as well. It was too long and too big, but Nicholas tugged it on, and in an instant, he might have been an apprentice out making deliveries.

Mr. Blair stood and stretched. "I'm cold and hungry." He spoke a tad louder so people could hear. "I've had enough of selling for now. Let's eat a hot dinner, and we'll come back later. Maybe the shoppers will open their purses by then."

"Yes, Father," Nicholas said.

He snatched up the silk fabrics and stuffed them into the satchel. Then he picked up the blanket, and they folded it together as if they'd done it a thousand times prior. Nicholas carried the blanket, while Mr. Blair hoisted the satchel over his shoulder. He laid a palm on the small of Nicholas's back, guiding him down the narrow, busy street.

In a flash Nicholas was free and away and once again being protected by Mr. Blair. He felt safer and more secure than he had in many, many months.

The door to Kat's chamber burst open, and Dmitri stormed in with a gaggle of guards behind him.

She'd been sitting in the corner, staring out the window, watching a light dusting of snowflakes drift by. Her women were knitting, playing games, but she was ignoring them. She was practically dizzy with plotting as to how to evade the marital noose that was choking her, and she couldn't abide more bickering with Dmitri.

She wondered if he understood the punishments he'd have to endure should his beloved Kristof die or lose the throne. Kat and her two siblings had suffered such insult and offense from Dmitri. Did he recognize the perilous spot in which he'd placed himself?

He was an idiot, so probably not, but he ought to pray each and every night that Kristof lived to be a very old man.

"Where is your brother?" he demanded.

"I have no idea. Last I saw of him, he was on his way to Kristof. I assume that's where he went."

"He did not arrive."

"My brother is thirteen now, as he constantly reminds me. I'm sure he's off enjoying his own pursuits, and he'll attend Kristof when he's good and ready. But he *will* attend him. I can't imagine why you're in such a dither about it."

"Where is your brother?" He bellowed the question.

Her ladies shifted uneasily, anxiously glancing at Kat, at Dmitri. With each passing day, palace affairs grew more tense, civil unrest more apparent. Dmitri's sour mood provided stark evidence that people weren't happy.

Kat rose very slowly, and Princess Morovsky surged to the fore. For too much of her life, she'd been meek and obsequious, so Dmitri regularly forgot who he was and who *she* was.

She sidled over until they were toe to toe. He was taller than she was, and he was a bully who liked to lord himself over others. Too bad for him but he would never be in a position to boss her, despite how he wished he could.

"Get out of my chamber," she furiously said.

"I will not leave until you tell me where you've hidden him."

"I swear, Dmitri, you are more deranged by the second."

"We have your sister," he spat.

She kept her expression carefully blank. "You *have* Isabelle. What is that supposed to mean to me?"

"She will be the King's insurance that the festivities proceed smoothly."

Kat smirked. So Kristof was nervous was he? So Kristof was afraid Kat wouldn't behave as he'd commanded her? Good. Let the stupid ass fret and fuss.

"Am I to presume," she asked, "that you're looking for His Royal Highness, the Prince of Parthenia, for the same reason? You and your paltry men are to keep him under lock and key?"

She barked the words, wanting all the spectators to hear her. Gossip about the incident would flow through the halls the minute Dmitri left.

"Yes, he will be locked in too," Dmitri admitted. "No matter where you've concealed him, we will find him."

"Is the King arresting them? My siblings are to be imprisoned—three days before my wedding?"

Behind her, several of her women tittered with affront, and Dmitri finally realized he was being a fiend, that rumors would spread like wildfire.

"No one is arresting them," he firmly stated.

"You couldn't prove it by me. Where have you taken my sister?"

"She's in her rooms."

"But she's not free to leave?"

"Well...ah..."

"Get out of here," she repeated. "I order you to go to my sister. Inform her that I will be there at once to check on her condition. She had better be fine."

"Or what, Your Grace?"

"You don't think I can do anything to you, do you? You view yourself as being so powerful and so smart. Shortly I'll be your queen."

"I don't serve you, Your Grace. I serve my king."

"As I serve mine," she seethed, and she shouted, "Get out!"

"Listen to me, woman."

"It's Your. Royal. Highness."

She started to spin away, and he had the audacity to reach out and, for just an instant, it appeared that he would lay a hand on her. Everyone, including his men, was aghast at the breach of protocol. He noted the frowns, and his arm dropped to his side.

He glared at her, his hatred exhausting, and she couldn't figure out why he disliked her so much. Before the coup, she'd always been courteous to him. Her father had always been kind. Somehow she'd made an enemy, but she wasn't bothered over it.

This was a battle she had every intention of winning.

"Your Grace," he said with a tight smile, "I can see your brother is not with you. We will search for him elsewhere."

He huffed out, his retinue trailing after him like trained puppies. Kat went the other direction, into her bedchamber where she could close the door.

"What to do? What to do?" she murmured to herself as she paced.

Isabelle was detained, and Nicholas was missing. She was so weary of Parthenia, and she was ready to depart and never return. Could she sneak away? Nicholas wanted to, but with him and Isabelle being watched so meticulously, it would be more difficult than ever to flee.

She'd been dawdling for months, trying to devise a plan, but in all actuality she'd been hoping Bryce would come, expecting Bryce would come. She absolutely could not believe that he'd forsaken her, but apparently he had, and she couldn't keep waiting for him to arrive and rescue her. She had to rescue herself. She had to rescue Nicholas and Isabelle.

She would not and could not marry Kristof. She would find a way out of the palace, out of the city, out of the country. She and her siblings would run so far and so fast that not even the hounds of Hell would be able to catch them. They would continue until they found a safe place, and they wouldn't stop until they did.

CHAPTER TWENTY-THREE

"I need to sneak into the palace," Bryce said, "but I won't leave you here by yourself."

Bryce looked over at Nicholas. They were in Bryce's rented room, discussing their options. Nicholas was eager to depart Parthenia once and for all, and Bryce was happy to take him, but first they had to rescue Isabelle and Kat.

With Bryce not having any friends to serve as back-up, and his one arm not as strong as it had been, he wasn't certain how he'd manage. If they had to stand and fight, it would be over quickly, and Bryce would only have made matters worse.

Nicholas was a fine boy who would grow to be a fine man, and Bryce was glad Valois had convinced him to travel to Parthenia. Even if he never managed to speak with Kat, he was relieved to know Nicholas had been watching for Bryce to arrive. He hadn't let Nicholas down, and he would try very hard to always live up to Nicholas's high expectations.

"If I wear a hat," Nicholas said, "I'm safe on the streets in town. I just oughtn't to go into the palace. My cousin, Kristof, isn't very bright. If he's searching for me, it would never occur to him that I'd be out among the rabble."

"We have to liberate both your sisters, but I'm having a difficult time figuring out how we'd accomplish it."

"We'll think of something." Nicholas's confidence in Bryce's abilities was much greater than Bryce's own. "I have every faith in you."

"I'm starving, so I'd like to find some dinner."

"I'm starving too."

"Then we should stop by a livery to see if we can buy or rent some horses. If we can get your sisters out of the palace—"

"*When* we get them out," Nicholas interrupted.

"I want to have horses ready. We'll have to ride like the wind. We can't putter along in a carriage."

"Agreed."

"Do your sisters ride?"

Nicholas grinned. "Like the wind."

"Wonderful."

"And don't forget. Parthenia is a very small country, so if we use the main road, it's about fourteen miles to the border. Once we're over it, Kristof's men can't follow us."

"Well, they weren't supposed to have much authority in Egypt either, but they managed to kidnap you and almost kill me. I'm not willing to assume that a mere border will give us any protection."

"You're correct of course," Nicholas said.

"Are you sure about this, Nicholas? If you flee, you're probably surrendering your father's throne forever."

"I realize that."

"I intend to proceed to England with the three of you. We'll race to Calais in France and cross the Channel. After we're in London, we'll have land and sea between us and Kristof. Even then I'm not positive how safe you'll be, but you have to be prepared to accept what you'll be relinquishing."

"Katarina keeps telling me the same, and I understand the consequences. For now I can't allow Kristof to harm my sisters. It's the only important issue. In a few years, when I'm an adult, I can fight my own battles. I'll be older and tougher, and I can retake my own throne. Katarina won't have to fight my battles for me."

"That's an excellent plan." Bryce smiled and patted him on the shoulder. "You're a good brother, Nicholas. Your father would be proud of you."

"Thank you."

He dipped his head, a regal gesture of acknowledgement, and Bryce was charmed as always. Nicholas was so mature and polite, so smart and interesting. He'd been raised to be a king, and he definitely showed it in his stellar manners and calm temperament.

When they'd been in Egypt, Bryce had recognized Nicholas was special, but he would never have guessed he was a royal prince. Or maybe he would have. Nicholas wasn't like any other boy Bryce had ever known.

"Let's eat," Bryce said, "then check on the horses."

"I'm coming with you then?"

"Yes. I don't think I should leave you alone, but if we bump into any guards, you have to slip away. We'll meet back here."

"I'll be fine. As I mentioned, I doubt very much they'll be looking for me among the common people."

They bundled up in sweaters and hats and went out into the chilly afternoon. It wasn't that cold, but after Bryce's extended sojourn in the desert, he was constantly freezing, and Parthenia was a mountainous country.

The town was nestled in a lovely valley, with the palace on a promontory up above. Off in the distance, he could see snow-capped peaks. It was late autumn, so without warning, a winter storm could blow in. He hoped—once he found a way to abscond with the Morovsky siblings—that they wouldn't be caught in an early blizzard.

With how his luck was running, he'd succeed in saving them only to perish in a snow storm.

They bought some meat pies from a street vendor, then kept on to a livery that was on the edge of town and the perfect place for a fast getaway. They were talking quietly, deciding Nicholas would wait outside while Bryce haggled with the owner.

They walked along, and they were marking alleys and alcoves where Nicholas could hide if he had to, and Bryce was fretting whether it would have been better to have left him at the inn. But what if guards had stumbled on him while Bryce was away? What was best?

For the moment, Bryce was determined not to let Nicholas out of his sight.

They approached the barn, and as they neared, two men exited the building. They were tall and dark-haired, and as Bryce glanced at their faces, he realized they were identical twins.

He scowled, abruptly swamped by the strangest feeling of disorientation. There was a ringing in his ears, the sound giving him such vertigo he was almost too dizzy to remain standing.

"What is it?" Nicholas whispered.

"I...I...know those men."

Nicholas tensed. "Should I run?"

"No, no, I have to be mistaken." Bryce scoffed at his foolishness. "I was thinking they were from London, but that's not possible. There's no reason for me to meet someone from home. I just...just..."

The twins hadn't noticed Bryce yet, but they kept coming in his direction. One of them peered over at Bryce, and Bryce murmured, "Michael...Scott? Is that you?"

Michael Scott was a renowned criminal and London gambling club owner who catered to the wealthy sons of the aristocracy. Rumors had always swirled that he smuggled liquor too, that he blackmailed and robbed. He was extremely wealthy from his illegal enterprises and was supposed to be incredibly violent too, but Bryce had never witnessed any misbehavior.

He had simply wagered at the man's club but had never been introduced. The last time Bryce had seen him had been at a musical soiree when Evangeline had been singing, and Bryce had accompanied her on the harpsichord. It was shortly before Bryce had sailed to Egypt.

Suddenly Bryce thought of the letter he'd received from Evangeline when he was still staying with Valois. His breath hitched in his chest.

She'd claimed she'd located their twin brothers. She'd claimed Mr. Scott was one of them, but that he was actually Michael Blair and his surname had been changed when he was a boy. The other, Matthew, was a soldier in the army.

Bryce's mind was awhirl as he tried to recall everything Evangeline had penned, while also trying to make sense of bumping into them in Parthenia. Fleetingly he wondered if he wasn't hallucinating, and he blinked and blinked, but the men were real and right in front of him.

Mr. Scott had stopped in his tracks. His jaw agape, he appeared as thunderstruck as Bryce.

"Oh, my Lord," Mr. Scott mumbled. "Bryce? Bryce Blair? Is it you?"

"Yes, it's me, Bryce Blair."

Mr. Scott's twin grinned. "We found you? Truly?"

Bryce was so stunned he couldn't move, and the twins were stunned too. The three of them were frozen in their spots, smiling, studying one another. Then Michael blustered over, his twin marching with him, their strides exactly the same.

"You remember me from London, don't you?" Michael Scott asked.

"Evangeline wrote to me while I was in Egypt. She said...said..." Bryce couldn't force out the words.

"So you know who we are."

"She said you're my brothers."

"She's correct."

Bryce was so shocked his knees buckled, and he collapsed to the ground. His heart was pounding so hard he worried it might simply burst out of his chest.

The twins leapt forward and grabbed his arms, keeping him on his knees so he didn't fall the rest of the way and land flat on his face. Poor Nicholas was terrified, and he cried, "Mr. Blair! Mr. Blair! What's wrong?"

"Nothing's wrong, Nicholas. I'm fine. I'm very, very fine."

Bryce's vision had faded, and it dawned on him that he was weeping, tears dripping down his cheeks. He swiped at them with his hand.

"Oh, my God, oh my God," he muttered over and over.

"Here now," Michael gently soothed, "there's no need to be so upset. Let's get you on your feet."

His brothers lifted him, and the three of them stood in a tight circle, Bryce scrutinizing their features. He had an old portrait of their father, and the twins looked exactly like him. There wasn't a whisker of difference.

Bryce had been five when his father had been killed, but on seeing the twins, he felt as if he was staring at the man, as if not a day had passed.

"I'm your brother, Michael," Michael said.

"You were Michael Scott in London."

"Yes, I was given the name at an orphanage. I was too young to realize I shouldn't have let them change it."

"All these years, we were crossing paths."

"Yes, isn't it strange? It's almost as if it was meant to be." Michael gestured to his twin. "This is Matthew. His surname was Harlow when he was growing up, but the past few months we've both become Blairs again."

"Matthew, hello." Bryce hugged him, then he asked them, "Do you recollect that morning at the docks when they took Mother away?"

"Not the actual event," Matthew replied, "but we have nightmares about it."

"Mother told me to watch over you, but I couldn't. Mr. Etherton sent me away, and I never saw you again. I'm so sorry."

"It's all right," they said.

"I've been sorry ever since."

"We thrived though," Michael pointed out. "We made it. It's over, and we can be a family now."

"But...what are you doing here? How did you find me?"

Matthew answered the question. "You mailed your itinerary to Evangeline, and we came to meet you. Parthenia was our last stop though. If we hadn't stumbled on you here, we were going to figure we'd missed you and turn around."

Michael added, "As to what we're *doing,* we couldn't wait to tell you the news."

"What news?"

"We've retrieved the estate and the title. We've retrieved what was stolen from us, and we happily give it all to you."

Initially he was confused over what they were claiming, then he gasped with astonishment. "Radcliffe is ours?"

"Yes," Michael said, and in unison they declared, "and Father is avenged."

Matthew said, "I hope his ghost is resting easier. It seems to be."

"So...*Lord Radcliffe*"—Michael had a definite teasing glint in his eye—"we are escorting you to your castle where you belong."

"Am I dreaming?" Bryce asked.

"No," Michael responded, "it's all very, very true, and we wanted you to be apprised immediately. It's why we decided to fetch you."

"We'll have to talk all night," Bryce said.

"I imagine it will take the remainder of our lives to straighten it out, but first we have to get you home. Evangeline is planning for all of us to spend Christmas at Radcliffe, so we can't dally in Europe. We have to get riding."

Bryce felt a tug on his coat, and he glanced down to see Nicholas, his gaze curious and intense. Bryce had been so overwhelmed that he'd completely forgotten Nicholas was there, and he'd been too polite to interrupt.

"Nicholas," he said, "this will sound very peculiar, but these men are my brothers. I didn't know them, and we've only just met."

"That is an extremely odd statement," Nicholas said, "and I'm eager to hear the tale behind it."

"Who is this?" Michael asked.

"This is Nicholas Morovsky." Bryce leaned nearer and quietly murmured, "He is the Crown Prince of Parthenia, and someday he will be His Majesty the King."

Michael and Matthew exchanged a shocked look, and Michael said, "You have some interesting friends."

"Yes, I do," Bryce agreed, "and at the moment, he's in trouble and in danger, so he's simply Nicholas, a shop boy and vendor's son."

Nicholas peered up at Bryce. "Might they help us to rescue Katarina and Isabelle? Can they fight?"

Matthew scoffed. "Can we *fight*? We invented fighting. Who is it who needs rescuing?"

"My sisters," Nicholas replied. "They're trapped in the palace and we have to get them out. Then we're going to England too."

"It appears we'll have quite a caravan," Michael said.

Bryce chuckled. "It's a long story."

"It certainly must be."

"I have a room at an inn in the town," Bryce said. "We can return there, and I'll explain what's happening."

They started down the street, Nicholas leading the way, the three Blair brothers walking shoulder to shoulder. Bryce was blond-haired as his mother had been, and the twins were dark-haired like their father. But it was their blue, blue eyes that set them apart, that marked them as siblings.

Bryce had lost them that morning at the docks. It had been the worst day of his life. Worse than the day they'd learned his father had been killed. Worse than the day their mother had been arrested. Worse than the day their home was forfeit and debt collectors had swooped in like vultures and seized all their possessions.

He'd sworn to his mother that he'd protect the twins, but he'd only been five. In his mind, he'd understood that it had been an impossible quest. Yet in his heart, he'd always felt he'd failed both his mother and his brothers. Servants had carted them away, had tossed them in a coach and left with them.

For a bit of time, he'd remembered them clearly, and with a little boy's determination, he'd thought he could somehow carry out his promise to his mother.

But years had passed, and memories had faded. Once he'd grown older and might have hunted for them, details had been so hazy that he'd had no idea where to begin. So he hadn't looked, hadn't searched. It was just one of the guilt-laden recollections that had plagued him.

But now...but now...

They were together, and no matter what else transpired in the future, he would never let them go again.

Nicholas glanced back at Bryce. "Are you really a lord?"

"Yes."

"What is your rank?"

"I'm an earl. I'm Earl of Radcliffe—as our father should have been before me."

"Hmm..." Nicholas mused. "You're not as high as I'd like, but when we're finished here in Parthenia, I might agree to your marrying Katarina. If she'll have you."

"It's always been the plan, Nicholas. Let's see if we can make it happen."

Katarina sat on the dais in the main hall with Kristof.

Supper had ended and dancing was about to start. Normally Kat would have loved to dance the night away, but Kristof was awful at it so he never participated. As the dishes were being removed, he'd ordered her not to embarrass him by joining in, so she probably wouldn't—although for once she was considering it.

In the months she'd been home, he'd relayed similar warnings, and she'd politely heeded them. Yet if she publically disobeyed him, what could he do?

Well, he couldn't do anything then and there, but there was likely plenty he could do later. Should she risk it?

She studied the crowd, trying to find a friendly face. It was an engagement party of sorts so people were pretending to be merry, but the gathering wasn't very cheerful. Various courtiers were delivering wedding gifts, offering felicitations, but Kristof was in a foul mood.

Dmitri had pushed him into matrimony much earlier than he'd intended so the gifts were paltry, the remarks insincere. There were no nobles from foreign lands, no dukes or princes to

HEART'S DEMAND

congratulate him.

Parthenia had an aristocratic class, but few of them had ridden in from their rural estates for the wedding. Since Parthenia was a small country and the weather continued to be mild, it was a horrid snub, and Kristof knew it. As each gift was tendered, he was muttering about the cheap workmanship or the low position of the person who had provided it.

She stared blandly, but in reality she was watching for Nicholas. Isabelle was in her room, under guard and unharmed, but Nicholas was missing. Kristof's minions had turned the palace upside down hunting for him, but they hadn't found him, and she was growing alarmed.

Had he run off? Was he hiding in a safe place?

She was anxious to sneak away, to grab her siblings and go, but she'd delayed too long, had ruined any chance to flee. For how smart she was, and how stupid Kristof was, he'd bested her constantly. It was humiliating.

There was a ruckus at the rear of the hall with people whispering and pointing as three men entered. From their traveling clothes and demeanor, it was obvious they were foreigners. Kat assessed them, being a tad dazzled by how tall they were, how handsome, broad-shouldered, and fit. They put the local men to shame.

They marched down the center aisle, and though there had been a line of supplicants waiting to speak to Kristof, they scooted out of the way as the foreigners approached. They exuded that type of power and charisma.

The Sergeant at Arms stopped them and asked their names, then he announced, "Your Majesty, Your Royal Highness, may I present the Earl of Radcliffe, newly arrived from London, England. He is accompanied by his brothers."

At hearing *Radcliffe,* Kat's gaze whipped to the man in the front. His hair was darker and he'd grown a bit of a beard, so he looked very different from the blond, clean-shaven fellow she'd known in Egypt. There was a nasty scar on his cheek that hadn't been there previously, as if he'd been injured since she'd last seen him, but those blue eyes didn't lie.

She swallowed down a squeal of astonishment, gripping her chair as tightly as she could so she didn't leap up and shriek with joy.

Kristof mumbled, "It's about time some dignitaries paid their respects." "Yes," she calmly replied, though her pulse was pounding in her ears, "isn't it marvelous that he's visited?"

"Your Majesty." Bryce bowed to Kristof, then shifted his attention to Kat. "Princess Morovsky. I'm delighted to make your acquaintance."

Kristof tried to appear officious and kingly. "Radcliffe, you say?"

"Yes, Your Majesty. My family seat is located in the north, on the Scottish border. It's quite a grand residence. Not as grand as your palace, but very fine all the same."

Kristof nodded his pleasure, thrilled to have a British lord admitting that Parthenia was superior.

Kat was struggling not to gape, not to let any of her excitement show. He had to have come for her, hadn't he? He had to have come to save her?

A more terrifying notion occurred. What if he was toying with her? What if he had no intention of assisting her? What if he simply wanted her to see that he'd been passing through and didn't care? Could Fate be that cruel?

"What brings you to our little corner of the world?" Kristof asked.

"My brothers and I have been on business in Rome. We are on our way to England, and we decided to stop in your beautiful country."

"Yes, it is very beautiful," Kristof agreed.

"We hear congratulations are in order," Bryce said.

"Yes, the Princess and I are marrying in three days. I hope you'll stay and grace us with your presence during the festivities."

"You're most kind," Bryce gallantly stated. "We are gratified by your invitation, and we will do our best to make your nuptials a celebration worth remembering."

Bryce bowed, his brothers bowed too, and as they backed away, Kat called, "Lord Radcliffe?"

"Yes, Your Highness?"

"The dancing is about to begin. Will you honor the court by leading me in the first set?"

Kristof bristled, but he couldn't refuse to let her proceed or he'd seem petty and jealous. And he'd want Kat to impress a foreign lord. He'd preen about it for weeks.

As to Kat, she couldn't guess how long or how ably she could maintain the ruse that she didn't know Bryce, that she didn't love Bryce, but she had to risk it. She had to get close enough to ask if he was there to help her. If he said he wasn't, she'd just die.

"I would be most pleased to lead off the dancing." Bryce grinned at Kristof. "With His Majesty's permission of course."

"Oh, of course," Kristof arrogantly huffed. "Be my guest."

"I will," Bryce said.

He and his brothers walked away, and the final courtiers left their gifts. Then the musicians struck up the introductory chords, summoning couples onto the floor. A servant held her chair and another escorted her down to Bryce. They stood at the head of the line.

The music started, and it was a popular country dance. She had no idea if he'd learned the patterns, but he joined in without missing a step. They promenaded down the center, the other couples prancing behind. The men and women separated, circled each other, moved back. She only had a few chances to twirl with him, then the partners would switch.

"I'm so glad to see you," she whispered as he made the initial turn, but that was all she had time to say.

"Nicholas is with me. He's safe," Bryce told her on the next pass.

"Thank goodness."

Their conversation continued like that, quick snippets as they locked hands and spun around.

"My brothers will protect him with their lives."

"I'm so relieved."

"I'm coming for you and Isabelle. Give me a day or two to figure out how."

"All right."

"You can't marry him."

"I won't. I can't."

"Nicholas has drawn me a map of the palace. Sleep alone tonight."

"I will."

"Don't let any of your women stay in your room."

"I won't."

"Be ready to travel fast. No bags. No nothing."

"I understand."

"We will likely leave on the spur of the moment."

"Fine."

"Make sure Isabelle knows."

Then it was over. They separated, and she partnered with the rest of the men down the line until the musicians sounded the last chord, and everyone was breathless and laughing. He bowed to her, and she curtsied, barely glancing at him, pretending they were strangers.

Bryce spoke to Kristof. "Your Majesty, this was a great honor. Your fiancée is beautiful and graceful."

"Yes, she is. You dance well for an Englishman."

"When I was a boy, my dancing masters always insisted I should learn—in case I was ever required to dance with a princess. They didn't want me to embarrass myself."

The crowd chuckled, and Kristof said, "It's lucky you minded your masters then."

"Yes. I'm nothing if not obedient."

He delivered Kat to a servant, and she was whisked up onto the dais. She sat, and when she dared to gaze out over the hall, he'd faded into the gathered horde, and she couldn't see him anywhere.

CHAPTER TWENTY-FOUR

Bryce stepped out of a dark stairwell and slipped into a dressing room. He tiptoed over to a door and peeked into a bedchamber.

From the map Nicholas had drawn, he was supposed to be in Kat's suite, but the interior of the castle was a warren of tunnels and dead ends. If he'd taken a wrong turn, if he awakened the wrong woman, it would very likely be the last idiotic move he'd ever make.

In for a penny, in for a pound...

He crept toward the bed as she sat up and whispered, "Bryce?"

"Yes, I'm here."

She reached out her hand, and he rushed over and clasped hold, climbing onto the mattress and stretching out on top of her.

Then he was kissing her and kissing her as if they'd never quarreled, as if they'd never been parted a single day. He'd never imagined he'd have an opportunity to embrace her ever again. It was like a dream, a slice of Heaven, and he almost pinched himself to ensure it was really occurring.

"Where have you been?" she asked as they caressed and hugged and kissed some more. "I've been waiting for hours. I decided you weren't coming."

"There are guards everywhere. I was nearly spotted a dozen times."

"Am I leaving with you? If guards are patrolling, how will we get me out?"

"It won't be tonight. I'm still planning things."

She slumped with dismay, her spirits flagging. "I want to go right now."

"I know you do, but we have to be careful. We'll only have one chance to escape, and we have to retrieve Isabelle too."

He started kissing her again, needing to fill himself up with her and being terrified that—should he botch his rescue—he would never be with her like this in the future.

He touched her everywhere, anxious to imprint her size and shape into his mind so he'd never forget. He reveled in the way she smelled, the way she tasted, in the soft, warm feel of her skin.

"I'm sorry," she murmured.

"For what?"

"For how I treated you that final morning in Cairo."

"It's all forgiven, Kat."

"My companion, Pippa, was spying on me for Kristof, sending him reports."

"That must be why all those Parthenian fellows were following you."

"Yes. Kristof insisted we return, but he figured I wouldn't meekly agree. So Pippa had Nicholas and Isabelle kidnapped in order to force me."

"My friend, Chase Hubbard, helped her."

"Was that how it happened?"

"Yes."

"Last year, after we sneaked away," she explained, "there were rumors that we'd met with foul play and that Kristof was responsible."

"I understand why people would think that." "He needed us home so he could show everyone we were fine. Pippa claimed if I didn't comply, he would torture Nicholas and marry Isabelle."

"Valois told me." He searched her eyes. "I haven't seen Miss Clementi anywhere. Have you gotten even with her? I hope you have."

"I left her on the dock in Alexandria, and we haven't heard a word about her."

"Good. Please tell me you're not feeling guilty or wishing you hadn't."

"I haven't suffered a moment of guilt."

Bryce grinned. "That's my girl."

"I was afraid I'd upset you too much, and you wouldn't come after me."

"Not come after you! Are you joking?"

"I watched for you every minute. I constantly studied the road behind us, but when I never saw you back there, I thought I'd wrecked everything and you didn't care about me anymore."

"For about one second, I was convinced that was the case. Then I realized you must have been coerced into being so horrid to me."

"I'm so relieved."

"I would have arrived immediately, but it took me awhile to leave Cairo. I had a bit of...difficulty."

She traced the scar on his cheek. "How did you get this?"

He stared for a lengthy interval, remembering that evil period when he'd been a captive, when he'd been flogged and starved and so dreadfully ill. If Valois and Chase hadn't rescued him, he couldn't imagine where he'd be. Most likely deceased from the fever and infection that had nearly killed him.

But he wouldn't admit any of it. Maybe he would in the future, but not now. Now it would only give her more to worry about, and he wanted her focusing on their escape and naught else.

"I had a fight with a brigand," he lied. "He managed a quick swipe with his sword before I repaid him."

She smiled, apparently believing the falsehood. "Tell me he ended up in worse shape than you." "Oh, he was definitely in much worse shape."

She sighed. "My dashing hero. I'm so lucky that you became my champion."

"I'm a fool for love, Katarina."

"Do you still love me, Bryce?"

"So much that I'm dying with it."

"Are you sure?"

"Very sure."

"I seem to bring an awful lot of trouble with me wherever I go."

He chuckled. "You certainly do."

"Are you positive I'm worth it?"

He peered down at her, and she was so beautiful, the most beautiful woman he'd ever met.

When he'd initially departed England, he'd been adrift and dissatisfied, with no goals or ambition. After learning about the crimes committed against his parents, he'd felt as if he was wasting his life, as if he was engaged in frivolous pursuits that were beneath the son of Anne and Julian Blair.

He'd been desperate to reinvent himself, to be a better person, a better man, and he'd discovered his purpose.

He would love Katarina Webster Morovsky. He would sweep her away to safety, would marry her and live happily ever after. He would take her and her siblings to Radcliffe. They would build a family, would fill the halls with the giggles and running feet of boisterous children.

They would revive the drafty, haunted place, would make it the home it should have been for Bryce and his siblings.

"I'm positive you're worth it, Katarina."

But suddenly it dawned on him that he was ready to implement those plans, but he hadn't asked her opinion. Did she want what he wanted? Was she interested in remaining with him as his bride?

If she wasn't, he'd help and protect her from her cousin, but he would be crushed if she'd changed her mind.

Tentatively he inquired, "Are you still willing to marry me?"

"Me!" She appeared stunned by the question. "Are *you* willing? After how I hurt you?"

"Yes, I want to, you silly girl."

She nodded ferociously. "Yes, absolutely yes. When can we?"

"As soon as I get you away from here. Will you come to Scotland with me? Will you come to Radcliffe as my wife and countess?"

"It's what I desire more than anything in the world."

She pulled him to her and initiated her own kiss, as if sealing their promise. He felt as if he was walking on air, as if he'd just won every prize. He was so glad, so content.

Their embrace grew more profound, more intense and reflective. They were both aware of their precarious situation, of all the details that could go wrong to prevent their fleeing. Would they ever have another chance to be together? What if they didn't?

Then and there, he swore their future would transpire. No matter the risk, no matter the difficulty, he would spirit her away. She was his, and her cousin could not have her. It would happen over Bryce's dead body.

When he'd first arrived, she'd been lying under the blankets as if she was asleep, but she was fully dressed, having been prepared to leave with him if that's what he requested. Gradually he was lifting the hem of her skirt, working it up her legs, his hips dropping between her shapely thighs.

Would he make love to her? Was he that brazen? Evidently the answer was *yes*. He didn't care that there were servants outside her door, didn't care that danger lurked in every hallway.

He unbuttoned the front of her gown to bare her breasts. He caressed one, then the other, and she swiftly responded to his ministrations.

He pushed at fabric to dip down and suck on a nipple. He laved it vigorously, as his fingers sneaked into her drawers, as he found her sweet center. He scarcely touched her, and she was pitched into a wild orgasm.

He clapped a palm over her mouth to keep her from crying out, from making any sound that might give them away. As she reached the peak, as she spiraled down, he was opening his trousers, freeing his cock so he could enter her.

There was an urgency to his moves, and a burgeoning excitement fueled by the hazards, by the possibility of discovery.

He slid into her, and she was relaxed, welcoming him, spurring him on. He began to flex, slowly and cautiously, not wanting any noises to carry, not wanting the mattress to creak or the bed frame to groan.

With her virginity no longer an issue, their coupling was so much easier, so much more potent. He didn't have to worry about her anxiety, about whether he was going too fast or hurting her.

He thrust, impaling himself to the hilt, then he'd pull all the way out only to impale himself again. She rocked with him, drawing him in, holding him near, both of them sensing that a special bond was being created. Though they hadn't spoken any vows, they understood that God had brought them together, and no one would ever tear them asunder.

He continued until he couldn't bear it. Finally his passion swelled, his seed shooting into her womb. Perhaps this time, it would take root. Perhaps this time, as they rode through the gates at Radcliffe, she would be increasing with his son.

Let it be so, Lord. Let it be so...

He flexed to the end, hating to have it over. He collapsed on top of her, and they sighed in unison, Kat stroking her hands up and down his back.

It was the most tender moment of his life, and eventually he rolled off her. They shifted so they were nose to nose, and they were smiling, struggling to remain silent, to not utter any of the words that were dying to be voiced.

"I have to go," he whispered.

"In a minute."

"I'm not sure if I'll visit you tomorrow night or not."

"Aren't we departing tomorrow?" She looked panicked. "If we don't, the day after will be my wedding day. I don't believe my nerves could stand to cut it that close."

"I'm leaving some clothes for you and Isabelle in the children's old nursery. In the toy box. Nicholas said you'd know where that is."

"Yes, I know."

"It'll be boy's clothes—for both of you. You don't mind? We thought it would help to hide you."

"Whatever you ask, Bryce, I am happy to do."

"It'll be the morning of your wedding. The palace will be chaotic, and the townspeople will be celebrating. We'll slip away in the confusion."

"If you think that's best, then I'm certain it is."

She was trying to be brave, trying to pretend Bryce's idea was viable, but he couldn't predict if they'd succeed. He was running in circles, making quick decisions and trusting Fate would provide a boost so everything would work out.

Would it?

"We'll be fine, Kat. We'll get you away. My brothers and I will see to it."

"You haven't failed me yet."

"And I don't intend to this time either."

In the outer room, two women were talking. Suddenly one of them knocked on the door and spun the knob. Thankfully Kat had barred it and they couldn't enter.

"Princess," one of them called, "are you all right?"

Kat's eyes were wide as saucers. Bryce's too.

"They spy on me for Kristof," she mouthed then—sounding grumpy and vexed—she called back, "Are you speaking to me? I was sleeping. How dare you wake me."

More tentatively the woman asked, "Are you all right? We heard someone."

"You're mad. I'm quite alone."

Goodbye, he mouthed.

Goodbye. I love you!

I love you too!

"Are you really Lord Radcliffe?" she whispered.

He grinned. "I wasn't yesterday, but I am today."

He slid away and tiptoed to the dressing room, straightening his clothes as he went. At the last second he touched his fingers to his lips and sent a kiss winging toward her. Then he crept into the secret stairwell.

In his final sight of her, she'd climbed out of bed and huffed to the door, prepared to yank it open and scold her traitorous servants. What a sad life she was leading! After witnessing it for himself, he was more determined than ever to rescue her from it.

"What is the meaning of this?" she barked at them.

He vanished into the dark and rushed away.

&   &   &   &

"Where is that wretched boy?"

Kristof hissed the question and glowered at Dmitri, but the man shrugged as if Nicholas's whereabouts were none of his concern. They were in the King's receiving chamber, with the citizenry popping in to file complaints, ask for favors, or offer wedding gifts, so Kristof couldn't display too much temper.

He was a day away from the ceremony, and instead of bothering with his subjects, he probably should have been meeting with his tailor to discuss the alterations to his wedding suit. Or he might have been wooing Katarina, trying to generate a spark that would carry him through the wedding night.

He didn't like her, couldn't abide her superior attitude, didn't physically desire her, and couldn't imagine fornicating with her. He was growing terrified that his disdain might render him incapable of performing the marital deed. Just from considering such a humiliation, his phallus seemed to shrivel.

"We've searched high and low," Dmitri claimed. "Nicholas is no longer in the palace."

"There are a thousand hiding places in this accursed building. You can't have checked them all."

"We have," Dmitri smugly replied.

"He must have fled. Katarina must have smuggled him out."

"She was completely surrounded by your spies, so she couldn't have helped him. He walked out of her rooms and disappeared."

"Might he be raising an army against me?" Kristof anxiously inquired.

"What army would that be, Sire? We have no army. We've never had an army. We've never needed an army."

"Maybe support has been mustered for him. Maybe he's found some allies."

"What fool would ally himself with a child? Stop worrying. It exhausts me."

Kristof's greatest fear was that things would fall apart before he could bind himself to Katarina. He was a nervous wreck and constantly wondered if disaster was approaching.

Dmitri's brother, the hapless Captain Romilard, was lurking in the corner, avoiding Kristof. He had been in charge of watching Nicholas, so it was his fault Nicholas was missing.

"Summon your brother," Kristof said. "I would have a word with him."

Dmitri motioned to the Captain, and he marched over, looking as if he was about to face a firing squad, which Kristof was beginning to think would be a fine idea. Kristof gestured for him to keep coming until they could speak softly enough to not be overheard by anyone nearby.

"Where is Prince Nicholas?" Kristof fumed.

"I don't know, Your Majesty. I have tried my best to locate him."

"Why was it necessary for you to search, Captain?"

"Because I lost him, Your Grace."

"Yes, *you* lost him, so let us review, Captain Romilard. Who was charged with guarding him?"

"I was, Sire."

"Precisely. You have an hour to bring him to me or I'll have your head."

Both Romilards gasped, then the Captain backed away and left. Dmitri leaned in and nagged, "Honesty, Kristof, if you alienate everyone, who will stand as your friend?"

"Shut up, Dmitri, or I'll execute you with him."

He peered over the crowd, looking for Nicholas, but looking for the British noble, Lord Radcliffe too. Since the evening he'd introduced himself, he hadn't returned, and Kristof made a mental note to have Dmitri learn where he was staying.

Kristof wanted him to visit again so they could chat and perhaps share a glass of wine. Not a single foreign aristocrat had ever called on him, and he was dying to impress Lord Radcliffe.

He was about to tell Dmitri he'd had enough of dealing with the public for one afternoon, was about to rise and leave, when a bedraggled woman pushed to the front of the line. She was thin and unwashed, her hair unkempt, her dress ragged and torn, and she wasn't wearing a cloak even though it was chilly outside.

She was intent on getting close to him, and she might have run right up to the throne if two guards hadn't stopped her.

"Kristof! Kristof! It's me! It's me! Don't you recognize me?"

He frowned. "No, Miss, I don't recognize you."

"It's me. Pippa."

"Pippa...Clementi?"

"Yes." She burst into tears.

Katarina had deserted Pippa in Egypt, and after that debacle, Kristof hadn't given her much thought. She'd proved herself a gullible dunce and had thus squandered any fond acquaintance they'd once possessed.

"Why are you bawling?" he snapped.

"I'm so glad to be home. My darling, Kristof, I didn't think I'd ever see you again."

As she voiced the inappropriate endearment, Kristof scowled at Dmitri, indicating he should handle the situation. Dmitri gestured to the guards who were holding her. They tried to pull her away, but she yanked hard and rushed to Kristof, falling to her knees and clasping his ankles. He could smell her hair and clothes, and it wasn't pleasant.

"I'm here now," she wailed. "We can continue on as we planned."

People were agog, watching with a sort of horrified fascination, and he said, "Miss Clementi, you seem distraught, and it's clear you've suffered some difficulties during your travels. Let's have Dmitri get you to your room. You could use a bath and a nap."

"I have had difficulties. So many of them! The only thing that kept me going was memory of all the rewards I had waiting for me."

"What rewards?" he scoffed.

"Why, the ones you promised me if I would sneak off with Katarina, if I would spy on her for you."

"I haven't the vaguest notion what you're talking about."

His reply agitated her. "You swore if I betrayed Katarina you would give me—"

He couldn't allow her to finish the sentence, so he leapt up and shoved her away. He seethed at the guards, "How dare you let her approach me. My God, the woman is unwell and unbalanced. Take her away."

"Kristof, Kristof," she whined, "don't be like this. Don't treat me this way. You said I'd sit by your side on the throne. I only had to spy on Katarina and—"

Kristof jumped over and clamped a palm over her mouth. "Go away, Pippa. I won't tell you again."

She skewered him with a glare. "Are you denying me? Are you pretending we had no bargain? Are you claiming there is no reward?"

Kristof whispered directly in her ear. "You failed in your role, Pippa Clementi. You were ordered to bring Katarina home, and instead you were tricked and left behind. If Captain Romilard hadn't been on his toes, the entire plan would have collapsed because of you." He pushed her away. "Get out of my sight."

"You don't mean it," she moaned. "You can't mean it! Not after what she did to me! Not after I've come so far."

"Dmitri, please!" Kristof said. "If your guards were ever trained to carry out a single task correctly, they must know how to escort a lunatic from my presence."

The guards, along with all of the onlookers, were mesmerized by Pippa and the secrets she'd let slip. Everyone was frozen in place, eager for more juicy gossip.

Kristof whipped away to storm out when several people cried out with alarm. He glanced over his shoulder, and to his stunned surprise, Pippa was clutching a small pistol.

"You liar," she fumed at him. "You dirty dog. You deceitful rat."

"Miss Clementi!" Dmitri shouted. "Are you mad?"

Numerous men lunged for her, but she managed to pull the trigger before any of them reached her. Kristof lurched away, but he was hemmed in by the throne and the curtain behind it. To his dismay, he learned he could not outrun a bullet, even one fired from a little tiny gun.

Fortunately her aim was poor so the bullet simply grazed his arm, but nevertheless a searing, hot pain doubled him over.

"She shot me! She shot me!" he shrieked, pointing out the obvious. "Arrest her! Hang her!"

Bystanders were so astonished that she was able to race to the rear doors. Hands grabbed at her, but she was very quick and evaded them all. As she was about to exit, Lord Radcliffe suddenly entered, and he was blocking her path.

She stumbled to a halt, and she studied him. Seeming to recognize him, she scowled in confusion. "You're supposed to be dead. Captain Romilard had you killed." She peered back at Kristof. "He was there, and he shouldn't be *here*. He must intend to cause trouble. They were in love, and they would have—"

Before she could complete her crazed comment, Lord Radcliffe wrenched the pistol from her fingers, then cold-cocked her with it. She collapsed to the floor in an unconscious heap, and his brave action propelled the guards from their stupor.

They rushed down the aisle, picked her up, and dragged her off to the dungeons. Dmitri and others ran to Kristof and eased him onto the throne. A kerchief was produced and pressed to his wound.

"Get a doctor! Get a doctor! Where is the King's doctor?"

Various spectators were repeating the question, and Kristof observed it all with a dazed detachment. Lord Radcliffe sauntered toward him, and he was calm, dashing, and every bit the *lord* he was. Kristof was insanely jealous that Radcliffe could be so courageous and composed.

Kristof couldn't have displayed such daring aplomb if he'd had a thousand years to practice.

"Lord Radcliffe," Kristof gushed. "You're a life-saver. Thank you."

"Who was that woman?" Radcliffe asked. "She was quite deranged."

"*Deranged* doesn't begin to describe it, but don't worry, you won't ever see her again."

"I'd say that's good for both of us, Your Majesty. You're lucky her aim wasn't any better."

"Yes, very lucky. She's been out of the country for an extended period. Evidently her travels have affected her mental capacities."

"They certainly have."

"You have our most sincere appreciation," Kristof regally said.

Radcliffe waved off the compliment. "It was nothing."

"You must attend my wedding tomorrow as my special guest. You'll be seated in the front row."

Radcliffe considered for a moment, almost as if he'd decline the honor, but ultimately he shrugged. "Why not? I wouldn't miss your wedding for the world."

He smiled, and everyone in the room smiled too. The tension lifted, and the crowd started to applaud him and his heroic act. He nodded, accepting their admiration as his due, while Kristof silently seethed and tried to appear pleased.

His injury was painful but slight, so he'd survive, but he'd suffered the mortification of being shot while the whole court was watching. His guards had behaved impotently, and a foreign stranger had had to ride to Kristof's rescue.

It was a humiliation too great to be borne, and he could only imagine how amused Katarina would be when she heard the news. Would his arm be in a sling during the ceremony?

How disgraceful! How unmanly! Why couldn't anything ever proceed as he planned?

CHAPTER TWENTY-FIVE

"The King commands you attend him immediately."

Kat stared at Captain Romilard and the cadre of guards who'd entered her suite. Her smile was carefully blank. "I was just about to fetch my sister so we can walk to the chapel and pray. I can't possibly accompany you now."

In reality, they were about to go to the old nursery to find the clothes Bryce had left for them.

"The King said *immediately,* Your Highness."

"Tell him I'll be there very soon, Captain Romilard."

For once, she was alone. Something had happened in the main hall, and there were wild rumors of a shooting or a murder, so everyone had hurried down to join in the excitement.

Kat felt so disconnected from all of it that she wasn't curious in the least. In her mind's eye, she was already halfway to England with Bryce.

When Romilard had knocked, Kat had come out to the sitting room to see what he wanted. Isabelle was in Kat's bedchamber, peeking through the crack in the door and listening to the conversation. Kat had told her to keep herself hidden until they found out why he'd arrived.

She was on pins and needles, every sound making her jump as she expected Bryce to sneak in and whisk her away, but so far there'd been no sign of him. With each passing hour, she was growing more unnerved.

She and Isabelle had decided, unless they heard differently from him, they would don the disguising clothes and wear them the next day under their wedding finery. If Bryce showed up at the last minute, they would be able to yank off their gowns, appear to be boys, and ride away from Parthenia forever.

"There has been an...accident," Captain Romilard said.

"What sort of accident?"

"Miss Clementi has returned from Egypt."

Kat was surprised at how little emotion the announcement generated. "Bully for her."

"She tried to assassinate the King."

It was always amusing to prick at Romilard's temper. "She tried to kill my brother, Nicholas?"

"You know who the king is, Your Grace."

"Oh, you mean my cousin, Kristof. Since you state that she *tried* to kill him, I take it he survived."

"Yes, he survived."

"What was her weapon of choice? Did she slice at him with a knife? Did she shoot at him with a pistol?"

Two slashes of red stained his cheeks. "She used a pistol."

"My, my, how very brave of her."

"Or mad," Romilard countered. "She seems a tad deranged."

"Does she?" Kat blandly asked.

"She suffered many difficulties on the road."

"How awful for her. I'm sure there must be someone in the palace who would commiserate over her story, but I guarantee you I am not that person."

He was spitting with offense, nearly choking on the scolding he wanted to vent over Kat leaving Pippa in Egypt. In the end, he bit his tongue. "As you wish, Your Grace. I won't bore you with the details." "Pippa shot, but she missed? Is that what you've come to tell me?"

"One of the things. The King was grazed in the arm."

"The poor dear." Kat oozed false sympathy. "I trust he's recuperating?"

"He's in his private chambers, and I have orders to escort you to him."

"Why? I hardly have any nursing skills, and I am on my way to the chapel. While I'm there, I'll pray for his speedy recovery."

He sighed, her recalcitrance irking him to his limit. "There has been a change of plans."

"What change?"

"The King feels there is too much unrest among the populace, and it might be dangerous to have a public event tomorrow. With tensions running high, he doesn't care to be out and about in crowds and riding in the scheduled parade."

"What are you talking about? You're making no sense at all."

"He will skip the elaborate celebration."

Kat scowled. "We're not marrying?"

"Yes, you're marrying. You're marrying right *now*. The priest is in the King's chambers. They're waiting for you."

"Marry...now? I couldn't possibly."

"You'll have to explain it to the King. I'm simply the messenger sent to fetch you."

Kat's heart was pounding so loudly that her ears were ringing.

Her wedding was supposed to be in about thirty hours. She was supposed to have the entire afternoon, evening, night, and morning for Bryce to proceed. The ceremony couldn't be held immediately. It gave her no time to get word to him, to warn him.

"The wedding is tomorrow," she mumbled like an idiot.

"No, it's today instead. I fail to see how it makes any difference."

"I can't go through with it."

"Why can't you?"

What answer could she provide that would be believed? "Have you found my brother?"

"No."

"It can't occur without him there. My sister must be there too. I insist. You'll have to locate them first."

"Again, Your Highness, you'll have to take it up with the King. But I must apprise you that—after Miss Clementi's shenanigans—he's out of sorts. You won't be able to dissuade him."

"No one can force me."

Romilard shrugged. "You can marry today or marry tomorrow. As I mentioned, I don't see how it matters."

Romilard's patience was waning, and she was frantic, trying to stall, but she couldn't think straight.

"What became of Miss Clementi after the shooting?" She wasn't really interested but hoped to lure him into gossiping, which would delay the inevitable.

"The British lord who's visiting, Lord Radcliffe? He caught her as she was fleeing the hall."

"Lord Radcliffe? How gallant of him."

"He was closest to her," Romilard grumbled. "I had already left or I would have gotten to her."

"Oh, I'm sure." Casually she asked, "Is he still downstairs? Perhaps I should speak with him to offer my thanks for his valiant efforts on the King's behalf."

"He was there when I departed, but there's no time for dawdling. The King awaits."

Romilard gestured to his men, and they moved to surround her. She stepped away and said, "One moment, please. I need to grab my shawl."

She whirled and went into her bedchamber where Isabelle was crouched in the corner.

"You heard?" Kat whispered.

"Yes."

"Find Mr. Blair. Tell him what's transpired. I can't refuse to leave with them."

"I know."

"Your Highness," Romilard called, "the King is in a foul temper.

We oughtn't make it worse by lollygagging."

Kat swept out to the sitting room, and she glared at Romilard. "I will go at my own pace, Captain. Don't command me. The King may be in a foul temper, but you haven't begun to see how angry I can become. You've been on my bad side for months. Might I suggest you consider getting on my good side?"

She sauntered by all of them, and while they were impatient and inclined to hurry, she strolled along, in no hurry at all.

&c&d &c&d &c&d &c&d

"We'll teach you to fight. Don't you worry about that."

Nicholas grinned up at the twins, Michael and Matthew Blair. They were his new chums, his new heroes. After Mr. Blair of course. No one could ever take his place in Nicholas's regard, but his brothers were a close second.

"I've always thought I should learn to defend myself," he said. "I won't be much of a ruler unless I can thwart my enemies."

"I absolutely agree," Matthew replied. "Every boy should learn how to defend himself, but how to muster a solid offense too."

"I'll teach you to fight dirty," Michael said as Matthew said, "And I'll teach you how to fight honorably and well."

Michael added, "You never know what type of punches you'll need to throw. You have to practice both kinds."

"Since you'll finish growing up in England," Matthew said, "we'll have to reflect on a stint in the British army for you. It would be beneficial. It would help you to acquire the necessary skills to come back here and seize what is yours."

"I would love to be a soldier," Nicholas said. "My father and I used to discuss it, but since I was his only son, he believed the risks were too great."

"Nonsense," Matthew scoffed. "We'll put you in a good regiment. My stepbrother, Rafe, is enlisted at the moment. By the time you're ready to join, I'll buy him a commission so he'll be an officer. You can serve under him, and he'll watch over you."

"I'd like that," Nicholas said.

They were in the palace, outside the main hall. Nicholas was dressed in the old sweater and knitted cap Mr. Blair had given him, so there was no possibility of his being recognized. And with the Blair twins towering over him, he felt very safe.

Not that anyone was paying any attention to them. There'd been an incident in the presence chamber, so people were running and shouting and it was extremely chaotic. Nicholas wasn't certain what had occurred, but it was thrilling to stand on the edge of it and observe the frenzy.

A footman rushed by, and Michael stopped him. "What happened in there?"

"Miss Clementi attempted to murder the King."

"Who is Miss Clementi?"

"A childhood friend to Princess Morovsky."

"Why did she shoot him?"

"I have no idea."

"Is the King dead?"

"No, just grazed in the arm. If you'll excuse me? I have to find the doctor."

Michael stepped to where Matthew and Nicholas were huddled in an alcove. He asked Nicholas, "Who is Miss Clementi? Do you know her?"

"She's the shrew who had us kidnapped in Egypt and brought back against our will. She might have been a friend of my sister when they were girls, but she's definitely not now."

Nicholas glanced over and saw Isabelle walking by. She was being furtive, trying not to be noticed, which wasn't difficult. With everyone in a panic, she might have been invisible.

"Isabelle," he murmured as she passed.

She peeked around, searching for him. He lifted his cap slightly, and her eyes widened with surprise. She hurried over.

"I thought you were with Mr. Blair," she quietly scolded. "You shouldn't be here."

"I'm fine, Belle. These are his brothers, Michael and Matthew Blair."

"Hello, Your Highness," the twins said in unison.

"You won't believe what happened," Isabelle told them.

"Yes, Kristof was shot," Nicholas said.

"Who cares about that?" she asked. "He was so shaken by the attack that he's decided to skip the big ceremony he had planned for tomorrow. He's ordered Kat to wed him immediately in his private chambers."

"What?" Nicholas gasped.

"Captain Romilard came to fetch her. She refused, but he took her anyway. She sent me to advise Mr. Blair that there's no time to delay. We have to save her."

"This makes things a tad more interesting," Michael mused.

"What should we do?" Nicholas asked him.

He and his brother stared at each other for a lengthy period, almost as if they were carrying on a conversation in their heads, then Michael peered down at him.

"Here's what I need from you, Nicholas."

"Just tell me what it is, and I shall see to it."

"Matthew and I will locate Bryce, and the three of us will rescue your sister."

"All right," Nicholas said.

"While we're occupied with that, you and Isabelle must sneak out of the palace. Stop by the nursery and retrieve the clothes we hid so she can change. Then scoot out as fast as you can. Have the horses saddled and wait for us at the secret spot we arranged."

Matthew asked, "Can you do that?"

"Of course," Nicholas scoffed.

"You'll have to be very brave," Matthew said.

"I am the Crown Prince of Parthenia. I was raised to be a king, and I will be a king someday. I've never been afraid of anything in my life, and I'm not afraid now."

Matthew nodded. "You'll be a fine soldier when you're a bit older."

"Thank you."

"Get going," Matthew urged. "We'll meet you at the secret spot."

Michael reached in his boot and pulled out a knife. He handed it to Nicholas. "If you have any trouble, use this. Don't dither. Stab like you mean it."

Nicholas stuck the knife into the sleeve of his sweater. "I will. Where my sister is concerned, I won't hesitate to protect her."

Matthew grinned at Michael. "I'm liking this boy more and more."

"Welcome to the family, Nicholas," Michael said. "You too, Isabelle."

"We're grateful that you'll have us," Nicholas replied.

He bowed to the two men, and Isabelle curtsied, then she strolled away. Nicholas followed behind her as if he was her servant. They been highly trained, reared in the royal way, and they knew how to play their parts.

"Where have you been?"

Kristof barked the question at Katarina. It had been an eternity since he'd sent Captain Romilard after her.

His head was pounding, his wound throbbing. The doctor had declared it to be a minor scratch, but it stung much more than Kristof could ever have imagined it might. He'd been doused with laudanum and had also downed three tall whiskeys. Opiates always made him nauseous, and the liquor being dumped on top wasn't helping.

He felt faint, and if they didn't get a move on, he'd either vomit up the contents of his stomach or fall asleep before he could complete the vows.

"Hello, to you too, Kristof." She sounded quite snotty. "I see you're in your usual sweet temper."

"I summoned you ages ago."

"You're constantly laboring under the impression that you can command me."

"I'm not in the mood for your haughty attitude, Katarina."

"And I'm not in the mood for yours." His royal arm was heavily bandaged and cradled in a sling, and she gave it a cursory glance. "I hear you had a problem with your chum, Pippa Clementi."

"The deranged woman almost killed me."

"It appears she missed."

"She didn't *miss*. A few inches to the left, and I'd be dead."

"Lucky for you Pippa never was good at anything. I hope you've had her locked in the dungeons, for I must tell you—after how she treated me in Egypt—I really shouldn't bump into her in the halls. It would be...unpleasant."

She flashed such a dangerous glare at Kristof that he could barely keep from flinching. How did she exude such imperious disregard? It was probably from being born to the title. She'd had twenty-five years to learn how to be imposing. He was only just figuring it out.

"You must cease your complaints about Pippa," he scolded.

"Never."

"When she was with you in Egypt, she was serving the Crown."

"Pippa is a traitor to my family and a disloyal shrew. Don't presume to extol her virtues. I won't listen."

Kristof tried to match her glare, tried to seem as forbidding, but he was feeling ill and was simply desperate for the horrid afternoon to end.

He gestured to the priest. "Let's get on with it."

"Yes, Your Majesty."

Kristof was seated in a chair and too wobbly to stand. He waved at Katarina so she'd come over and stand next to him. Instead she sat in a chair too.

"What are we doing?" she asked.

"We're holding the wedding ceremony."

"I'm not speaking any vows."

"You are, Katarina," he fumed. "Don't argue over it."

"We're supposed to have a grand celebration with the whole country fêting us. Yet you want to slink off and do it in secret. Why?"

"The masses are restless. I don't wish to stir the flames of discord."

"You're scared of our citizens?"

"At the moment, when my arm is throbbing and I could have died? Yes, I'm absolutely terrified of them."

"Our people don't like you? I wonder why not?" She smiled a cocky smile. "They love me, and I demand the wedding I was promised."

"Well, you're not having it," he snapped.

"My brother and sister aren't here either. I won't proceed without them. Nicholas planned to walk me down the aisle."

"We're not waiting for them." He motioned to the priest, but the idiot hemmed and hawed. Kristof bellowed, "Get on with it!"

"Majesty," the toad groveled, "if the Princess is opposed, I can't possibly carry on."

Kristof glowered at Dmitri. He was the only other person in the room with them, would be the only witness.

"Dmitri, you have sixty seconds to explain this dunce's role to him. If he's not ready to begin by then, it will be the last ceremony he ever performs."

The priest blanched and started leafing through his prayer book, looking for the correct page.

"I won't marry him," Katarina said to the priest. "He can't force me, can he, Father?"

"Ah...ah..." the priest mumbled.

Kristof scowled at Katarina. "I have Nicholas in my custody. If you refuse me, he will pay in all the ways I swore he would."

"You don't have Nicholas," she smugly retorted. "I know exactly where he is and he's not with you." She stared at the priest again. "Are we finished?"

Suddenly there was a pounding on the outer doors to Kristof's suite. No one was there to answer. Everyone was down in the presence chamber, gleefully gossiping about the shooting.

"Oh, for bloody sake," Dmitri grumbled, and he spun as if he'd march out to learn who had interrupted.

Before he could though, the inner doors burst open and Lord Radcliffe bustled in, his twin brothers flanking him. Katarina rose and went over to them. Lord Radcliffe murmured in her ear, then shoved her behind him so they were blocking her from Kristof's view.

Dmitri spoke up. "I'm sorry, Lord Radcliffe, but this is a private meeting. You're not welcome."

Radcliffe ignored Dmitri and kept his gaze locked on Kristof. "We heard there's about to be a wedding."

"Yes, there is, Radcliffe. The Princess and I are marrying."

Radcliffe frowned. "Katarina is marrying you?"

Kristof bristled at his using Katarina's Christian name. "Yes. In light of today's excitement"—Kristof pointed to his sling—"we thought we should avoid any pomp and circumstance. If you'll excuse us...?"

Radcliffe didn't budge, and Dmitri said, "Really, Lord Radcliffe, you're being a boor. I'll just escort you out."

He huffed over to Radcliffe as if he'd manhandle him, but the twins stepped in his path. They engaged in a staring match Dmitri could never win, and he skulked back a stride or two.

"You can't wed her," Radcliffe told Kristof.

"Why can't I?" Kristof snidely inquired.

"Because she's already married."

The priest and Dmitri gasped, as Kristof demanded, "To whom?"

"To me," Radcliffe boasted. "We were wed in Cairo before she left."

"That's a lie!" Kristof raged.

"No, it isn't," Radcliffe claimed, "and I hate to tell you this, but I believe she's increasing with my child. You wouldn't put my son on *your* throne, would you?"

The priest shut his prayer book and hurried out without a word.

Kristof felt as if he'd been punched in the stomach. He studied Radcliffe and his brothers, loathing how handsome they were, how tall, dashing, and dynamic. How dare they be so spectacular! How dare they ruin everything!

"Is it true?" he snarled at Katarina. "Don't think to further deceive me."

She peeked around Radcliffe and her expression was impish. "Yes, I've been married for ages."

"Why didn't you confess it?" Kristof roared. "Why persist with the ruse that you might ultimately be my bride."

"You had threatened Nicholas and Isabelle, and I couldn't risk that you might harm them. I've simply been waiting for my husband to arrive to save me from you."

"Where has he been all this time?"

Radcliffe answered for her. "Your Captain Romilard ordered my murder in Egypt, but as you can see, I'm fine."

Kristof was incensed. With Katarina. With Radcliffe. With Captain Romilard who never seemed to accomplish any task he was assigned.

"Dmitri," he seethed, "summon the guards. I want these men arrested."

Radcliffe chuckled. "You actually imagine they could succeed?"

He nodded to his brothers, and in a quick minute, Dmitri and Kristof were tied to their chairs and gagged so they couldn't call out.

Radcliffe towered over Kristof, and as a final insult he said, "We've spread the story everywhere of how you treated Nicholas and Isabelle. We've told everyone that Kat was wed to me, that you tried to have me killed because of it, that you tried to force her into matrimony when she'd been adamantly opposed."

Lies, all lies! Kristof complained behind the gag, his hatred wafting out of his eyes. *I am King here! You shall not belittle me this way!*

"Rumors about us and *you* have been circulating," Radcliffe continued. "Soon the entire country will know what you did to the Morovsky heirs." He scoffed and taunted, "May the rest of your reign be as stable and productive as the first part has been."

One of the twins sarcastically said, "I've heard the first part hasn't been all that grand."

The other said, "I'm betting the remainder of it won't last too long."

Katarina couldn't leave well enough alone either. "Goodbye, Cousin Kristof. Nicholas is a boy now, but he won't always be. He'll return one day and recover what you stole from him. You have a few years where you'll be safe, but you'd best keep looking over your shoulder."

The group whipped away and marched out, Katarina in the center of the trio and obviously protected by them in a manner Kristof could never have offered. They pulled the door shut and spun the key in the lock.

Kristof and Dmitri sat in a stunned silence, listening as their strides faded down the corridor. Then they started to kick with their feet and struggle against their bindings. But they couldn't seem to generate much noise and—as if they suddenly hadn't a friend in the world—no one came to assist.

Bryce rushed Katarina toward the rear of the palace. They had hidden clothes for her in the nursery, but there wasn't time to retrieve them. It was more important to get her to the horses and ride off. The border was fourteen miles away, and while guards could follow them, he'd feel much better once they were in another country.

They rounded a corner, and to his dismay, they ran into Captain Romilard. Thankfully he was by himself, his usual contingent missing. The halls were abnormally quiet with everyone downstairs, clucking over the shooting, bragging about what they'd witnessed.

Bryce bristled with offense and dislike. Romilard hadn't attacked him in Cairo, hadn't beaten him within an inch of his life or sold him into slavery. But he'd ordered all of it done.

"Your Grace," he said to Kat. "Or is it Your Majesty now? Is the ceremony over?"

"Yes," Kat smoothly lied. "Lord Radcliffe and his brothers are accompanying me to my rooms."

"That's odd." Romilard's smile was cunning and sly. "Your suite is in the other direction. You're going the wrong way."

Kat glanced up at Bryce. "Lord Radcliffe, this oaf has always been insolent and impertinent to me. His brother is Kristof's chief advisor, so he feels free to disrespect and disparage me."

"Does he?" Bryce replied.

"Turn around, Princess," Romilard dared to command. "We'll speak to the King and ask him if you're supposed to be traipsing off with these men."

Kat scowled at Bryce. "See what I mean, Lord Radcliffe? He is the most rude, impudent dog I've ever met."

"I see that," Bryce agreed as the twins stiffened, ready to deal with the prick so Bryce wouldn't have to. But Bryce was more than happy to ensure Romilard never insulted a female ever again.

Bryce assessed Romilard and couldn't conceal a blanch of astonishment. He had a sword on his hip. It was an ancient weapon made from gold and polished steel with jewels in the hilt. It dangled from a delicately-tooled leather sheath.

"That's a fine sword you have there," Bryce said.

Romilard put his hand on the hilt, sensing a fight coming too. "Yes, it is. It's very fine."

"Where did you get it?" Bryce hissed.

"It was a gift from my men. They took it off a criminal in Egypt." Romilard stared into Bryce's blue eyes, and he frowned. He'd only glimpsed Bryce in passing at Valois's villa, and he asked, "Don't I know you from somewhere?"

"No, but *I* am the criminal your accomplices stole it from in Egypt."

"Bugger off, Radcliffe," Romilard crudely retorted. "It's mine, and I'm not inclined to part with it."

He had the audacity to grab Kat's arm as if he'd pull her away from them, and Bryce couldn't decide if he was deranged or if his ego was so inflated that he assumed he could beat Bryce and his brothers in a brawl. But no man could. Not when they stood shoulder to shoulder like a brick wall.

"Let's go, Princess," Romilard said, "to your husband, the King."

Kat jerked out of his grasp, and Bryce hit him as hard as he could. He collapsed to his knees and hovered there, blood dripping from his nose. He braced and would have leapt up, but Michael was on him before he could, a hand on his throat, a knee crushed into his back.

Bryce peered over at Matthew. "Would you escort Kat to the horses? Michael and I will join you in a minute."

"Certainly." Matthew's steady gaze apprised Bryce he understood precisely what was about to transpire.

"What is it?" Kat asked. "What's happening?"

"The sword on Romilard's belt belonged to my father," Bryce said. Michael and Matthew gasped with surprise, saying together,

"What?"

"A man who befriended me in Cairo, he knew Father well. Years ago, Father left it at his house, and he's had it all this time. He gave it to me. It's a priceless memento, and Captain Romilard doesn't get to keep it."

Kat looked as if she'd argue that she should stay and watch the ending, but Bryce nodded to her. "Go, Kat. I'll be with you shortly."

"We shouldn't dally, Princess," Matthew told her. "They can finish up without us."

Kat bit down on whatever her comment might have been, and Matthew hurried her out.

Once she was away, Michael yanked Romilard to his feet. Bryce leaned in so they were toe to toe, but he was many inches taller and much more robust than the pathetic little tyrant.

"The sword is mine," Bryce informed him.

"You'll have to kill me to take it," Romilard blustered.

"I intend to."

Romilard opened his mouth to call for help, but before he could murmur a sound, Bryce was holding his father's weapon. He stabbed Romilard straight through the heart, then casually stepped to the side as his life's blood drained out.

"Asshole," Michael muttered as he released Romilard. He dropped like a rock, his head smacking the stones with a muted thud.

Bryce wiped the blade clean on Romilard's trousers, then he sliced the belt and retrieved the sheath. He attached it to his own belt.

As he glanced up, Michael was studying him in an odd manner.

"What?" Bryce inquired.

"Matthew once asked me what you were like, and I claimed you weren't anything like him and me."

"What is that supposed to mean."

"I claimed you weren't the type to stab somebody in the heart and blithely walk away."

"I hate this guy."

"That's obvious," Michael mused.

"Someday I'll tell you what occurred in Egypt. I barely survived."

Michael pointed to Romilard. "He was responsible? He harmed you?"

"His men did, but they were simply carrying out his orders to murder me."

"Bastard," Michael spat.

"And I am Julian Blair's son. No one can take from me what is mine." He gestured down the hall. "Let's go. I need to catch up with my fiancée. I'm not ever letting her out of my sight again."

The two brothers rushed off, Romilard a forgotten lump on the floor.

CHAPTER TWENTY-SIX

"Goodbye, Calais. Goodbye, France. Goodbye, Europe."

Kat stood at the bow of their ship, smiling at Isabelle who was throwing flowers into the water. The wind was catching the sails as the captain maneuvered them out of the harbor. In a few hours, they'd be in England.

"Do you miss Parthenia?" Kat asked her.

"No," Isabelle scoffed.

"Would you go back someday?"

"Maybe if Nicholas was sitting on the throne, but not while Kristof is pretending to be king."

"I agree."

"Life was grand when Father was still alive. I hate how Kristof wrecked everything."

"So do I."

"Will the people ever tire of him?"

"Yes," Kat said, "and I imagine it will happen very soon. When we departed, they were already growing restless."

"I'll never understand how someone could pick Kristof over Nicholas."

"I'll never understand it either. Father would have been so angry. I'm glad he wasn't there to witness what occurred."

"I'm glad too," Isabelle said. "I could never bear to have him upset."

Kat reached over and ran her fingers through Isabelle's hair. It was a pretty chestnut color, but it used to flow to her bottom, and Kat had spend many years brushing and braiding it. But now it was cropped at her shoulders, swinging loose and free and too short to even be tied with a ribbon.

On the afternoon Isabelle and Nicholas had sneaked out of the palace, when they'd gone to saddle the horses for Bryce and Kat, they'd stopped by the nursery so Isabelle could change into the boy's clothes that would conceal her identity.

She'd ordered Nicholas to cut her hair, and though Nicholas had put up a fuss, Isabelle had won the argument. He'd taken a knife and sliced through the braid so Isabelle could don a knitted cap like his, so she could pull it over her eyes and hide her face. Then she'd dropped the lengthy rope of hair into their old toy box and shut the lid.

Occasionally Kat thought about that hair, lying alone and forlorn. Would Kristof ever wed and have children? Would they ever play in the nursery and open the toy box? What would they think of that shorn braid tossed inside?

She spun and stared at the receding coastline, the receding town. They were about to leave the quieter bay and move out into the Channel.

The captain had warned her that the seas would be rougher, that they might be nauseous at the start, but he swore the waves would even out and carry them to their new life with no trouble at all.

Toward the stern, Nicholas was huddled with the twins, and on seeing them together, Kat sighed. He'd bonded with the two men, and they were constantly in deep discussion, talking about fighting and strategy and tactics. Matthew Blair had been a soldier since he was very young, so Nicholas was particularly fascinated by his stories of bravery and battle.

Apparently she'd have a brother join the army before too much more time had passed, and she couldn't decide how she felt about that. Nicholas insisted he needed the training and discipline the army would provide, and Matthew insisted he'd learn leadership skills that would serve him well when he went back to Parthenia.

At the moment, with her home country naught but a distant memory, she didn't want him to ever go back. Nor could she imagine returning herself. Her future was in England and Scotland with Bryce.

She understood Nicholas's yearning to reclaim what was his though, and she would always help him to achieve that goal. She suspected—with the Blair brothers offering their protection and advice—Nicholas would succeed at whatever he chose to do in Parthenia. How could Kristof hope to keep what he'd stolen?

Bryce climbed out of the hold and onto the deck. He looked very grand, but then he always looked magnificent. Their weeks of riding across Europe had lightened his hair so it was once again a golden blond. He'd begun shaving too, so the beard was removed. Attired as he was in tan breeches, a flowing white shirt, and knee-high black boots, he might have been a pirate about to commit mayhem.

He came over, and he had a wool blanket woven in a beautiful plaid of dark greens and reds, a purple and white stitch thrown in to add intrigue.

He leaned down for a quick kiss, then he wrapped the blanket around her so she discovered it wasn't a blanket after all, but a long swatch of Scottish tartan. It was very warm and instantly warded off the cold wind. She grabbed Isabelle and drew her close, wrapping the tartan around her too.

Bryce pointed to the fabric. "Michael and Matthew brought it from Radcliffe Castle. It's my family's pattern."

"It's lovely," Kat said.

"If I was any kind of Scot, I'd have dressed myself in it, but I'm not certain how the blasted garment is supposed to be worn."

Isabelle peeked up at him. "After we're in Scotland, you'll have to ask the elders in the castle. They'll know how."

"I'm positive they will," he agreed. He gazed at the receding coastline. "I can't say I'm sad to see France disappearing."

"Neither can I," Kat said.

"Might Captain Romilard follow us to England?" Isabelle nervously inquired. "Should we be on the lookout for him?"

"No, Isabelle," Bryce assured her. "He wouldn't dare follow us to England. He's too scared of me and my brothers."

"As he should be," Isabelle regally stated.

She'd posed the question a thousand times, and he'd furnished the same answer a thousand times. But evidently she was more anxious by all that had happened than she liked to let on. She'd been raised to be a princess, to take things in stride, but she was only ten. The past two years had been a nightmare of upheavals and drama that no child should have to suffer.

Bryce gestured to Nicholas who was still huddled with Michael and Matthew at the other end of the ship. "Why don't you ask if they're ready? Will you give me a minute alone with Katarina?"

"I will." Isabelle giggled. "But not too much kissing!"

"I wouldn't dream of it," Bryce said.

"Not until you're married."

"Which will be very, very soon."

Isabelle ran off, and Bryce snuggled next to Kat, being enveloped in the warmth of the wool. It was December and the temperature icy. The wind made it feel even colder.

Once Isabelle had skittered away, Kat said, "Tell me the truth. Did you kill Captain Romilard?" So far on the trip, he'd refused to confide any details of the encounter.

"Will you be upset if I say *yes*?"

"I won't be upset. I will be delighted."

"Then *yes*. I killed him for what he had done to me in Egypt, for every insult he ever leveled at you, and so he couldn't rush to Kristof's chambers and release him one second earlier than I wanted him released."

"My hero." She batted her lashes at him. "If Romilard is dead, I don't have to worry about him, but what about Kristof? Will he send guards to England? Will he try to take us back?"

"The road behind us has been empty ever since we left Parthenia. Maybe he convinced himself that you aren't worth the bother."

"Maybe, but I'm concerned about Nicholas and Isabelle. Remember in Egypt? We had several kidnapping attempts."

"We'll spend most of our time in Scotland, so any foreign strangers would stick out like a sore thumb. They wouldn't be able to get within ten miles of Radcliffe without someone notifying us."

"I'll hope that remains true."

He pulled her close and kissed her cheek. "Don't be afraid. I would never let anything bad happen to you."

"I know."

They stood silently for a bit, enjoying the sway of the ship, the caw of the gulls overhead.

"I'm happy," he said.

"So am I."

"I didn't think I'd ever marry."

"I thought I would, but I figured it would be a political union, forged under a treaty to some aging despot whom I couldn't abide."

He grinned. "I saved you from that fate at least."

"And I will always be grateful."

"Are you sure about this?"

"Of course."

"There's no going back," he reminded her.

"There's no going back for you either. If you wake up some morning and decide it's exhausting to have a house full of royals, I don't want to hear a word of complaint."

"I'm starting to like it," he claimed.

She snorted. "I'll ask you in six months and see how you reply."

He pointed to their four siblings, who were merrily chatting. "My family is growing by leaps and bounds. For so long, it was just me on my own. I never believed I could change my situation."

"You were likely wary of changing it too. After discovering how quickly stable things can fall apart, it definitely makes a person cautious."

"It definitely does," he concurred.

In their frantic dash across Europe, he'd shared the heartbreaking tale about his parents. Kat couldn't imagine what it must have been like, especially for Anne Blair, with her husband deceased, her children being so little, and her not being able to stay with them.

Kat wished she could argue that her own family was better, less cruel and less greedy, but the Morovsky clan had no right to brag. Kristof had proven her kin possessed as much avarice and malice as anyone. Yet Kat had only had to suffer tragedy and turmoil for two years. Bryce had suffered from the time he was a tiny boy.

He was such a fine man, strong and faithful, steady and devoted. He'd overcome every obstacle, had raised himself to heights that seemed impossible when his rough beginnings were considered.

His brothers were the same, had both achieved remarkable feats. What extraordinary men they all were.

Their sister was searching for their mother, optimistically hoping the woman might still be alive. If Evangeline could locate her, she intended to bring her to England, to have her pardoned and reunited with her children. Kat secretly vowed—as an unspoken wedding gift to her husband—that she would spend any amount of her fortune necessary to find out what had happened to Anne Blair.

It would be a way to show her immense gratitude to the Blair family. When she and her siblings had been alone in the world, when they hadn't had a friend who would dare to stand by them, the Blair brothers had stepped forward. The Blair brothers had offered their loyalty and protection. Kat could never fully repay that debt.

Bryce was nervous about Kat's decision to wed him. He assumed he was too far beneath her, that she'd ultimately regret it. *He* thought he was reaching too high, but Kat was the one who'd garnered much more than she deserved.

Who wouldn't want to marry Bryce Blair? He was handsome, dashing, brave, trustworthy, and wickedly fun. Who wouldn't want him? Who wouldn't love him?

She probably should have left him in peace, should have let some other woman have him. But it was her heart's demand that—for once—she not be selfless, that she not be noble. For once, she would take what she desired—without reflection, without apology.

She'd cherished the title of Her Royal Highness, but she couldn't wait to be Mrs. Bryce Blair and Lady Radcliffe instead. She was a princess who no longer had a home or a country or a place to call her own. Yet she had Bryce Blair, which meant she had much more than she would ever need.

The ship maneuvered past the jetty, the waves growing bigger as they headed into open water. The sails cracked and snapped in the sharper breeze. Sea spray splashed over the bow, wetting them, and they laughed and twirled in circles.

The captain approached and asked, "Shall we proceed, Lord Radcliffe?"

Bryce smiled at Kat. "Last chance. Are you still sure?"

"Yes, I'm sure."
"You'll be mine now."
"And you'll be mine."
"I like the sound of that."

Matthew, Michael, Isabelle, and Nicholas came over and stood behind them. Isabelle had a few flowers she hadn't tossed into the ocean. She gave them to Kat, and Nicholas clasped her arm and turned her to Bryce.

"She's yours, Mr. Blair," he solemnly said. "Swear to me you'll always take care of her."

"I always will, Your Grace," Bryce responded just as seriously. "Don't worry for a single second. I will go to my grave taking care of her."

Michael grinned at Bryce. "I'm trying to picture Evangeline's expression when we walk into Radcliffe Castle not only with you, but with an entire family in tow. What will she have to say?"

"She'll say she had no idea I was smart enough to make myself so happy." He gazed at Kat. "Are you ready?"

"I've been ready my whole life."

They faced the captain, and he opened an old, tattered prayer book, but he didn't need to glance at the words to recite them. It was an abbreviated version of the vows, but the most important parts were all there. And it was just as binding as it would have been if they'd been standing in a cathedral in London.

"Dearly beloved..." he began.

Bryce squeezed her hand as tightly as he could. "That's what you are. My *dearly* beloved, and you always will be."

Kat peered up into his blue, blue eyes, and she felt safe, protected, and adored.

When the captain asked, "Your Highness, Katarina Victoria Sasha Webster Morovsky, do you take this man, Bryce Blair, Lord Radcliffe, to be your lawfully wedded husband?"

She could only answer, "Oh, yes, I definitely do. For now and forevermore."

EPILOGUE(S)

"A princess—of all things!"

"Yes, a real princess. What do you think of that?"

Evangeline smiled at Bryce. "Of all the surprises you might have brought home, it's the last I would have expected. But, dear brother, a princess is precisely what you deserve."

"I can't believe she agreed to have me. My head is still spinning over it."

"In the bargain, we get to help raise a royal princess and a king. We've certainly come up in the world from where we were when you left for Egypt."

"We certainly have."

Evangeline gazed around the main receiving hall of Radcliffe Castle. It was packed with people, the Christmas supper about to be served. Servants were running, guests laughing, drinking, and jesting. The Yule log burned in the grate, and musicians were seated in the corner and playing carols.

Christmas morning had started at the chapel in the village with Bryce and Kat repeating their vows. They'd wanted to speak the words with Radcliffe residents looking on, and they'd been intent on writing their names in the church's Bible where all of the previous earls and countesses had signed after their weddings, their ancestors going back hundreds of years.

In light of the road she and her brothers had all traveled, in light of the difficulties they'd overcome to have Radcliffe returned to them, it had been a poignant and emotional moment.

After the meal was concluded, there would be dancing, cards, games, and other entertainment. She'd invited the important neighbors, the merchants in the surrounding villages, and most of the tenant farmers.

Gradually the castle was blossoming, shucking off its aura of misery and bad luck. The greatest news of all was the title and rank of Bryce's bride. She had been trained in all the social graces, would know how to manage such a large, sprawling abode. Evangeline didn't have to worry anymore about how the place would be rebuilt and refurbished to its prior grandeur.

Over the past week, the entire family had arrived, and the fact that she could claim an *entire* family was particularly thrilling.

Her husband, Aaron, was at the head table, chatting with Katarina. Evangeline and Bryce would join them in a few minutes.

Also at the front, Matthew and Michael sat with their wives, Clarissa and Magdalena. Aaron's brother, Lucas and his wife Amelia, were seated with them too. Everyone had babies now, with the little ones upstairs and put to bed for the night. The old nursery was packed with so many youngsters Evangeline had had to hire five women from the village to care for them all.

King Nicholas and Princess Isabelle were off at a side table with the other children, and Evangeline thought it an excellent sign that Kat insisted her siblings be seated there, that they not be given special favors or treatment.

Already Nicholas had won over the children in attendance. He was a charming, magnetic boy, and Evangeline expected he would have an amazing future.

"What a fine looking family," she mused. "We must have good bloodlines."

"The very best," Bryce replied.

"When we first crossed paths, did you ever imagine we would end up with such a mob of relatives?"

"No," Bryce said. "I felt awfully fortunate just to have stumbled on you."

"I told you I'd locate everybody else."

"I didn't believe you."

They hadn't found her mother though, but Evangeline had learned she'd survived the treacherous journey to Australia. If she'd survived the trip, why couldn't she still be alive?

Evangeline had sent many inquires to the foreign country, had hired lawyers and investigators, and she was waiting for any information. It was frustrating that the Earth was so huge and the mail so slow. It took forever to receive a single response.

Evangeline sighed with delight. "Husbands, wives, babies."

"Step-siblings, in-laws."

"The room is filled to overflowing. We're so lucky."

"Yes, we are." Bryce grinned down at her. "Have I thanked you for arranging to have Christmas here?"

"Only a hundred times."

"Make it a hundred and one. Thank you. For all of this. I never thought we could retrieve what was ours."

"I know, you horrid pessimist. You ran away to Egypt rather than try, but it was much simpler to accomplish than I could ever have predicted."

"Considering all that happened to me there, I'm wishing I'd remained at home."

"Then you wouldn't have met Kat."

"There is that, I guess."

"Will you ever tell me how you got that scar on your cheek?"

"No, and if you think that one's bad, you should see the ones on my back."

She scowled. "Are you joking? What happened to you? Tell me the truth."

"Well, I nearly drowned, starved, and perished from typhus. I lost all my possessions. I had to hire on as a laborer. I was set upon by brigands on numerous dire occasions. I was nearly murdered or robbed whenever I turned a corner. I was flogged, sold into slavery, left for dead, and my best friend and I split apart after a dreadful quarrel." He paused. "Hmm...have I forgotten anything?"

Her scowl deepened. "All of those disasters could not possibly have occurred."

He chuckled. "Some of them did. I'll let you decide which of them transpired and which didn't. But I will say this: I'm staying put. I've seen the world, and I don't need to see it again."

"I'm glad you made it back safe and sound."

"So am I. You have no idea."

Aaron gazed down from the head table, and she gestured to him, visually apprising him she was ready to begin the ceremony she'd planned. He banged his goblet on the wood, like a Viking lord, and the gathering grew silent.

She and Bryce walked down the aisle and stopped at the fireplace where the Yulelog was burning with such cheery flames. She waved to Michael and Matthew, and they rose and joined her. The four Blair siblings faced the crowd.

"As you know by now," she said, "our father and mother should have been earl and countess here."

There were nods and murmurs all around.

The tittering died down, and she continued. "Before Bryce departed for Egypt, we were investigating our past. An acquaintance gave us portraits of my parents that my father had commissioned for their wedding. I've had them hung in the hall so we will always be able to glance up and see them watching over us."

The paintings were covered to keep them hidden until this unveiling. She motioned to the servants, and they tugged on the cloths, drawing them away.

And...there they were, so young and gorgeous and extraordinary.

People gasped, clapped, smiled, pointed, and beamed with pleasure.

Her father, Julian, was tall, dark, and handsome. He was attired as the adventurer he'd been in a flowing white shirt, a jaunty kerchief circling his neck. Dangling from a belt on his hip, he wore the sword Bryce had brought with him from Egypt. He was so dashing and charismatic he might have been a hero in a romantic novel.

Her mother, Anne, was beautiful, her exuberance and charm seeming to leap off the canvas. She was dressed in a sapphire gown, and the artist had captured her verve and spirit, her flamboyance and splendor. She appeared merry and mischievous, as if she had spent her life laughing with joy.

Bryce had seen the portraits, but Michael and Matthew had not, so this was their first glimpse with the rest of the room.

The twins looked exactly like their father, while she and Bryce looked exactly like their mother. Both parents had had the most fabulous blue eyes, and their children had inherited those eyes, the Blair eyes. It connected them. It bound them to each other and to their parents.

"Oh, my Lord," Michael mumbled. "How absolutely stunning."

"Where did you get them?" Matthew asked.

"Mr. Etherton's niece had them. She kept them for us."

Etherton had been their father's friend. He'd been the only one who'd stood by their mother during her difficulties. He'd arranged for all of them to go to boarding school, had checked on them and watched over them as best he could—which hadn't been very well at all. The twins had vanished for most of three decades.

She stared at her brothers, such incredible, remarkable men. How had they persevered? How had they thrived?

It had to be due to her parents' blood running in their veins. It had helped them to carry on and prosper beyond anyone's imagining. They had been three little lost lords, cast to the winds of fate. But destiny had brought them together again, guiding them to the place they were meant to be.

They were home now—at Radcliffe—where they belonged.

"I've had copies made," she told the twins. "It's my Christmas gift to you."

Matthew turned to her and gave her a tight hug. "Sissy, it's wonderful. How can I thank you?"

"I agree," Michael said, "and I'd say it's a few steps beyond wonderful."

Evangeline smelled the scent of roses, so her mother was close by, letting her know she was happy for what Evangeline had done.

Bryce peered over at the twins. "Did you feel that?"

"The hand on the shoulder?" Michael asked.

"Yes." They often perceived their father's presence too, and

Bryce peeked up at the ceiling. "I'm glad you're here, Father. I'm glad you approve."

Suddenly a burst of wind whistled down the center aisle, and Evangeline worried that the doors had banged open. It was snowing outside, a blizzard possible by morning, but the doors were shut. They were all cozy and warm inside the large chamber.

The gust whipped by and proceeded directly for the fireplace. It blew on the hearth, almost as if a blacksmith was pressing on his bellows. Sparks flew, the flames billowing up, and for a moment, the paintings glowed as if they'd been gilded in golden sunlight.

Then the light waned, the fire calmed, the wind abated, but an eerie sensation lingered, the air charged with an odd energy. People nervously glanced at one another, brows raised, shoulders shrugging.

Bryce looked out at everyone. "I think my father just stopped by to say hello."

"I think he did too," Matthew said.

Scotland was a land where ghosts were common, so no one was surprised. The crowd laughed, the tension eased.

"Welcome to my home," Bryce declared for the first time ever. "While I have always been Bryce Blair to my acquaintances, in the future I plan to call myself Lord Radcliffe, and I hope all of you will refer to me as Radcliffe. When you do, I will know that you fondly remember and honor my father."

Evangeline smiled. "That's fabulous news, Bryce. I mean, Lord Radcliffe."

"I'll call you Radcliffe," Michael said, "so long as you don't grow annoyingly cocky about it."

"And *I* will call you Radcliffe," Matthew said, "no matter how you act. As far as I'm concerned, you can be as cocky as you want."

From over at the children's table, King Nicholas stood. "Lord Radcliffe, might we have the servants start serving supper? Your guests are getting quite hungry."

"A fine idea, Your Majesty," Lord Radcliffe replied. "Let's eat. Let's eat together—as a family."

The four Blair siblings walked to the front of the room.

        &x;   &x;   &x;   &x;

Lord Radcliffe strolled outside to tarry under the gates of his castle. He'd felt the need to survey his domain, to remind himself it was real. He perused the lush landscape, the rolling hills, the thick forests. Through the trees, he could see the church steeple in the village, could see smoke from chimneys as the day began.

It was a gray morning, the ground white. It had snowed all night and was still snowing lightly. It was very quiet, very peaceful.

He'd been away for almost two years. He'd gone to travel the roads his father had traveled. He'd viewed sights he'd never imagined, had lived through dangers he probably shouldn't have survived. He'd learned to fight and win, had killed and maimed, had loved and wed and taken on the responsibility of raising another man's children, and not just any children, but royal children.

The prior months had been exhausting and exhilarating. The mad trip from Parthenia had been wild and perilous, but filled with joy too. He and his wife had come home to the spot that would always be theirs, the spot where they would always belong. They would never be alone again, would never stand isolated, without friends or allies. They had each other now.

Christmas Day had been perfect. He'd married Katarina again and had hosted his first banquet in the main hall. His father's and mother's portraits were hanging on the wall. Their ghosts had visited.

He was happy, but sad too, and the sadness never really left him. In some ways, he would always be that five-year-old boy on the dock in London, wailing with dismay as the guards had forced his mother onto the ship. He would always be that little boy who'd tried to prevent Etherton's servants from leaving with the twins. He'd always be the little boy who'd given his sister their mother's ivory statue so he could use it to identify her should he be able to find her in the future.

He'd journeyed to Egypt to figure out what he should do with his life, to figure out the man he was meant to be. But he hadn't needed to trek so far to discover the truth. He was the son of Julian and Anne Blair, and that's all he'd ever needed to comprehend about himself.

He peered down the road that led to the village. There was a woman walking toward him. She was wearing a heavy cloak, her wool-lined boots kicking at the snow, the sound of her crunching feet echoing in the silent air. Her hood was up, so he couldn't see her face, but she was small in stature, short and slender.

There was a man with her, walking slightly behind as if he was a servant or companion. He was a bit younger than Lord Radcliffe, and he was dressed all in black, like a pirate or a bandit. Lord Radcliffe didn't know him and, not liking strangers to approach unannounced, he frowned.

They seemed a peculiar couple to be out so early when everyone else was just breaking their fast. What could have lured them out on such a cold, snowy morning?

The woman stopped and studied the castle. She hadn't noticed Lord Radcliffe watching her, and he wondered as to her purpose.

She glanced over her shoulder and murmured to the man who

was with her. He nodded stoically and gestured for her to continue on. She turned toward Lord Radcliffe again, and she lowered her hood.

She was older, perhaps fifty or so. Her hair had once been blond, but it had whitened to a striking silver color. She wore an odd pair of spectacles, the lenses tinted.

Finally she saw him. For an eternity, they were frozen in place, and as Lord Radcliffe assessed her, a surprising sense of recognition settled in. She was someone he knew. She was someone he had always known. She was someone for whom he'd always been searching, someone who had come to find him. And she had.

He stared and stared, breathless as she reached up and removed her spectacles. She swiped at her eyes, and he realized she was crying. But he also realized that her eyes were very, very blue.

"Mother?" he gasped, and he began to run.

THE END

ABOUT THE AUTHOR

CHERYL HOLT is a *New York Times*, *USA Today,* and Amazon "Top 100" bestselling author of forty novels.

She's also a lawyer and mom, and at age forty, with two babies at home, she started a new career as a commercial fiction writer. She'd hoped to be a suspense novelist, but couldn't sell any of her manuscripts, so she ended up taking a detour into romance where she was stunned to discover that she has a knack for writing some of the world's greatest love stories.

Her books have been released to wide acclaim, and she has won or been nominated for many national awards. She has been hailed as "The Queen of Erotic Romance" as well as "The International Queen of Villains." She is particularly proud to have been named "Best Storyteller of the Year" by the trade magazine Romantic Times BOOK Reviews.

She lives and writes in Hollywood, California, and she loves to hear from fans. Visit her website at www.cherylholt.com.

Printed in Great Britain
by Amazon